JAMES E. HONAKER

Beyond Good and Evil I

The Horizon's Edge

Copyright © 2024 by James E. Honaker

All rights reserved. No part of this publication may be reproduced, stored or transmitted in any form or by any means, electronic, mechanical, photocopying, recording, scanning, or otherwise without written permission from the publisher. It is illegal to copy this book, post it to a website, or distribute it by any other means without permission.

This novel is entirely a work of fiction. The names, characters and incidents portrayed in it are the work of the author's imagination. Any resemblance to actual persons, living or dead, events or localities is entirely coincidental.

Second edition

This book was professionally typeset on Reedsy.
Find out more at reedsy.com

To my brothers and sisters in Theta Sigma Tau.

"Around a hero everything becomes a tragedy, around a demi-god everything becomes a satyr play; and around God everything becomes-what do you think? perhaps the 'world'?-"

-Friedrich Nietzsche

Contents

Acknowledgments	ii
Prologue	1
1 The Moon and the Sun	4
2 Lunar Strain	18
3 Umbra and Penumbra	35
4 Wisdom of the Winds	49
5 The Blossoming Breeze	62
6 Whorl of Intrigue	74
7 The Hurricane's Eye	87
8 Smoldering Shadow	99
9 Storm Seeker	113
10 Rolling Thunder	131
11 Lightning Runner	146
12 Earthbound	160
13 Snowblind	175
14 Frozen Dominion	189
15 Winds of Winter	203
16 Contest of Clouds	217
17 Luminescent Spires	233
18 The Pinnacle of Light	250
19 The Door of Destiny	265
Epilogue	279
About the Author	281
Also by James E. Honaker	282

Acknowledgments

While writing is largely done by oneself, many people help to bring a book to life at the end.

Thanks go in particular go out to three people who helped me with beta reading on various versions of this book: Lawrence Honaker, Sebastian Savaric, and Kelwyn Graham. Kelwyn's help with my book cover was also a great asset in getting this project across the proverbial finish line, and those two overall were the greatest specific help.

More general thanks go to my brothers and sisters in Theta Sigma Tau, my assorted Internet friends near and far, my various teachers through school (especially Shirley Thornton, my junior high English teacher), and all of the people who encouraged me and provided moral and immoral support both.

Last, but certainly not least, my mother Colette merits special praise for being simply the best in many regards, and she's always encouraged me to purse the things I'm passionate about.

Prologue

There once was a great war.

The people were embroiled in devastation, subject to a brutal campaign of carnage and subjugation overseen by a figure calling itself as a dark god. Its powers were terrifying and formidable, and it had brought its conquest to this world unprovoked and unexpectedly. It was vicious and ruthless, and the land itself was ruined and ravaged, wracked with the scars of battle.

In their desperation and hoping to turn the tide, the people called upon a savior, a divine figure. They emerged from the heavens and descended into the fray, called to action by the desperate pleas of those who believed in it and gave it strength. The Almighty, protector of all, rose to defend the world it governed from the evil that imperiled it.

The battle that ensued was long and arduous, and the Almighty fought back the darkness with all it had. As it fought, it crafted islands in the sky, far above the battlefield of the land below, and it placed its charges on those for safekeeping while it tried to vanquish the evil at hand.

After a long and ruinous struggle, the Almighty managed to overcome the evil, and the self-styled dark god was defeated. In its defeat, though, the foul entity's remains exuded a malfeasant pall that radiated across the surface, blanketing it in a corrupting miasma that ruined all it touched.

Desperate to protect the people, the Almighty constructed a thick, impenetrable sea of clouds to blanket the surface, to contain the miasmatic influence of the dark one and to prevent further assaults from any of its forces that had not fallen. For now, the people had been saved, and the Almighty had tone their job.

As the battle wound down, though, it became clear that the dark one had injured the Almighty in a most grievous way, and despite their best efforts, the Almighty started to succumb to the wounds it had sustained. The people, not wanting to lose the one who had saved them, knew they had to act expediently if they wanted to save them.

And, so, it came to be that the Almighty had a stone tomb constructed for them, said to be lined with all sorts of tokens and totems the people felt would expedite their healing. The Almighty bade the people farewell as it disappeared into the rock, promising to return one day in the future, a day when the people needed them among them anew and when it had recovered from the wounds wrought by the dark one.

The story of the Almighty, the war that was waged against the great evil in opposition, and the history of the tomb that houses them is a story that has been disseminated to the point of ubiquity. Every child learns a variation of the story, the story that explains how they came to live on the islands in the sky and why the sea of clouds exists, though particulars differed in the retellings that were given.

The years passed, generations came and went, and the memory of the civilization that lived beneath the cloud sea had long faded, consigned to books that had a knack for getting misplaced. To many people, the Almighty was but a story that had little relevance to their lives, while others saw far more value in it.

The people were divided between six cities on large, skybound land masses, with subsidiary islands for agriculture and pastoral use as needed. Airships came to be used as the main means of transport, flying vessels to transport cargo and convey information, and the physical separation allowed each city the opportunity to develop a unique character. The Tomb of the Almighty, guarded fastidiously and unerringly by its custodians, sat at the approximate center of the islands, almost as if to keep watch over the people the Almighty had traded their vitality for.

The guardians of the tomb attended to the rocky monolith, keeping all others out of Aracoras in hopes that it would aid and abet their sacred calling, all while hoping for a sign that their guardianship of the Almighty might one day come to an end. Once the Almighty had recovered fully from their wounds, the tomb could be opened; when freed, the grateful and gracious divinity would see fit to reward those in attendance.

Nobody knew what day that would come, the day the Tomb of the Almighty would be opened for the first time since it had been sealed. To most, though, the Tomb of the Almighty was but the last and most spurious part to a story they were taught as children, an ephemeral and legendary rock that may not even exist beyond the imagination of their forebears and their teachers. Whether or not the stone existed was immaterial, inconsequential to their lives above the sea of clouds.

Legends, though, sometimes have seeds of truth to them, and many who had been captivated by stories of lost treasures within or ancient relics suffused with immeasurable power would wonder if the day of the Tomb of the Almighty being opened was near, or if they could open it themselves. The answers to both queries were nearer than they realized, and in a form that none of them expected…

1

The Moon and the Sun

The sun hung high in the sky, shining brightly as the airship left behind the still blue skies and touched down in the sky harbor of Lunaria. An official-looking entourage awaited its arrival, and they all looked as if they had been forced to wait longer than they would have liked. Harbor workers scrambled about to ensure the airship had been properly docked, while the aforementioned officials glowered impatiently. People walking by stopped to look at the airship, an ancient model that stood out against the sleek, modern ships in the harbor.

After a sufficiently fashionable bit of lateness, the party they were receiving stepped off the airship. Clad in white, formless robes that billowed in the light wind, the just-arrived party contrasted sharply with the rather decadent trappings and attire of the party they were meeting. From each of the groups, a man stepped forward to meet the other.

"Visitors from Aracoras," said the most opulently-dressed man of the receiving party. "I bid you all welcome to Lunaria, the grand city and the crown jewel of the skies. Truly, your visit is a time for celebration and revelry, as we come together ahead of a grand and glorious union between our families and our cities." His tone sounded like he had practiced the words incessantly during their wait, dripping with a forced cheer and enthusiasm.

"But of course," the other man said, matching the forced cheer with his own. "The alliance between our grand cities, Aracoras and Lunaria, is to be strengthened immeasurably in the days ahead, tempered and reinforced by the bonds of holy matrimony."

"Verily. The groom-to-be is among your cohort, correct?"

"That he is. Come here, Venser!" the white-robed man called back.

From the back of the group stepped forward a young man whose robes had been drawn up to cover his head. He had a posture that was submissive and meek, suggestive of someone not wanting to be there. He made his way to the front of their group, joining the man at the front.

"So, this is your son, the groom-to-be?" the man asked, looking over the slouching man. His expression was impassive, and his voice was an incredibly diplomatic tone that aimed to hide any semblance of how he felt about the man before him..

"That he is. Is the bride-to-be here, to receive us?"

"She is not, as we felt it imprudent to force her to wait for your arrival in discomfort. She waits back at the castle, where she and her father will receive you and your companions. Lord Hessler dislikes letting her leave the palace."

"Cannot say that I blame him. I do not like letting my daughters out more than is absolutely necessary myself." The man chuckled, met by polite laughter from the other party.

"Shall we be off, then? We've prepared carriages for you and the rest of your retinue."

"That sounds agreeable. Come along, everyone! Let us not tarry in this place any longer than necessary." He motioned, and his retinue followed his lead.

The party from Aracoras was divided among the available carriages, and Venser found himself in a carriage with a couple of the party members that weren't his father. He liked this, because he wanted some time to think before having to be social again. By request of his father, the carriages they were riding in had been installed with opaque curtains, and those curtains had been drawn shut and fastened tight. Contact with the "outside world", as it was dismissively called, was strictly prohibited unless deemed necessary.

The reason for the visit to Lunaria was to finalize the plans and arrangements for Venser's marriage, one he'd had no say in. Arranged marriages had been part of life in Aracoras for as long as anyone could remember, used as a means to further enrich families and keep power tightly wound around several axes, with Venser's family being the principal axis. He'd certainly seen his siblings partnered off in arrangements meant to maintain order and keep his family's grip on power tight, but this arranged marriage was a bold experiment. Venser was being made to marry an outsider, the daughter of the paramount leader of Lunaria, and accordingly bring together the ruling families of Aracoras and Lunaria.

Venser was left wondering why he was being made to take up the mantle for this, since he was the eighth of ten children and unlikely to ever have any sort of claim to leadership, and so his "value" to the leadership of Lunaria was lessened. Then again, that may well have been why he was chosen for this role, being seen as expendable to the Aracoras side of the equation while still acceptable to whatever end Lunaria had in mind. However the calculus was, the fact remained that he was still a piece on a game board moved around by those at the table above him.

Unable to look out the windows, he slumped into his seat, hands folded in his lap and hood drawn down around his face. A low hum formed the soundscape, coming from the carriage bringing them to their destination. He was going to meet the woman he was betrothed to, having only heard about her in passing before. He heard of things like her supposed piety and being a good and subservient daughter, the things his father cared about. Nothing else about his bride mattered to them, and Venser *certainly* had no say in the matter. He was the child, and children obeyed their parents without question in Aracoras, an arrangement said to buy favor from the Almighty. He wondered if and how things were different in Lunaria, aside from the situation with his prospective fiancée, but that was more idle musing than anything else. Idle musing was all he had as the carriage clattered through the city, the blocked windows tempting him with a forbidden world strictly forbidden to him and everyone else he traveled with.

The ride through the city terminated in a place darker than where they had wound through, in what seemed to be a tunnel. The carriages came to a shuddering stop, and he was ushered out with the rest of the entourage, positioned towards the back of the procession with his father at the front of it. They were in a dimly lit, featureless room situated beneath the surface, a space both dank and disorienting.

"It does appear that everyone is accounted for," said the man who headed the welcoming party. "Follow me. I'll take all of you to meet Lord Hessler."

The group was corralled and funneled into a series of snaking hallways, and Venser walked quietly with the group through the labyrinthine hallways. There was a weirdly sterile, empty feeling to the part of the building they were in, a feeling that felt intentionally disorienting, and it did not sit well with him. He walked along silently, looking at the ground so that none could reprimand him for wandering eyes.

The group emerged from the tunnels and into a spacious and sprawling hall, the size of which seemed meant to intimidate and daunt anyone who was in there. The windows were positioned high, so as to not allow people to look in properly, and the decoration was intended to convey a sense of sheer power. Towering, menacing statues lined the sides of the room. Venser definitely did not feel comfortable, which was probably the point.

"Welcome, esteemed guests!" He heard a voice from the back of the room, and he looked up to see who it came from. An imperious man stood in front of a throne; he was both large and opulently attired, a stately gentleman who clearly wanted everyone to know that he was in charge.

"Lord Hessler, it has been too long," Venser heard his father say. He saw him step forward to meet the other, coming up to the end of the carpet in the throne room and pulling back the hood of his robe to reveal his golden blond locks.

"Indeed, it has." Every word that Hessler said seemed to hang in the air, his booming brogue demanding attention. "Victarion, High Priest of Aracoras, I welcome you and your companions to Lunaria. I understand that the one betrothed to my lovely Leondra is among you today?"

"That he is, Hessler. In addition to my aides and advisors, my son is here."

"May I request that he step forward?" It sounded like a question, but Venser knew the answer to this was not going to be no.

"Yes, you may. Come up here, Venser!" Venser stepped away from the pack and up to where his father was standing, still trying to not look up.

"Ah, so *this* is your son." Venser looked up in response to this, looking directly at Lord Hessler. The man was as daunting physically as he had seemed from afar, built like a mountain and with a grim, humorless expression on his face. His eyes were the thing that most stood out to Venser, and there was something unsettling about how they didn't seem to reflect any light. He had never seen eyes like Hessler's before, and it was disquieting.

"That he is. I trust that he will be acceptable?" Victarion asked.

"Certainly! More than acceptable, really. He and my daughter will make for a lovely pairing. His eyes, though…they are *interesting*. I seem to recall hearing that the rest of your children have blue eyes."

"Venser has…he always has had different eyes from the rest of my children, but I can assure you that, as one of the sons of the paramount member of the Council of Elders, he is a faithful servant of the Almighty all the same."

"Of course, of course! I have no doubts about that, none at all. The people of Aracoras have always been known for their unwavering devotion and piety, and I imagine the son of the paramount of the Council of Elders is no different. Still, he has *remarkably* green eyes."

Venser had always been conscious of the fact that he had differently-colored eyes from the rest of his family, but nobody ever talked about it openly. So a stranger bringing it up, compounded with the unnerving gaze of Hessler, made him feel like he wanted to disappear into the floor he was standing on. That being implausible, he settled for silently standing there and nodding in affirmation, all while yearning for the sweet release of death.

"There will be time enough to talk on and attend to other matters, I imagine, but I suppose we should introduce our betrothed to one another," Hessler continued. "She should be coming in here as we speak, I do believe."

As he said those words, a young woman was escorted into the room. She appeared to be Venser's age, and she was dressed like someone of her stature might normally be attired, a fancy-looking dress with a conservative tailoring. She did look like she had been forced to hurry, and she was slightly out of breath.

"Sorry for the delay, my dear father," she said, bowing in his direction. "I had to help attend to something that came up."

"We can discuss it later," Hessler said dismissively, more caring that she was there and not how she got there. "Anyways, Leondra, I wanted to introduce you to your fiancé."

"Oh, he arrived today?" she asked, turning to look at Venser and his father. Venser noticed her eyes; they were brown and plain, but there was a mischievous sparkle alight in them, one lacking in her father.

"Yes, they did. Not too long ago, in fact."

"I'm sorry for not introducing myself sooner, gentlemen," she said, walking up to them and bowing properly. "I was attending to affairs before you got here. I am Leondra, daughter of Hessler. And you are…?"

"I am Victarion, High Priest of Aracoras," Venser's father said, making himself known. "My son is Venser."

"It is…a pleasure to meet you, Leondra," Venser said, returning her bow. He spoke carefully, saying no more than necessary and trying not to stammer.

"Speaking of meetings," Hessler said, "I believe that now would not be an unreasonable time for me and High Priest Victarion to discuss some of the items we need to talk about, in advance of your nuptials and…other events to come. Leondra, might I ask that you take Venser somewhere, so that you two can get acquainted with one another and we may discuss pressing matters privately?"

"Will the two of them be appropriately supervised?" Victarion asked, his voice showing concern over the risk of his son being dragged onto the wide and pleasant.

"We will not be alone and unsupervised, sir," Leondra said, bowing.

"I see." Venser could tell that his father was already not a fan of Leondra; his tone was very icy, the voice he adopted when he was being addressed by someone he perceived as his inferior.

"All right, you two, be off," Hessler said, motioning. "As always, you are to remain on the castle grounds, doubly so with Venser with you. Understood?"

"Yes, Father. Well, Venser, shall we?" She motioned for Venser to follow, and he felt he didn't have a choice in the matter. The two left the hall, with their fathers watching as they left their sight.

"Well, *that* was an interesting meeting," Leondra said. Once the two had gotten out of the throne room, Leondra had motioned the Lunarian guards to follow at distance, and she was leading Venser through another corridor.

"How so?" Venser asked.

"It felt like we were more of an afterthought to my father, while your father had us foremost on his mind."

"I...you know your father better than I do, but I think you are right, regarding my father." Venser was slightly taken aback by Leondra being so forward and so frank.

"My father surrounds himself with all sorts of interesting people, people not too dissimilar from your father among them. This is the first time I can recall seeing him, but I suppose I could have seen him a long time ago and it left no impression."

"I see. Do you...uh, does your father tell you about...the people he meets with?"

"Absolutely not! I have my own ways of figuring out about them. My father tells me nothing, says that things like that are too far over my head. He's wrong, but he needn't know that."

"I...I see."

"Your father doesn't tell you anything, either?"

"He...he definitely does not," Venser said. He was surprised by Leondra's tone and temperament, which were a lot livelier than he was expecting from his prospective bride. Maybe his father wouldn't have assented to the union if he'd have gotten to know her first, what with his preferred ideas of how children were to behave (and especially female children).

"In case you were wondering," she said, "we're headed to the library. It's a public space with enough privacy, so we can talk while keeping those two off our backs."

"I...that sounds good. I like that idea."

The palatial library wasn't the most spacious room, a fairly tight and windowless trove of books that rarely saw traffic. Still, there was space enough for Leondra and Venser to be in the room and at a distance apart that their retainers would approve of; after all, contact prior to their nuptials was, at least to Venser's father, an egregious transgression deserving of punishment. They were seated in separate chairs in one of the corners of the library, behind a bookshelf, and they each were able to get a good look at one another.

"I have to say, Venser," Leondra said, leaning forward, "you're nothing like what I was expecting."

"What *were* you expecting?" Venser asked. The way she said it gave him pause.

"Based on the reputation of the people from Aracoras, a well-rounded mess with long blond hair, blue eyes, and a haughty demeanor. Sort of like a younger version of your father, really. You *do* have long blond hair, but that doesn't look like a natural blond if you ask me."

"Uh...it is not. My hair...it is normally brown, but they...Mother, she insists on dyeing it so that I blend in." He wondered how she was able to pick that up.

"So, brown hair and green eyes, reserved, and built like a beanpole. If it wasn't for your attire or that I literally saw who you'd come here with, I wouldn't be able to tell that you were from Aracoras."

"Really?"

"Really," she repeated, sitting back. "Seeing as how you don't look like you're from there, I'm wondering if there's another reason for our planned marriage, if we're just pawns in some kind of game our fathers mean to play."

"Some...game? You mean, they have some other reason for wanting to marry us off to one another, one that is not just facilitating a wedding between our families?"

"I think so. My father's been pretty insistent on this union. Says it's his way to get to the Tomb of the Almighty."

"Tomb of the Almighty…" Venser's voice trailed off as his mind fixated on the name. Into his head came the vision of a large, floating mountain of rock that was situated near Aracoras. A bridge connected the main land of their city to the "Tomb of the Almighty", but it was usually closed to everyone outside of specific events during the year.

"Does the name mean anything to you?" Leondra asked.

"I…it does. There is…well, there is a mountain of sorts, a floating rock that's located near Aracoras proper," he said, speaking haltingly to let his brain fill in details of the image he was trying to remember. "They call it the Tomb of the Almighty, and it was guarded, said to be the holiest site in all of the city. We were not allowed on or near it unattended. A couple times a year, we would go there to a shrine on top of the tomb and pay tribute."

"What even *is* that?" she asked. She furrowed her brow as she spoke. "The Tomb of the Almighty, that is. No book I've been able to find ever gave me anything beyond a name. I overheard it once and tried to look into it, but nothing illuminating came up."

"We were…we are taught that it was the resting place of the Almighty, the divine protector of all of us and the force keeping evil at bay. Many generations ago, the Almighty was engaged in…a battle against a great malevolence, a 'god of darkness' who claimed to hail from a world of infinite evil and who sought dominion over this one. The Almighty succeeded in defeating the dark god, but they…the battle came at great cost to them, and they were wounded gravely in the process. The children of the Almighty, unwilling to merely sit by and let them suffer, put them in a tomb, the Tomb of the Almighty, to allow them to slowly recover their strength and undo the damage done to them when they clashed with such an indomitable evil." Venser took a breath, having recited that more or less straight from memory. For her part, Leondra took a moment to digest the speech before she replied.

"So, the Almighty is entombed in a rock guarded by Aracoras, and my father is fixated on it," she said. "What could it mean? Does he want to get access to it?"

"That…I suppose that could be the case," Venser said, furrowing his brow.

"According to the laws of Aracoras, you are not allowed near the Tomb of the Almighty for any reason unless you are of Aracoras, as we are the custodians of the tomb and charged with protecting its sanctity." As he said that, though, it clicked for both of them.

"They mean to marry us off so that my father can get access to the Tomb of the Almighty, then. Why would that be so important to him, though? What would he get out of it?"

"Apparently, on the day the Tomb opens, the Almighty will shower their most faithful servants and attendants with puissance unbounded and life eternal, an apt reward befitting their sworn defenders. I...do not know how, or if, it would open, but maybe he knows something we do not."

"That certainly sounds like something my father would want to get in on," she said, shaking her head. "My father seems to be particularly obsessed with staying young and fit, so that he can rule forever. At least, that's the impression I've gotten, and while he makes overtures about preparing a successor, he's not serious about it and would rather be his own successor. To that end, he gets a lot of people to advise him on how to achieve that, with each one getting his ear by promising a new lead on prolonged life and vitality, and he's recently been particularly fixated on the Tomb of the Almighty as the means to this end. And awakening the Almighty and getting their blessing might do the trick, because being there would let him shape the narrative to his own ends."

"Has...uh, has he always been like that?" Venser was envious of how frank she was regarding her father.

"So far as I can remember, he has. Nobody's told me stories otherwise about how he *used* to be, at least. Then again, there aren't many people left to ask. Staff turnover is remarkably high here, and people find themselves fired for the thinnest reasons. That makes it hard to learn anything conclusive or reliable at times."

"I...I see."

The two fell back into silence, trying to think about what it all meant on their own terms. Venser had certainly learned a lot already, and it wasn't even dinner time. He wasn't entirely sure how all of this connected, or the exact role he had in all of this, but it seemed towing back to the Tomb of the Almighty and the awakening of whatever laid in it.

That evening, in honor of their esteemed guests, Hessler had ordered that there be a banquet to honor both Venser, his soon-to-be son-in-law, and Victarion, High Priest of Aracoras. It was suitably lavish and grandiose, with all sorts of extravagant and exotic dishes on offer. Venser and his father were seated at the head of the table, near Leondra and Hessler, and the rest of their contingents were all stationed towards the back of the banquet hall.

"So, Venser, I trust you and Leondra got to know one another today?" Hessler asked. His plate featured a massive slab of meat, drenched in a buttery sauce of some kind.

"That we did, sir," Venser said. He spoke steadily, not wanting to stutter. "Your daughter is lovely to talk to."

"Is she, now? That's good to hear! All of her tutors used to tell me she talked a lot, so it's nice that all her talking got her somewhere." He tore a massive chunk of meat off with his teeth, which Venser found alternately impressive and a bit off-putting.

"On a related tangent," Victarion said, putting his fork down, "I believe that, in preparation for the upcoming ceremony, I will need to briefly return to Aracoras to get plans for the wedding moving in a satisfactory fashion. Confirm with the Council of Elders that the nuptials will be going ahead, and…any details of the celebration that are necessary to set in motion. I presume the engagement is to your satisfaction, Hessler?"

"Of course it is, Victarion! I was afraid you were the one who might have misgivings. Your son will make for a fine son-in-law, and I have no objections to the proposed union."

"Any…misgivings I may have about the union are largely trivial and mostly irrelevant, Hessler. The union will be a blessed one that will benefit both Lunaria and Aracoras and will…enrich the standing of both of our cities." Venser noted how his father's voice hung a bit. He could tell that Leondra had irked him already, but he wasn't in position to refuse. That made Venser wonder what they were getting out of it if Leondra was objectionable *enough* for him to pick up on his father's displeasure, and for his objections to be largely overruled.

"I should certainly think so! Will the young master be returning with you to Aracoras?"

"I…believe, given that Venser and Leondra are soon to be wed, that it would be better that, if you are willing to provide him the necessary environment, he remains here in Lunaria until I return to collect the groom and bride. This will give the two more time to become acquainted with each other, and it may well give Lady Leondra time to adjust to her impending role." He spoke slowly, his tone rehearsed.

"I think that's a reasonable idea," Hessler said, setting down his hunk of meat. "What say you, Leondra?"

"If it's your decision, I would be happy to have more time to get to know my future husband," Leondra said. Her voice was appropriately deferential and demure, Venser noted, and he noticed that it lacked the fervor and lively tone from that afternoon's conversation.

"Sounds like a grand plan, then!" Hessler said. He was smiling, but Venser felt a bit uneasy seeing the smile. It felt somehow oddly disingenuous, like there was *something* beneath the surface that he couldn't pick out.

"A plan, indeed," Victarion said, picking up a piece of a tart with his fork. Venser could tell that his father was not thrilled with the idea of leaving his son on Lunaria, but seemed to have had his hand forced.

Venser nodded, then turned back down to his food. He was curious as to the particular impetus behind his father agreeing to both the union and to leaving him here while he made final arrangements. Unfortunately, asking the questions he wanted to ask would, at best, earn a stern reprimand from his father for not "knowing his place", so he kept his silence and focused on the food.

That night, Venser was laying in bed. The rest of the evening consisted of him being left to his own devices while his father and Hessler continued their negotiations, and Leondra had retired early under the auspices of "the day being too exhausting". Venser had been given his own room, and it was nice to finally have time to breathe without needing to keep up appearances. If nothing else, the bed here was a lot more comfortable than the rock-solid mattress he had back home, and he could have a night without listening to his brother snore.

Like everywhere else he had been in the castle, there weren't really windows Venser could look out. One small one hung high in his room, giving him a glimpse of the moon. It was a waxing gibbous, so it seemed the full moon was coming in a couple days. He'd always found peace in the moon and how it looked, its phases a soothing constant in a world that he had little control in.

Control, indeed, was something Venser rarely had. Aracoras was a place that tended to have very particular visions and roles for its people, and as one of the sons of the High Priest, Venser's options were constrained in terms of having to contribute in a similar role. But he was the eighth child of his family, much less the black sheep of the family in being *different*, and he was far enough down the totem pole that he had few actual prospects available.

He sighed, rolled over, and tried to sleep. His mind was still racing, though, and immediate sleep proved elusive. He was supposed to marry Leondra, but he didn't want that. She was a nice woman from what he had gleaned, but he didn't like the idea of calling her his wife. He didn't even really know what a husband and wife were supposed to be, because his family had a particular dynamic that was nearly inscrutable even from inside and because there was an expectation of their service to the Almighty being the primary focus. His mother was tasked with taking care of the children, and he rarely got the chance to see his mother and father interact. His siblings that had gotten married rarely came back to interact with the ones of them who had yet to be married off…which was, at this point, the three youngest of them.

What did *he* want? That was the question at the front of his mind, but did it ultimately matter? It felt like he didn't have any say whatsoever in whether or not he wanted to marry her, or what he wanted to do. His life had been akin to that of a bird in a gilded cage, unable to escape or live a life truly his own, and he was being moved from one cage to another.

There would be more time for solipsism and regretting his lot in life later, and so Venser finally drifted to sleep. His sleep was a troubled, tumultuous mess of dark images and shadowy figures that he tried to fend off, none of which stuck with him after he woke up. All that remained by the time he had awakened the next day was a generalized sense of unease and discomfort.

2

Lunar Strain

The next morning, Venser saw his father off bright and early. The men convened in the main hall of the palace of Lunaria, with the retainers Victarion had brought with them. It was to be just Venser left behind, and everyone else seemed eager to make the return visit. Not that they would say so much out loud, as they rarely spoke to Venser, but he could tell from their demeanor.

"Remember, Venser, your conduct reflects on Aracoras," Victarion said, puffing himself up to his full height to make his point known. "Behave in a way that reflects well upon us, for the union between you and Leondra is paramount to our continued vitality and success."

"I...I understand, sir," Venser said.

"I shall return to collect you as soon as preparations on our end are ready. Until then, be mindful of your conduct, and behave in a manner the Almighty, and I, would be pleased by."

With that, Victarion disappeared into the tunnels that snaked under the castle. As the footsteps echoed fainter, it sank in for Venser that his father was actually leaving him here, marking the first time neither of his parents was there to monitor him. It was a strange feeling, and he felt like he might need time to process his relative freedom.

Before he could do that, he heard some noise from behind where he was standing. When he turned to face the noise, he saw Leondra and another, younger man with her. It looked like he could be the sibling that she was attending to shortly before he arrived, Venser thought; they had similar features, sharing the same shade of sandy brown hair and bright brown eyes.

"Your father left already?" she asked.

"He did," Venser affirmed.

"Is this guy going to be your husband?" the younger man asked, turning to Leondra.

"That's what the plan is, apparently," she said. "Oh, I haven't introduced you two yet, have I?"

"You have now," Venser said. "Is he your brother?"

"I am! My name is Lionel, and I'm going to be the leader of Lunaria some day! Probably. Not tomorrow, at least." Lionel had a lot of exuberance to him, which impressed Venser.

"It is good to meet you, Lionel."

"He's really nice, Leondra," Lionel said."I thought people from Aracoras were supposed to be rude."

"That's what I thought as well, and his father definitely is, but Venser's not anything like I was expecting." Leondra said. She turned to look at Venser with a bit of a sheepish expression, almost like she was apologizing for her brother.

"His father is here? What is he like?"

"Well…he's just left. and it's fair to say that we might not get along."

Venser chuckled, amused that Leondra had figured that out quickly. He also noticed that Lionel had a fair number of queries; he'd been used to people shutting questions down whenever he posed them, so having Lionel get answers was a change of pace.

"Anyway, Venser, I was wondering," Leondra said, dropping her voice so that only Lionel and Venser could hear, "if you would want to go into town with me."

"Uh…what? Go into town? As in, leave the castle?" This offer shocked Venser. He remembered hearing clearly that he was not supposed to leave the castle under any circumstance.

"Exactly that." Leondra had a bit of a wry smile on her face "I don't imagine you'll have seen Lunaria before, and it's never a bad idea to broaden one's horizons, right?"

"I...uh...well...honestly, I would like that," Venser said. "If it is okay...and if my father won't find out."

"I certainly won't tell him."

"Nor will I!" Lionel said. "We're actually not supposed to leave the castle, either, but we think that's a stupid rule."

"Why are you not supposed to leave?"

"Our father thinks," Leondra said, "that we're exposing ourselves to the vulgar riff-raff, and that we must distinguish ourselves by being above the people. Lionel and I disagree."

"At any rate, we should probably get going if we want to be back in time for supper," Lionel said, perking up. "Are we going to tell Father that Venser's with us today?"

"If he asks, since we're 'not leaving the palace'. Not sure if he would ask, but that would work as an explanation."

"And is he really going to go out dressed like *that*?"

Venser was still dressed in the robes he had from Aracoras, which were white and very ill-fitting. They would stand out very glaringly, which seemed counterproductive to the idea of slipping out of the castle unnoticed.

"Uh...I do not have anything else to wear," Venser said.

"Let me take care of that," Leondra said, a smile on her face. "I have a solution."

Just after midday, a small group of three people emerged from one of the many doors leading into the tunnels beneath the castle of Lunaria. Two of them, appearing to be a brother and sister, were dressed in inconspicuous plain clothes, while the third looked the part of a guardsman. Leondra had managed to find a uniform that fit Venser well enough, who had weirdly lanky proportions in spite of a relatively average height.

As they made their way out, Venser finally got a proper look at Lunaria, and he was impressed. The city was a bustling collection of buildings, with streets winding through them. Buildings rose several stories from street level, and there were visible signs of life in the form of people talking, interacting, and just milling about. It was weirdly simple and commonplace to the people of Lunaria, who would instead be taken aback by the austere sterility of Aracoras, but this was all mind-blowing to Venser, who looked around with a wide-eyed wonder he hadn't felt in a long while.

"Are you all right?" Lionel asked, tugging at Venser's hand.

"Me? Oh...yeah, I am fine. Sorry to worry you. It's just..." Venser's voice trailed off as he tried to think of the words to capture what he was feeling. It was like he was experiencing a completely new world for the first time, and it was one that his father and everyone else on Aracoras had tried to hide from him.

"Is it a lot to take in?" Leondra asked.

"I...think so. I...yeah, I will be fine," Venser said, shaking his head.

"Good. Follow me closely, then. I'll give you a bit of an overview of the city."

Venser quickly learned why Leondra had cautioned him to stay close, because the city's winding streets were disorienting to him. The streets were rather narrow and brimming with people, and he could see a mix of stores and street activity. The city was very much *alive*, and he was trying to mask that all of this was a bit overwhelming.

They soon entered a plaza, which had the form of a central wheel with spokes jutting out of it. A fountain sat in the middle, and the trio saw a strange-looking contingent occupying a prominent space in front of it. They were clad in black robes, and it looked like they were trying to offer *services* to anyone who passed by.

"Oh, it's *them*," Leondra said, the distaste in her voice evident.

"Who is 'them'?" Venser asked.

"They call themselves the Coven of Unholy Nocturnal Terror. They present themselves as a traveling group of entertainers, but they're more nuisances than actually entertaining. They like to offer fortune-telling that isn't especially accurate and various...titillating services." As she said this, one of the robed figures from the aforementioned Coven of Unholy

Nocturnal Terror sauntered up to the group.

"Oh, 'ello, 'andsome!" she purred, addressing Venser with a conspicuously fake accent she seemed to think would get people to open their wallets. "You are *such* a stunning specimen! Truly a gentleman of lordly caliber! Might I interest a stud like you in…the *puff-puff*?"

"Uh…'puff-puff'?" Venser had never heard the term, and the way she said it suggested he wouldn't be keen on finding out.

"Oh, you 'ave not 'eard of the *sensual* wonders of the *puff-puff*? It is…a *magical* experience! Those who taste the fruit of the *puff-puff* are *never* truly the same!" As she said this, she positioned herself in a way that allowed her to conspicuously squeeze her breasts together in what she thought passed as an alluring show of sex appeal.

"I…I am not interested, sorry," Venser replied, He wasn't wholly sure what he was being offered, but she had not sold it particularly well, and he had the feeling that no *had* to be the answer.

"Ah, alas, *such* a tragedy," she said, her practiced feelings of hurt coming off as inauthentic. "Should you change your mind, 'andsome, we shall be waiting!"

"I…thank you, I guess." He wanted to get away before another one of them made him uncomfortable. Leondra saw this, and she ushered him and Lionel away from the pernicious posse.

"They seemed more…audacious today than usual," Lionel said, frowning. "Audacious feels like the right word, I think. I don't think they usually will stand in broad daylight and offer their *services*."

"I don't recall seeing them do that before, either," Leondra said. "They like to wait until it's a bit later before they come out to play. Might be worth looking into why they're so brazen today."

"They normally are not out on the street?" Venser asked.

"They're on the street a lot later at night most days, if they're out and about," Leondra replied. "I've seen them out when I've been out in the evenings, still offering whatever the hell their 'puff-puff' things are and other services. Like this weirdly-named 'Cleavage Divination'. Please don't ask, because I have no idea, and I'm happier not knowing."

"I do not think I want to know, either," Venser said. He was equal parts curious and horrified.

"I don't know either, and I want nothing to do with them," Lionel added. "They're weird and creepy."

Venser frowned, a thought coming to him. "Pardon the question, Lionel, but how old are you?" he asked. "You are younger than me and Leondra, I think."

"By a bit. I'm not yet considered an adult, but I'll be there soon enough!"

"Anyway, let's get some lunch," Leondra continued. "I know a nice little place where we can sit, eat, and watch the people passing by. And talk. I have a couple of things to talk about."

"That sounds like a plan to me," Venser said. He didn't have another itinerary to suggest, so hers would do the job.

The establishment the trio had parked at was a small cafe not terribly far from the harbor. It had reasonably good food for a reasonable price, and it also was private enough that they wouldn't need to worry about being overheard. Leondra explained that a lot of palace staffers and officials who might recognize the two of them would frequent establishments closer to the palace, and everyone knew about this.

"Lionel can't go with me when I'm out in the evenings," she said, putting a fork down, "but I can still learn tidbits to bring back to him. If he's going to be in charge, he really should be informed, even if others have other perspectives that way."

"And I appreciate it," Lionel said. "Father tells me nothing interesting, and he's told everyone else to tell me nothing."

"Why is that?" Venser asked. "To…well, to be fair, my father also tells me nothing, but I do not really have ways of finding out what he's not telling me beyond a vague sense of exclusion."

"To be blunt," Leondra said, "he wants us to mirror his views and perspectives exactly. Father certainly does not like dissenting opinions or people questioning his decisions, and he's treated people who disagree with him poorly."

"That sounds like my parents. My father, at least. Mother...she just mirrors Father."

"What's your family like, Venser?" Lionel asked.

Venser sighed. "They are...it is hard to really describe the dynamic we have," he said. "I was not ever really close with any of my siblings. I am the eighth out of ten, and both of our parents were always busy. Mother usually is worrying about my younger sister and brother, and Father is busy with what he terms as 'the business of running Aracoras'. The trip here with them is the most time I have spent with him in a long while. I guess I sort of got lost."

"Ten kids is a lot," Leondra said, shaking her head. "There's just three of us."

"I have not met your other sibling, I believe."

"That's because he's 'Daddy's Special Little Treasure'," Lionel said, the distaste in his voice. "They spoil him."

"Pretty much, he's kept separate from me and Lionel," Leondra said. "Father divorced our mother and remarried, and his new wife insists on special treatment for her child. Lionel and I are full siblings, but we're half-siblings with him."

"I...see."

"As an upside, it gives us room to do our own thing, to a point," she said, between bites. "To be fair, Father's been incredibly occupied with things of late, like his current ad persistent obsession with the 'Tomb of the Almighty'."

"That's on Aracoras, isn't it?" Lionel asked. "Maybe he wants to get into the tomb?"

"That is what we're both thinking," Venser said. "The Tomb of the Almighty is supposed to be a sacred site that nobody is allowed near under most circumstances, outside of guards. But besides that, only the people of Aracoras are allowed there, and it is possible that he thinks that us getting married will allow him access to the Tomb of the Almighty."

"Can't they just waive their restrictions to allow him in?"

"They would not, not unless they got a lot out of it."

Leondra shook her head. "I bet a dowry is involved, and a rather immodest one," she said.

"A dowry?"

"Basically, the family of the bride pays the family of the groom money, usually a rather hefty sum of it. It's a time-honored custom, especially when people are in higher stations."

"Well...a lot of money *would* be attractive, I guess. I...several times, I can recall hearing Father complain about not having the funds for specific purchases, at least not readily available. Though...he did not know I was listening at that time when he said as much. If he had known, he might not have complained outwardly."

"That might help answer one question, in part," Leondra said. "Aracoras could use the money, and my father wants to open the Tomb of the Almighty to get at what's inside. My question is what's actually in there."

Venser frowned. "You are thinking the stories of what is in there are lacking?" he asked.

"The first time I heard about the Almighty literally being sealed away in there was from you. Nowhere else have I found any sources telling what actually could be in there, even if it was the Almighty. There might be something more than what they're telling us, and I'm doubting that I'd find answers here on Lunaria."

"Here on Lunaria..." The tone of her voice made Venser think she was about to suggest something interesting.

"So what are you going to do, Leondra?" Lionel asked.

"I was thinking that I need to ask someone who might know more than I can readily access here," she said. Her tone was cagey and evasive.

"Are you talking about Uncle Yamato?"

"Uncle Yamato?" Venser repeated.

"Yamato is the paramount leader of Sorocco, the city nearest to us," Leondra said. "He's not *actually* our uncle, I don't think, but he's always been friendly and helpful to us. He's also incredibly knowledgeable, and he would either know what I'm looking for or where to find it."

"How would you ask him?" Venser asked.

"I'd go to see him," she said. It was very matter-of-fact.

"In Sorocco?"

"Yes, in Sorocco." She was smiling, amused by how seemingly flustered Venser was getting.

"How…uh, how would you get there?"

"I'd take an airship."

"But given what you have told me about your father, would he let you take an airship?"

"I couldn't use one of the official ones, but he wouldn't need to know if I were to, say, pay for passage aboard another airship, right? There are public passenger services to anywhere you could want to go besides Aracoras, and there's the option of hiring private pilots. I prefer the latter when I travel, and it doesn't hurt that I have several friends who are involved in cargo hauling."

"She has a number of friends that way," Lionel said. "I don't ever go with her, because we really don't want to raise more suspicions than absolutely necessary, but she brings me back souvenirs, and I've even gotten to meet her friends."

"The ones I've flown with are a reliable lot, even if some of them have their…eccentricities," she said. "There are a couple who are more questionable, but that's to be expected."

"She's told me about this creepy man who calls himself the 'Chairman of the Educational Guidance Council'. She avoids him."

"That is…a mouthful of a title," Venser said. "What even is the 'Educational Guidance Council'?"

"Nobody knows. Honestly, it might just be something he made up to make himself sound more important," Leondra replied.

"I think he tried to get an audience with Father once," Lionel added. "He was laughed out of the palace."

"Enough of talking about delusional people with grandiose titles. Let's finish up here and head home. I'm going to be going back out tonight to meet up with who I think I can get passage with. You'll be coming with, Venser?"

"I…yes." It was presented as a choice, but he knew it was better to not debate acquiescing.

"Excellent. Let's get back, then!" she said, standing up. "Let me just pay the check, and we should be good to go."

Venser sat and watched, making mental notes. He'd never been occasioned to deal with money or with restaurants like this, though he had read about them in books he was not supposed to have had access to. There was a lot he could still learn, he thought, and he liked to observe the things that he'd never seen before.

Venser sighed and sat down in a chair. He'd just gotten back in, and his legs were sore from all the walking. While he was used to some walking, this was above and beyond what he had been used to. He took off the helmet that he'd been wearing while dressed as a guardsman and set it down, and he stretched out in an attempt to loosen up.

It wasn't long before he heard some commotion, taking the form of a seemingly haughty diatribe. His plan to nap was interrupted, but he wasn't keen on getting up, so he just kept sitting there. The source of the ruckus manifested itself shortly: a young boy who was rampaging through the palace, screaming for attention and sweets. He was dressed in fancy clothes, with a seemingly expensive haircut, and Venser noted that he looked a bit like Lionel.

"Which one of you useless guards is actually going to get me candy?" he whined. "I'm going to be the next paramount leader of Lunaria, and I'm going to have you all executed if you don't get me my candy *right now!*"

It was here that the boy saw Venser, still dressed as a guard, and stormed over to get his attention. "You, get me candy, *now!*" he yelled.

Venser was normally inclined to try and defuse situations, but the way the kid was yelling reminded him of one of his siblings, and he didn't like that. So he sat up, turned to face the kid, and shook his head "no".

"How *dare* you tell me no! I'll have you fired now! I'll have you executed! Bring me candy! *Right now!*" he screamed.

"You're welcome to try and get him fired," came the voice from the other end of the room, "but it won't work. He doesn't work here." Venser and the screaming boy looked over to see Lionel, who had an apologetic look on his face.

"What do you mean, he doesn't work here? He's dressed like a guard!"

"He doesn't have any other clothes he can wear right now. His clothes are in the wash, and we loaned him the outfit to wear for now."

"Who is *he*, then?" The boy put his hands on his hips haughtily, as to demand the answer.

"He's a guest who's visiting. Do you always treat our guests like that?" Lionel asked.

"But *I want candy*!"

"You're not getting candy, Lucius. Especially not after you screamed at our guest and demanded he be fired from a job he doesn't even hold. You can scurry back to your mother to get the sweets you desire, but neither he nor I will be getting candy for a spoiled, whining brat."

"I'm *not* a spoiled brat!" Lucius screamed back. "I'm going to be the leader of Lunaria, and when I am, I'm going to have you *executed*!" Even as he yelled, Venser could see the tears welling up in his eyes, not accustomed to being told "no".

"You're not the leader *now*," Lionel retorted.

It was clear to Lucius that he wasn't winning the argument, and so he stormed off, sulking and bawling alternately. Lionel came over to Venser to check in on him.

"Sorry about that spectacle," he said, shaking his head.

"It…it is okay, I suppose," Venser said. "Is he your brother?"

"Yes…well, half-brother. He's the spoiled brat that Father's second, and current, wife bore."

"I see."

"Anyway, Leondra told me to tell you to meet her where we set out from earlier today after supper. She's going to be busy for the rest of the afternoon, or so she claims."

"All right. Thank you."

Lionel headed back in the direction he was originally headed, and Venser settled back in to rest a bit more. Hopefully Lucius wouldn't bother him further. There had been a headache that lurked at the back of his head as he dealt with Lucius, but it faded as he stormed off, and Venser could just chalk it up to Lucius being loud and unpleasant.

That evening, through the same way they had gotten out of the palace, Leondra and Venser stepped back out into the city. Their supper had been light and uneventful, with just Leondra and Venser there and an apology that Hessler was "busy".

At night, the city had a slightly different aesthetic, Venser thought. Its liveliness was channeled more towards revelry, and there was a particular energy to everything, between the lights and the various participants in evening antics.

"The taverns and bars are generally where people tend to congregate at night," Leondra said. "There's one in particular that gets a lot of airship pilots there."

"You are looking for someone particular?" Venser asked.

"Not just a singular someone, but there's a crew I like to travel with, so any of them would do the job. Turns out that most of them tend to frequent the same bar, which is helpful."

"That is convenient. Where is the bar?"

"It's down near the harbor."

"I…uh, I guess that makes sense."

The two snaked their way through the streets and towards the harbor, making their way past various individuals aiming to entertain those on the streets or those merely offering the seductive pleasures of *"puff-puff"* and the like to those so inclined. Venser wondered exactly how successful such entreaties were, but he was not keen on finding out.

The bar that was their destination was a large, brightly lit establishment called the "Crimson Flower", and the first thing Venser was greeted by was the dank, stagnant stench of the establishment. He tried to not gag.

"All right, the first thing to do is speak to the bartender," Leondra said, gesturing. As she moved, Venser followed, and they made their way back towards where the drinks were dispensed. She got to talking with the bartender, while he took stock of where he was and who all was there. It was an interesting group of patrons, divided in weird configurations that didn't immediately make sense to him. There also was someone chaotically playing a piano in the corner, livening up the atmosphere with jaunty tunes and shenanigans. It was equal parts overwhelming and exciting, and while he hoped that they wouldn't be here for *too* long, there was something about being in here that made him feel alive.

He felt a tap on his shoulder, and turned to face Leondra. "The bartender tells me that he saw one of them come in with her boyfriend, and we can find them over there," she said, pointing to a table nearby. There were, indeed, two people sitting at the table, a man and a woman.

"That is a good thing," Venser said. If nothing else, they wouldn't have to go looking for them, and that could be tedious. He followed her as she moved through to the table in question.

"Hey, Sebastian, look who it is!" he heard the woman say, with her pointing to Leondra.

"It's Lady Leondra! Haven't seen you around here recently," the man called Sebastian said, standing to greet her.

"Sorry I've been scarce of late," Leondra said. "Things have been a bit crazy recently for me. My father's been trying to marry me off."

"Marry you off? Is that the reason for your companion tonight?" Venser noticed that they both were looking at him, and this did not make him feel comfortable.

"It is. It's a long story."

"Arycelle and I have nothing better to do for now, if you want to catch us up."

Leondra and Venser joined them at the table, and Leondra started to tell them about how her father felt that she needed to be married off, and that neither party was especially enthusiastic about it. The two listened, nodding as she spoke. The man had a messy mop of brown curls, and the woman had a head of straight, brown hair; they were fairly unremarkable in terms of appearance, though they did have a rather jovial disposition from what he could tell.

As she spoke, Venser found himself agreeing with her overall reluctance and her lack of interest. She was *nice* and a lot of fun as a friend, but marriage to her was not what he thought he wanted, and it certainly wasn't what she wanted. He did notice that she was deliberate with not telling them that he was from Aracoras, and he surmised that this was a fact he shouldn't freely offer up.

"So, you want to hitch a ride with us to Sorocco to meet with your uncle?" the woman called Arycelle asked, brushing her hair back behind her shoulders. It wasn't especially long, but Venser noted it was a bit longer than his own when it wasn't firmly ensconced in his helmet.

"If at all possible, and if you are all headed that way," Leondra said.

"I think it should be doable," Sebastian said. "I know we wouldn't object to having you with us, though I'm not sure we can guarantee that our return to Lunaria would be immediately afterwards."

"If not, that's perfectly fine. I have a couple other contacts I can talk to, if not my uncle, to get back before anyone notices. Lionel's pretty good at providing cover."

"Will he be joining you?" Arycelle asked, gesturing towards Venser.

"He will be, if that's fine."

"We have room, if you two are fine sharing the one room. You'll have your own beds, at least."

"That is...uh, it is fine with me," Venser said. He hadn't ever been occasioned to sleep in the same room as a woman before, something that had been firmly forbidden by the laws of Aracoras prior to marriage, but there was a first time for everything.

"If he's fine with it, I'm fine with it," Leondra said.

"Anyway, I don't think we've been properly introduced," Sebastian said, offering a handshake to Venser. "I'm Sebastian, and my girlfriend is Arycelle. We're crew members on board the merchant vessel *Alamithea*, an airship of no small repute."

"It...uh, it is nice to meet you both," Venser said, returning their handshake. "Call me...Victor." Victor was the name of one of his childhood friends, though they'd drifted apart after Victor had gotten betrothed to, and later married to, a rather unpleasant girl known for being possessive and clingy. Given that Leondra had insinuated that his true identity might be a liability, he felt a different name was good cover, and he went with the first name he thought of that wasn't his own.

"Victor, eh? Nice name," Arycelle said. "As for our plans, we're looking to depart for Sorocco the day after tomorrow, if that works for both of you?"

"It should work perfectly," Leondra replied. "I'm guessing I should speak to Marianne first, though?"

"It might be helpful to do so," Sebastian said. "And speaking of which…"

They noticed a drop in the din of the bar just then. Venser looked up and saw someone in the doorway of the bar, a broad and imposing woman with flame-red hair. Her presence was very commanding, which could be felt even halfway across the room.

"That's Marianne, all right," Leondra said, craning her neck to get a look at the person in question. "She looks to be in good spirits today."

"We've had a pretty good run up until recently," Sebastian said. "I imagine she just got a spot of good news. It's unfortunately been a bit of a weird spell of late, though, and business has been more erratic than any of us like. Poor Matthias has had trouble scrounging up the funds for his various…vices."

"We can probably avoid talking about those for now." The looks on all of their faces suggested to Venser that he really shouldn't ask.

"All in all, that was successful," Leondra said. The two were leaving the Crimson Flower; she had just gotten done talking to Marianne, and the pilot had indeed agreed to give the two of them passage to Sorocco on their next run, which was two days away.

"That was a pretty interesting establishment," Venser said, looking around as they were leaving. The dark streets still bustled with activity, and it looked like the Coven of Unholy Nocturnal Terror had moved their *"puff-puff"* offerings closer to the harbor.

"They attract interesting clientele. Anyway, let's get back to the palace. Tomorrow, we've got a couple of things I want to get done before we fly out. Like getting you some clothes that aren't your robes from Aracoras or that guardsman uniform."

"That sounds like a good idea. We will be back in town?"

"So goes the plan. I might have trouble procuring new clothes to fit you in the palace, at least clothes that'd fit you. We can also change up your style, if you'd like."

"Change up...my style? How do you mean?"

"If you want a haircut, or to not wear that awful dye in your hair... something in that vein. Seriously, I haven't seen a dye job that bad in years, and I know from past experience." He could tell she had a smile on her face here.

"Well...I suppose it would be nice to change things up," he said. "I have never had a different hairstyle, and it could be fun to try a new one out."

"No pressure. But it would help you to not stand out, if such is your choice."

"That is true." There was a weird bit of irony in that the long hair and dye were how Venser tried to fit in back in Aracoras, but both were now more of a liability away from there.

"Anyway, let's get back. I met the people I needed to, we made the arrangements we meant to make, and we should have no issues going out tomorrow."

"That is a good plan. I...truth be told, I am not used to so much walking."

"It's not so bad, once you get used to it."

"I think it'll be better tomorrow, though my legs might be sore when I lay down tonight."

As they got back into the palace, they heard commotion from the floor above. Venser couldn't make it out exactly, but it sounded like Lucius screaming at someone.

"Some things never change, I suppose," Leondra sighed.

"Should we investigate? Venser asked.

"I can handle it. You should go to bed, I reckon. You look tired."

She was right. He was tired, and the day had definitely worn him out. After a final word of parting, he headed back to his room, getting the help of a maid to take him there. He collapsed onto his bed and fell asleep almost instantly.

As his mind wandered, Venser realized that he never did get a clear answer as to what those Coven of Unholy Nocturnal Terror members were offering in terms of *"puff-puff"*. Truly, some knowledge rested beyond mortal reckoning.

He also thought about how everyone had talked to him, a manner that was refreshingly informal. That would be something he would want to adopt for himself, so as to allay any suspicion of him being from Aracoras.

3

Umbra and Penumbra

"Are you okay in there, Venser?" Leondra called. The two, with Lionel along for moral support, were in a clothes retailer's shop right off the Lunarian main street.

"I think so…yeah, I'm fine," Venser said. He was in a fitting room, trying things on and trying to figure out what he liked. "I'm sorry I'm taking so long. This is…it's all pretty new."

"It's okay, Venser. Take your time. We're in no rush."

Finally, Venser stepped out of the changing room, and he was decently satisfied with his choice in outfit: comfy trousers, a sharp-looking shirt, and a small scarf around his neck. He liked how it looked, but he felt like his hair still stood out, and he definitely wanted to get it taken care of. Still, he was pleased with how it all looked, and it was also comfortable.

"Looking good," Leondra said, smiling.

"Yeah, those suit you better than that guardsman outfit," Lionel added. "Or that other thing you were wearing."

"Good to hear that," Venser said, looking around. "I like how it looks, as well. Thanks for letting me pick these out."

"Hey, you needed *something* to wear that wasn't either of those options."

"It's appreciated."

"Anyway, what's next?" Lionel asked.

"Well, I was thinking we could visit a barber shop, if that works for you?"

Leondra asked, directing the offer at Venser. "Change up your appearance a bit more, getting that bad color out of your hair and attracting less attention with it."

"That sounds good to me," Venser said. He tried to not sound too eager; he had always hated the fake color he had been made to wear.

The bad blond dye job was stripped out at the barber's shop, replaced by his natural brown, and the shoulder-length locks had been styled and trimmed into something shorter and more manageable. It was a pretty radical transformation, all things considered, and Venser himself was surprised to see how different he looked after something so simple.

"Hey, Venser, what's that necklace?" Lionel asked. He was pointing to a little silver pendant Venser wore around his neck, a metal charm in the shape of a stylized sun with a small, inlaid red gem at the center. He and Venser were still in the barber shop while Leondra was off "doing things"; she'd seen fit to head out while Venser got his hair done.

"This? It's the necklace I got when I completed my education, meant to symbolize joining the ecclesiastical order of Aracoras. All men receive one, because we are immediately inducted into it at that point. It's a symbol of devotion, meant to be a constant reminder of what they call our 'calling.'" These were memories that came back almost instinctively, and Venser could recite a lot of what he'd been taught without mistake. His teacher would have been proud, were it not for him getting a haircut and frolicking among vulgar scoundrels, but there was at least that.

"And what was your 'calling'?"

Venser frowned, looking at his haircut in the mirror and trying to think of a response suitable to Lionel's question. It was then that it occurred to him that he might never have had a proper calling, not like everyone else. He remembered hearing from his brothers and sisters about the spark of divine inspiration that struck them and drove them towards whatever they ultimately pursued. Such a bolt had never come to him, and he'd felt aimless long before being betrothed.

"I...I guess I never found one," he said softly.

"Why not?"

"They told me that a calling was a sort of bolt of inspiration, gifted by the Almighty themselves to guide us on the path we're supposed to follow. While everyone else apparently heard that word of divine inspiration, the thing they were destined for and towards, the years passed and I heard nothing of the sort. I'm not sure why I never received one, and I wonder what it was like for those who did."

"I don't think we've ever really had those sorts of things in Lunaria, outside of anyone in the noble families being pushed to follow in their parents' footsteps. I'm supposed to be the paramount leader of Lunaria some day, but I don't know if Father will ultimately hand power to Lucius."

"Why not Leondra? Is there a restriction on women taking leadership?" Venser knew that there was such a prohibition in Aracoras, but Leondra had seemed like a good potential leader.

"I don't think it's a formal ban, but it's more of a historical bar to power. I guess it was taken for granted that she couldn't and wouldn't take over. Father wouldn't allow it. He seems to have ideas of what girls are supposed to do, and being in charge is not part of those ideas."

"That sounds like my father. As well as all of the other members of the Council of Elders."

"The Council of Elders? I think I heard the name before in passing, mostly someone complaining about not knowing who to contact."

"The Council of Elders is the paramount authority of Aracoras, and my father holds the head position. It's five old men who basically dictate the fate of all of us on Aracoras. What they allow in, who they allow in, what we're allowed to do, and all that."

"That's pretty restrictive," Lionel said, frowning. "And it doesn't sound very fun."

"There were always ways to get around them and their edicts, but it took a deft touch and knowing the right people. You could try to get novels and books, and I certainly got a couple of them, but you'd get punished pretty severely if you were caught by them. Someone was pretty severely beaten for being caught with a copy of *The Fisherman's Wife*."

Lionel snorted in response. "Of course it was *The Fisherman's Wife*," he said.

"Uh…have you read it?"

"I'm not allowed to read it. It's banned from the palace. I've heard about it, though, and it's legendary bit of reading, shall we say." His smile connoted more familiarity with it than he was willing to openly admit to.

"I…well, I suppose that's unsurprising." Venser vaguely recalled seeing the cover once. Tentacles were involved from what he could remember. He didn't want to know more.

"Not too late, am I?" Leondra asked, returning to the barber shop.

"No, not at all," Venser said.

"Looks like your haircut turned out well, I'd say. Are you satisfied with it?"

"I like it." He ran a hand through his hair: it was short enough to stand up a bit on its own, with a bit of fluffiness.

"If I didn't know better, I couldn't tell you were from Aracoras," she said. "More so than when I initially met you, at least."

"That's…a good thing, I suppose," Venser said. It was a strange sentiment, but one that felt appropriate.

"Anyway, while you were getting your hair done, I figured I'd swing by the Crimson Flower and make a couple final arrangements with Marianne for tomorrow. She usually uses the bar as her base of operations while in Lunaria, so it's not too hard to track her down."

"Everything's still good to go for tomorrow?"

"It is. We leave for Sorocco not long after midday, and we should be there in a couple days."

"That's less time than it took to get from Aracoras to Lunaria," Venser said. "I think it took us five days of flight time."

"Well, Aracoras tends to insist on using their own airships for transit, and their airships are an old, archaic model that tends to be far less efficient. I think it's slightly farther to Aracoras than to Sorocco, but their ships are slower."

"I'm surprised you weren't attacked by sky pirates," Lionel said.

"I doubt they'd frequent that particular air corridor," Leondra said. "Ships are uncommon, and the cargo they would carry is not all that valuable. Especially one outbound from Aracoras."

"That makes sense," Venser said. He hid his displeasure at hearing about the risk of sky pirates. "You'd have to be pretty desperate to try and hit the handful of ships that come by."

"Most would-be sky pirates aren't that stupid. Most. There's one who is famous for making really poor decisions, but that's a story for another day. Shall we get out of here, though? I think it makes sense to head on out."

As the trio left the barber shop, they were greeted by another spectacle: robed members of the Coven of Unholy Nocturnal Terror, confronted by Lunarian guards.

"Come now, fine sirs, can't we offer you the seductive and sensual pleasures of the *puff-puff*?" one of them could be heard asking. "I'm sure we can come to an agreement about a *substantial* discount on services rendered."

"Look, lady, we're here to keep you from causing a commotion and get you away from bothering all these people," the guard at the front of the group said. Even still, Venser thought he could see some of them showing signs of countenancing their offer of discounted *puff-puff*, whatever that was.

"We do not bother anyone unwillingly and non-consensually, good sir! We're just chaste maidens attempting to practice our trade in a cruel, cold world!"

"Look, boss," one of the other guards in the group said, "I'm sure they didn't mean to bother anyone. We can probably let them go with a warning, right?"

"And this would be at least the thirty-fifth warning I've issued to them by this point!" he snapped, turning to face the other guard. "Don't think that I don't see what you're doing in trying to get them off."

"But they're offering a discount!"

"I don't care what they're offering! I'm not letting them just go with a slap on the wrist!" As he turned back around, though, the Coven of Unholy Nocturnal Terror had dispersed, escaping into the crowd.

"That...was not meant to happen," said the guard who argued for leniency.

"Well, if you don't apprehend those trollops, you're going to have a major problem brewing! Go find them!" The leader sulked off while his contingent of guards sheepishly moved into the throngs of people to try and accost the purveyors of *puff-puff*.

"They're just going to get themselves what those floozies were offering," Leondra said, shaking her head.

"They're not going to get them?" Venser asked. "I mean, didn't their boss tell them to track them down?"

"Lunarian guards are sometimes a bit of a joke," Lionel said, shaking his head. "Father insists that they not be highly paid in order to get people who really want the gig, but all that's done is lower the standards of the guards we do have."

"He's exactly right," Leondra confirmed. "I wouldn't be surprised if one of the guards was getting his *puff-puff* as we speak."

With that, the three started back towards the palace. They'd gotten done what they wanted to do, and aside from Lionel grabbing a small bit of sweets for himself, there was nothing else on their agenda.

"I've been wondering...what *is* 'puff-puff'?" Venser asked.

Leondra sighed. "My understanding is that *puff-puff*, as those ladies offer it," she said, "consists of them thrusting the hapless subject's face between their breasts."

"Uh...okay." Venser didn't understand the appeal, and it definitely sounded far more boring than their dramatic proclamations insinuated.

"It's apparently big business in places. I've heard that there's a place called the 'Palace of Perpetual Pleasure' in Electrum that offers the 'finest *puff-puff* known to man', which is nowhere I have any interest in going."

"That name is a mouthful."

"I heard about one of the guardsmen who saved up his money to go there on vacation," Lionel said. "He sent back a letter of resignation sometime after. Not sure what ever happened to him."

"Shortly after, Lunarian guardsmen were officially forbidden from visiting there, but there's no way to enforce it outside of Lunaria," Leondra said, pursing her lips.

"That sounds extreme," Venser said.

"That's our father for you."

The rest of the evening proceeded smoothly, and Venser found himself in bed after a leisurely palatial supper and listening to Lucius and Lionel snipe and scream at one another. He was almost impressed by how different they were, with Lionel being more seemingly put-together and Lucius being a spoiled brat. He also noticed Hessler hadn't joined them for the meal; Leondra explained that their father usually took his suppers alone, and he had dined with them that first evening to come off as a gracious host.

It would probably be Lucius who took over, Venser thought, since he seemed more pliable and obedient regarding their father and his wishes. He thought back to his family and his oldest brother, Veldrane; they'd rarely interacted, but he was the one lined up to be the successor to their father on the Council of Elders. From all that he saw, it felt as if Veldrane had never had an original thought that wasn't sourced from someone else (especially if that someone was their father), and it seemed like every action he took was geared towards garnering adulation and praise. Seeing as how the next two brothers, Vectoringame and Visserion, were also potential successors, should Veldrane somehow fall out of their father's good graces, it was in Veldrane's best interest to play nice if he wanted to be assured of the role he felt entitled to.

On that chain, Venser was far enough down to not be in any sort of serious consideration. He was the eighth child and the second-youngest son, and he was generally overlooked for things because of his generally quieter demeanor and different appearance.

In a way, getting away from Aracoras was what *he* needed. He couldn't have imagined a few days ago that he'd be off to Sorocco on the morrow, to be fair, but this was a chance to, maybe, find who Venser was. Not who the eighth son of Victarion, High Priest of Aracoras was, but who *he* was, independent of his father's legacy and burden.

And on that thought, his mind finally shut off for the night. The day ahead promised to be a big one.

The next day, Venser and Leondra made their way back through the winding Lunarian streets. Venser had the chance to muse on how they almost looked the part of a normal couple; she was dressed in a comfortable pair of pants and a nicely classy blouse, while he was in the outfit he'd gotten the day before. One thing he made sure of, though, was to tuck his necklace under his shirt. While many might not know what it meant, those who *did* might invite unwelcome attention.

The harbor soon came into view, populated with airships of every possible size and shape. The sea of clouds stretched out just beyond the edge of the harbor, a threatening expanse that disappeared into the horizon beyond, but that could be contemplated later. More immediate to their interests was the massive, gleaming airship prominently positioned in the harbor, a cherry-colored vessel with a sleek-looking varnish and massive engines. The name *Alamithea* was prominently painted on it, indicating that this was the vessel they were looking for.

"You got here early," they heard. The two turned around to see Marianne walking up to them. She was still imposing, a broad ginger figure who carried herself with a lot of class and distinction.

"I figured it's better to get here earlier than later," Leondra said, nodding.

"I do like people who think that way. This is the man you told me about the other night?" She was looking directly at Venser, her blue eyes proving to be rather piercing.

"He is. Father's trying to marry me off to him."

"I see. He seems nice enough. Victor, was it?"

"Uh...yes, I'm Victor," he said, conscious to try and not stammer.

"At least he's not ugly," Marianne said, her tone blithe. "An arranged marriage would be worse if they weren't nice to look at."

"I suppose," Leondra said. Venser held his tongue, unsure of how to respond.

"Anyway, we're wrapping up preparations to set out, and everyone should be on board already. Go on up."

A movable staircase stood next to the *Alamithea*, and Venser and Leondra took it up to the deck. The bridge of the airship sat near the bow, a closed door standing between them and the flight center, while a passageway below deck was back near the stern. Standing on the deck were Arycelle and Sebastian, the two people Venser met the other day, along with a third person, a rather squat-looking man wearing glasses.

"Oh, look, our guests have arrived," the other man said, gesturing to Leondra and Venser. "Good to see I wouldn't have to go collect them from 'Chez Le *Puff-Puff*' after all."

"And that would be *such* a hardship for you, Matthias," Arycelle said, rolling her eyes.

"If anything, we're the ones who'd have to extricate you from that den of debauchery," Leondra said, stepping forward to greet them. "I can remember one time when we had to drag you out of that…unfortunate place."

"Unfortunate? How was it unfortunate?" He had a wry, mischievous smile on his face.

"We can discuss that later. Anyway, Matthias, here's the man who my father's trying to get me to marry. He's coming with me on this jaunt."

"New people are fun," he said, coming up to Venser. "I'm Matthias, first mate and second-in-command of the *Alamithea*. I'm sure we'll have a chance to get to know each other better on our short sojourn, right?"

"Uh…yeah, I guess we will. I'm Victor," Venser said, returning the handshake he was offered.

"Nice name. Your room should be the first one on the right as you go down below deck, if you want to check it out. The other crew member might be sleeping, so I'd recommend that you don't disturb him. He needs his beauty sleep."

"He does like to nap, I do recall," Leondra said.

"Go ahead and settle in," Sebastian said. "We've got some final things to prepare before take-off, but we should be in the air shortly."

"Sounds like a plan. Shall we, Victor?"

The two headed below deck and to their room. It was sparsely decorated, with a bunk bed and a desk, along with a window to look out. Venser took a look out the circular porthole and saw the activity of the harbor going on outside, people scurrying around to prepare other airships for departure and unload cargo from recent arrivals. He was reminded of his arrival, though he couldn't remember seeing any activity in the harbor beyond the group there to meet him, and he wondered if that had been a deliberate move asked for by his father.

"How are you feeling?" he heard Leondra ask.

"Oh, I'm…doing fine. Sorry, I'm trying to not be overwhelmed," Venser said.

"I know the feeling," she said. "My first airship trip was really exhilarating. It was definitely scary at first, but that fright went away."

"This isn't my first time on an airship, but it feels so different this time."

"How about you take a look around below deck?" she suggested. "See what all is where, and take your mind off of the departure."

This sounded like a sound idea, and Venser tentatively stepped back into the hallway. Most of the doors were shut, but he could see the lavatory and the kitchen area from a quick jaunt. The below-deck area was linear, a welcome change to the labyrinthine airship he'd ridden to Lunaria on, which was an archaic and windowless vessel that seemed to have been held together with harsh language and a lot of hope.

The sound of machinery starting up startled him, and he appreciated that nobody saw his little jump. The engines roared to life, and it finally sank in that he was doing this.

He briskly walked back to their shared room, finding Leondra sitting at the desk. She had a notebook open, and she was writing in it. He walked over, sat on the bottom bunk of the bed, and waited for them to take flight. His mind was racing, and there definitely was that feeling of trepidation mixed with dread, but Venser was excited most of all.

The sun sat high in the sky as the *Alamithea* lifted up off of the ground, beginning its ascent out of the harbor. Venser watched out the porthole window as the features of Lunaria grew smaller and smaller. It was up here that he finally got a sense of how sprawling Lunaria was, as he'd only gotten to see the quarter that the airship harbor was situated near. The palace served as a sort of centerpiece, with the city sprawling in many directions out from it and with that same aesthetic he'd experienced.

Everything on the ground continued shrinking, and he noticed that the airship was beginning to move laterally. They were soon above the cloud ocean, moving towards their destination, and the undulating and billowing white clouds stretched ahead of them.

"You seem impressed," Venser heard Leondra say.

"This is all new to me," he responded. "The airship I came to Lunaria on didn't have windows or a way to look outside."

"That's an interesting, though unsurprising, thing." Venser looked over to see that Leondra had finished writing, and she closed her notebook up.

"I'm going out to talk to whoever is out and about," she said, standing up carefully. "You're free to come along, if you'd like, but it's also fine if you're not comfortable moving around the ship yet."

"Give me a bit to get used to being in the sky," Venser said. He hoped he didn't sound too pitiful.

She nodded, then left the room, letting Venser sit down at the desk to gather his thoughts. This was a lot for him to take in, and it all was sinking in at once. If his father would have had his way, Venser would have stayed cloistered in the palace of Lunaria until he got back from Aracoras, and then he and Leondra would have been shuttled back to have their "proper ceremony". Instead, he was flying further away from Aracoras than he ever could have imagined.

He sighed, then stood up gingerly. The floor had a slight vibration to it, and he could still hear the drone of the engines. It was a lot quieter than the pre-flight routine might have suggested, but that constant din was new to him.

Venser turned to the door, and he noticed the door across from their room was open. Standing in the doorway, stretching, was a man he hadn't seen before. The man was tall and muscular, presently bereft of a shirt, with spiky brown hair and facial hair that formed a chinstrap and ended in a goatee. He cut a very impressive, imposing presence, and Venser was awe-struck by him.

"I see we have guests," the man said.

"Yes," Venser replied, trying not to stammer.

The man just grunted and headed out of his room, closing the door behind him. Venser caught sight of him disappearing into one of the other closed doors, presumably to another part of the ship he shouldn't go.

"I see you met Basch," he heard. Arycelle and Sebastian both were coming below deck, appearing in the stairway, and it was Arycelle who made the remark from the sounds of it.

"I did," Venser said. "He seems...friendly."

"He's a bit brusque and prickly, especially to people he's not familiar with," Sebastian said. "But he is very reliable, responsible for all the weapons systems on board and fending off would-be ill actors."

"How often do they show up?" Venser's face flickered with concern.

"It depends on the route," Arycelle said. "Lunaria to Sorocco is usually pretty light on threats one might have to fend off."

"You needn't worry too much about it, Victor," Sebastian said. "We're competent and capable, and the *Alamithea* has the best protection money can buy."

"That's good," Venser said. His nerves weren't completely assuaged, but they were helped by the two of them.

"Anyway, I'm going to check in on the engines, while Arycelle gets started on food for the evening. She's the most skilled cook out of us."

"You're just saying that," Arycelle smiled, tousling his hair playfully. Venser noted that Sebastian had brown hair that naturally curled on top of his head, while Arycelle had tied her brown hair into an elegant-looking braid. They also had more of an affectionate vibe than he was accustomed to seeing, but he figured he should keep to himself his not being used to outward affection.

That evening, following an uneventful suppertime filled with lots of banter and chatter, Venser was laying in bed. He wasn't comfortable with the idea of sleeping in the top bunk, so Leondra took that spot.

"So, how was your day, Venser?" he heard Leondra ask.

"A bit overwhelming," he said, "but it was fine. The crew of the airship has all been really friendly."

"They're an odd bunch, but they're good people."

"Yeah, I can see that."

A bit of silence set in, Venser looking up at the bed. There was a very faint light from a lamp on the desk, what looked to be a stone set in a holder, and it kept the darkening room from getting too dark.

"So, what is Yamato like?" Venser asked.

"He's very no-nonsense," Leondra said. "It's been a while since I've spoken to him at length, but he's always very lucid and rational. Sort of the opposite of my father in a great many regards."

"Are you going to tell him who I am?"

"Knowing my father, he's probably already started telling everyone, so I imagine he's already up to speed on you being my fiancé. But I don't think we would need to conceal who you are with him."

"Probably not, no. What are you looking to talk about?"

"I want to ask him about the Tomb of the Almighty and why Father is so insistent on opening it. There's a lot of questions I have about it, but I can't find the answers I'm looking for in Lunaria."

Venser sighed. "I wish I could help you more there," he said. "I just know what I was taught in all those boring lessons back in Aracoras, which probably amounts to not all that much."

"It's been helpful all the same, Venser. I just need a bit more than what you've shared."

They fell back into silence, thinking about the next lines of conversation.

"What *do* you think is in the Tomb of the Almighty?" Leondra asked.

"I...I guess the Almighty is there, recovering from their fight against the great evil," Venser said.

"You think that's all that's in there?"

"I guess I haven't thought about what else might be in there with them. Maybe it's just the Almighty? If they were as wounded from the battle as they told us, they might need a lot of space to convalesce."

"You might be right, Venser. There's just something I can't wrap my head around, though. Why can't I find any books in Lunaria that attest to that? There's been a surprising lack of information about the place, even as Aracoras gets mentioned in them."

Venser frowned. "I guess we…I mean, Aracoras is protective of what information gets out or is allowed to be disseminated to the broader public," he said.

"That doesn't seem like something they would have reason to tightly control, at least to me."

They went silent again, and Venser felt himself drifting to sleep. He could have sworn he heard the door across the way creak and click shut, even through their closed door, but it could have just been unfamiliar sounds playing tricks on him.

4

Wisdom of the Winds

The next morning, Venser was in the kitchenette area of the *Alamithea*. He'd been told that he was free to help himself to breakfast when he felt up for it, and he was in there to get a bite to eat. As he looked over the foodstuffs available to him, his eye fell onto a book sitting on the table, one that had rather eye-catching artwork.

"What's this?" he muttered, picking it up. "Let's see...*The Fisherman's Wife: The Tentacular Deluxe Edition, Now With 69% More Tentacles*. What in the..." He looked properly at the cover of the book, and it featured a naked woman being accosted by conveniently-placed tentacles of various shapes and sizes. He then opened the book to a point a third of the way through, saw even more tentacle action on the pages, and realized that this was not a book for him, closing it as quickly as he opened it.

"Oh, hi, Victor," Matthias said, choosing this time to saunter in. "I was going to ask if you'd seen my book anywhere, but it looks like that's been answered."

"This is yours, then?" Venser asked, handing the offending book to him.

"You know it. I do quite like literature of that particular persuasion, and *The Fisherman's Wife* truly is a classic of its genre." He had a sly grin on his face, that of someone who knows they've been naughty and without any particular repercussions to said naughtiness.

"I'll...uh, I'll take your word for it." Venser found himself both intrigued and appalled by Matthias and his taste in literature.

"It's not for everyone, I suppose, but it certainly appeals to me. I do have a soft spot for the sequel, *The Fisherman's Wife 2: The Re-Tentacling*, but that one isn't nearly as popular. Hence why they re-issue this one all the time."

"I...see." Venser still wasn't wholly sure why such a work would have appeal, but he was beginning to understand why that person was severely punished for possessing it back on Aracoras.

"Anyway, enough about my taste in fine literature for now. I'll leave you to grab food while I grab a bite for me and for Marianne. Our pilot needs her sustenance, after all."

"That sounds reasonable."

As Matthias worked on gathering food, Venser got a better look at the man. He was fairly stout and, as he would describe himself, "well-rounded", with a messy mop of slightly curly brown hair and a perpetual twinkle in his eye.

"You definitely are an interesting choice for a fiancé for Leondra," Matthias said as he gathered things.

"How so?" Venser asked.

"You mostly don't match anything about what I have come to understand her preferences are. That said, I suppose it wouldn't be so easy for her to have a marriage arranged to someone she was attracted to, since a lot of the choices for those *would* be pretty unappealing, from what I gather."

"Unappealing...uh, it sounds right." He thought of his brothers and of his brief run-in with Lucius, and that was an apt descriptor for them. He also wondered what Matthias meant by "her preferences".

"I'm sure we'll have more time to talk, if you're up for it later. That said, I should probably get this food to Marianne and put my book away where it won't disappear. It was nice talking to you, Victor." Matthias scurried off with a basket of food in hand.

"What an interesting man," Venser muttered, turning back to where the food was. It was then that he noticed that what *The Fisherman's Wife* had rested on was a magazine called *Ogler's Digest*, featuring a seductively-attired woman making an especially suggestive pose. This time, he wasn't going to take the bait and pick it up. Matthias could clean up after himself.

The rest of the day passed by rather smoothly, even when the issue of *Ogler's Digest* was discovered by Leondra around lunchtime. Venser spent much of the day below deck, relaxing and looking out of the windows, observing occasional passing airships and small bits of rock. He was still too nervous to spend time on the deck, and he appreciated that everyone seemed understanding of his anxiety.

Night fell, and as he settled in, Venser found that he was a bit too anxious to sleep. They were scheduled to alight in Sorocco tomorrow, and his mind was racing with scenarios and possibilities over what they would find there. He thought it a good plan to move around and try to quell his racing thoughts.

He got up, stretched, and gingerly stepped out of the room. All of the cabin doors were shut, though he noticed a faint light in the kitchen that piqued his interest. He quietly walked to the room with the light, and he peeked inside to see Matthias and Sebastian sitting at the table, poring over the issue of *Ogler's Digest* that he and Leondra had called out earlier that day.

"Hey, look at who came to join us," Matthias said, looking up. "Sebastian and I were just perusing the issue I got during our latest stop in Lunaria."

"I see," Venser said. He was trying to not convey his confusion over their interest.

"Can't sleep?"

"No, I couldn't. I'm not really used to sleeping on an airship, and I'm nervous about tomorrow."

"You and Leondra are going to meet up with the leader of Sorocco tomorrow, I hear. You haven't ever met him before, Victor?"

"I haven't. I...actually, I've never been to Sorocco before." He thought at least that much was safe to admit.

"I sometimes forget that we're outliers with how much we travel," Sebastian said, holding up the magazine to the light.

"A lot of the more 'noble' families tend to stay where they hold their

51

power," Matthias said. "They have everyone else get the things they want to get from the other cities. I should know, because I've been tasked with it at times."

"Like copies of *The Fisherman's Wife*?" Sebastian asked, his tone clearly joking.

"Look, it's not my fault that Yamato's son wanted…oh, what was the right term…'examples of the female figure to help in drawing practice'? Yeah, that's the term!"

"You realize that it was probably a thinly-veiled excuse for him to get his hands on contraband smut, right?"

"I mean, that's what made it especially funny!" Matthias grinned.

Venser couldn't help but smile at the absurdity of their discussion. He also wondered if the son in question would be someone he'd encounter, but that certainly wouldn't be answered right now, of all times.

"Anyway, if you want to, feel free to have a seat, Victor," Matthias said. "It'd be rude to not offer you a spot. Even if you're not keen on perusing the latest issue of *Ogler's Digest*, we like the company."

He wasn't anywhere near tired, so Venser accepted the offer and sat with the two men as they chatted, pointed at various scantily-clad women, and engaged with him in conversation. Venser was surprised by how at-ease he was with them. They weren't concerned about impressions or putting forward a certain appearance, just…ogling some women and enjoying themselves. He knew he couldn't let his guard down completely, but there was something refreshing about the utter lack of pretense from the two men.

It wasn't the most thought-provoking night, but it was a decently enjoyable one, and when Venser returned to his room to try and sleep, he conked out this time, that conversation having done the trick.

A slight change in the pitch of the engines' noise roused Venser from his sleep, and he got up to notice that the next day had begun. He walked over to the window and noticed that, from the right angle, he got a look at a mass of land, though it was hardly the most impressive sight.

He relocated to the kitchen area to see if that afforded him a better view, wanting to see where they were without wanting to go out on the deck. It did, and he got his first look at what he presumed was Sorocco.

From what he could see, the architecture of the city was markedly different from what he was used to, emphasizing and suiting a more dispersed population compared to Lunaria's bustling density (and whatever was going on in Aracoras). Buildings were shorter, and a healthy number of trees were worked into the landscaping. Lunaria's color palette was very much a mix of earthy, neutral tones, while Sorocco emphasized bolder, brighter colors like reds and blues that stood out in sharp contrasts. He couldn't tell much more from up in the sky, but the vibe was already very different from Lunaria (and Aracoras).

"There you are," he heard Leondra say. He turned to face her; she'd already gotten her possessions and looked ready to disembark.

"Not long until landing, I take it?" he asked.

"It shouldn't be, no," she said.

She was accurate enough in her forecast, and the airship touched down in the harbor as gently as a vessel of its size could. As the engines powered down, Venser finally ventured out onto the deck, and he saw that Sebastian, Arycelle, and Matthias were all there and waiting for the "all clear". That came with the engines winding down.

"All right, we're here!" Matthias called out, turning to the duo standing near the deck entry.

"We could tell, Matthias," Leondra said.

"Look, calling out the obvious is part of my job description sometimes. Go on ahead and get going to the palace, since that's where you have your business. We need a couple moments to wrap up at the harbor, all of the fun paperwork and the like. Do you want to maybe meet up this evening and hang out?"

"We should be free to do so," she said. "I'd also like to talk to Marianne, but I know she's probably going to have her hands tied with those procedures and that paperwork this afternoon."

"All right, that should work. There's a bar called the 'Azure Moon' we'll be at this evening, if you want to track us down."

With that, Venser and Leondra stepped off of the airship and onto Sorocco. The first thing Venser noticed was a bit of a cool breeze blowing. The image he'd gotten of Sorocco from up high wasn't too far removed from the one he had on the ground, between the architecture standing out with its bright colors and the prevalence of trees. He realized that trees were surprisingly uncommon in Lunaria, but they were ubiquitous here and almost all uniformly lush and vibrant-looking.

"You seem impressed," Leondra said.

"Um…yes, I am," Venser admitted. "This is…it's nothing like the other places I've been."

"Every city has their own unique quirks, and Sorocco has more of a connection with the natural world. Lunaria is a city that runs from the past, while Sorocco looks to it for inspiration. Which is maybe a good part of why I'm hoping this trip will be fruitful."

"You're hoping they have the information you're seeking?"

"I do, and even if it's not exactly what I'm looking for, at least I can get more here that I might not have gotten in Lunaria. Let's head for the palace. My uncle will be waiting. I did send notice ahead that I'd be coming, so he should be expecting us today."

Compared to the cramped and narrow streets that wound through Lunaria, Sorocco's avenues were generally broader, but with fewer people on them. The vibe was peaceful, but not in a sort of "forced" peace like Venser was used to.

Much like Lunaria, the palace was in the center of the city, and it was easy to get to from where they had started. Two guardsmen stood outside it, and they snapped to attention when they saw the approaching guests.

"You appear to be Lady Leondra," said one guard. "Is this correct?"

"You are. I suppose it's good that I've left an impression," she said.

"But of course. Yamato told us you might be coming today. Is this person you have with you…"

"He's the man I told him about, my fiancé. Will he be allowed in with me?"

"That he will, so long as he behaves himself." The two guards made sure to look right at Venser as they said this.

"I can vouch for his good behavior, and he will cause no problems. Unlike the occasional dodgy antics of some of the people I've traveled with, but they have their charms," she said. "Might we come in?"

"Certainly. We'll send word that you've arrived. It's possible Yamato might not be immediately available, though. We heard he had a meeting with a visitor earlier today."

"A really hot one," the other guard said, before realizing that this was something he maybe shouldn't have divulged.

"Fair enough," she said. "Let's head inside, Venser. I think we might be able to make ourselves comfortable. I'd like to meet with my uncle first before we get to exploring the city proper."

"That suits me," Venser said. He was looking forward to seeing the city proper, but this meeting was more important, and he followed Leondra's lead.

The palatial compound was made most remarkable by a large, sprawling tree in the center of the courtyard. Its girth was like nothing Venser could ever recall having seen, and it also had a bit of red ribbon tied around it.

"One of the traditions of Sorocco," Leondra said, noting Venser looking at the tree, "is that they mark trees thought to have a strong spiritual connection. This particular tree is the largest and longest-lived tree of them all, if the stories have heard are to be believed, so the spiritual connection is thought to be the strongest."

"I see. It's certainly impressively large…I can't say I've ever seen a tree so big." Most of the trees he could remember from Aracoras were small things, carefully manicured and kept deliberately diminutive.

"Agreed. There's certainly nothing this big on Lunaria, at least in terms of trees. But even the trees outside of the palace are nice."

The two stood there, looking at the tree and reflecting on things that had happened while they waited to hear that Yamato was free to see them. As they passed the time in silent contemplation, they heard an argument taking place in the rooms above their level. Two voices were involved in the argument, a booming one and a peculiar one that seemed to ooze a level of seduction, but neither one of them could quite pick out what was being said by either party. It didn't sound like mere pleasantries, though.

"I think one of those voices sounds like Uncle Yamato," Leondra said, frowning. "He sounds rather passionate."

"Do you recognize the other?" Venser asked.

"I can't tell for sure. It doesn't sound completely unfamiliar, I just can't place it any better." It was still more than Venser had, because neither voice was a voice he recognized.

The voices got louder and more prominent, though it was still hard to pin down what they were saying. Their tone was raucous enough, though, and it certainly sounded like the two were coming towards where they were.

"You are *such* an unimaginative, stuffy old lizard," they finally heard, coming from the female voice that Leondra thought she might have recognized. Venser saw Leondra contort her face in thought, trying to dredge up a memory from somewhere. For his part, a strange, dull headache took hold in his temples. It was not incapacitating, but it was definitely irritating.

"Try cajoling and insulting me all you want, hussy, but you shall find that it will be to no avail. I have no interest in what you're offering," said the other voice, the man Leondra picked out as being Yamato.

"Hussy? You would call me a hussy? Your words hurt me, Yamato, and I feel *very* aggrieved by such words. Still, I would be willing to overlook that bout of rudeness. The offer I make is one that will benefit all sides, and all I ask is that…"

"No. The answer still is no, Hellvira."

"Suit yourself, old man. Just don't come crying to me when you're left out in the cold."

From around the corner came the woman, strutting in a way that oozed sex appeal. She was tall, with comically overwrought proportions that were accentuated by an immodestly-cut dress.

"Oh, it appears you have guests, Yamato," the woman said, her voice coming out as a strange mix between a sultry purr and a seductive coo.

"No wonder you wanted to kick out poor little Hellvira."

"Go away," Yamato said. This was not a suggestion.

"But I'd like to introduce myself first! Your guests seem *so* friendly and cute." She strutted over to get a good look at the two of them, and Venser got more of a look at her. Her skin was extremely pale, with just a bit of red make-up in the right places, and her black hair was held up in a beehive. Her dress barely qualified as much, a red number that plunged below her navel and offered a side slit all the way up to her hip. Her eyes were particularly peculiar, though, not seeming to reflect light in a natural way.

"Ah, I recognize one of you," Hellvira said, turning to Leondra. "You're Lady Leondra of Lunaria, aren't you? Hessler's daughter."

"I think we have met before," Leondra replied. "It was in passing, though."

"That *is* true. While I might like to talk, alas, my time here is just about up, and I fear I am needed elsewhere. Might I ask who is your companion on this day?"

"Uh…" Venser was a bit dumbfounded by her, not knowing exactly how to respond.

"He's Victor, my fiancé," Leondra said.

"I see. You may call me Hellvira. I am…a traveler, of sorts. Who knows, our paths may well cross again. For now, I bid you two adieu."

Hellvira walked past them, and Venser felt a strange, dull wave flicker between his temples. It was a weird feeling that compounded with his headache.

"What a strange woman," Leondra said. "There's something more going on than what meets the eye with her."

"You felt it too, I see." Yamato uttered these words as he stepped out into the courtyard to meet them. He was not a very large man, a bald-headed figure with pronounced eyebrows. Still, Venser had a sense that he was both wise and rather firm.

"Uncle Yamato, I've come to see you," Leondra said, bowing. Venser followed her lead.

"It has been a while, but it's good to see you. I presume your father was not informed of this trip?"

"I did not see the need to trouble him so, and I also suspect he would not have assented."

"The old adage I recall you being so fond of comes to mind. The one about how it is better to beg forgiveness than to ask permission." He smirked as he repeated those words.

"I suppose I might have said that once or twice. Maybe even thrice." Leondra smiled sheepishly.

"It was more than thrice. But we can reminisce later. Let's return to my study, where we can catch up. I heard you had something you've been wanting to ask about."

Venser found himself sitting in Yamato's study, listening to Leondra and Yamato talk about recent developments. He'd learned a lot about how things were: apparently, Hellvira had shown up in Lunaria not too long ago after what people had described as a substantial gap between visits, and her return had coincided with the sudden rise in interest by her father in the Tomb of the Almighty. Hellvira's appearance had reminded Leondra of her past encounter.

"So, your father thinks opening the Tomb of the Almighty will reward him with...what, exactly? Power and eternal life?" Yamato asked. "That sounds like Hessler. He's always wanted a bit more power than what he had, and I suppose he might be concerned about his mortality."

"He wants to open it, that much I know," she said. "What concerns me is that I haven't been able to find any information about what's *in* the Tomb of the Almighty."

"What do you mean? There are no books in Lunaria to illuminate the answers you seek?"

"None that I have found, and I've been trying to check every nook and cranny. I want to, if possible, look through your archives. Sorocco's library is the best available, and since I can't go to Aracoras to learn for myself, this is the next-best option."

"Wouldn't you go to Aracoras for your wedding?"

Leondra and Venser looked at each other, and Venser had a strange feeling about what was to follow.

"Well…I'm afraid that I wouldn't have the chance to actually learn what's in there before they open the tomb. And I…don't want to get married, I suppose."

"Well, that was a given," Yamato said. He was looking right at Venser. "You hardly seem like the type to sit down and get married, or at least get married to who your father would tell you to get married to without there being romance."

"Venser's a sweet man," she said, "but…I don't think we'd work as a couple."

"What say you, Venser?" An eyebrow was raised as he said this, as if to emphasize his curiosity.

"Uh…I guess I…well, I agree with her, sir," he said.

"I see." Yamato's gaze remained piercing and probing, and Venser was uncomfortable under it.

"One thing that surprised me," Leondra continued, "is how different Venser looks from what I came to expect from the people of Aracoras."

"You mean the blond hair, blue eyes, and generally well-rounded appearance?" Yamato asked. "None of which are present in Venser here."

Instinctively, as a sort of defense mechanism, Venser reached under his shirt and pulled out his necklace, the symbol of devotion of Aracoras. Yamato noticed this and leaned over his desk.

"That certainly looks like the symbol of devotion," Yamato said. "Even if you're not someone who looks like they're from Aracoras, that symbol would confirm your lineage to anyone who knows its significance and its meaning."

"It's that well known?" Venser asked.

"Not to the general public, but those in charge of each city would know what it means, if nothing else. Along with a couple assorted people here and there, so the sharing of that information may be best done with discretion."

"I understand, sir."

"I do believe that there's a lot that we all will need to talk about in the next couple of days," Yamato said, standing up. "First things first, let's get you access to the library, Leondra. I'll start making the arrangements for you to get in there, and hopefully you'll be able to find the information you seek."

"Thank you, uncle," she said, bowing respectfully.

"For now, go ahead and show Venser around the city. I would imagine he's interested in seeing the sights. You can stay in the palace for your stay here, since that should be easier than working around securing lodging elsewhere."

"Again, thank you. And we'll do just that."

With a motion, she and Venser got up and left Yamato's study. They were getting ready to return to the courtyard when they ran into someone else who recognized Leondra.

"Oh, Leondra! I didn't know you were going to be here." It was a young man about their age, looking similar to Yamato with an actual head of hair, and he scurried over to greet them. He had a topknot ponytail that bounced jauntily, and his features were well-defined.

"Sorry I didn't have a chance to tell you in advance, Isamu," she said. "This was maybe not the longest notice I've had before making a trip."

"I can imagine. Why are you here, anyways?"

"My father's trying to marry me off, and I've had some questions about his motivations that I'm trying to find answers to. And I figured the library here might give me the chance to find the answers I seek."

"I see. Might I help in any way?"

"Nothing comes to mind right now, but I imagine we might need help to look through all the books."

"Let me know if I can help with that," Isamu said. "Speaking of which, who's with you?"

"He's the man my father's trying to marry me off to," Leondra said. "His name is Venser, and he's one of the sons of the paramount member of the Council of Elders in Aracoras."

"Really? He's from Aracoras? He just looks like a random bum off of the street from Lunaria, to be perfectly honest." Something in the tone of his voice irked Venser, a flippant and dismissive attitude that could not be bothered with him. As he listened, Venser noticed that Isamu was holding a book with a familiar cover.

"That book looks interesting," Venser said, pointing to it. His speaking startled Isamu, and he dropped the book. Venser's suspicion was right: it was a copy of *The Fisherman's Wife*, complete with an embossed cover featuring the titular character and a surfeit of tentacles.

"Oh, look, a copy of *The Fisherman's Wife*," Leondra said, bending down to look at it. "And here I thought your father had thrown out your copy of it recently." She spoke loud enough to draw attention to Isamu's scrambling to try and hide the cover.

"Be quiet, woman! Don't get me in trouble! It's…that's for anatomy study!" he hissed.

"Oh, it's for *anatomy* study? Much like those copies of *Ogler's Digest* were? Or those copies of *Juicy Jumblies Quarterly*? I'm *curious* as to what parts of the anatomy you're focusing on!"

By now, a crowd had gathered to watch the spectacle, and Isamu was both aware and uncomfortable.

"Why are you doing this, Leondra? They don't need to know about the… anatomy study guides I have!"

"Maybe you should have thought about how you phrased your comments before you were rude to Venser!" she snapped. "You've always been like this, Isamu, making flippantly rude comments to people you think are beneath you."

"I do not!" he huffed, but the crowd clearly agreed with her.

"Anyway, we should leave you to peruse your anatomy study materials. Can't wait to see your drawings!" Leondra swept out of the lobby as Venser followed, letting everyone make comments about Isamu's taste in literature as he scrambled to get the book put away before his father could notice.

5

The Blossoming Breeze

"Are you and Isamu longtime friends?" Venser asked. The two had left the palatial compound for the nonce and were strolling down the main street, looking around the city.

"We…yes, you could say we know each other," Leondra said. "Despite our differences and the fact that our families tended to not interact regularly, we wound up friendly. Nothing more than that, of course. In particular, when Yamato came to Lunaria on business, Isamu was the only person close to my age in their entourage, so we spent time together."

"That makes sense." Venser noticed that her tone was a bit careful, like she was trying to say things without saying something she might come to regret. It was a tone he was all too familiar with.

"Enough about that and about him for now. I'm sure we'll run into him this evening, though. He likes to enjoy the nightlife of Sorocco." Her tone suggested the conversation's change in subject was not negotiable.

"His father approves?"

"Isamu has rarely changed his behavior based on his father's approval."

The city was still less bustling than Lunaria, but it felt like there were more people on the street than when they'd arrived. The overall vibe of Sorocco was very placid and charming, and the free-standing buildings stood out for having less of a constricted, cluttered vibe. Venser noticed a couple of birds sitting on buildings, preening themselves.

"Over there is the library," Leondra said, pointing off to their left. It was a massive structure, easily the tallest building outside of the palatial complex. It was both tall and wide, occupying a healthy amount of space overall.

"That's certainly impressive," he said. "I can see why you want to look in there for the information."

"It's the biggest library that I know of, and their collection is broad. I'm not sure that I *will* find what I'm looking for there, but it's certainly my best bet for finding anything meaningful."

"Why do you need permission to go in there?"

"I don't need permission to just go in and browse," she said, "but I do need permission to access certain collections, ones with far older books that they have particular interest in preserving. I'm not wholly sure where I need to look to read about the Tomb of the Almighty, but I think I'd want to cast the widest net possible."

"I understand."

Venser thought back to the main library on Aracoras, which was a tightly guarded, carefully curated, and meticulously subdivided cache of texts. Very few books were available without special permissions from the Council of Elders, divided into several tiers of permission, and they usually said "no" to those asking for permission without very clear reason for such an ask. He hadn't gotten to explore Lunaria's library with any sort of depth, and he wasn't sure what libraries were present besides the palatial one they'd spoken in, but if Leondra thought this one was worth the trip, that said a lot for what she felt was missing from that collection.

Evening came before long, and Leondra and Venser made their way to the bar Matthias had mentioned earlier, the "Azure Moon". The atmosphere of the bar was different from the last one they'd visited, a bit quieter and more orderly than the Crimson Flower on Lunaria. Even still, there was a bit of boisterous activity going on, and it appeared that Matthias was the source of much of it.

"That man wastes no time," Leondra said, shaking her head. "And it looks like he has friends, too." Sebastian and Arycelle were part of the revelry, and

Isamu had joined them. Their current activity was leading the bar patrons in singing a slightly vulgar drinking song.

"He does this a lot?" Venser asked.

"He does it enough for it to be a well-known trend. Matthias is certainly known for his ability to start a party or bit of revelry wherever he goes."

"Oh, Leondra, so glad you and Victor could join us!" Matthias said, noticing them and waving them over. "Marianne's off doing things and stuff, but we got Isamu in on the merriment."

"You gave him that book, didn't you?" Leondra asked, a wry smile on her face.

"Look, the man wanted reference materials, so I gave him what he asked for!"

"And I'm *sure* he wanted tentacle references."

"Eh, it's a nice bonus. Anyway, enough chatter about literary proclivities and the finer points of literature. Pull up a seat and all!"

As the revelry continued, with Matthias starting up another drinking song, Venser noticed Basch sitting alone at a table near the group, observing them with a look of wanting to not be associated with them. The partying was too much for Venser to be comfortable, and he told Leondra that he'd sit away from Matthias and his pernicious posse. She voiced understanding, and so he sat down at the table with Basch.

"Why are you here?" Basch asked, looking up at him. "The party's over there. Not much going on over here."

"It's too loud over there," Venser said. "I'm not used to such noise and such revelry."

"I suppose you wouldn't be."

There was something about Basch's voice that struck Venser as concerning, but he said nothing. He'd gotten a glass of water, having no appetite for alcohol, and he took a sip from it. They sat in relative silence, observing as Matthias continued to drive the party with another choice drinking song, this one about a girl named Carloota who had the biggest rack he had ever encountered.

"So, you're going to get married off to Leondra, I hear," Basch said, breaking the silence.

"That's what the plan is," Venser said.

"How do you feel about it?"

"About the plan? I...I guess how I feel doesn't really matter, so I haven't allowed myself to feel a particular way."

"Why not?"

"It's an arranged marriage, set up by our fathers."

"Arranged marriage, he says." Basch lifted up his glass and swirled it around a bit. "I suppose those are still a thing between the idiots and despots who hold an iron-clad grip on each city. Put more puppets on your strings, watch them dance to your preferred tune, and make sure nobody ever is in position to take the reins of power from you."

"That's a bit bleak," Venser said. Basch wasn't *wrong*, but it was certainly far more blunt than he was used to.

"Those with power like to do what they can to keep the power, it being both a means and an end. They certainly would rather concentrate the power than risk its dilution. Some are better at hiding their hand than others, though it sounds like you and Leondra might be dealing with people who have all their cards on the table, challenging others to try and trump them."

"I...I guess you could say that. We're trying to figure out what those cards are, and figure out if we can beat their hand."

"Fascinating, as politics often can be. That said, one question I have, that I think the others don't care to ask or think is too rude to ask," Basch continued, "is why you, in particular. At least as far as I can tell, there would be more value in Leondra being married off to someone important. Like that idiot Isamu, actually. I'm almost surprised their fathers haven't tried to arrange a marriage between them by now."

"I'm honestly not sure why me, either," Venser replied.

Basch smirked in response. "You're rather coy about things," he said.

"What do you mean?"

"Most of those noble, high-class types would jump at the chance to defend their lineage from attack, to prove their status. I know Isamu and Leondra would. Even if they don't play the part sometimes, they're fiercely protective of what their birthright has afforded them."

"I see," Venser said. Basch did have a point; a lot of people would defend their high-born status, especially his siblings. He remembered one of his brothers got into a fist fight with someone else over that particular point.

"I might be off the mark, but I have a theory. It's not an airtight one, but my guess would be that you're from Aracoras, which would explain some things and ask a lot more questions." Basch had dropped his voice and leaned in as he said this.

"...what would make you guess that?" Venser asked, trying to keep his voice down and not sound too shocked by this query.

"I asked Sebastian and Matthias about you, and they both said you tended to be more inclined to listen to conversations and that you didn't talk about yourself. Leondra also hasn't explicitly mentioned it to us, but she demurred whenever asked about you, beyond just mentioning you were her fiancé. I also overheard you talking with Leondra the other night on the *Alamithea*, which was the seed for this entire line of thought, but I wanted to see if I could gather the information more directly, to corroborate all of this."

So *that* was the weird creaking noise he'd heard the other night. Basch was apparently listening in on them surreptitiously.

"Do you make it a point to eavesdrop on all of your passengers?"

"Only the cute ones," Basch replied. "And I've said too much. Must be the drink."

Venser sighed. "Is this information you're going to spread?" he asked.

"It's not my business to, and all of this is just rumors and hearsay besides. Sometimes, there is value in keeping one's tongue in their mouth, waiting for when to speak. But I do notice you're denying none of it, which tells me a lot."

As Basch said this, a loud, cacophonous crash rang out near where the cavorting was most intense. It appeared that Matthias had fallen in a way that ensconced himself in the bosom of a waitress, and this naturally caused quite the commotion.

"Not again," Basch groaned. "I suppose I need to try and get that drunk twit back to the *Alamithea* before he gets himself, and all of us, into even more trouble." He got up and, with a final nod, left Venser to think about that conversation. He probably also needed to get back to the palace for the night, if Leondra and Isamu were ready to go…though it did seem like everyone was ready to disperse after that climax.

The trio headed back to the palace to escape the commotion at the bar. Leondra had worked up a nice bit of a drunken buzz, while Isamu was nicely plastered and needed a bit of guidance to get back to the palace.

"Oh, Leondraaaaaa, why do we…hic…why do we have to go baaaaack," he said, his voice slurred. "I want to…hic…paaaaarty. I want to party with…ulp…with all those fun people."

"You've had too much to drink, and your father would not like you to have to be treated for alcohol poisoning. Again."

"But…but…I don't waaaannaaaaaa," he whined, clinging to her arm and trying to not fall over. "It's way too…hic…way too early to go baaaaaaaaack for the night."

"I really don't care what you think it's time for," she said, shaking her head. "We're going back to the palace."

"You're…hic…you're no fun. You're a *fun sponge*."

Venser followed quietly, amused by their dynamic. It definitely seemed like they were old friends, regardless of if there was anything more there than that. Isamu also seemed to have a problem with impulse control, but he'd not say that aloud.

"If I were to let you go off and do what you please, I'd probably have to extricate you from a brothel the next morning. And, yes, I'm speaking from experience."

"But they were sooooo nice…hic…to me. And sooooo pretty."

"Well, you probably should have gone to them first if you wanted to spend the night there. Not that your father would be more pleased by you getting it from every buxom babe in the brothel."

There was a lot of history there, Venser thought. It'd be nice to have someone to rely on when something like Isamu getting hammered happened.

He didn't have that in Aracoras, partially because people liked to leverage those little misdeeds and miscues into prime positions; despite an outward appearance of piety, things could be incredibly vicious and ruthless.

They finally got Isamu back to the palace and left him in the care of several staff members, who all pledged to take care of him in spite of his attempts to hit on the women among them. Leondra and Venser retired to their own room, which was a front-facing guest room with two beds.

"I maybe had a bit more than I was planning to," Leondra said, "but that was a fun enough night. Did you enjoy yourself, Venser?"

"I had a decent time," Venser answered. He didn't want to mention everything he'd heard from Basch, but it was still accurate to say as much.

"I'm surprised Marianne wasn't there, actually. She's often in the bars with the crew, or so I think I remembered."

"Maybe she was at a different bar?"

"Quite possibly. Or she was busy with business dealings. She's always been more business-minded than the rest of the lot. They're reliable in their own right, of course, but Marianne is definitely the businesswoman of them all, always working towards bettering their status. Sometimes she gets too focused on the bottom line, but that happens."

"I suppose someone needs to handle the business side of things." Venser laid down in bed and looked out at the sky, a clear view of the window from his bed. The moon hung large in the sky, with a couple scattered clouds and a smattering of stars.

"It frees Matthias up to supply pornographic novels to nobles, that's for sure."

"Is *The Fisherman's Wife* pornography?" His idea of the genre was cheap magazines he saw some of the people sneaking around Aracoras, tattered tomes that featured lovely ladies in provocative positions. They *didn't exist*, of course.

"Depends on who you talk to." He heard Leondra lay down in bed. "Some would say it is, others might have a broader definition that excludes it. All the same, it's the kind of book that probably should not be passed around in polite public, which is *exactly* why Matthias does so. Or part of the reason.

He loves that sort of shock value."

"That sounds like him, all right," Venser said.

They started drifting off, sleep coming quickly to Venser. He wondered if he'd see much more of them, or if this would be where they'd part ways for good. The latter seemed likely; he had no idea how long Leondra would need to be here for research, and they didn't seem like the type to stay longer than they absolutely needed to.

Eventually, they'd have to go back to Lunaria. He hoped that they would be back before his father returned, because the firestorm would be hellacious if they weren't there. He did wonder about Basch, the man he'd talked to in the bar, but he figured that nothing would likely come of it; they'd be gone soon enough, and he wouldn't be occasioned to see the man again.

Sorocco's library was, Venser discovered, as impressive from the inside as it was from the outside. It reached high in the sky and deep underground, filled with all sorts of works of both literary merit and historical merit. The archives Leondra wanted to access were one at the top of the library tower and one in the basement. She had a small team of scholars loaned to her by Yamato, and they were presently cloistered on the top floor while Venser was free to explore. He wasn't inclined to explore much, instead settling into a nice corner with a couple novels to keep him company.

It was, by all accounts, a perfect afternoon for him. He'd always loved reading, but his past experiences had always been trying to hide books from prying eyes at all hours of the night. He and the people he spent time with always were trying to sneak around with literature they weren't supposed to have, and getting caught was definitely a mark of disgrace.

There was none of that, though, and it was nice to just sit and *read*.

The sound of rain could be heard on the sides of the building, carrying through as a steady drumbeat of sorts. He'd heard that there was a chance of rain, and it was panning out today. Rain wasn't common in Aracoras, but it was generally unwelcome because of a tendency to make everything uncomfortably humid and moist. That feeling of dampness and stickiness that was prevalent on Aracoras wasn't to be found here, which was a nice change of pace.

Every once in a while, he'd see a scholar scurry out from where Leondra was researching, and he wondered what they were doing and where they were going. Scholars returning to join her were slightly less frequent, but still something that happened.

Finally, Leondra emerged. Venser saw that she had a notebook filled with what looked like dense, spidery notes, and her face bore a curious expression. It didn't look triumphant, but it wasn't completely defeated.

"How did it go?" he asked.

"I don't completely know," she said, looking down at her notebook. "There's a lot of information that we gathered, that's for sure. The problem is that it's a weird, circular web of contradictions, and there's no way it can all be right."

"That's…well…interesting." Venser wasn't sure what to say in response to this.

"I need a break, though. I've been staring at pages for too long. If you're free, how about we walk, and I tell you what I've learned?"

"I like the sounds of that. I'm done with the book I was just reading, so it's excellent timing." Indeed, Venser had finished an entire novel while Leondra was researching, which both spoke to how quickly he read and how long she was in there.

"Let's start at the beginning," Leondra said. The two were in the public gardens; she had procured an umbrella, and the two were huddled under it as a light drizzle fell.

"Good place to start," Venser said. "At least, if there is a beginning."

"There is one, at least. The Tomb of the Almighty dates back a long way. I've found lots of references to it in historical logs and records, and it's at least older than we both are. So it's been there, and people see it as important. Where the contradictions start coming in is why it exists, why it's important, and what's inside it."

"The story I know is that the Almighty was entombed there to recover from a battle against evil. What do the works you've read say?"

"Lots of different things, lots of theories that can't all be correct together.

One book says that there's nothing inside it, that the Tomb of the Almighty is just a hunk of rock assigned a sacred role by people wanting to subjugate the masses. Another story is that the Tomb is actually a cache of rare, magical weapons sealed away to prevent misuse and abuse by people who would be enthralled by the promise of power. Another is that it houses a mindless, voracious monster called a lhurgoyf, but that was an especially vague statement without much detail to it."

"That is…a wide range of possibilities," Venser said, shaking his head.

"There were two theories that stood out to me. One of those is that the Tomb of the Almighty houses what you told me was in there, the Almighty convalescing after their battle against a great evil. The other is that the Tomb actually houses the great evil itself, confined there after the battle to best it failed."

"If that's the case, then where would the Almighty be?" The idea that the Tomb of the Almighty might not hold what was promised was a deeply disturbing thought.

"If anywhere, the book posits that the Almighty lives in the world beneath the sea of clouds," she said. "Trapped beneath a veil held together by malign means, unable to fully vanquish the evil entombed within. Of course, the inverse may also be true; the book saying the Almighty is in the tomb bearing their name says that the great evil they fended off is trapped on the surface, unable to continue their conquest and working to rend the sea so that they might resume where they left off."

"That is certainly a wide range of possibilities. And your father is operating off of the Almighty being there?"

"The weapon cache theory may also be one he's banking on, claiming a number of powerful weapons with which to secure further power, but he thinks he'll benefit greatly from it being opened and being there when it's opened. The book espousing the theory says that, when the Tomb of the Almighty opens, they will emerge and reward their most faithful servants with many benefits, and prolonged life is a commonly-listed reward."

"Is your father that faithful a servant?"

"I doubt it," Leondra said, smiling grimly. "Outside of Aracoras, none are all that faithful or devoted anymore. But being there lets him shape the narrative to his benefit."

Before Venser could talk more, they came upon a pair of women in the rain, getting into a heated argument. They looked like they were from the palace, and they were having quite a disagreement. Venser swore he could hear one of them call the other a "scullery skank", which was quite an insult and one new to his ears.

"We should probably change direction," Leondra said, motioning. "Those two seem to be having a disagreement, and it's better if we don't get caught up in it."

"It sounds like it, and it certainly looks like it," Venser said. "They're from the palace, aren't they?"

"I think so. They might be arguing over Isamu and one of them getting googly eyes from him the other day. He has a reputation for flirting with a lot of the maids, and some of the less-experienced ones tend to mistake his casual flirting for something with meaning."

"He's a womanizer?"

"And a notorious one. His father's tried to get him to change, but nothing's stuck. He'll behave for a while before going back to his old habits, shallowly flirting with the maids and breaking their hearts. And instigating plenty of fights, when they realize that he's done this to all of the maids."

"That's almost…uh, impressive." He wasn't sure if that was the best word for Isamu's antics, admittedly.

"Impressive certainly is *a* word for it."

They turned and walked in the opposite direction as they heard a "splash" near where the women were arguing. Neither one looked back, and neither one thought it'd be a spectacle worth their time.

Sorocco looked a bit different in the rain, Venser thought. There was a bit of mist in the air, providing some shrouding to the buildings. While the red accents still stood out, providing a bit of framing, how it looked was very picturesque.

The two returned to the library, and Leondra threw herself back into a stack of books, hoping that the answers she sought were just within reach, a morsel of information that rested between covers she had yet to explore. Venser was left with another novel and his thoughts, and he wondered if there would be clarity yet in the search for figuring out what, exactly, was in the Tomb of the Almighty.

There was a lot to think about. What was beneath the sea of clouds? The story he had heard from his schooling was that it was a world that had been twisted by the machinations of evil, that the defeat of the dark deity opposing the Almighty had nevertheless poisoned the world to the point of being uninhabitable. Much like the Tomb of the Almighty was meant to allow the Almighty time to heal and recover, the cloud sea was meant to give the land time to heal and recover from the damage done.

How long ago had all of that happened, though? It was just described as having happened "in the past", a vague time frame with no further specificity. He wondered how many generations ago it all happened, and if there was any way to get clarity beyond that vague sense of it having happened some time before all of them were there.

Many questions remained unanswered, and he hoped that there would be some progress to figuring out the answers that were missing. Both for the questions he knew about and the ones he hadn't yet thought to ask, whatever those were.

6

Whorl of Intrigue

Yamato had extended a dinner invitation to both Venser and Leondra that evening, an invitation brought to them by courier, and they accepted. It did not seem like an invitation to be refused, though they were not inclined to refuse it. Leondra had filled a second notebook with spidery, narrow writing by the time they were to be off for supper, with some insights spilling into a third volume, and Venser was impressed by how much she had compiled in just the day.

"That's a lot of notes," Venser said, the two walking out of the library. "Did…uh, did you learn anything further about what you're trying to find out?"

"I think so," Leondra answered. "It's a…well, it's a bit of a mess, and I just wrote down everything that looked worth making note of. There's a surprisingly low amount of cohesion between all of the stories and tales I've been coming upon. I'm definitely going to need to sort through it, figure out what's actually the case or what might plausibly be the case. It's certainly as much work as I was expecting, if not a bit more, but I think I can put it all together into something that makes sense."

"You're really throwing yourself into this." Venser was impressed by her dedication to this.

"My tutors told me that as well, with my studies. I think that sometimes it's worth going in and digging deep. And here is the place and time for such, at least in my eyes." She was smiling as she said this.

"Hopefully the threads you've found all make sense when you can put them together."

"I hope so, too. I just need to figure out how it all comes together…or *if* it does, I suppose. Maybe talking about it with Yamato will help. I've found, in the past, that talking about complex topics helps, particularly with having to process what's being said."

Venser nodded and said nothing further. He'd have liked to have discussions like the ones she was describing, but instruction in Aracoras always consisted of being taught and accepting without question, and questions were both discouraged and punished if they were deemed "dangerous".

They returned to the palace, and they were met by the sight of Isamu arguing with a maid. It was a spectacle of an argument (as attested to by the amassed audience, and it seemed like she was holding something of a vaguely salacious nature.

"Come on, baby, be gentle with that!" Isamu whined.

"Don't call me 'baby', you lecherous and disgusting twit!" she screamed. "You're not supposed to have those vile magazines!"

"Hey, you don't need to be so loud! And…uh, those magazines, they're for my anatomy study! Nothing wrong with that, right?"

"Oh, you're definitely *studying* anatomy, all right! Probably paying particular attention to their breasts!" She aggressively waved the magazine around, showing everyone that it was a copy of *Ogler's Digest*.

"Be gentle with the pages! Those…uh, those are some prime study materials! I can't get the most of them if those pages get wrinkled!"

"So you *really* must like that 'Oglette of the Month'! What was her name… oh, I remember! It was 'Carmelita the Cock Destroyer', and last month's was 'The Jugtacular Jessica'!"

It was here that Isamu saw Leondra and Venser. "Excellent timing for you to show up, Leondra!" he said. "I'm having an…argument with this *lovely* maid here, who seems to find some of my drawing reference materials objectionable."

"That's maybe because they *are* objectionable?" Leondra said, glaring at him.

"Not you, too!"

"Your father told us all that *Ogler's Digest* was not to be allowed in the palace, and I distinctly recall you voicing your assent to this rule! And what do I find in your room? A copy of the accursed periodical, open to *this* page!" The maid showed the offending pages to the crowd, featuring a well-endowed woman (apparently the aforementioned "Carmelita the Cock Destroyer") wearing naught but a jaunty hat and a smile.

"Keep it down, or Father will wind out!" Isamu hissed.

"Find out *what?*"

Everyone turned to see Yamato standing behind his son, observing this all with an inscrutable look on his face.

"Oh, Father! I...did not see you standing there," Isamu said, stuttering. "When did you get here?"

"While you were arguing with her," he said. "Might you be so kind as to hand that to me?" The maid stepped over and handed the *Ogler's Digest* to Yamato, still open to the especially offensive page, and over Isamu's stammered objections.

"I...you were not supposed to see that I had that," Isamu continued. His voice was desperate, clearly the sound of someone who knew they had been poorly-behaved. "I was...you see, I am using that for anatomy practice, for my drawings!"

"The last time you were caught with a copy of this periodical," Yamato said, glaring, "you told me that you were reading it for the articles. Which *would* be interesting, given that several of the articles had titles like 'How to Get Her to Climax More Reliably' and 'Livening up the Bedroom with Fruit.'"

"How do you remember all of these?" Isamu yelped. Everyone else had a look that melded disgust with horror.

"You mentioned the literary value of the issue, and I wanted to see it for myself. I had heard of the periodical's reputation, and sometimes it's good to confirm things for oneself. The titles were...memorable, to say the least, and the prose was remarkably florid and loquacious. I certainly regret reading the words on the pages, but the titles were *very* descriptive."

Isamu didn't have any response to this. He hung his head, cheeks flush with shame.

"This is something we can talk about later, your *proclivities* towards such periodicals," Yamato said. "For now, I ask that you take this time to reflect on *why* I might be so displeased with you bringing such…literature into the palace. I would like to talk to Leondra about what she has learned prior to supper, and I fear that your face would do little else besides fill me with *disappointment*."

That last word hung in the air, and Isamu took this time to slink back towards his room, which was enough pretext for the crowd to disperse. Yamato glanced down at the magazine, sighed, and closed it up before turning back to his guests.

"I apologize for you two having to see that spectacle," he said. "While I might hope that Isamu has learned his lesson from having his literary interests revealed, I doubt it."

"He hasn't the last couple of times he's gotten into trouble," Leondra said.

"So it would seem. He's a talented young man, but his lechery may prove his undoing at some point. Anyway, enough of that. I'm curious to see what all you've pulled from texts today, Leondra."

"I'm looking forward to sharing those notes, sir. Shall we?"

Supper was still being prepared, and Yamato was listening to Leondra present what she'd learned from the texts. The first part of the findings was what she had told Venser earlier, the conflicting theories about what the nature of the Tomb of the Almighty was. She then got to the newer tranche of information, which was about the nature of the seal on the Tomb of the Almighty.

"So, the nature of the Tomb of the Almighty's seal is up for debate, at least according to the books you read," Yamato said, stroking his chin.

"The common thread I can gather," Leondra said, "is that the seal is, at minimum, tied to Aracoras. The strongest force holding the seal on the

Tomb of the Almighty originates in Aracoras."

Venser frowned as he heard this. "I remember hearing," he said, speaking slowly, "that the Tomb of the Almighty is bound by what they called a hieratic seal, one that can't be broken by mortal intervention."

"How would you break it, then? *Could* it be broken?"

"That much, I'm not sure of. We were just told it was sealed by a force beyond our ken, and that its opening would only be through divine intervention."

"I have heard word," Yamato said, "that there existed several implements that could break open seals of an arcane nature. The locations of them have been lost to history, though, as have the mechanisms by which they operate. Whether or not they still exist is up for speculation."

"So, if you have one, you can forcibly open the Tomb…correct?" Venser asked.

"I don't know," Leondra said, shaking her head. "There's just a lot of hearsay and innuendo about how they work and how they'd open the Tomb of the Almighty."

"Are they the only way to open the Tomb of the Almighty?" Yamato asked.

"That's something I couldn't pin down, I'm sorry. There were lots of nebulous statements, lots of words that seemed to be deliberately obtuse in their meanings. That appears to be one way to open the Tomb, but there may be more avenues to that effect."

"No need to apologize. This is all information that's good to have, and it's nice to have it all compiled. In summary, we know that your father wants to open the Tomb of the Almighty, that he wants to be there when it opens, and your planned nuptials are part of the impetus for this to happen." Yamato was pacing as he said this.

"That all sounds in agreement with what I've been putting together," she said. "The question, I suppose, becomes if there's a way to keep it from happening."

"There might be ways," Yamato said, his tone cryptic and his eyebrows raised as he made the remark. "For now, though, we should eat. I suspect supper is ready."

That cagey remark stuck with Venser through supper, which was a rather low-key affair. The food was good, albeit not what he was used to, and it was punctuated with Leondra and Yamato continuing to talk about her research and where she was looking to take it. Isamu wasn't present at dinner, probably reflecting on the shame he had brought upon himself earlier that day. Or quite possibly finding ways to bring further shame upon himself, but nobody could really know.

The rest of the day proceeded without incident, and Venser and Leondra retired early. He didn't mind an evening less chaotic than their bar misadventure, though he was reminded of it when he heard commotion deeper in the palace. Maybe Isamu had gone out to drown his sorrows or drink away his shame after all, which would largely nullify the point of his father reprimanding him earlier.

Venser woke up on his own around the middle of the day, noticing that Leondra had already left. Likely back to the library, no doubt, he thought. All the same, it'd be good to get up and rendezvous with her.

He got up, stretched, and became aware of an argument outside his window. He looked to see Isamu chasing after a woman, with her holding a book and him desperately trying to get it back. Some things never changed, it seemed. He stepped out of the guest room and was swiftly greeted by a maid.

"Master Venser," she said, bowing respectfully, "Yamato requests your presence in his study. Might I have the privilege of taking you there?"

"Uh...yes," he said, surprised by her being there. He wasn't expecting such a greeting, but if Yamato wanted to see him, it seemed ill-mannered to refuse. He followed her through the corridors, thinking that he recognized her but was unable to exactly pin down where or when it was.

As they arrived, Yamato was at his desk, writing. He looked up in response to the sound of the maid's entry and saw the person he had called for.

"Your timing is excellent," he said, motioning Venser to one of the seats in front of his desk. "It so happens that I've been able to, with Leondra's help, make some *arrangements*."

"What…uh, what kind of arrangements, sir?" Venser asked. He was a bit leery of how Yamato said "arrangements".

"Let's start from the beginning. Leondra told me that your father returned to Aracoras the day after your arrival, and the flight time to Aracoras with the airships used by members of the Council of Elders is roughly five days."

"That…yes, that's correct."

"You father should have arrived back in Aracoras yesterday, if the chronology you two have told me is correct. That means that he may well be returning to Lunaria in short order, though I wouldn't know the exact date he would start his return trip. He would, of course, be headed there to pick you and Leondra up to take you to the ceremony, held in Aracoras."

"…yes, he would be. I believe both he and Leondra's father agreed on that much, that the ceremony was to be held there."

"That said, if you *weren't* there when he got back, the wedding might not happen, right? There would be no groom, and thus no pair."

Venser started to figure out where this was going, and he was nervous. "You're suggesting I not go back to Lunaria," he said.

"Exactly. Leondra *would* need to return to Lunaria, of course, but you might not need to…return with her, thus preventing the marriage. That said, you staying here would not be without peril, as I believe it would fray already fragile ties of diplomacy, so I would rather not have that."

"So, what are you suggesting, sir?" He knew it wasn't much of a suggestion, but it sounded better than the alternative.

"I'm *suggesting* that you take a flight out of Sorocco and to a nearby city, laying low and out of sight of the people of Lunaria and Aracoras. And it so happens that the crew you and Leondra traveled with are planning to travel to Gran Moria on the morrow."

"That is…interesting, an interesting development. You have already arranged for my passage with them, I presume."

"Yes, I have. They've been promised a princely sum for looking after you, both from my coffers and from Leondra's personal trust, as well as a very positive recommendation as to their capabilities for use wherever it's suitable. I think all of this is worth it to make sure this goes off, and we have time enough to unravel all the little irritating details of Hessler and Victarion's machinations before it's too late to. After the wedding, it will be far too late to do this, and we need to try and put up resistance now."

Venser knew that he didn't *really* have a choice here. He was going to Gran Moria tomorrow, with or without his assent. So, he reasoned, it was better to make peace with it, because sometimes sacrifices needed to be made in the short term. Not that it was necessarily a sacrifice, because he wouldn't be thrust into a marriage he wasn't ready for, but he wished for a say in the matter he was unlikely to get.

"I'll do it," he said. He tried to project confidence he didn't have in his voice.

"Glad to hear your agreement," Yamato said, smiling slightly. "I understand that we put you in a tricky situation, but your assent is welcomed. I do have a request I'd make of you for when you get to Gran Moria, but that can come later today. For now, though, you may want to meet up with Leondra in the library. She should be in the basement archive today."

"I see. I'll go to meet her." Venser slowly stood up, ready to get going.

"Before you go, I have one more question. Have you seen Isamu at all today?"

"I believe I did. He...I saw him out of a window. He was chasing a maid into the city, and it looked like the maid was holding a book."

Yamato frowned. "I see," he said. "If you run into Isamu, please tell him that I would like to have a word with him."

Venser had an idea of the kinds of words he wished to exchange with his son. He bid Yamato farewell for now and left the palace. The city sprawled before him, almost a daunting prospect alone.

"Let's see, it's the tallest building over there," he said, pointing to the towering library in the distance to orient himself. "She's in the bottom floor archives. Let's get going."

A light breeze drifted across the city, carrying a mix of scents from all around. There was a sense of idyll that Venser appreciated, one that felt a bit less affected than the forced peace of Aracoras. The chaotic clamor of Lunaria was memorable in its own way, but he found himself liking Sorocco a good amount from what he'd seen.

The streets weren't bereft of activity, but compared to the crowds of Lunaria, it was definitely far less chaotic and congested. The walk to the library tower was a pleasant one, and Venser took in both the sights and the other sensations. The breeze tousling his hair, smells of food from various establishments, and occasional bouts of song from birds all made for an enjoyable jaunt through the city, and he almost forgot the unfamiliarity of the place he was walking through.

It was almost a pity he was leaving, but he thought he understood why he couldn't stay. Diplomacy was sometimes a thin line that had to be walked, and if they discovered he was on Sorocco when he was definitely not supposed to be, that could prove *problematic*. So that left the option of going back to Lunaria to await his marriage, or go wherever was offered to get away from it.

It wasn't much of a choice, and going into the unknown was scary, but he didn't like what was waiting for him in the known.

He made it to the library without incident; while minor, Venser was still mildly pleased with himself for having accomplished that much. Scholars were milling about as he walked inside, talking among themselves.

"Oh, you're the man who's with Leondra," one of them said. "She's currently in the basement collection, which is at capacity. We're rotating out in shifts."

"It's a small space," one of the other scholars added.

"That's fine," Venser said. "If you tell her that I'm here, I should be fine waiting for her."

They nodded, and one of them scurried off. Venser found a chair and settled in; he didn't know how long Leondra would be, but there would probably be time for reading and generally relaxing.

By the time Leondra had emerged from the archive for the day, the sun had begun to set. She looked exhausted and like she didn't want to see another dusty tome for the rest of the evening.

"Sorry it's taken me this long to come up and say hello," she said, addressing

Venser. "I got a bit absorbed in the research, and I lost track of the time."

"It's fine," Venser said. "Was it productive, at least?"

"I think it was productive. If you don't mind, though, can we get going to get some food? I'm not sure I can talk on a stomach as empty as mine is."

Everybody scattered away from the library, with Leondra and Venser headed into the city. He saw that she had several more notebooks filled with writing and notes, and he wondered what she had learned from today's delving.

"That hits the spot," Leondra said, taking a bite of sandwich. They had grabbed sandwiches from a small streetside food stand as something tide them over until supper proper, and they were walking as they ate.

"They are good sandwiches," Venser nodded. He also hadn't eaten recently, so it was welcome.

"So, Yamato caught you up on our plan, right?"

"He did."

"I'm sorry we sprang this on you, but it's the only way we can think of to delay the nuptials without igniting a diplomatic row of epic proportions." She looked apologetic, Venser thought.

"I understand. I...I guess I wasn't sure if I wanted to get married."

"To be honest, I didn't. Not to you, no offense. Not that I find you objectionable, because you're not! You've been nothing but sweet and lovely, but...I don't *feel* anything, and I'd rather not just be part of the cycle of getting married for diplomacy."

"That's a familiar cycle to me, at least from the outside." Venser was remembering all of his siblings' marriages, and all of them were for political reasons. "I can't blame you, though, and I feel the same way."

"Don't worry about your father and his reaction. I'll figure out how to weather the storm. Father might not be thrilled with things going differently from how he was expecting, but I have enough experience with him to soften the landing, at least."

"That's good, then," Venser said. He was more concerned about how his father would react, as his temper was known to be volcanic and volatile, complete with his face turning unmentionable shades.

As the two walked and talked, they happened upon Isamu, currently attempting to sweet talk another "lovely lady". She had a look of disinterest, one that didn't budge as Isamu continued to run his mouth.

"Come on, baby, you know I only have eyes for you!" he said. "You're easily the prettiest girl I've ever met."

"You told that to my friend the other day," she retorted.

"No, I didn't!"

The woman sighed and walked away, leaving Isamu to ponder what part of his approach might have failed this time. He looked up and saw Leondra standing there, arms crossed, and he jumped.

"How long have you been standing there?" he yelped.

"Long enough to know that you really should try out a new playbook," she responded. "Sounds like your old song and dance aren't cutting it anymore."

"That's none of your business!"

"Uh, your father asked me to tell you that he wants to talk to you," Venser said.

"He's been wanting to talk to me for ages now, so that's not new!" Isamu responded, his tone clipped and short. "He tells me that I need to get serious about things and stuff and…things. Quit trying to get girls, quit trying to have fun…"

"More like he's trying to get you to not get in trouble," Leondra said. "You *can* have fun, but you're coming off as alternately desperate and lecherous. How do you think all the girls you're talking to feel when they learn about your extensive 'Oglette of the Month' poster collection?"

"How do you know about *that*?"

"You showed it to me. Repeatedly."

Isamu laughed, though the tone was definitely a nervous one. "I guess I did, didn't I?" he stammered.

"Your father might be different, but I'm not asking you to change overnight, Isamu. Just tone down the antics, and…well, the girls might actually listen to what you're telling them instead of thinking you're just telling them all the same thing."

"…you're probably right, Leondra," he said, sighing. "I've been a handful, haven't I?"

"You've always been a bit of one. I kinda appreciate that about you."

He smiled. "Thanks, Leondra. I think I'm going to go back and talk with my father. I'll see you later."

As he walked away, Leondra shook her head. "I know he means well, but he can't help himself," she sighed. "He's had these periods where he turns over a new leaf, behaves, and then is lured back into his normal patterns with an issue of *Bounteous Buxom Babes* or *Ogler's Digest*. Or *Fantastic Breasts and Where to Find Them*."

"Maybe he might finally have gotten the message?" Venser asked. The titles were certainly interesting, but not in a sense of wanting to learn more about them.

"I'll believe it when I see it. Let's get back to the palace for now. I need to catch you two up on the day's discoveries."

Compared to the day before, the discoveries Leondra shared were relatively sedate. The main new piece of information was that the Tomb of the Almighty would be able to be opened in several different ways, if believable. The one that stood out was needing some kind of key to open the vault, but there were few details on what the key would look like, what it might be called, or where it would be. All the same, the volume of texts suggested that the Tomb of the Almighty, at least, was *not* empty.

Venser was trying to fall asleep that evening, wondering what it all meant. He did accept an offer to have his clothes washed prior to setting out tomorrow, so he was in a borrowed sleeping gown. It wasn't uncomfortable, but he was trying to get used to it.

After they had finished recapping Leondra's discoveries, Yamato had given Venser a letter to give to the leader of Gran Moria when he got there, explaining what was happening in summary and vouching for his identity. Yamato mentioned, seemingly in passing, that they could be *difficult* on Gran Moria, and he hoped that the difficulty wouldn't be terribly hard to get over.

He and Leondra had also briefly met with Arycelle, who mentioned that she would be to the palace early to pick Venser up. She still had no idea of who Venser *actually* was, unless she was hiding it. Basch had seemed to pick up on things, aided by a bit of eavesdropping, but Basch also seemed to be a bit more cynical and distrusting than the others.

Tomorrow, he'd be back in the skies, on towards another adventure. It was scary, especially when he reflected on how much Leondra had smoothed things over for him in Lunaria and Sorocco, but he'd have to learn to handle things himself. Having others was a gift he realized he hadn't really experienced before, but he didn't want to keep being a burden to everyone.

Maybe if he was able to do things without a guiding hand, he'd feel less like a piece to a game, being moved around the board by the hand of someone else. That was, in a sense, what he had been to this point, a piece for his father and now for Yamato and Leondra. At least they had the courtesy to ask before moving him.

Finally, he fell asleep. He needed sleep, and tossing and turning wouldn't help that any. His dreams were an unpleasant, threatening morass of shadows and threats, almost like it was his guilt over having fled from his fate in Lunaria. He wondered if it was sent by the Almighty somehow, to show the wayward lamb the error of its ways. He'd been drilled about the ruthlessness of the Almighty against those who strayed from the path, and while he had normally felt his conviction waning, these nights of nightmares and turmoil rarely helped.

7

The Hurricane's Eye

"Well, looks like we're here early," Arycelle said. She, Leondra, and Venser were standing in the harbor of Sorocco, looking at the *Alamithea* and the people scrambling to load cargo last-minute. Arycelle had shown up early, and the walk back to the harbor was not particularly long.

"Better early than late," Leondra said. "I know Marianne is very much not a fan of waiting."

"You remember correctly. She loves punctuality....or, rather, she loathes a lack of it. Same difference."

"Of course I love punctuality," they heard. Marianne had shown up behind them, and Venser tried not to jump in surprise. "Time has value of its own, and I detest when people waste mine or the time of others."

"I can understand that," Leondra said. "There's a lot of 'hurry up and wait' going on in my life."

"You know," Marianne continued, "if you ever want to run away from your life and join our crew, I'd be fine with that. Not that you'd accept, I suspect, but it is a standing offer."

"With how things are going, I may yet take you up on that." Leondra was smiling, but it was a grim sort of smile.

"At any rate, we're finishing up pre-flight preparations, and it should be an hour before departure. Victor can settle into the quarters you used to come over here, and we'll finish what we need prior to departure."

She walked off, while Arycelle disappeared into the ship. Leondra turned back to Venser. "So, it looks like it's farewell for now," she said. "I'm sorry that we're doing this with you, but I think we need to try and keep them from opening up the tomb for as long as possible, not until we can confirm for sure what's inside it."

"I...I think I understand," Venser said. "I wish I could be more directly helpful to you all."

"You've been helpful enough, just by being yourself and being there. Don't worry about doing more, because you're doing enough.

"Before I forget, take these." She handed him a small bag, one that held the letter Yamato had drafted up the day before, as well as a notebook. "The notebook can be for you to write in, in case you have things you want to put down. Thoughts to reflect on, things to remember, or whatever comes to mind."

"Thank you, Leondra."

Leondra then took Venser's hand and pressed something into it. "And take this as a good luck charm of sorts," she said. "It might be helpful to you."

With that, the two bid farewell. Leondra was off to the library to resume her research, and Venser watched her walk away. Once she was out of sight, he climbed up the steps to board the *Alamithea* and returned to the cabin he had been in for the flight to Sorocco. It looked like it had when he was last there, with a sitting desk and a bunk bed, though the sheets had been changed.

He sat down in the chair at the desk and finally took a moment to look at the thing Leondra had pressed into his hand. It was a metal ring, silver and emblazoned with what he thought looked like the sigil of Lunaria. It was a stylized crescent moon, somewhat similar to the style of the sun on his symbol of devotion. He slid it onto a finger; it wasn't a perfect fit, but it was good enough, he reckoned.

"Oh, you're here already," Matthias poked his head in as means of greeting.

"Hello, Matthias," Venser said.

"Just got back here myself. I had a...*delivery* to make before we left, if you catch my drift." He raised his eyebrows suggestively, and Venser was struck by a thought.

"Forgive me for asking, but...are you the one who supplied Isamu with those books and magazines?"

"Which ones? ...oh, I see. Looks like Isamu might have left them where he wasn't supposed to. And after he complained to me about the maids finding his stash of *Ogler's Digest*, too!" He had a mischievous smile that confirmed Venser's question.

"He seems to be bad at hiding them."

"His problem, not mine. He asks, I supply, he pays. The cycle of life and death, and all that."

"Matthias has a pretty lucrative side-gig selling his filth wherever he goes," Basch said, appearing behind Matthias. He appeared to not be wearing a shirt again, which stood out.

"It's not *filth*! It's classy, bespoke literature!"

"Tentacles and nude girls aren't 'bespoke', Matthias."

"And *you're* the reason arts education is on the decline!"

"If arts education is the reason we have things like *The Misadventures of Stripperella and Booblinda*, I think I'm fine letting it go down further. And, yes, that is an actual title," Basch said, answering the question he saw Venser was about to ask.

"That's a classic of the literary corpus!" Matthias retorted.

"You have a fascinating definition of 'classic'. Anyway, we should finish preparing and let our guest settle in." They left Venser to wonder about how Matthias knew of books with such spurious titles, a thought perturbed by the sound of the engines roaring to life.

The *Alamithea* rose into the sky, and Venser saw the red roofs and lush trees of Sorocco fade away. It slowly began to sink in that Venser was leaving Leondra behind and, in the process, he was leaving behind everything he had known to that point. It was certainly overwhelming in a sense.

The early day passed uneventfully. Venser still didn't want to venture out onto the deck of the airship, and it seemed like everyone was unavailable, so he had time to think and reflect on how things had gone. He tried to put pen to paper, but found his thoughts were garbled and ill-suited for cohesive writing, so he settled for sketching a couple of small drawings. It wasn't much, but it was satisfying and soothing in its own way, to distract from thinking about the sea of clouds beneath and everything he was running away from.

Nightfall brought supper, and with it interaction with people. Basch had grabbed his food and left, while the trio of Sebastian, Arycelle, and Matthias were gathered in the kitchenette. Venser accepted an offer to join them, and he sat and listened to their lively conversation.

"So, Gran Moria's next on our agenda," Sebastian said. "A job is a job, I suppose, though I can't say I'm thrilled by the idea."

"I don't think any of us are, save maybe Marianne," Arycelle replied. "Though I'm sure she has her own reasons for trying to avoid the place."

"Why do you want to avoid Gran Moria?" Venser asked.

"Ah, that's right, you haven't been there," Sebastian replied. "It's…well, I'd describe it as not being very lively. The city's always had this sense of gloom about it."

"You only go to Gran Moria because you have to," Matthias added. "Were I picking our destination, we'd go straight to Electrum and I'd hit up the *puff-puff* parlors."

"Of *course* you would," Arycelle said, glaring at him. "I swear, the only head you think with sometimes is what's between your legs!"

"I do not!" Matthias huffed. Venser tried not to laugh.

"Says the man who single-handedly managed to keep a massage parlor in Balmung from going out of business," Sebastian added.

"Do you two *really* have to bring this up in front of our guest?"

"Look, *you're* the one who brought up going to get your head ensconced in a big pair of jiggly jumblies," Arycelle said.

"Anyway, the bottom line is that Gran Moria is boring. It's also rather dirty there, so be ready for air pollution like you wouldn't believe."

"I see," Venser said. He wasn't sure what that'd be like, since the air in Aracoras was almost sterile in how clean it was, but he'd certainly find out soon.

"Also be ready for Matthias to complain endlessly about all the action he's not getting there," Sebastian said.

"I'll get *plenty* of action there, thank you very much!"

Arycelle and Sebastian both looked at Venser and shook their heads, seemingly telling him that this was not going to pan out like Matthias thought it would. Venser said nothing, unsure of how to respond in such a scenario.

Night had fallen, and Venser was lying awake in bed. He wasn't tired enough to sleep through his mind racing, wondering how things were going in Sorocco and how they *would* be going in Lunaria shortly. He couldn't do anything about them, but he couldn't help being troubled by them, which was the worst place one could possibly be in that regard.

He turned over and noticed that the door to Basch's room, directly across from his, was open. This was surprising, as it had been permanently closed the last time he was on board. Unable to sleep, he figured that he'd get up, stretch, and see if he could figure out if Basch's door being open was intentional.

A faint light was visible in the room, and Venser quietly looked in. He saw Basch sitting at his desk, seeming to be working with something. Lining the room were small little figures that each gave off a faint glow.

"Can't sleep?" Basch asked, still looking intently at what he was working on.

"Not yet," Venser said.

"You have a lot on your mind, I take it."

"You...yeah, I do."

"If you want to talk about it, I guess I can listen."

"You don't mind?"

"I like my privacy, that much is true. But you're nowhere near as annoying as Matthias is, at least in my experience so far, and I've sometimes found that certain things are better if you talk about them. So until you prove me wrong, I'm open to listening."

Venser nodded, and he sat down in a chair next to Basch's desk. He could better see what Basch was working with, a glowing stone-like material. It was the same material the figures around his room were made from, though in an array of colors.

"What is that?" Venser asked.

"It's called skystone," Basch said. "It's a mineral that's used to power modern airship engines and reactors. Skystones don't last forever, and you can tell their effective lifespan by how brightly they glow and their color. When they're depleted, you can either dispose of them or use them for artistic purposes. Carve them, turn them into paints, or any number of other things, though they are pretty brittle if you're not careful."

"I see. We...I don't think I've ever seen a skystone before. Not that I can remember, at least."

"Fully charged skystones can be a bit volatile, and you don't want to mess with them more than necessary. And given where you're from, or at least where I *think* you're from, you might not have reason to deal with them. Or even see them."

Venser tried to not wince. He recalled that, in the bar in Sorocco, Basch had called out his potentially being from Aracoras.

"You mean, with all the old airships that are used there?" he responded, tacitly confirming Basch's supposition.

"In a sense, it's impressive that they have airships there that are so old and in working condition, even if they're hopelessly outdated."

"I suppose so, though 'working order' is a stretch." He'd heard complaints from his father about how some of the Aracoras airships were considered so unsuitable for air travel, they had to get special permissions to land at some of the harbors. There had also been complaints about procuring the old parts necessary for their maintenance, which were apparently *very* expensive and part of why trips had become scarce.

"Airships are almost uniformly powered by skystones, save the ones in Aracoras and a couple other hobby crafts that rarely go far afield. Most of the depleted skystones, save the small amounts saved for artistic purposes, are disposed of by being dropped into the cloud sea. Some people have tried to figure out ways to recharge them to be reused, but nothing has yet been figured out, and it's cheaper and easier to mine new ones anyways. The largest skystone mine is in Gran Moria, but there's another one in Calaveras, and those two are responsible for the vast majority of skystones."

"I see. Are the mines in danger of running out?"

"Not that I've heard, but seeing as how they're the main economic activity of those cities, they wouldn't want to risk alarming potential customers about a shortage." Basch continued to work with the stone as he spoke; Venser couldn't quite tell what he was making yet.

"The way you're talking suggests that my read on where you're from was accurate," Basch continued.

"I am from Aracoras, yes," Venser said, sighing. "Is it that obvious?"

"It's not immediately obvious, no. I put it together in response to all of the contextual clues I had to work with. That said, I was a bit surprised to realize that much about you, because you look nothing like the others from Aracoras I know of."

"Have you met other people from Aracoras?" Venser asked.

"Once or twice, in passing," Basch said. His tone was a bit breezy and clipped, suggesting that this was not a topic he was keen on expanding upon right now.

"Trips out of Aracoras used to be more common, I think."

"Why did they dry up?"

"I don't know the exact reasons for that. I wasn't privy to such information, at least not directly."

"They don't tell their subjects much?"

"No, they don't. I...well, Father would sometimes mention things, but we're not supposed to actually know things, and we wouldn't ever talk about them."

"Interesting enough." The tone Basch had seemed to imply he had more questions, but he wasn't going to ask them presently.

"Can I ask about you?" Venser asked. "I feel like I've talked a lot about myself, but you've volunteered very little. Besides finding Matthias annoying."

"I'm not a very interesting person, I don't think," Basch replied, rotating his figure. "I'm originally from Balmung, an accursed little rock of ice and misery. I left years ago and drifted for a bit, before settling into this job."

"Balmung...I've heard of it, but not much specific. Visitation and communication, so far as I can remember, usually was with Lunaria."

"I don't think there's much to talk about regarding it, but my impression is that Aracoras is pretty closed-off unless they need something, so it makes sense you wouldn't have heard much about unusual trade partners."

"That sounds about right." For being a mere airship crew member, Basch seemed to know a *lot*, Venser thought. But he also seemed reluctant to say more, and he didn't want to press for information that wouldn't be volunteered.

"So, do you have any plans for when you get to Gran Moria?" Basch asked. "My understanding is that they're paying for us to just take you with us on our travels, for whatever reasons those are."

"They...I was asked to, if possible, deliver something to the leader of Gran Moria," Venser said.

"Sounds sufficiently vague, but reason enough, I suppose."

The two fell back into silence, Basch continuing to work on his figure and Venser pondering what awaited him when they got to Gran Moria. Matthias had not spoken highly of the city, and nobody seemed excited to go there, but there was still some excitement and intrigue to be had in visiting a new place.

Eventually, Venser made the decision to turn in, and Basch wished him a good night. The conversation had helped him to feel drowsy enough to countenance sleep, and sleep was exactly where he went. There were lots of questions to ask and things to talk about, but those could wait until the next day, at least.

There was to be a day of travel prior to the *Alamithea* arriving in Gran Moria early the day after, so Venser found himself with an entire open day and nothing particular to do. He started the day by going to the kitchen area for food, only to discover a book with an *interesting* cover on the counter.

"*The Fisherman's Wife 2: The Re-Tentacling...*" Venser read, picking it up.

"Did Matthias leave his book in the kitchen again?" He shook his head and put it back down, not keen on discovering for himself the tentacled horrors between the covers.

"Matthias does like leaving his books around," Sebastian said, coming into the kitchen just then. "He then complains when he can't find them, mostly because Basch or Arycelle hid them."

"I suppose he wouldn't have them go missing if he kept better track of them," Venser said.

"He has some he's very particular about keeping in pristine condition, but he has the copies he's a bit more cavalier about."

"I see."

"Anyway, I'm going to be in the engine room for a bit. Do you want to see what goes on there, Victor?"

"Uh...sure, if I won't be a bother."

"As long as you don't mess things up, it'll be fine."

It turned out that there was a third level to the airship; while the living quarters were immediately below deck, there was a level beneath that housed the engine room and the weapons suite. The engine room was an impressive array of machines and apparatuses. In the majority of them, Venser could make out the presence of glowing skystones, each shining brightly. He could understand what Basch meant when he said that fresh skystones were more vibrant in color, as these all brimmed with energy.

"The *Alamithea* has a lot of redundancy built into its systems and its machinery," Sebastian said. "We were able to get two of everything, and I have it staggered so that we won't need to replace skystones all at once. These power pretty much everything, from the engines to the on-board amenities."

"How long do skystones last?" Venser asked. It was the first cogent thought he could vocalize, as he was otherwise rather awe-struck.

"Not terribly long, unfortunately. We can usually get a couple of days to a week of flight time with fresh stones, and you can tell when they'd like to be replaced." He pointed to a dull-looking skystone that was sitting on a bench, its orange luster noticeably muted.

"Do the colors mean anything?"

"To a point. In my experience, redder skystones will last longer, but their power output is lower. The ones that are more blue to purple last nowhere near as long, but their power output is higher. So I like to try and balance out with red and orange stones and with purple and blue ones, one of each." He gestured to what looked to be the main reactors of the airship's engines. They could see two skystone holders in each one: one pair held an orange and a purple skystone, while the other held a red and a blue skystone.

"That makes sense." Venser was trying to conceal how impressed he was by all of it. He stood a reasonable distance back as Sebastian made his rounds to check all the stones; he wound up replacing one, but the rest were deemed serviceable. The task done, they left the engine room and ran into Matthias, who seemed to be making rounds of his own.

"Fancy seeing you both here," he said. He seemed to be holding a publication of some kind, the cover angled so that neither could see it.

"Did you come down here to do some reading?" Sebastian asked, raising an eyebrow.

"Why would I need to come down here to read?"

"So that you don't get bothered and distracted from…your literature."

"I always handle my duties with aplomb, I'll have you know!" As he said this, Venser noticed he was trying to not reveal the cover of what he was reading.

"Uh-huh. Victor and I will leave you to…whatever those duties are." Sebastian walked off, and Venser took that as a cue to follow, leaving Matthias to his literary pursuits. He did glance back to see Matthias open up his piece of literary accompaniment, which appeared to bear the title of *Slymenestra Hymen's Breast In Show*. He didn't want to know any more than that.

"So, we're going to be in Gran Moria tomorrow," Basch said to Venser. The two were in Basch's room for another conversation, under the cover of night. Venser couldn't sleep, and Basch's door was open again, so they had another conversation while Basch whittled away at his figure.

"I wonder what it's going to be like," Venser replied. "I...I never thought I'd be this far away from home."

"You're not *that* far away from Aracoras. Think of the cities in the sea of clouds as mostly resting on a circle. Aracoras is at the center of that circle, so it's roughly the same distance from Gran Moria to Aracoras as it would be from Lunaria to there." Basch set what he was working with down and used his hands to mime out what he was describing.

"So Aracoras is at the center? I guess that makes sense, with the Tomb of the Almighty."

"I've heard of that, of the Tomb of the Almighty." Basch frowned, as if trying to bring back a memory long forgotten. "The name's not unfamiliar, but I just know only the name. What is it?"

"It's the holiest site in Aracoras, a large mountain of rock floating next to the main island," Venser said. "We were taught that the Almighty is resting there following their battle against a great evil, recovering their strength from the brutal confrontation."

"The Almighty is resting there, eh? I wonder what they're like."

"I guess, given that they were in opposition to a great evil, that they have to be benevolent."

"Or just that they're less evil than the force they were against," Basch said, resuming work on his figure. "History often is written by the ones who hold power, the ones who won the war, and they tell us what they want us to believe to underscore their right to rule."

"...I suppose you're right, but you're rather pessimistic."

"Some say pessimist, others say realist, and there's not a lot of daylight between the two. But it's good to have some optimism and hope for the future, or you wind up jaded and bitter like me."

"I don't think I ever grew up with optimism as a persistent feature," Venser said. "There was always a sense of fear, that we were all doing something to offend the Almighty."

"If the Almighty was sleeping, I doubt they'd care much about our affairs, much less the particulars of what one random person is doing. But it'd still be an effective tool to rein in the people, that fear of divine retribution."

The way Basch talked continued to suggest to Venser that there was something deeper there, but he didn't think it prudent to pry.

"Before I forget," Basch continued, "I think you should take this for now." He set his figure down before her reached over and lifted something off of his bed. It was a scarf, long and gray.

"A scarf?" Venser asked.

"Gran Moria is known for its…very poor air quality, and I believe you might have a hard time adjusting to the air there. That scarf is one that, if you wear it around your face, should help a bit with getting you used to the air. It filters out a lot of the dirt and grime."

"Thank you," Venser said. He put it over his shoulder, not needing to wear it at the present.

"Before you ask if I'll miss it, I generally don't need it unless I'm spending a lot of time there, or in Calaveras. We shouldn't be there for long enough for me to need it."

"Why is the air so bad there?"

"Mining is a dirty business, and they certainly do a lot of mining there. Since they need to sell skystones and other ores in order to be able to secure foodstuffs and other goods, they tend to be very gung-ho about extracting what they can sell."

"I see." Venser wondered what Aracoras did in order to be able to afford things, since he couldn't recall ever seeing stores or marketplaces.

"The hour is starting to get late, though," Basch said, stretching in his chair. "At least late enough to matter. We should both sleep. Tomorrow might be a long day."

With that, Venser went back to his room to sleep. He saw a light in the kitchen, but he wasn't keen on finding out which manner of egregious publication Matthias had deigned to share on this fine day.

8

Smoldering Shadow

From the window of his room, Venser could tell as they crossed into Gran Moria's air space, as the air started getting dingier and dirtier, with the window attracting a bit of grime to it. Even still, he could see out as they approached.

Unlike the colorful architecture of Sorocco, everything in Gran Moria was a muted color of some kind, usually a mix of gray, beige, and brown. The architecture was more about sharp angles and flat surfaces than gentle slopes, and the overall aesthetic was a very unwelcoming one.

Venser stepped outside of his room to see Matthias emerging from the kitchen. "Ah, there you are," he said. "I hear you're going up to the main governmental building today, to do Stuff and Things."

"That's right," he answered.

"Do you want someone to go with you? If it's your first time in Gran Moria, you might get lost if you're unfamiliar."

"If...if it wouldn't trouble you any."

"Let me check to see if Arycelle is free first," he said. "She's better at those sort of...delicate negotiation things than I am," Several minutes later, Matthias returned to confirm Arycelle did, indeed, say that she'd be free to accompany Venser. He felt a bit of relief, because the big city was daunting in its own right.

The *Alamithea* touched down in the harbor, and the crew disembarked in an orderly fashion. As he stepped onto the deck, Venser could see what Basch meant about the city's air, a hazy and dingy pall hanging over. He'd wrapped Basch's scarf around his face, which had a pleasantly woody scent about it, and he and Arycelle passed by Marianne on their way off the ship.

"Matthias and Sebastian told me that they're looking to spend some time at one of the bars this evening," Marianne said.

"Probably the 'Vermilion Hammer', right?" Arycelle asked. "That's the one Matthias likes in particular."

"That name sounds right. I'll be busy, so I'll see all of you when you get back to the ship tonight."

With that settled, Venser and Arycelle set off towards the high-looking building at the center of the town. It was up several hilly portions, an imposing monolith that seemed to leer unpleasantly. Where Sorocco had buildings that tended to be fairly low and spread out, Gran Moria's buildings all sat narrowly and were very vertical in their orientation.

Venser looked around, impressed by how the city looked. Large, mountainous crags rose throughout the city, with buildings sometimes set into their sides. Those looked to potentially be the various mines, he thought, as he saw carts of gleaming stones being pulled out of openings.

"The city has mines strewn throughout," Arycelle said, noticing his looking around. "They'll discover lucrative skystone and mineral deposits and seek to capitalize, and building plots are narrow to make room for more mining. I've heard of stories of buildings being torn down to make room for mines if a deposit is discovered."

"How do they find these?" Venser asked.

"They have instruments that find them, using unique properties of the desired material when compared to the rest of the surrounding rock. They'll also occasionally enlist the 'guidance' of people who claim to have the power to divine deep into the earth, to mixed results."

"I see."

"There was a case I heard about a rather notorious miss by one of the hired oracles. The families whose houses had to be taken out to dig were not happy."

SMOLDERING SHADOW

"They wouldn't be, no." He was left to wonder how such a mistake could have happened.

The city's narrow avenues and drab colors were disorienting, and Venser was thankful he had a guide to keep him from getting lost. The citizenry also seemed rather dour and disinclined to offer advice or assistance, instead choosing to glare at the two of them.

"Shouldn't be too far, I think," Arycelle said, pointing in a direction. "Unless I'm mistaken, but I like to think I'm pretty good at navigation."

Her read wasn't wrong, and the two emerged onto the top of the hill their destination was on. Like the rest of Gran Moria, the palatial complex was a drab, austere building with sharp angles and a generally threatening aura. Small windows and sharp angles on the facades helped to add to the aura of imposition, and Venser certainly felt appropriately intimidated by it.

"Well, we're here," Arycelle said.

"We sure are," Venser replied, trying to hide how awe-struck he was. At least his scarf hid that from people.

"You have what you need to share, right? The letter from Yamato?"

"Yes, I do." Venser felt around in his bag and felt the envelope he had been given.

"All right, let's go up to the guards and see what they say." They walked up to the guards, a pair stationed in front of the gate to the palatial compound. Instinctively, they spread themselves out to provide more of a physical presence.

"State the business that you are having, unwelcome guests!" one of them squealed. Despite being a broadly-built man, he had a high voice with a thick accent.

"Uh...I brought a letter from Yamato, lord of Sorocco, to the leader of Gran Moria," Venser said. He was nervous, but he spoke deliberately, so as to not flub his delivery.

"You are bringing communication, messenger boy? We are wanting to have the proof that the tidings you are bringing are authentic!"

He pulled the letter out of his bag and handed it to the guard who said this. The two began to look over it, muttering among themselves. He thought he could hear "da" and "nyet" as the most common sounds. Finally, they looked up.

"We are bringing this to the esteemed Tsangarvides, and he will be making the assessment as to what is to be done. You will be waiting here, da?" he asked, though it certainly sounded more like a command than a query. The other guard disappeared inside, leaving Venser, Arycelle, and the loquacious guardsman.

From where they were, Venser could look a bit better out at the city, and it looked much the same from higher as it did below. There seemed to be a noticeable cloud of soot and ash over the lower part of the city, and a couple of hills had residences meant to be for the people able to afford life above the dirtiest parts of the city. The overall vibe was very eerie to him, but he dared to not say this aloud, lest he irk the guard. He glanced back at the guard, whose expression resembled that of someone sucking something sour.

After a seemingly interminable wait, the guard came back out and began muttering to the other guard again. It was a long mutter session.

"You two, you are coming with me inside," the talkative guard said, motioning to Arycelle and Venser. They obliged, following him into the palatial compound. The inside was as aesthetically brutal and harsh as the outside, with few decorative elements to soften the edges.

"We have been telling the great Tsangarvides that there are two of you, but he is telling us that the one he is wanting to see is the man out of the two of you. We are asking that the woman will be doing the waiting while they will be having the meeting," the guard said. "Do not be doing the worrying, as there will be snacks."

"Snacks, huh?" Arycelle said. "That's reasonable enough. Hopefully there are other things to be done besides gorging on snacks."

"There will be the entertainment to do the entertaining," the guard said. "For now, we are asking that you are following the woman there while the man will be following me to meet with Tsangarvides."

Arycelle followed the woman the guard gestured to, and Venser followed the guard deeper into the compound. Their footsteps echoed through the cavernous halls, a rhythmic cadence that filled Venser with unease. It reminded him of the halls of Aracoras, and he wasn't sure he wanted to be reminded of such.

The door that was their destination was ornately decorated, though still not out of place for the city as a whole. The guard opened it and bade Venser to go inside, and he found himself face-to-face with an imposing mountain of a man. He was tall and broad, with a shaved head and formidable mustache.

"Esteemed Tsangarvides, I am bringing to you the man who you are asking for the meeting with," the guard said.

"Thank you. You may leave," was the reply. His voice was sonorous and baritone, carrying well. The guard stepped out, leaving Venser and the man called Tsangarvides in the room together, alone.

"So, you were the one who brought me the letter," he said, looking right at Venser. His gaze was piercing, his eyes dark and inscrutable. "I must ask, do you know what the letter says?"

Venser took a breath, to try and calm his nerves. "I have a rough idea, sir," he said, "but I do not know its exact contents."

"What do you believe it to say?"

"I...I believe it tells you about my impending nuptials, intended to unite Aracoras and Lunaria and allow Lord Hessler unfettered access to the Tomb of the Almighty."

"So that's his latest ruse. Fascinating." Tsangarvides stroked his chin contemplatively.

"Uh...might I ask what you mean by that, sir?"

"You should have a seat. We have much to discuss."

"Let's start at the beginning," Tsangarvides said, leaning over his desk to look at the seated Venser. "Hessler has been the ruler of Lunaria for as long as I can remember. Or, for that matter, for as long as any of us can remember. But he's always had an obsession with youth and vitality, and he'll pursue any avenue that will give him the chance to rule for as long as possible."

"I understand," Venser said. He could think of several people like that, though none of them seemed motivated to go out of their way to extend their lives.

"The contents of the Tomb of the Almighty are up for debate, which I understand is what your fiancée is trying to find out. We were always told that the Almighty was sleeping there after their battle against a great evil, so I'm left wondering why it's to be opened now."

"I...I think Lord Hessler thinks the tomb's opening will reward him somehow."

"That if he's responsible, the Almighty will reward him with eternal life? That would be in character, and I suppose that it would make sense. *If* the Tomb of the Almighty contains what is claimed, and I don't know that we have proof of it."

"That's what Leondra...uh, my fiancée is looking into. She's scouring books and materials in Sorocco's library, to see what she can learn."

"Yamato was kind enough to offer a brief summary of the developments to that point. That there are several theories as to what is in there, some benign and some malignant. But no theory seems especially sturdy, and I wouldn't be surprised if the truth lay somewhere between all of the extremes."

"I suppose nobody would have a way of knowing what's in the tomb for sure," Venser said. "Not until it's opened."

"I strongly suspect that it being opened is something we *don't* want to happen," Tsangarvides said. "It's been sealed for a reason. If they are wrong as to what's in it, particularly concerning their assessments of how benign whatever inside is, that would be potentially cataclysmic."

"Can we stop it?" Venser asked. "I mean...can it be stopped?"

"I'm not sure how far this plan is in its execution, but it seems like the key is that Aracoras would need to agree to it being opened. One of their sons marrying into the foremost family of Lunaria would do the job, since it would provide a pathway towards rectifying their financial situation."

"Aracoras has never been especially well off, that's true. At least, not consistently." While Venser and his family were all largely insulated from the see-sawing financial situation, he could get an idea of how much money they had by how much care was being paid to the "Garden of the Heavenly

Ideal", a massive spectacle that they took great pride in. Leaner years would cause the plants to be more modest, while richer years saw an ornate and elaborate topiary that they thought was the envy of all the other cities. Not that they would see it, given a lack of visitors, but still.

"The dowry for a marriage would be formidable. But I'm left wondering why they'd pick you for the groom, because you look nothing like the average person from Aracoras."

"I guess it's because I was never their favorite," Venser said, his tone self-effacing.

"Sometimes families are bad at hiding hierarchies," Tsangarvides said. He had a slight smile on his face, though Venser couldn't quite tell the emotion. "Where are you in your family's lineage?"

"Uh…I am their eighth child, and the second-youngest son, if that's what you're asking. Anyone older than me is already married."

"I see. Is your younger brother at the age to be married?"

"He would be, but I don't think Mother would approve of such. Not that she would have much of a say that way, but he's always been her special child, and she's very protective that way."

"What ultimately happens with them is something I imagine we'll discover in due time, and I'd not be surprised if, presuming you're not on hand for a wedding, they found another groom for Lady Leondra. Is she back in Lunaria yet?"

"I…do not believe so, sir. She wanted a couple more days to do research."

"I see." Tsangarvides stood up and walked over to a window, looking out it and seemingly contemplating things. Venser wasn't sure if he should say anything.

"The letter you brought has some interesting elements to it," he finally said. "I believe that I would like some time to consult with my advisors about its contents. Would you be so kind as to wait at the palace while we peruse it?"

"I can do that," Venser said. He was just hoping he wouldn't be bored during the wait.

Venser was led out of Tsangarvides' study, and he saw Matthias talking animatedly with Arycelle in the lobby. This surprised Venser, partly because Matthias did not seem to be someone they'd let into the palatial compound willingly.

"He had a 'special delivery' to make," Arycelle said, preempting Venser's question. "How'd your meeting go?"

"It went okay, I think," Venser said. "He wants time to ponder what it all means and talk with his advisors. He wants to meet with me later this evening."

"Well, that's almost perfect timing," Matthias said. He was smiling, but it didn't appear as jovial as usual, and his tone had a strange bite to it. "We need to talk. Something has…come up."

"Come up?" Venser felt a chill run down his body as he repeated that.

"Let's go into a room to talk and get out of the hallway," Arycelle said. "More privacy."

Venser obliged, following them. Any time there was a "need to talk", bad things often followed, at least in his experience. Matthias seeming a bit more on edge suggested that this was the case.

"So, let's catch you up on things, because things have been moving *very* quickly," Matthias said, looking right at Venser. His tone was very direct, with none of the usual lightness Venser was used to hearing. "It seems that your cover has been blown."

"What do you mean by 'cover'?" Venser asked.

"Your identity…your *true* identity, that is, has been revealed to Marianne and, by extension, us. Along with that your actual name is Venser, but that matters less. We can forgive that, I think."

"My true identity…what do you mean by that?" Venser was still confused.

"The information that got passed to Marianne, and then to us, was that you are one of the sons of the foremost member of the Council of Elders in Aracoras. I've never heard much about it, but I came to understand they run the place."

"That…that's correct. How did that get out?" Venser's emotion had changed to a mix of horror and surprise.

"Turns out that a certain rather loathsome little runt, known for his ability to stick his abnormally large proboscis places he really should not stick it, learned this information from someone else, and he went scurrying back to Marianne in an effort to get into her pants. Or, at the very least, her shirt."

"Was it *him* again?" Arycelle asked. Her face expressed disgust, and it sounded like she knew who the likely culprit was.

"It was *him*. I'm curious as to how he could have possibly gotten that information, but I suppose rodents are good at finding caches of treasure when they snoop around, and he certainly is notorious for his ability to scrounge together information. If he used his powers for things other than trying to get laid, maybe we all wouldn't hate him so much!"

"Fat chance of that, Matthias. Poisonous toadstools don't change their spots."

"So true. Interestingly, Basch seemed to already know that you were from Aracoras, but he certainly didn't tell us, and he would never tell *him*."

"How *he* got the information ultimately isn't relevant, I think," Arycelle said. "However it happened, he found out, and now we know. But we can figure that out later. What I want to know now, and what we need to figure out, is what Marianne plans to do with it."

"What do you *think*? She wants to turn our friend back over to the people in Aracoras for what she presumes will be a massive bounty," Matthias said, his tone grim. "She's making plans to set a course for Aracoras as soon as possible."

This was not what Venser wanted to hear, and he involuntarily shuddered. He did *not* want to go back.

"She'd really do that? It'd be suicide for all of us!" Arycelle yelled. "Our reputation would be ruined! Who would want to work with a cargo crew who betrayed their employer? Yamato and Leondra already made a deal with us, and I'd rather stick with that. If we go along with this, that's the last time anyone will work with us!"

"That's what I tried to tell her, but she's not listening. Not to me, not to anyone else. She wants to, in her words, 'wash her hands of this business of nobles and their twaddle' and get a fat paycheck to boot."

"She's not going to get anything from them," Venser whispered. "That's not how Aracoras works. All of you will be arrested and sentenced to death for, in their words, 'defiling their sanctified grounds.'"

Now it was Arycelle and Matthias's turns to look suitably mortified, and they stood for a moment in silence to allow their horror to marinate.

"Well, that escalated," Arycelle said, breaking the silence. "By a lot."

"So, not only would we lose our reputations, we would also lose our lives in the process," Matthias hissed. "Bravo, Marianne. You're the best. Your idea is going to get us all killed, and I can guarantee you that she'll dismiss Venser's warning as an attempt to scare her."

"What *can* we do, though? Leave him here? Abandon the ship and let her hire a crew to replace us all?"

Matthias shook his head. "We can't do that, no. That ship's ours as much as it is her ship, and I'm not going to abandon the man we were asked to take care of. I just need time to think," he said, tapping his foot frantically. "But we don't have time!"

"Do Basch and Sebastian know?"

"Basch actually was the one who came to me with this update, and he told me that he was going to find Sebastian to catch him up. I tracked down Marianne myself to confirm her plan and try to talk her out of it, though you can probably guess how fruitless the last of those parts was."

Just then, a guard poked his head back in. "Master Venser?" he asked. "Lord Tsangarvides will be wanting to do the meeting with you."

"Huh? Oh, yeah. I...uh, I'll be there," Venser answered. He tried to project calm and confidence, two things he lacked utterly at the present.

"He is also telling me that your companions may be doing the accompanying, as he will be having his advisors there."

"Really?" Arycelle asked. Both she and Matthias looked at each other. "That'll be good, actually."

"I certainly think so," Matthias said.

"I'd be happy to have them with me, if they want to come with me," Venser said.

"We do," Matthias affirmed. "In particular, I have some things I want to talk with Tsangarvides about as well in light of recent developments."

The ensuing meeting was long and boisterous. It started with Matthias and Arycelle being brought up to speed on what had happened with Yamato and Leondra in Sorocco, as well as with the business surrounding the Tomb of the Almighty, which took up a fair bit of time and involved questions aplenty. Venser was surprised that Matthias had dropped his usual jovial, jocular demeanor and was serious, asking actually insightful questions and trying to learn as much as he could. He certainly appreciated that Matthias wasn't slipping in references to the *Ogler's Digest*, though.

"So, your captain is intending on turning your charge over to Aracoras and their people, even though you have an agreement with Yamato and Leondra to keep him safe and away from Lunaria and Aracoras," Tsangarvides said. "That's accurate, I presume?"

"That is the gist of what I have come to understand, yes," Matthias said. "This is a very recent development, precipitated by her finding about his identity through unknown channels, and she intended on doing so without informing him of this."

"Has she been promised funds or compensation for his return?"

"I do not believe so, no. Not explicitly. She plans to show up with him and demand ransom. Such is my understanding."

"You can't deal with Aracoras like that," Venser said, shaking his head. "They would arrest her and have her executed. As well as the rest of the crew. I might share their fate, if they felt I had become irrevocably corrupted and tainted by exposure to the 'outside world.'"

"Well, that's certainly no way to treat you," Arycelle said.

"How does the rest of the crew feel about this?" Tsangarvides asked.

Matthias pursed his lips. "There are four of us on the *Alamithea*. Discounting the captain, of course. I can affirm that the weapons operator is vehemently against the plan hatched by our captain and spoke passionately against it. The engine specialist is her boyfriend, and while I haven't spoken to him directly, I feel he'd be on our side," he said. "You know our positions already, I think."

"He'd be against it, I know," Arycelle said. "Especially with the details of potential execution awaiting us."

"So," Tsangarvides said, settling back into his chair, "it seems like we're at an impasse of sorts. Your captain wants to fly Venser back to Aracoras, to your dooms. As your captain, you're obliged to follow her lead, even though you disagree with her completely. I'd offer Venser space here, but the peril in such a decision is similar to the one I understand Sorocco faces, and I would rather not make an enemy of Lunaria and Aracoras without reason, which would happen if he were to be discovered."

"We don't have a ship of our own, else we could escape with Venser," Arycelle said. "We certainly can't desert the *Alamithea*, least of all because our captain is certainly petty and would make sure we'd never get hired again."

"Those are true points. All the same, though, you *do* have a ship."

"What are you..." Matthias started, but he fell quiet. A smile dawned on his face, one with mischievous intent.

"There is much to be done today, and while I apologize for making it seem like I am rushing you onward, I suspect you know what is to be done in order to make this happen."

"Why go to such lengths for us, though?" Arycelle asked. She had picked up on what was being insinuated, it sounded like. Venser wasn't completely sure of the insinuation, but the way they were talking gave an idea.

"Sometimes, the way forward is not on the illuminated path, but the one steeped in shadows. To be caught directly would be a massive blow, and this is a situation in which actions taken without official capacity are actions that stand a better chance of panning out." Tsangarvides had a bit of a twinkle in his eye, and Venser wondered if he was enjoying this.

"So, what *is* the plan?" Matthias asked. "I believe I already know, but I want to hear it from you first. Just to make sure we're on the same page."

"Of course, I am speaking none of this," Tsangarvides said, leaning in. "How this will go..."

"You're back late," Marianne said, standing in front of the *Alamithea* to greet the returning trio. The sun had mostly set by this point, and the only light was from the city itself. Even through the dingy pall, lights twinkled through windows and along streets.

"Apologies for our delay," Matthias said. "Arycelle had to pull me away from this *lovely* bookstore I found. Got so caught up in it, I forgot to go to the bars."

"Lovely, I'm sure. And here I thought you'd be busy figuring out your conquest for the evening."

"Come, now. I'm not *that* much of an animal."

"So, I presume we're leaving tomorrow?" Arycelle asked.

"You presume correctly. I have a time-sensitive shipment that needs to get to its destination. In Electrum." Venser noticed that Marianne's body language felt evasive, and she seemed a bit more on-edge. He wasn't too familiar with her normally, but she had previously carried herself with ease and confidence that were missing here.

"I suppose it makes sense, and I can't argue the point. We don't usually stay in Gran Moria very long, anyways. Not a huge loss, but it is what it is," Matthias shrugged.

As they spoke in front of the *Alamithea*, a trio of guards walked up. "Which one of you is being the one named Marianne?" one of them asked, their voice high and reedy.

"I am she," Marianne said, stepping forward. "What is it?"

"We are to be informing you that the paperwork that you are filling out is having deficiencies, and as you are making the preparations for a departure at the start of the day tomorrow, we are to be asking that you are making the corrections tonight."

She sighed mightily. "I swear I had it all taken care of. Damn bureaucrats. All right, I suppose I'll go off and do it now, so that we don't get held up in the morning. Lead the way." Two of the guards escorted her off, while the third remained behind momentarily.

"I am to be telling you that the window for you being departing is here," they whispered, making sure Marianne was out of earshot. "And, now, I am wishing you the best of luck and I am also to be going."

As he scurried off to join the others, Matthias looked at the other two. "Well, here we go," he said, smiling. "Time to put Operation: Commandeer into action!"

"Is that what you're calling it?" Sebastian called out. He and Basch were waiting on the deck, having emerged to watch Marianne walk off.

"Yes, we are," Matthias said. "You know what we're doing, right?"

"I have an idea, as does Basch. We're both ready." Basch nodded in agreement.

"Thank you. Time is of the essence, and we can talk once we're in the sky. To your stations, everyone!"

Arycelle and Matthias both went to the bridge, while Venser, Sebastian, and Basch headed below deck. Venser went to the room he had been occupying; without a role in the crew, he just had to sit and wait for departure. And sure enough, the engines roared to life in their familiar sequence.

Finally, after what felt like an eternity, the airship shuddered, then jerked skywards. He watched out the window as the lights of Gran Moria rapidly receded into the darkness. As they rose higher, he slowly began to reflect on what had happened. In less than a day, they had wound up commandeering the *Alamithea* and were flying somewhere else. He had no idea where they were off to, but he knew it was going to not be Lunaria or Aracoras, and that suited him just fine.

As they lifted skywards, he thought he could see a figure running beneath them in the harbor. It was too dim to tell, but he wondered if it was Marianne. Should he feel bad? He didn't, he realized; Marianne was all but threatening to get them all killed, and he had a hard time empathizing with her as a result.

He flopped onto his bed and fell asleep, too exhausted to stay conscious and too wound up to dream. What a turn of events, he thought. He also hoped that he'd have a chance to see Gran Moria again, with less of a whirlwind tour, but what could be done on this occasion about that?

9

Storm Seeker

"A meeting on the bridge?" Venser asked. Morning had broken and Basch had come to fetch him, as Matthias (now captain of the *Alamithea*) called for a meeting. Venser's presence was requested, in spite of him not being on the crew.

"Indeed," Basch said. "Let me guess, you're scared of being on the deck while we're in the air."

"...maybe?"

"Just hold my hand. You'll be fine. Nothing's going to happen to you."

Swallowing his fear, Venser agreed to it. With that, Basch led Venser across the deck, the wind providing an interesting sensation. He couldn't marvel at the clouds, because he had his eyes shut all the time, and they stayed shut until the sensation of the wind was gone.

"There you are!" Matthias said. "Sorry for calling you up here. I can't leave the flight deck unattended, and I figured it was good to have a meeting with all five of us."

"It's okay," Venser said, opening his eyes and looking around. The bridge was filled with all sorts of meters, levers, knobs, and buttons that were impressively daunting. All four of the crew members were there, and while it wasn't the most comfortable fit, they had room enough to not be crushed.

"So, we've stolen the *Alamithea* and are fleeing Gran Moria," Sebastian said, shaking his head. "Not how I'd imagined things would go."

"Excuse you, 'stolen' is such ugly phrasing! I prefer 'liberated,'" Matthias protested. "We 'liberated' her from the nefarious clutches of a greedy harpy intent on leading us to rack and ruin! And not the good kind of rack."

"That's...a bit florid," Arycelle said.

"Eh, probably. I blame the schools. Anyway, we have things to discuss besides the terminology for what we just did. Let's start at the top, the minor things related to airship business. We need a new name for this vessel, as calling it the *Alamithea* would be a bit problematic in terms of expectations, and might attract people thinking this vessel was stolen and not liberated!"

"And you sound like you already have a name in mind," Basch said.

"But of course, dear Basch! I propose we call it...the *Naglfar!*"

He pronounced this with a dramatic cadence everyone couldn't help but laugh at. Once the laughter abated, the consensus was that nobody had a name that quite matched the absurdity of the one proposed, and that the name was perfectly reasonable to all of them.

"With that settled," Matthias said, "let's move on to crew and crewing decisions! As the new captain of the *Naglfar*, I have an open vice-captain position."

"I don't want it," Basch growled.

"How about Arycelle?" Sebastian asked. "If not Basch, then it's me or Arycelle, and I think she'd do a better job at it."

"Excellent proposal! Arycelle, do you accept?"

"Uh...sure?" She was surprised by how quickly this happened.

"That's settled! As for our passenger, Venser...I'm going to make him a crew member, if there are no objections!"

There were none, not even from Venser. He had no idea what it all involved, but if nothing else, formally joining the crew could potentially provide him some protection that way. And there was something thrilling about being part of an airship crew.

"I...I have no idea what's entailed, but I'll accept," Venser said.

"Perfect! It looks like our business is concluded here, outside of catching Basch and Sebastian up on all the minutiae of what happened on Gran Moria between now and our arrival in Electrum...or I would say that, if it weren't for a bogey that might need to be disposed of right quick." He pointed to a screen, which seemed to be a sweeping radar of some kind. Venser had no idea what it was, but he could see a dot approaching rapidly from behind their position.

"Let me check something," Sebastian said, stepping outside the bridge briefly. He popped his head back in, shaking his head in disgust. Matthias seemed to know what he meant.

"Looks like we need to deal with something before we move on to story time," Matthias said. His tone became serious, which was impressive in how quickly it happened. "If you would, Sebastian and Basch, take your stations. Venser and Arycelle, stay here with me."

The two men nodded and left the bridge. Venser was still confused, but he said nothing. What was going on?

"We're being pursued by someone," Arycelle said, noticing his confusion and offering an explanation. "Might have to beat them back."

A loud hiss rang through the flight deck, startling Venser. Matthias seemed to know exactly what it meant, and he began to twist knobs and flip levers instinctively. Through the hiss, Venser heard a voice taking form.

"Attention, larcenous and absconding scoundrels of the skies, transgressing criminals beyond the hope of redemption, you have been apprehended in your commission of a grave and grievous injury inflicted against the most buxom of all sky pilots!" came the voice. It was an affected mix of whine, pompous grandiosity, and general unctuousness. "It is prudent for you to concede your imminent defeat and relinquish the *Alamithea* and the special cargo you have in your possession at once!"

"Yep, it's *him*," Arycelle whispered. Matthias shook his head in response, then pressed a button and began to speak.

"Arrrrrr, you ain't talkin' to the *Alamithea*, you presumptuous runt," he said, affecting a voice of his own that sounded in line with a stereotypical pirate, drawl and all. "This here's the *Naglfar*, and we don't take too kindly to presumptuous little twits like you!"

"How *dare* you speak back to me in such an affected, base, vulgar, and lowbrow tone, a conspicuously fake and false front you have adopted to mock all that is dignified and divine! You clearly do not know who you are dealing with, so allow me to enlighten your boorish mind! Like a flower that blooms in the soil of our carnal and corrupt society, I shall administer retribution to the straying vermin that graze upon the land! For I am the Chairman of the Educational Guidance Council...*Archduke Emperor Pope Guillaume XIII!*"

Trying to suppress laughter, Venser thought some of what the annoying man was saying sounded familiar, but he couldn't immediately place where. He still had many questions, like who gave him all those titles and what the "Educational Guidance Council" was. Matthias and Arycelle seemed like they knew who this person was, and they didn't like them.

"Arrrrr, the crew of the *Naglfar* don't know what no 'Educational Guidance Council' is, but it's probably as stupid as you are!"

"Cease your affected drivel and stammering immediately, gibbering buffoon!" Venser could hear the unctuous sleaze dripping from the speaker system. "Should you not immediately tender your surrender of the *Alamithea* to Archduke Emperor Pope Guillaume XIII, you shall face extermination at the hands of the *Divinisher*, the divine instrument of heavenly retribution, and justice shall be meted out amidst a rain of heavenly bloodshed and *glo*rious violence!"

"That sentence there had too many syllables, an' you're gonna apologize for that, runt!" Matthias shot back.

"*That does it*! Your window for amnesty and mercy has expired, a closure expedited by your uncouth and appalling mien! It is time for your extermination, sky vermin! Pray long and hard for clemency and mercy from whichever false idol or heathen effigy you worship, because it shan't come from Archduke Emperor Pope Guillaume XIII!"

The sound of gunfire rang through the air, and Venser thought he could feel very slight vibrations on board. It felt ineffectual, though, and nobody was panicking.

"When you gonna start firin'?" Matthias teased. Venser saw him reach for a button.

"Clearly your armor is in violation of universal standards of armor thickness, else my firepower would have penetrated you beyond belief!" came the whining complaint. "Your punishment shall…"

His statement was interrupted by gunfire, this time originating from their ship. Venser couldn't see what was happening, but yelps from the other end of the communication channel could be heard.

"Your armaments clearly are more contraband than your armor!" Archduke Emperor Pope Guillaume XIII whined. "Your alliance with illegal suppliers and fell entities has clearly empowered you to beat back divinity's champion!"

"Only thing *you're* championing is a floating hunk of junk barely able to stay in the air at this point!"

"*Silence!* Clearly I need time to rearm and prepare for the next epic confrontation against the coffin of iniquity you pilot! Whilst I am loath to return to the most buxom of aviators without news of my absolute victory, it has proven elusive on this day! Mark my words, lowborn scum: I shall return!"

Venser could see an airship zipping ahead of them, a compact aircraft decked out in a lurid blue-and-orange color scheme. Smoke seemed to be streaming out of several holes in the hull, likely the work of Basch firing on the irksome twit.

"Well, that was annoying," Matthias said, sighing. "He did confirm that Marianne noticed our…liberation of the vessel."

"Uh…was that from the talk of the 'buxom aviator'? Venser asked.

"Right on the money. Despite his talk about being a vanguard of morality, which he didn't get into as much *this* time, that Guillaume person is a skirt-chasing pervert who likes to ogle women and lord over them whenever he has the chance to."

"He has a massive crush on Marianne, one that's extremely one-sided," Arycelle said. "She's made use of this sometimes. Like now, it turns out. Promising him the pleasure he seeks if he succeeds in taking back her ship."

"All the same, he's out of our hair, so we can call this good for now," Matthias said. "If you want to get Venser back across the deck, Arycelle, I think we'd all appreciate it, and you can also take the time to get Basch and

Sebastian filled in if they're not already. We'll be in Electrum later tomorrow evening, so plan accordingly."

"Thanks, Matthias," Venser said, nodding. He took Arycelle's hand and made it back below deck; he was still not ready to open his eyes crossing the deck, but he at least felt safe with these people, which was surprising to him.

"I have to say," Basch said, "things have been a lot more lively since you got here, Venser." The two men were in the kitchen area that evening, eating. Their flight had been uneventful since they fought off Archduke Emperor Pope Guillaume XIII, and there were no forecast interruptions between now and their arrival in Electrum the following evening.

"Is that a good thing or a bad thing?" Venser asked, setting his fork down.

"I'd say it's both. We've been lacking in excitement. Not sure I'd call getting caught up in a grand ploy to resurrect the Almighty the kind of excitement I'd have signed up for, but you take what you can get, I suppose."

"This is definitely more exciting than anything I've experienced in the past."

"Aracoras is that boring?"

Venser nodded. "I'd say so. There are tight restrictions on what we're allowed to do, in general. But the more prominent your family is, the tighter the restrictions. My siblings and I were rarely allowed to associate with others, and we'd take our tutoring sessions in private, with no more than one other person at times. I...even though I'm very far down in terms of my importance, I had the same restrictions as my siblings."

"Really? That is an impressive amount of control to have exerted on you."

"When your father is the foremost member of the Council of Elders, they really want to make sure you don't bring shame to the familial name or open up your father to what they see as exploitation."

Basch whistled in response to this. "That's interesting enough," he said. "So why would you travel to Sorocco under an assumed name? I can't imagine your name alone would raise suspicions."

"I wasn't even supposed to leave the palatial compound in Lunaria, truth be told. Leondra had suspicions she wanted to investigate in the library in Sorocco, she took me with, and here we are now."

"So *that* explains a bit," Matthias said, choosing now to saunter in. "Sorry to bother you. I needed a break, so I had Arycelle take over for now."

"Food break, or a break to peruse the finest literature you have?" Basch asked, the sarcasm dripping from his voice.

"Why not both? The soul needs nourishment as much as one's tum-tum." Venser noticed Matthias had a different issue of *Ogler's Digest* in hand.

"Not sure that tit periodicals count as 'soul nourishing', but I suppose that's something we'll disagree on."

"Indeed! The things that bring me joy differ from the things that do for you, though I've yet to discover what those are. You *do* keep your secrets."

"I don't see the need to open my mouth as wide as you claim you get the ladies to open their legs, Matthias."

"Hey, they do! There's no 'claim' about it." Venser tried to not break out in laughter, but he was not wholly successful.

"Changing the topic," Matthias continued. "Venser, do you have any plans for when we get to Electrum? If I may be so bold as to offer a suggestion, it would benefit you to go tell the people in charge what's going on."

"How much do you think they'll already know?" Venser asked.

"My hunch is 'not much'. From experience, news circulates on a 'need to know' basis, and even with as spicy as things have gotten, I doubt all of this is a talk of the town. I'm still wondering how news of you got around in the first place, because it felt like you and Leondra were keeping a tight lid on it."

"I am, as well."

"I have my suspicions, and I imagine that certain parties are keen on disseminating everything they know to everyone they know of. I doubt they'd get everything right, though, or get to the ears of people who would want to hear it."

"Come to think of it, we ran into a dignitary from Aracoras once," Basch said. "It was just in passing…maybe in Electrum, if I'm remembering, but I certainly recall that they were completely insufferable. Arycelle, in particular, got him all flustered."

"He wasn't used to a woman being so strong-willed, I suppose," Matthias chuckled.

"No, he wouldn't be," Venser said. He wondered if he knew who they were talking about.

"We'll probably need a couple of days in Electrum all the same, though. Tsangarvides was gracious enough to offer some…forms to process a change in registration of our lovely vessel," Matthias said. "We can use that time to figure out what and where we should go after this, if anywhere particular."

"That's fine with me," Venser said. "It'll be nice to get a chance to look around."

"Yeah, you didn't really have that on Gran Moria. Sorry about that. You'll have plenty of time to explore Electrum, and it's more suited to such."

"If my sense of chronology is right, though," Basch said, "Venser's father should be getting back to Lunaria in the next couple of days. We may want to lay low."

"Probably prudent, though at least they wouldn't have concrete information about where we are without talking to the right people. And on that, I should probably leave you two and go off to amuse myself." With a snack now in hand, Matthias sauntered off. Basch and Venser weren't too far behind in leaving the kitchen, having finished their food. With their arrival imminent on the morrow, both men wanted to get some sleep before then.

As dusk started creeping in on the following day, following an uneventful day of flight, Venser noticed that there was a seemingly abnormal amount of light in the night sky. He looked out the window to see, much to his surprise, a brightly-lit city, with towering forms. He couldn't quite tell what was going on, or anything in particular about the buildings, but it was an incredibly vertical alignment from what he could see.

"You seem impressed," Sebastian said, poking his head into the room.

"That's Electrum?" Venser asked. "I…how does it look like that?"

"The city apparently has a lot of proprietary technology involving skystone-based reactors, and they don't like to spill their secrets. Which is why Electrum is so brightly-lit where nowhere else is."

"It's…beautiful."

"It has its charm, to be certain. I definitely was taken aback the first time I came to Electrum. We'll be landing soon enough, so get ready to see it up close and personal."

The *Naglfar* touched down in the harbor with all the grace Venser had come to expect, and he joined the rest of the crew on the deck. The city was a brightly-lit array of lights and signs of all sorts.

"You look impressed by it all," Arycelle said.

"I am," Venser nodded.

"All right, we're here," Matthias said, bounding out of the bridge. "Venser's probably going to want to go to the main governmental complex, but they close in the evenings to the public, so we should do that tomorrow. For now, though, I vote that we do a bonding activity!"

"Oh, no," everyone but Venser groaned in unison.

"Come on, it's not going to be to 'Stripperella and Booblinda's Breastacular Café'! Yet. I know a pretty classy establishment that we can grab dinner at. They even usually have live entertainment."

Everyone agreed to this, mostly so that Matthias would not have pretext to whine about it the next day. As a group, they disembarked and, after a brief stop to talk to harbor officials about handling business tomorrow, they were off through the city. While both Gran Moria and Lunaria had some verticality in their constructions and sense of height in their architecture, Electrum took the cake with its towering skyscrapers, packed tightly. It was almost disorienting, and Venser had to shut his eyes occasionally to abate the feeling.

The establishment Matthias had picked out was a classy-looking place called the "Lightning Lotus", and it even advertised free entertainment. They settled in and started in on food while waiting for the entertainment to start. Venser noted that the food was definitely on the more "extravagant" side, though it delivered somewhat on the promise of it being worth eating.

After a while, an emcee came onto the stage at the front of the bar. "Ladies and gentlemen," he said, "it is my great pleasure to bring to you the traveling troupe, the wandering warblers, the voluptuous vagabonds! Without further ado, I present to you the inimitable talents of Blood Countess Erzsébet Báthory and her Coven of Unholy Nocturnal Terror!"

Polite applause rang out as Venser tried to remember where he'd beard the name. At least, he had heard part of it before. He had time to reflect on this as a posse of black-robed figures filed onto the stage, armed with an array of instruments and implements. One figure stepped forward, a frumpy-looking character with a distinctive pair of red-rimmed spectacles.

"Thank you for the warm welcome!" they said. The voice was feminine, high, and lisping. "We are the Coven of Unholy Nocturnal Terror, and I am its leader, the Blood Countess Erzsébet Báthory! We are pleased to present to you an evening of entertainment in honor of the great and ma...benevolent Astaroth, the one true deity! May Astaroth's spirit and presence touch you all as we honor his name!" She punctuated this with a laugh, a strange and shuddering giggle that almost sounded orgasmic in nature.

The performance put on by the Coven of Unholy Nocturnal Terror was, in a word, unusual. It consisted of strange musical numbers with ill-defined parts that were performed by an accompaniment of cacophonous instruments, interpretive dancing that felt stilted and wooden, and vocal performances that combined soprano range with abysmal enunciation. One could call it "art", to be sure, but the merits were dubious and the talents questionable.

"Okay, this is nowhere near as entertaining as I thought it would be," Matthias said. "At least the food's good."

"Yeah, the food is good enough, but we could have gone somewhere else," Sebastian added. He winced as one of the musical saws let out a particularly cacophonous squeal.

"Did you come here because you thought there would be hot girls?" Basch asked, raising an eyebrow.

"No! Uh...I mean, maybe?" Matthias was grinning awkwardly.

"Well, there are girls, but probably below your desired level," Arycelle said.

Venser was listening to them and the performance in silence, not entirely sure of what to make of it all. They were met with modest applause after each number, but it was more a smattering of polite applause in the vein of "we acknowledge you, now please get off the stage". Venser remembered the feeling of sitting through various "divinely-inspired productions" as a child, with heavy-handed moralizing and nonexistent entertainment, and the applause here reminded him of the applause there.

Nobody had any track of the time, and it had felt like the Coven of Unholy Nocturnal Terror's performance had gone on forever. After another number that sounded like the rest, a soporific dirge in praise of Astaroth's qualities that was delivered in an incomprehensible lisping soprano, the emcee from the start of the evening stepped onto the stage before they could start their next number.

"So sorry, ladies, but I'm going to have to end the set here," he said, the sleaze positively dripping from his voice. "An *opportunity* has come up, and we had to book them so as to not lose out to those bastards at the 'Wired Weasel'!"

"Excuse you? We paid for the entire evening, and we're not even a quarter of the way through our set!" squealed Blood Countess Erzsébet Báthory.

"But you see…"

"We will not stand for this injustice! How *dare* you try to end our set prematurely! We have not yet lavished sufficient praise upon the great and terrible Astaroth! You are an uncultured, discriminatory, and sexist pig!"

"That's not…"

"We will not acquiesce to your unreasonable demand!" The rest of the performers squealed in solidarity.

"Perhaps *I* might be able to help?"

The voice wasn't from someone on the stage, but it sounded familiar. It was a woman's voice that dripped with seduction, and Venser tried to both find where it was coming from and remember who it was from.

To answer both questions, onto the stage then strutted a familiar woman, a towering figure with ebony hair, ivory skin, and an immodestly-cut red dress with high thigh slits and a plunging neckline that barely avoided indecency. Venser also became aware of a bit of a dull headache that took hold acutely, but he didn't want to focus on that.

"Allow me to introduce myself," she purred. "I am Hellvira, and *I* shall take over as your entertainment for the evening. I trust there are no objections?"

The emcee and the members of the Coven of Unholy Nocturnal Terror all didn't respond, staring at Hellvira lustily and with rapt looks of euphoric bliss plastered on their faces. Venser looked around and saw both Matthias and Sebastian had similar looks of dazed ecstasy, while Basch and Arycelle were also trying to figure out what was going on.

"Ah, excellent!" she purred. "Just sit back, relax, and…enjoy." A sleazy, seductive beat started to play as Hellvira began to dance, a series of gyrations and tricks that were simultaneously more impressive than the Coven had displayed and unnerving, particularly with *how* fluid they were. She stepped over to the emcee and caressed his face with the back of her hand, and he collapsed immediately into a puddle of bliss, moaning euphorically.

"What's going on?" Venser whispered. He looked to Arycelle, who had a similar look of confusion. It was here that he saw Basch getting up and moving to the exit, to get out of the venue. Something told him he should follow Basch; if nothing else, a bit of air might clear up his headache, a dull and nagging discomfort that made it hard to think.

"I'm going after him," he told Arycelle.

"I'll keep an eye on these two," she said, gesturing to the googly-eyed gentlemen raptly watching Hellvira.

Venser slid out of his seat and tried to inconspicuously work his way out of the room, though he went largely unnoticed by the throngs of slack-jawed gentlemen and female companions trying to rouse them. He thought he could see Hellvira go into a sequence of movements that involved her winding up on the floor, culminating in her spreading her legs as a flash of light emanated from somewhere between them. He didn't want to know.

Venser left the thumping bass of the Electric Lotus behind, stepping into a light drizzle. This took him aback slightly, as rain was not something he was used to. He was also pleased to notice that the dull headache was no longer present, but he wondered where Basch had gone. He looked around and saw a figure walking down one of the avenues. Not knowing where else he could go, he followed them.

In the rain, the streets had a weird ambiance about them, heightened by the lights cutting through the darkness. As the figure walked, Venser continued to wind through the streets. He hoped that it was Basch; the couple of glimpses from lights suggested it was him, but he couldn't be sure. The rain was slowly picking up as he walked reaching a steady downpour at that point.

The figure stopped when they got to a park. It was the first somewhat open space Venser had seen since leaving the harbor, getting away from the dense streets. The figure stopped and seemed to be looking at a tree in the middle of the park. Venser decided to step forward and see if he could figure out who it was, attracting their attention when he stepped audibly into a puddle.

"Venser?" It *was* Basch, and he had noticed. "What are you doing here?"

"I needed to get out of there," he said. "My head was hurting, and I thought fresh air would help."

"I see. I couldn't stay there. I guess...seeing that woman and her performance brought back memories and feelings I hadn't wanted to revisit."

"How so?" Venser walked up and stood next to Basch. It was still raining, but he was under a bough that mitigated some of the rainfall.

"I've met that woman before, Hellvira. In passing. She's...always had that effect on men. When I lived in Balmung, I remember encountering her...there was an incident of her trying to seduce her way out of a situation. I tried to tell her no, but she got through by finding someone else she could sink her claws into. That...contributed a bit to me ultimately deciding to leave, though that was...one part of many that pushed me to that decision."

Basch was speaking slowly, and he seemed to be weighing his words. Venser thought he knew what he was trying to say, and the direction he was going in, but didn't want to interrupt.

"I...uh...well...damn it, I'm not good at this." He turned to face Venser. "What I'm trying to say is, I think...I've always thought you were cute, Venser. A bit mysterious, but cute. But I couldn't tell you, because..."

"...because I was supposed to be getting married, and you didn't think I was going to be around, right?" Venser asked.

"There was that, yeah. I didn't know how to tell you, and I didn't know how you'd take it, and I know people react violently sometimes if you tell them, and…"

Venser had always thought Basch to be rather stoic and emotionless, but here he was, pouring his heart out, and he could tell Basch was starting to get emotional.

Venser took Basch's hand to try and comfort him a bit. It was warm and well-worn, a contrast with his being rather soft. He wasn't sure as to if it was helping, but Basch let his voice trail off and interlaced his fingers with Venser's in a sign of appreciation, and the two stood in the rain in silence, reflecting on things.

Basch had admitted to Venser that he had a crush on him, and Venser realized that the feelings were mutual. He'd always been intrigued by Basch, especially once he got past his initially prickly exterior, and now that he was with the *Naglfar*'s crew for the long haul, he needn't hide his interest when the other party expressed it, as well..

Basch then drew Venser into him for an embrace, and the two stood under the tree for a while, the rain intensifying. They were otherwise quiet, and it was peaceful in spite of them getting wet.

"Thank you, Venser," he said. "I…thank you for following me, and thank you for listening."

"You're welcome," Venser replied.

They'd need to eventually get back to the Electric Lotus to check on things, but this was a moment all to themselves. And that, Venser thought, was worth as much as anything.

The two made their return to the bar, with Basch leading the way, to discover that Hellvira had vacated the premise and the duo of Sebastian and Matthias were both in a climactic, catatonic stupor. After getting an update from Arycelle (a rather detailed, blow-by-blow retelling of her final set of tricks, consisting of a handspring into what she described as a "death drop" that brought everyone to climax), the three worked on getting the two back to the

Naglfar. Basch carried Matthias, while Sebastian was handled by Arycelle and Venser together. The two continued to moan pleasurably, making for an awkward experience.

"You two didn't miss all that much," Arycelle said as they all trudged back, through the intensifying rain. "She finished her number and really did a number on everyone."

"It certainly sounds that way," Basch said.

"Who *is* that woman, anyways? I've heard about her and her antics, but it's always in the form of hearsay, tales spoken in whispers and vague phrasings."

"I…Leondra and I ran into her in Sorocco," Venser said. "It was in passing, though, and she seemed to be arguing with Yamato before we got there."

"What reason would she have to meet with him, though? She just seemed… extremely slutty, if I'm being perfectly honest. Not that there's anything intrinsically wrong with that, but is there more to her than just her trying to seduce every man she comes across?"

"I think there's definitely more going on there," Basch said, "but I have no idea what. Let's get these nimrods back to the ship for now, though. We don't have lodgings otherwise, and Matthias is a bit well-rounded anymore, so I'd rather not carry him longer than necessary."

They got back to the *Naglfar* and deposited the men in their rooms. Arycelle mentioned that she'd keep an eye on Sebastian, who already was starting to awaken, while nobody was keen on waiting with Matthias's wall of *interesting* posters to keep them company. At least Venser got to see his extensive "Oglette of the Month" poster collection, which was as impressive as it was appalling.

With the two catatonic men accounted for, Venser got back to his room, sighing with exhaustion. On top of being tired from carrying them back, he was still quite soaked, and he wondered if there was a way to get his clothes dry. It didn't help that he didn't have many options for things to wear besides these clothes.

"You're trying to dry off?" he heard Basch ask. He turned around to see Basch in the doorway, and he was just wearing a towel around his waist.

"Yeah," he answered.

"Your clothes aren't going to dry off very efficiently with you wearing them, and you'll catch a cold. Take them off and wear this for now. I can get them started with drying off." He handed a robe to Venser; it was sized to fit Basch, so it was big on Venser, but it was welcome all the same.

"Thanks." He closed the door, slipped out of his clothes, and slipped into the robe, which was indeed roomier than his clothes and with a slightly woody smell. His clothes were soon drying off in the machinery room, on a drying rack set up for such a purpose, along with the drenched clothes of everyone else.

"They should be good to go and wearable by the time you plan to head out tomorrow," Basch said, coming back from the lower level. "So…uh…do you want to continue where we left off earlier?"

"Define 'continue'," Venser said, smiling.

"I was thinking that…well…we established that we like each other, and I was wondering if…we could see where it goes." There was a sense of what almost felt like bashfulness, like Basch was too embarrassed to complete his train of thought.

"…I would like that, Basch."

Basch leaned towards Venser, and Venser followed his lead. Their lips met, a first kiss between them, and it was like a surge of electricity hit them both.

As they connected, Basch's towel and Venser's robe both fell off and onto the floor, leaving the two men completely naked. One kiss became ten, and the two men were furiously making out. Basch led Venser into his room and had him set up against the wall opposite the bed, their bodies warm against each other as they made out. Venser could feel Basch's hardening cock, possibly the most impressive he had beheld in his limited experience, starting to rub into his crotch and against his own rapidly stiffening member, and waves of pleasure coursed through his body that manifested in euphoric moans. Fully naked, Basch and Venser made for quite a contrast; Venser was slender and lithe, while Basch was muscular and solid.

Basch pulled Venser away from the wall and onto his bed, pulling Venser down to be on top of the man he was making out with. The two continued to kiss furiously as they writhed around against each other.

This kind of experience wasn't wholly new to Venser; there was some adolescent "experimentation" he had done back in Aracoras with Victor, the man whose name he had borrowed. Those had been the surreptitious activities of two unsure boys who had no idea what they were doing and who were unsure of how they felt about each other, though, and this was between two men who actually had feelings for one another. Venser wasn't entirely sure what he was doing, but Basch seemed eager to lead, and he was more than happy to follow.

Basch's lead led to his lips being wrapped around Venser's cock, and he vigorously sucked at it while Venser moaned, pleasure rippling through his body. He couldn't hold back the sounds of pleasure that involuntarily escaped, and he could feel the climax nearing.

Seeming to sense he was nearing climax, Basch pulled off and resumed kissing Venser on the lips, using his hand to continue stroking. Venser followed his lead, curling his fingers around Basch's turgid cock and jerking him off. Venser didn't last very long, though, and he moaned sharply as he erupted all over Basch's chest. Basch joined him, his orgasm a sticky geyser followed by a cadence of gasps. Thoroughly spent, Venser flopped into bed next to Basch, panting heavily.

The two men laid in silence, breathing heavily and basking in the proverbial afterglow. Rain continued to hit the window, creating a nice ambiance in both the sound of the precipitation and the sight of it rolling down the window.

Finally, Basch rolled over and kissed Venser again. "That was amazing," he murmured.

"It was," Venser replied, still trying to catch his breath.

"Uh...you know, if you want to spend the night here..."

"...I'd love that."

Basch just smiled and kissed him again. They quickly fell asleep, still slightly sticky from the night's fun, and Venser snuggled up in Basch's arms. He hadn't known what he was getting himself into, but snuggled up in a lovely man's arms on an airship, listening to the rain fall, was as nice a place as he could have hoped for.

10

Rolling Thunder

Venser stood on the deck of the *Naglfar*, stretching and taking in Electrum under the light of day. His clothes had dried off, he had gotten a wonderful night of sleep, and a new day awaited him. He was greeted by the sight of Matthias on the deck, nursing a headache and overseeing a bit of a paint job on the hull of the *Naglfar*.

"Ah, you're up," Matthias said. "Hopefully I didn't bother you, what with all the noise and activity. I figured now was a good time to get some work done on the ship."

"You weren't a bother," Venser said. "What are you doing?"

"Some airship maintenance and upkeep. Highlights include changing the name of the vessel to its new and glorious sobriquet, as well as touching up some armor plating and improving it. I suspect someone might, when the time comes, be trying to specifically counter the armor they knew we had, so I want to surprise her. Women *love* surprises, take it from me."

"I see." He didn't completely understand, but he figured there was a solid enough reason underlying his plans.

"The entire job should take a couple days, so long as nothing weird happens, so we'll be here until it's done. Which suits me just fine, because I like Electrum."

"It's...well, it definitely is an interesting city. A bit overwhelming to me, really."

"I can understand that, considering what I would imagine you're used to. On a related subject, what's your plan for the day?"

"Well...I should probably take the letter from Tsangarvides to whoever is in charge of Electrum. See what comes of it, share the state of things as they've been shaping up, and maybe learn of what they've learned."

"That's a reasonable plan," Matthias said. "If you're going that way, could I ask that you drop off something?"

"What is it?"

"It's the paperwork to re-register the *Naglfar* under its new name and updated ownership, along with a form updating the crew registry to strike our deposed captain and add you to it. The lovely people of Gran Moria were kind enough to give me a head-start on that, and it's good to get it done now."

"I can do that, sure."

"Excellent! I'll still need to go there myself to finalize things, but I can properly oversee the painting of the hull today and go when that's done."

"You're not putting a naked lady on the hull, are you, Matthias?" Basch asked, emerging from below deck.

"And good morning to you, Sunshine," Matthias quipped. "To answer your question, I'm not having a naked lady painted on the hull of this noble vessel. Not least of all because we couldn't agree on important qualities of said hypothetical naked lady, like what color her hair would be or what provocative pose she'd assume."

"In your mind's eye, she'd be wrapped in tentacles."

"Hey, you don't need to say it out loud!"

"Anyway, what's on the agenda for the day, oh dauntless captain? I'm seeing that Arycelle and Sebastian have gone off already."

"You'd be right. They're both off running errand-type things. Venser was getting ready to head to the main government building to drop things off for me and for himself, while I'm getting some airship modifications done."

"I see. Mind if I join you, Venser?" Basch asked.

"I don't," Venser said, trying to not answer too quickly.

"Wow, Basch actually wants to spend time with someone," Matthias said.

"Never thought I'd see the day. Might have to note it on the calendar."

"Just because I find *you* annoying doesn't mean I spurn *all* human contact," Basch shot back.

"Fair point, I suppose. You just spurn *most* human contact."

The two men left the ship, passing by the crew Matthias had contracted for painting over the name of the vessel once known as the *Alamithea*. Leaving the harbor and emerging into the proper city, Basch pointed out the tallest of the skyscrapers, mentioning that it was likely to be where they would want to visit, and so they set out for it.

"This is still rather maze-like," Venser said, looking around, "but it's at least not as hard to get my bearings now. I'm surprised I didn't get lost last night."

"Electrum does have unique things that make it harder to track position," Basch said. "A lot of the buildings tend to blend into each other."

"So I should stay close to you, so I don't get lost?"

"I mean...I wouldn't mind." Venser thought he saw Basch smile.

The two made it back to what Venser thought was the park they had their heartfelt moment in the night before, this time populated by members of the Coven of Unholy Nocturnal Terror. As was their wont, they were desperately trying to peddle their services to anyone passing by.

"Ah, bonjour, 'andsome!" one of them squealed, directly addressing the two. "Might we interest you two in...*puff-puff?*" They made a show of squeezing their chest seductively, as if to tempt them with their bounteous bosoms.

"No," Venser and Basch said, in unison. They looked at each other, amused by their timing.

"Oh, come on, gentlemen! It is a pleasure beyond measure! Though if that does not grab your attention, maybe you would like to borrow our talents in the service of augury and divination?"

"Your fortune-telling is *notorious* for its inaccuracy," Basch said.

"Where have you heard that? Our basic level of offering, Cleavage Divination, is at least 38% more accurate than our competition!" They were starting to panic in their efforts to get the sale to go through, hoping that one of them would say something that would stop Venser and Basch from walking away.

"You *do* realize that 38% better than zero is still zero, right?"

"Lies, slander, and slanderous lies! Clearly mistruths spread by our competitors, jealous of our success! Maybe we can offer you a discount on…"

"No."

The two men walked away, leaving the tittering members of the Coven of Unholy Nocturnal Terror to wonder what of their sales pitch was inadequate.

"They're shameless," Basch said. Venser looked back and thought he saw them starting their sales pitch anew, hoping to use their bounteous bosoms to draw in an intrigued customer.

Their destination was not too far ahead of where the park was, and the building clearly marked itself as such. Immediately inside was a reception desk, and Venser figured he needed to go there first.

"Welcome to the central governing offices of Electrum," the receptionist said, sounding thoroughly bored and wishing they were anywhere else. "What do you want?"

"I have two things today," Venser said. He spoke calmly, trying to not panic too much. "First, I'm turning in a registration form to change the registered ownership of an airship, along with a name change."

"Simple enough." They took the papers Matthias had asked Venser to turn in. "We'll begin processing this at our next possible convenience. What was the second thing?"

"I have something I mean to give to the leader of Electrum, from Tsangarvides of Gran Moria." He handed over the envelope, inscribed with the official seal of Gran Moria.

"An official letter," they said, looking the envelope over carefully. "At least, it looks the part. And you say this is meant to go directly to the leadership?"

"Uh…yes, that is correct."

"If you'll wait, I'm going to personally deliver this. This seems important enough that it needs to be delivered now instead of waiting." They got up, put a little sign on their desk that said "be back soon" with a smiley face, and then went into the room that the reception desk sat in front of.

"That's…interesting," Venser said, frowning. "From my experience, that means they're going to be gone for a while."

"Almost certainly. Let's have a seat until they get back," Basch said. "No sense in standing around, and no sense in going off in case the wait is shorter than expected."

"You're right."

A pair of chairs made for a suitable enough resting place, and it gave Venser and Basch time to rest and reflect before whatever else would happen. The room was rather sparse in its layout and decoration, meant to not keep people there and to usher them to wherever they were going.

The receptionist had been gone for a while, and their spot was taken by an equally-disgruntled replacement. They offered no further information, merely giving the gentlemen (and anyone else who dared perturbed them) a scowl of disapproval, and so they continued to wait patiently. Venser found himself holding hands with Basch as they sat there, which was a delight in and of itself, but he would still welcome something happening in a productive manner. Finally, the receptionist they had spoken to originally came back.

"Your presence is requested," they said, pointing to Venser.

"Uh…me? Just me?" he asked.

"Are *they* with you?" they responded, gesturing to Basch.

"Yes, he is."

They signed. "I guess they can come with you, but I make no promises as to if they'll be admitted into the meeting. Now, if you would, follow me."

They stepped into a small room, and Venser was startled when the room started to move upwards. The receptionist explained that this was an "elevator", and that it helped transport things vertically. They were apparently unique to Electrum, as the plans and schema for them were a closely-guarded secret, which explained a bit to Venser in terms of their novelty.

A "ding" preceded the doors opening, and Venser realized just how high up they were. Only the very tops of the other skyscrapers could compare to where they presently were, and there was more height than that above them. He tried to not think about that, so as to not trigger his acrophobia more than necessary.

"I don't think I've ever been this high up," Basch said, looking around. "At least, not in a building this high. Airships are a different beast that way."

"I definitely haven't," Venser said. He noticed a weird bit of pressure behind his temples, the formation of a potential headache, but he wasn't sure where it was from.

"If it helps, don't look out the windows, and it's like you're in a building of regular height." Basch gave Venser's hand a reassuring squeeze.

"Lady Elessa is currently busy," the receptionist said, "but her meeting should not last much longer."

"Lady Elessa," Basch muttered. "So, the old man handed power off, I see."

"Do you know them?" Venser asked.

"No, not personally. Not beyond a passing encounter here and there, at best. The man who used to be in charge of Electrum was Erdwin. But I think he'd been dealing with recent illness, and so they were transitioning power away from him. He had a few kids, and I think they were competing for pole position."

"How do you know all this?" the receptionist asked. They bore an expression of surprise that this random man off the street could know about their back-room politicking.

"I hear things." Basch's tone was flippant, not wanting to expound further.

"What happened to the other kids?" Venser asked.

"Who knows. Some might have stuck around to try and capitalize on potential windows to take power, while others might have quit Electrum entirely. I think Erdwin had five kids…two boys and three girls, if memory serves me."

Before anyone could respond to this, the door they were waiting in front of flew open, and a familiar figure strutted out. It was none other than the inimitable Hellvira, still wearing her immodest red dress and still possessing the same self-assured attitude from previous run-ins.

"I'll be in touch, Lady Elessa," she called back, her voice a silken purr that oozed seduction. "And what have we here, more guests? I thought Elessa would have an *open* schedule today."

"We got here late," Basch said. Venser noticed his tone was surly and brusque, a lot like when they first met. He also noticed that the receptionist had a rapt look of pleasure on their face, utterly captivated by the charms of Hellvira.

"I can see that. You two little fine specimens look…familiar, somehow. We've met before, I'm sure of it, but I just can't place where it was…ah, I know where I met one of you, at least!" She was looking right at Venser.

"Uh…we met in Sorocco, right?" Venser asked.

"I do believe we did. Your name was…Venser, was it not? You were with Lady Leondra then, and I'm surprised to see you without her."

"She…uh, we parted ways."

"Parted ways? With your fiancée? I hope you two didn't have a fight or falling out! That would be *tragic*!" Hellvira gasped dramatically, but in an exaggerated way that betrayed a lack of authenticity.

"Why we went our separate ways is not your concern," Venser replied, starting to get annoyed by her and by his headache.

"You're right, I probably shouldn't pry. Though I shudder to think what might happen when they come to pick you up for your wedding and…surprise, the groom isn't there!"

The way she was talking was unnerving to Venser, and he also didn't think he had mentioned his name to her in their past meeting. Something was up with Hellvira, but he didn't know what.

"I do have a question for you…Hellvira, was it?" Basch started. "My companion's identity is not particularly well-known, I would say, and it wound up being the source of some scrambling in Gran Moria. Did you, perchance, encounter a rather sanctimonious fellow, and did you tell them anything?"

"I run into a good many disagreeable persons in my travels, my little cabbage," she purred. "Though if we're thinking of the same person…

perhaps, yes, I did encounter them. They would have been *desperate* to please someone, so I might have passed along a choice morsel or two of information to help them along their way."

"I see." Basch said nothing further, but he definitely seemed to be thinking about what she said.

"Alas, my time is valuable, and while I would *love* to continue our conversation, this is where we must part ways for the nonce, my little treasures. I *do* hope we our paths cross again." Hellvira strutted past them and to the elevator, making sure to caress the receptionist so that they collapsed into an ecstatic, quavering mess.

"Something's up with her," Venser said. "I don't know *what*, though."

"I'm not sure myself, either," Basch said. "Let's mull over that later, though. Elessa's waiting."

The room the two men stepped into was rather plush and lavish, though still geared for business. Elessa sat at the desk at the head of the room, a young-looking woman Venser thought might not be too much older than either of them. She had sleek, black hair that reached her shoulders, and she was smartly dressed.

"Ah, our visitors," she said. "I hope that you weren't kept waiting too long."

"Not terribly so," Venser said as the two sat down in chairs opposite her.

"That's good, then. Sometimes I'm bad about keeping track of time. Let's get to it, shall we?"

Following introductions, Venser and Elessa began to talk about the contents in the letter, the events that led up to this point, and the plans to open the Tomb of the Almighty. She was attentive, listening patiently as Venser retold how he was betrothed to Leondra of Lunaria, they figured out that the Tomb of the Almighty was in the plans, that they still weren't completely sure what was in it, and that impending nuptials were the pretext to open the Tomb of the Almighty.

"You tell a fascinating tale," Elessa said. "One that matches what I have heard on the winds of late, actually. Hellvira, the woman I just got done meeting with...she wanted to regale me with information about the Tomb of the Almighty and what was within. That she would volunteer the information so readily strikes me as curious, as does the issue of where she got it."

"She has ulterior motives, you mean?" Basch asked.

"I can't rule it out. The way she spoke about it suggested that she wants it opened."

"Is she working with the people in Lunaria and Aracoras?" Venser asked. "I...we met her in Sorocco, and Leondra also mentioned having encountered her in Lunaria."

"So, she's getting around, then," Elessa said. She was frowning, trying to put the pieces together.

"If she wants the Tomb of the Almighty open," Venser continued, "wouldn't that suggest she stands to benefit from it? And if she does, I can't see how that's *good*. Something about her has me ill at ease."

"You too, then? We're on a similar page, then. There was this weird sense I got from Hellvira, that there's malign intent somewhere beneath that surface."

"If we're thinking similarly with regards to her," Basch said, "then we should take action, right? I think we can't just let things happen the way they look to be going."

"I agree," Elessa started. "But..."

"...let me guess, it's not that easy."

"I've only recently taken over as paramount leader of Electrum, and I fear that other leaders do not yet respect me. Both for my youth, and because I am a woman. Not to say they'd necessarily listen to Father, but that's one issue," Elessa said, with an almost rueful smile.

"Another probably would be me," Venser said. "I may have the symbol of devotion, but I look like an impostor, and they would further disregard my words as being from one who has strayed too far into sin."

"Speaking of which, Venser," she continued, "what *will* happen when your absence is noticed by your father?"

Venser frowned as he thought it over. In terms of chronology, his father would be returning to Lunaria any day now, which would cause all hell to break loose.

"I imagine that, besides demanding my return," he said, "they would insist on a solution to get the wedding to happen. Lunaria wants whatever is in the Tomb of the Almighty, and Aracoras wants...no, *needs* the dowry they would get from Leondra being married."

"Would they marry her off to a brother of yours?"

"I do have a brother, Velgrand, who is younger than me. That said, my mother would be adamantly opposed to such a marriage. All my older siblings are already wed, though."

"So, your absence might not stop a marriage, but it would make for a lot of distrust and chaos in the lead-up to the nuptials," Elessa said. "Leondra and this Velgrand fellow would be the 'happy couple', the means to the end. They would then open the Tomb of the Almighty at the climax of the ceremony, letting out whatever is in there. Which we don't yet know concretely, but given that Hellvira wants it open, it can't be good."

"That...I'd say that about sums it up," Venser said. "I'm not thinking the Almighty is what awaits us in the Tomb of the Almighty...not anymore, that is. There's something weird about it all."

"I suppose the Almighty *could* be in there, trapped with whatever they were fighting. But, as far as I know, we don't have any texts in Electrum that would provide clarity in that regard. I could be in error, but that seems like a subject beyond our expertise."

"It's sounding to me like someone, or something, *doesn't* want us to know for sure what's in there," Basch said. "They can then use the ambiguity to push us to keep it sealed...or to unseal it, as appears to be the case here."

Elessa stood up and walked over to the window, stretching a bit. "I suspect you may be on to something," she said. "If Leondra has discovered so many conflicting theories and stories about the Tomb of the Almighty after a short research stint, who knows where the truth truly lies? You two have given me a lot to think about, to be sure. Might I ask that we continue this conversation tomorrow? I need time to think and consult."

"Certainly," Venser said. "I don't believe we were leaving on the morrow, so we can pick this up then." Basch nodded to confirm agreement with this.

"Excellent," she said, smiling. "I shall see you then."

"So, you mean to tell me Electrum is ruled over by a hot chick, *and* the hot chick is giving us lodging for the night in some swanky digs?" Matthias asked. "Man, hiring Venser was the best decision I've made as captain!" Basch and Venser had made it back to the harbor, and Elessa had given word to relevant parties that they were to be put up for the night as "official" guests. Matthias was certainly not displeased by this.

"The catch is that we have two rooms to divide between the five of us," Venser said.

"Oh, that's fine! Even if I have to share a room, it'll be a soft bed for the night. And it'll be nice to not be looking at the *Naglfar* for a night." The paint job Matthias had commissioned had gone well, and the new name gleaned from the hull.

"I take it you got everything done you wanted to on the ship?" Basch asked.

"Mostly, but not all of it. Today was the painting of the hull, because that's easy enough and I had a headache. Tomorrow, we're looking to have the hull touched up with some thicker armor."

"Right, you did mention wanting that done, just in case,"

"But, if nothing else, lodging in town will let me get to where I need to for finishing up registration-type things."

"Do I hear right, that we're staying in town tonight?" Sebastian asked. He and Arycelle had just gotten back to the *Naglfar*.

"Pretty impressive, if that's the case," Arycelle said. "I know some of those places can be hard to get into, even if Matthias might prefer staying at the 'Palace of Perpetual Pleasure' most nights."

"Look, I know not to pass up a prime bit of luxury," Matthias said. "Besides, I can pay the ladies of the Palace a visit when the opportunity strikes, right?"

"Oh, we all know that," Basch said, rolling his eyes. "I think we're surprised you haven't made time to go there yet."

"I've been busy today, dear Basch! And the hour is still early, and stuff. Plenty of time to go to all the important places, like Stripperella and

Booblinda's Breastacular Café."

"Is that *really* a place that exists?" Venser asked, everyone else around him groaning.

"Of course it exists, dear Venser! Their lunch specials truly are the 'breast in show.'"

"It's mediocre food you pay a premium for because the waitresses are all wearing tops that show off their busts," Arycelle said.

"How about, instead of quibbling about the merits of the restaurant," Sebastian said, "we go check out our lodgings for the night?"

"I'm on board with that," Matthias said.

"The *Naglfar* will be fine, right?" Venser asked.

"Don't worry. The cabin and bridge will both be locked, and I did have those locks changed out as part of today's activities. Guards also patrol the harbor."

"We'll do a proper go-over before we depart, too," Sebastian said. "Always good to have that assurance."

"Verily. Anyway, shall we be off? Lead the way, whoever is leading the way."

As they left the harbor, they immediately ran into a familiar sight: the Coven of Unholy Nocturnal Terror, who seemingly had relocated to try and lure in people who had just gotten to Electrum.

"Ah, bonjour, 'andsome!" one of them squealed, starting their usual sales pitch directly to Basch. "Might I…"

"No," all five said in unison. They kept walking, ignoring the tittering offers of *puff-puff* and Cleavage Divination and whatever else they came up with. Matthias mentioned that their auguries were all notorious for being inaccurate and vague, and he did *not* know this from experience, thank you very much.

The accommodations that the quintet were put up in were certainly impressive to all of them. Barely a proverbial stone's throw from the main skyscraper, they were in a rather posh-looking hotel (called the "Verdant Wind") with all sorts of luxuries. The best part was that they were to have their lodgings covered for three nights, which Matthias hoped would be enough time to finish all of the tweaks and to finish any additional business that needed finishing in Electrum.

"A hotel like this is certainly impressive," Matthias said. Evening had set in, and the five had gotten back from an excursion that included supper. "Maybe not where I want to spend all of my time, but nice for a change of pace."

"This is all a bit too pricey for us to do more than occasionally," Sebastian said. "I don't think I want to know how much it'd cost to stay here if we had to foot the bill ourselves."

"None of us do," Arycelle said.

Venser nodded in affirmation as he looked around. While the palace in Lunaria had been impressive, from the brief time he'd spent there, the sense of grandeur from the hotel was different, meant to impress from the inside instead of merely from the outside. The clientele of the hotel definitely looked the part, put-together and self-assured, and they made sure to regard them all with measured disdain and displeasure over the presence of such riff-raff.

"Excuse us," a rather haughty man said, walking up to them, "but I am not sure what you lot are doing in an establishment such as this. Are you lost?"

"We're staying here," Basch said.

The man chuckled, his tone condescending. "I find that hard to believe," he scoffed. "You'd not even be able to afford to breathe the air in here!"

"We were invited to stay here by Lady Elessa herself," Venser said, stepping forward. He was annoyed by the man's demeanor.

"Really, now? Also unbelievable. What could she want with a lot of urchins?"

Venser pulled out the letter that had gotten them the accommodations in the first place, the one Elessa had given him. "Our business is our own, and we would appreciate it if you would leave us alone," he said. He spoke firmly, his tone saying that this was not a conversation he was keen on having.

"Excuse us, what is the problem here?" asked one of the hotel staff, walking up to them.

"We're being harassed by this disgusting old man who thinks we're not allowed to stay here," Matthias said. He had a wry smile, knowing that this would irk the man in question, and it did indeed have its desired effect, as the man sputtered in protest over being labeled as "old" and "disgusting".

"I can confirm that they are our guests here," the staffer said, glaring at the man. "I would ask that, in the future, you keep your nose out of the business of others and do not harass them." She walked away, and the red-faced man continued to sputter in protest.

"Come on, everyone," Arycelle said. "Let's go."

As they walked by, the man tried to spit out a mealy-mouthed apology, the standard "sorry if I caused you offense" non-apology. None of them acknowledged it, feeling it better to let him stew in his humiliation than to offer him the closure he wanted.

The rooms they had were on the highest floor. Arycelle and Sebastian took one room, Basch and Venser offered to share another room, and Matthias decided to go with Sebastian and Arycelle and sleep on the fold-out bed in their room. Partly out of Basch finding Matthias annoying in large doses, and also partly so that Matthias and Sebastian might be able to chatter about the latest periodicals.

"What a day," Venser said. He and Basch were in the room they'd taken, and he sat down on the edge of the bed to gather his thoughts. "Started with a meeting with Elessa, and ended in a hotel room more expensive than I would have dreamed to experience."

"You're a long way from Aracoras anymore," Basch said, sitting next to him. "At least in a metaphorical sense."

"The more I see, the more I realize why they tried to keep it away from us. The more I've learned and the more I've experienced, the less I've wanted to go back."

"I can understand that. I don't think the idea of what was home is anywhere near as inhospitable for me as it is for you, but I can definitely understand you not wanting to go back and not having reason to go back."

"I suppose there *are* reasons to go back, if I look hard enough and lie to myself, but I have more reasons not to." He looked at Basch as he said this.

The two leaned in, and their lips met. The passion that had taken hold the night before flared to life anew, and their clothes made an unruly pile on the floor as they made out, furiously kissing and writhing about with one another. Venser forgot about everything else in that moment, and the world fell away around the two of them for that night, between his sucking off of Basch, the frenzied frotting as they mad out on top of each other, and the blasts that covered their chests afterwards.

As they laid in bed together, spent and naked, Venser realized that this was where he finally felt like he belonged. He'd never felt like he belonged in Aracoras, but this motley crew was one where he was free to be himself. He nestled into Basch's arms and fell asleep.

11

Lightning Runner

The sun rose over another day in Electrum, and the crew of the *Naglfar* all got to work. Sebastian and Arycelle took it upon themselves to oversee the upgrading of the hull's armor, while the other three went to the central skyscraper for their tasks.

"Lucky you, not having to wait around," Matthias said. They had arrived to behold quite a formidable line for the bureaucratic process, while Venser was being actively waved over to the elevators. "I'm going to need to wait here as they go over all of the paperwork. It's pretty voluminous, and I need to make sure everything is properly accounted for."

"You're pretty serious when you want to be," Venser said.

"The key is to always know when I *need* to be, dear Venser," he said, smiling.

Basch and Venser left Matthias behind as they were ushered into the elevator. Venser tried to not think about the functioning of the elevator or about how high up they were, a mantra he kept repeating as they returned to the upper chambers they had been in the day prior. As before, they were left to wait while Elessa finished a meeting, this one with a businessman of sorts.

The two weren't left waiting long, and the door opened to reveal none other than the same man who'd been rude to them in the hotel. He started strutting out of the room, seeming pleased with himself, when he noticed that there were people waiting for a meeting.

"Oh, looks like some urchins got in off the street," he huffed, looking at them disdainfully.

"Not surprising you don't recognize us," Basch said. "Probably keen to forget your mistreatment of us last night, right?"

The man stopped and looked at him. "Have we met before?" he asked, making sure the disdain dripped from his voice.

"We did, in the hotel. It was five of us, and you tried to tell us we weren't guests there."

"Oh, that? That was a silly little misunderstanding. Nothing more."

"What's going on?" Elessa asked, having made her way to the door.

"We ran into this man last night," Basch said, "and he was just as rude and uncouth then as he was to us just now."

"Really." She looked at the man, who was still trying to project confidence.

"Me, *rude* and *uncouth*? I was just voicing my doubts about the *importance* of people as shabby-looking as they are."

"Ah, so you're one of *those* people. Someone who sticks their nose in the dirt for people they see above them and pushes faces into the dirt if they're below them. I understand," Basch said.

The man turned red with displeasure. "How *dare* you presume to know anything about me, you little rat!" he spat, marching over to Basch and getting in his face. It clearly was an attempt to intimidate. "You should be lucky that I don't have you drowned like the scurrying little vermin you are!"

Just then, he remembered where he was and who he was in front of, and he saw Elessa and Venser looking at him. Elessa's face displayed marked distaste.

"I'd heard rumors about how you treat your subordinates," Elessa said. "And, I have to say, I am *appalled*."

"A-a-appalled? What do you mean?" His tone had gone from haughty confidence to a meek, almost pleading whine. "I assure you, this is not who I am!"

"I'm not so sure it's *not* who you are," she responded. "Let's just say that threatening my guests is not conducive to staying in favor. Those plans we talked about *might* have to be reconsidered..."

"Please, no, not that! If I caused offense, I'm sorry! Deeply sorry!" He was clearly desperate, something Venser had seen aplenty in the past.

"You're not sorry," Basch retorted. "You're only regretful that you couldn't get away with it this time."

"Quiet, you rat!" he spat back, an instinctual response.

"Could you escort him out of the building?" Elessa asked, addressing the receptionist that was there and pointing to the man. "Please have him removed from the premises." The man continued to try and plead his case as he was dragged away, whining about the injustice being wrought against him.

"I'm so sorry about that," Elessa said, bowing. "He's one of the operators of the biggest entertainment establishment here in Electrum, and he was making a case for a grand expansion. Economic expansion isn't a bad thing...but I have heard about his mistreatment of people who work under him."

"I noticed that people tended to treat those above them well," Venser said. "Those below them are different, though."

"Or the people they see as below them, at least. Anyways, let's head inside. There's much to be discussed."

The conversation with Elessa felt, to Venser, like one he'd had before in different cadences. It featured a detailed explanation of what Venser knew about why Aracoras might benefit from the opening of the Tomb of the Almighty, Hessler's focus on it, Leondra's trying to learn about what was in it, and all the competing theories of what was in there.

"I did have the chance to ask my father if he had any insight, and he unfortunately had nothing further to offer," Elessa said. "He did mention that he's heard about the Tomb of the Almighty several times over the years. And, apparently, the wisdom at the time was that 'we would know when the time was right' as to if, and when, we should open it. But he was also taught that the decision should not be made lightly, and that it should be an agreement among all of the great cities."

"It doesn't sound like it's the case at all, that there is agreement among everyone to open it," Venser said.

"Though it's funny that you should mention that now, because this morning, I got something fascinating by mail." She reached across her desk and pulled out an envelope, one with ornately-done lettering and bearing the seal of Lunaria on it.

"That looks threatening," Basch said. His tone was joking.

"Maybe not 'threatening', but ominous indeed. In a sense. It's a notice of nuptials. Informing us that there is to be a grand ceremony tying together the ruling family of Lunaria and the family of the foremost member of Aracoras' Council of Elders. In particular, one Lady Leondra of Lunaria and Lord Venser of Aracoras…they are to be united in holy matrimony with expediency and under the benevolent gaze of the Tomb of the Almighty itself." She looked down at the letter as she read it, trying to capture the grandiloquent tone they had employed.

Hearing this made Venser realize that, indeed, that was what was waiting for him. Or, rather, what *had* been waiting for him.

"It doesn't quite sound like a proper wedding invite," Basch frowned. "Not the kind I'm familiar with, though the parties involved might be given to more florid phrasing."

"From my experience, they send out these notices as a heads-up as to that a marriage is being scheduled, and then the actual ceremony invites are issued closer to time," Elessa said. "Give enough advance notice so that schedules can be cleared. Of course, Venser's absence might complicate matters."

"That sounds like quite the understatement," Venser said.

"Of course, you're not *here*, not in any official capacity. Which I imagine is starting to wear on you a bit, being passed around like a bit of contraband and unable to settle in."

"I'd be lying if I said it was completely fine. But I suppose I've gotten used to it, for lack of appealing alternatives. And I'm with a good group of people, which helps a lot."

"I saw you're actually part of the air crew of the re-registered *Naglfar*. I have to say, that's a shrewd move on your captain's part, in terms of keeping you safe. Under conventions governing trade and commerce, people can't be forcibly removed from airship crews by external forces, unless they've committed misdeeds that would demand prosecution."

"I suppose Matthias has a good idea every now and again," Basch said. "I'm not sure what the laws of Aracoras say in that regard, but your mere presence is not necessarily illegal. Just...highly inconvenient."

"I suppose that's apt phrasing, indeed," she said.

Venser closed his eyes, trying to remember the laws about people who had left Aracoras. There were the laws prescribing death to any and all who violated their sanctity without official leave, as well as laws mandating death to those whose purity had been compromised irrevocably, but they had not enacted laws to make it illegal to leave. You just *didn't* leave, because to leave would inevitably invite claims of impurity by that one irksome bureaucrat with a grudge against you.

"So, obviously, Venser's not going to be allowed to stay here, at least in an official capacity," Basch said. "But there has to be *something* more we can do, right? Because if we let them just go and figure out a work-around that works for them, the Tomb's still opening up. If we're presuming that it's a bad thing, of course."

"I'm inclined to believe that it's nowhere near the windfall that's being promised, in terms of a world without suffering and strife," Elessa said. "Seriously, I received an envoy from Lunaria a few days ago who told me that we were on the verge of a glorious turning point, one that would thrust us into a utopia. They didn't say *what* it was, but hearing about the Tomb of the Almighty from you makes it make more sense."

"All right. So, tomb opening equals bad. What now?"

"Venser, you've been to Sorocco and Gran Moria before here, correct?"

"I have," he confirmed.

"The grand cities you have yet to visit, Calaveras and Balmung, might be reasonable stops, if you can finagle such an itinerary. I'm unsure of what their respective leaders may have heard about what Lunaria and Aracoras have in the works, but they'd like to know, I would imagine."

"The itinerary shouldn't be a problem," Basch said. The mention of Balmung has seemed to irk him slightly, Venser noticed. "I suppose...we should talk it over with everyone today, just to make sure it works."

"I think that's a good idea," Elessa said. "We can then plan to meet again tomorrow, I presume?" They confirmed their meeting on the morrow would work, and the two men got up to head out.

"Ah, there you are," Matthias said, greeting them as they left the elevator. "I thought to wait up for you. I got the paperwork done, so that's one less thing to do, right?"

"That's good," Venser said. "Did it go smoothly?"

"Smoothly enough. I also think I saw that asshole who was in the hotel last night, the one who was rude to us. He seemed nicely rattled."

"He was rude to us, Elessa heard, and it might have cost him a contract."

"Ah, comeuppance. Always satisfying. Basch seems a bit distracted, though."

Basch sighed. "A bit," he said. "I suppose we should catch you up on what happened." The two gave a quick rundown to Matthias about both what they learned and what their recommended course of action was.

"So, she wants us to go to Calaveras and Balmung? I suppose the latter being on the agenda is why you're not thrilled."

"If we have to go there, we have to go there. I'm not happy about it, though. I'd rather not go back there, but I suppose that's not a luxury we have."

"You're sure it's okay?" Venser asked.

"It'll be fine. It's going to be a short visit, if nothing else. My suffering won't be long and drawn out."

"Speaking of long and drawn out..." Matthias started, grinning.

"Is this a joke about your dick again?" Basch groaned.

"Not unless you want it to be! But we should tell Sebastian and Arycelle all of what has happened today. We can make plans to alight the day after tomorrow to Calaveras, which is the closer of the two."

"More time to mentally prepare for my impending torment. That should work. Let's meet up with those two and catch them up on the details."

They left the building and headed back towards the harbor, winding through the streets and avoiding as many of the street side vendors as they could. Their offerings were varied, ranging from foodstuffs to souvenirs to promises of *puff-puff*, and the overall level of activity was certainly impressive to Venser. The only real point of comparison he had was Lunaria's streets, and those hadn't seemed as frenetic and frenzied as these.

"How are you holding up, Venser?" Matthias asked. "You seem pretty awe-struck."

"All of this is still pretty impressive to me," he said. "I couldn't have imagined anything like this while I was home."

"It would be pretty far away from what you're used to," Basch said. "At least, based on what I've heard."

"What have you heard?" Now Venser was curious.

"Lots of hearsay, stories that filter through a lot of different people and distort along the way. That they don't let their women outside, that men and women aren't allowed to be alone together before marriage, that you spend at least half of each day in reflection and prayer..."

"Those all sound pretty accurate, if slightly exaggerated. In particular, women are allowed outside, but with strict supervision as to...I think the phrasing is 'protect the fragile vessels and enable them to flourish into their divinely-prescribed role.'"

"I imagine Arycelle would tell them where they could shove their 'divinely-prescribed roles,'" Matthias said. He craned his neck as they walked by a bookstore with specifically salacious offerings, volumes featuring various scantily-clad ladies and tentacles in compromising places, likely making a note for later.

They got back to the harbor, and the hull of the *Naglfar* did look remarkably shiny, at least more than Venser could remember. He didn't rule out it being a trick of the light, but it was still impressive.

"Well, it looks like they got the hull treated," Matthias said, walking over and tapping on the hull with his knuckles. "Sounds good, anyways."

Basch walked over and did the same motion. "You're right.Definitely sounds a lot more rigid," he said. "Hopefully it's as sturdy as the acoustics suggest."

"So, did Sebastian and Arycelle leave already?" Venser asked.

"They might have, but I suspect they're still here. On board. In their room." Matthias had a mischievous grin on his face.

"...right, they *would* have had free time after overseeing things." Basch also was smirking.

"Should we tell them we're back?" he asked.

"Probably," Matthias said. "Let me go get them. Hopefully they're not in the middle of something, though we can wait if they are." He scampered onto the deck, leaving Basch and Venser on the ground of the harbor.

"I'm sure Matthias is going to catch them in the middle of something," Basch said.

"That sounds about right, from my experience," Venser said. "There was a scandal I remember of someone getting caught making out in a room, and they were pretty severely punished for it."

"We should probably make sure they don't catch us, then." Basch slipped a kiss onto Venser's head, which segued into a quick lip lock. The timing coincided with hearing commotion on the *Naglfar*, which almost certainly meant Matthias interrupted them.

The plan had been finalized, and Calaveras was to be the *Naglfar*'s destination. Following a rather leisurely evening by all parties, the five of them all headed to meet with Elessa on their last day there. They had heard that she wanted to meet with all of them, together, if they were free to do so. Not wanting to miss the opportunity, they agreed, and they were packed into the elevator.

"I don't think we've ever been this high up," Sebastian said, getting off the elevator and looking around. "You can see just about everything from all the way up here."

"Makes you realize just how much of Electrum has been taken up by pleasure parlors of varying types," Matthias said. "I think Erdwin, the last paramount leader, tended to let anyone set up shop if they were willing to pay expenses and taxes, and it turns out that he permitted a lot more establishments of…interesting character."

Venser nodded. It was an interesting approach, but he wondered how much everyone seemed to agree with it. As before, Elessa was in a meeting, and her schedule was often pretty jam-packed, so they were left waiting.

The door opened, and for the second day in a row, the haughty-looking businessman walked out, this time flanked by a couple of intimidating-looking associates. He did not look pleased in the slightest, like he had failed to get done what they had intended.

"Fancy seeing him again," Basch said, making sure it was loud enough. The man looked up, and his face turned red with anger.

"What are *you* doing here?" he spat. His associates stepped forward, making themselves appear large and intimidating.

"We're meeting with Elessa," Matthias said. "As for *why*…well, you're not worth our time."

"How *dare* you take that tone with me, whelp! I am the richest man in Electrum, and you will understand that you are…"

"And we don't care how much money you have, especially with someone as morally bankrupt as you are," Arycelle cut in, not giving him a chance to respond further. "Money can't buy you respect, and with as badly as you treated us, I don't think we'll *ever* give a damn about how much money you claim to have."

"Speaking of that," Matthias said, a mischievous smile on his face, "your friends look familiar. I think I saw them last night…I remember! I saw their faces when I was passing by where the Coven of Unholy Nocturnal Terror was set up, and they were getting a Cleavage Divination! At the very least. Might have been more, come to think of it."

The two of them looked panicked, as if this was something they did not want to get out, and the businessman turned even redder than Venser thought was possible.

"I have to say, getting Cleavage Divinations from *them*?" Basch said, shaking his head. "That's just desperate."

"Enough! I'm not going to stand here and be belittled by all of you!" the businessman spat.

"You just were," Matthias said.

His response was to scream and storm off, bringing his sheepish associates with him. With that taken care of, they went in to meet with Elessa. They all made it a point to remind Matthias that his ogling should be kept to a respectable minimum, which he agreed with.

"It's a pleasure to meet all of you," Elessa said as they filed in. "I do hope that my last guest was not overly unpleasant. He may have been *displeased* by my decisions recently, and he thought that his associates might be able to convince me to change my mind."

"Subtle, that," Sebastian said. "Anyways, you haven't met the three of us, I don't think. I'm Sebastian."

"I'm Arycelle."

"...oh, yeah, I'm Matthias. Captain and all that stuff." Matthias had lost himself and was, indeed, briefly ogling.

"Pay him no heed, Lady Elessa," Arycelle said, shaking her head. "He has a thing for the ladies. *Quite* the thing."

"I'm fine now," Matthias said, glaring. "Sorry about that. Let's get to business, shall we?"

"Yes, let's." Elessa's expression was between amusement and bewilderment, and she sounded keen to move on.

"So, let's do a recap. Venser's scheduled to get married to Leondra, and him not being there might impede that somewhat," Elessa said. "We still need to figure out how to keep Hessler and Aracoras from opening the Tomb of the Almighty. It turns out that my father knew of a couple old books that might be of use, and he had those retrieved."

"Well, that's intriguing enough," Venser said. "Did you learn anything?"

"We're not completely sure of the validity of the information, but the books haven't been disturbed in a long while, so they're not likely fabrications. Unfortunately, they're suggesting that what's in the Tomb is...not good."

"How 'not good' are we talking?" Matthias asked, pursing his lips. "Not good is a pretty broad spectrum."

"The implication is that the Tomb of the Almighty holds a great evil. In particular, it's the great evil that was said to have been defeated by our ancestors, the force the Almighty was said to have fought off."

They fell into silence, contemplating this. Venser felt a great unease inside him, particularly given that he'd been taught that the Tomb of the Almighty held just that: the Almighty. What was in there if not them, and how bad *were* they?

"So, that's the very far end of 'not good,'" Basch said.

"How evil are we talking?" Arycelle asked. "If they've been sealed away for however long they've been sealed away, I'd have no idea how powerful they are."

"Unfortunately, specifics are light. All I know, if these books are accurate, is that whatever is in the Tomb of the Almighty is something that should not be let out. They detailed the lengths they had to go to in order to seal them away, as they were unable to completely defeat it, and that does sound like information that could be useful in the future."

"Probably," Sebastian said. "So, for now, what are we to do?"

"Venser and Basch told me that you want us to meet with the leaders of Calaveras and Balmung to get them up to speed," Matthias added. "Presumably, to get them on our side, and by that I mean 'not Lunaria and Aracoras.'"

"One other question I have," Elessa continued, "is if that weird woman, Hellvira, fits into this somehow. She came to me, telling me about the riches and glory waiting in the Tomb of the Almighty."

"Hellvira...that trollop from the club the other night?" Arycelle asked, narrowing her eyes.

"I remember her, a bit. But that entire night was a blur," Matthias said. "My memory after she stepped on stage feels like a big hole."

"I...I ran into her in Sorocco, too," Venser said. "And Leondra mentioned seeing her meet with her father at some point. And we met her as she finished up a meeting with Lady Elessa."

"Something's up with her," Elessa said. "Between her effects on those intrigued by the female form, her travels, and what she's apparently been telling people, me included, I bet Hellvira has her hands all over the plans to open the Tomb of the Almighty. I don't know where, exactly, she fits into it, but something tells me that she's not a coincidence."

"I suspect we'll all find out when it's most detrimental to all of us," Basch quipped.

"Any good schemer holds their cards for the time it most benefits playing them," Matthias said. "I suppose we just have to hope that we can answer whatever is in their hand."

"On that note, I suppose I should give you this." Elessa motioned one of her attendants to walk a pair of letters over to Venser. "I took the initiative to have these drafted up, and I think they'll help explain our position. Not that I suspect we'd have too much trouble, as Lunaria's generally domineering behavior has won it few actual friends."

"So, it's stopping by to make sure we all agree to disagree with them?" Matthias asked. "Simple enough. What after that, though?"

"Well...my hunch is that there might be the long-awaited nuptials between the two families, with or without Venser there to take part. If they *are* going ahead with it, they're almost certainly going to invite delegations from each city to the ceremony, for the pomp and circumstance of it all. And I can't imagine Hessler would want to have us miss out on his presumed ascension to whatever he thinks the Almighty will bestow upon him."

"Ooh, a wedding," Matthias said, grinning. "I hope there will be cake."

"I can't imagine we'd be let in, though," Arycelle said. "And I'm not keen on testing that out for myself, not with their apparent fondness for capital punishment."

"On your own, almost certainly not. Not even with the presumptive groom, which likely would just ask more questions. However, with this..." Here, she picked up a thing off of her desk, an official-looking medallion. The crest on it was one Venser had seen, a weird sigil that looked like a hand holding a ball of fire. The style was similar to his Aracoras pendant and his Lunarian ring.

"We'd be part of the wedding delegation from Electrum, then?" Sebastian asked.

"Exactly. In conjunction with an accompanying letter, the medallion will be proof enough to get you into Aracoras as our guests. Of course, you would be representing Electrum, and so I'd ask that you behave in a manner befitting that," Elessa said, looking right at Matthias.

"When it comes to things that matter," Matthias said, "you'll find that I can behave myself, Lady Elessa. It's more fun normally, though."

"I can imagine." She was smirking.

"On a related topic," Arycelle said, "Venser's father should be getting back to Lunaria, or should be back there already, and we can probably expect to hear something about it at our next destination, correct?"

"I believe so," Elessa nodded. "They certainly won't miss Venser's absence, even if they've tried to hide it. What will come after that, I'm not entirely sure. But you should have enough time to get to where you need to and talk to who you need to."

Thus concluded their business, and everyone parted ways with final words of wisdom. Matthias planned to arrange for a potential cargo shipment to Calaveras to coincide with their trip there, and everyone else dispersed to get any last bits of things done in Electrum.

Venser walked out of the room with his new pile of things to carry, the letters to the leaders and their proof of affiliation with Electrum. He almost felt like a glorified messenger boy, but that had enough merit in and of itself. He had a goal in mind, trying to stop the opening of the Tomb of the Almighty, and he was hoping each step he took was in that direction.

Following an evening of revelry and merriment, Venser laid in the bed in the hotel room, Basch next to him. Matthias had convinced everyone that it would be a good idea to visit "Stripperella and Booblinda's Breastacular Café", and while it was amusing to see the waitresses wearing as little as could be gotten away with, he couldn't help but wonder if the "group bonding" was really just an excuse for Matthias to enjoy some scenery. Besides that, it had been a pleasant enough day; he had gotten another set of clothes, so that he didn't need to keep wearing the same thing, and several of the men had all gotten touch-ups at the local barber shop. That said, he wasn't wearing his new clothes now…or much of anything, besides a bed sheet.

Calaveras awaited, he thought. He rolled over and wrapped an arm around

Basch, falling asleep rapidly. He tried to think about what awaited, but sleep beckoned, and he could ponder such things tomorrow.

12

Earthbound

Shortly before midday on the following day, the engines of the *Naglfar* roared to life once more, and it began its ascent out of Electrum's harbor. Loaded with all its passengers and a small shipment, its bow swung in the direction of Calaveras, a journey of just over a day on the agenda.

Not long after departure, excitement popped up, and Venser was startled by the sound of a siren. It was a deep, sharp sound that caused him to jump, and he turned to the doorway as Arycelle's head popped into view.

"That sound means we have a likely bogey, someone who's approaching in a threatening manner," she said. "I'm headed to the bridge to see what's up. Want to come with?"

"I'd like to," he said. They made it across the deck and into the bridge, Venser holding on to her hand for dear life, and they saw Matthias looking at screens and checking gauges.

"Excellent timing," he said. "Arycelle, can you handle this?"

"Uh...what?" She was confused. As if to respond, a voice crackled over the speakers.

"Like a flower that blooms in the soil of our carnal and corrupt society, I shall administer retribution to the straying vermin that graze upon the land! For I am the Chairman of the Educational Guidance Council...*Archduke Emperor Pope Guillaume XIII!*"

"Not him again," she whispered, her face showing distaste. "You want me to talk to him?"

"Yes."

"Larcenous weasels in collusion with malfeasance, you have been accosted by the vanguard of divinity, Archduke Emperor Pope Guillaume XIII, and it is time to exact my vengeance for your refusal to acquiesce to your impending demise previously!" the voice came, still the same simpering whine. "Your punishment shall be swift, unerring, and decisive, and the *Alamithea* shall be returned to its rightful and buxom owner once your festering existences have been erased from the skies!"

"Uh, this is..." Arycelle started, her voice immediately cut off and interrupted by a long and loud scream of "Wooooooooooooomaaaaaaa aaaaaaaan!" from the other craft.

"What the...?" Venser asked, unsure of what had just happened. Both Arycelle and Matthias shared looks of shock and horror.

"Verily, my ears have picked up the presence of a lovely and chaste maiden, doubtless a distressed damsel and exemplar of absolute and intangible virtue absconded with by the thieving scoundrels who made off with the *Alamithea*!" The tone of Archduke Emperor Pope Guillaume XIII's voice had changed completely, now sounding like the aural equivalent of brown-nosing.

"What are you talking about?" she asked. Her face expressed disgust.

"You needn't say more, fair maiden! Your dulcet tones and melodic timbre tell me all that I need to know! Your present abduction and captivity by the slimy, sin-choked, and transgressing nimrods aboard the commandeered *Alamithea*, likely to be in the service of debased debauchery, is soon to be ended, and you shall be taken aboard the *Divine Divinisher* and afforded the respect and care a vessel as fragile and graceful as you is due!"

"I'm telling you, I'm not..." Arycelle tried to speak again, but she was cut off.

"Indeed, once I have liberated you from the bastion of filth and squalor you presently are ensconced in, you shall be afforded the luxury and care a voluptuous and ravishing specimen like you deserves! Your existence shall be an exalted one, none holding a spot before you in my boundless heart!"

"Is this guy for real?" Matthias whispered. "Who tells women they're 'fragile vessels' that need special care and protection?"

"It sounds like something I would hear in Aracoras," Venser whispered back.

Arycelle shook her head. "You're not listening to…" she started, cut off again.

"Words are very unnecessary! It has come time to express my love for you, fair maiden, through liberation! Vermin of the absconded-with *Alamithea*, I hope you're listening and regretting the poor decisions you have made to this point, because this shall be the final day of your existence! Come to me, fair maiden! Free yourself from the shackles of malfeasance, and permit me to ensconce myself in your bounteous bosom!"

The "rat-ta-tat-tat" cadence Venser recalled from their last run-in with Archduke Emperor Pope Guillaume XIII filled the air, and he thought he could feel a slight vibration beyond the usual operation of the airship's engines.

"How can this be? My firepower is inadequate to liberate the chaste and virginal maiden I am aiming to free from the wretched claws of sin?" they heard. This time, Arycelle, tired of trying to talk to someone who cut her off, pressed a button, and the much-louder cadence of the *Naglfar*'s guns rang out, with many yelps lighting up the airwaves.

"Once again, I am thwarted by illicit airship armament!" he whined. "I regret that I am unable to deliver you from evil on this occasion, radiant beauty of the skies, but I shall return to you with utmost haste! I hope it will be soon enough to stave off the tears of sorrow! If you're hearing this, fetid rats of the ill-gotten *Alamithea*, I shall return to terminate your foul existence when least you expect it!"

The communication channel fizzled silent, and they could see another airship zip off into the distance. Like before, it was a lurid orange and blue color scheme, and it looked like it had seen better days.

"Was he waiting for us?" Venser asked, frowning.

"Probably," Matthias said. "We were in Electrum for a while, long enough for his ship to catch us and try to spring the trap as we left."

"He builds his airships for speed more than for actual utility," Arycelle said. "Basically all engine, no anything else. And those engines are pretty inefficient at that."

"Anyway, sorry about that, Arycelle. I wanted to see if he'd say anything interesting if he spoke to a pretty girl instead of me. I...don't think he did, nothing beyond him wanting to still please Marianne dearest."

"Just don't make me do it again. I felt like my brain cells were dying just listening to him cut me off and prattle on about how he needed to save me from you." Arycelle looked equal parts amused and traumatized.

"How does he get away with that?" Venser asked.

"He's a terrible listener. Someone tells him no, he ignores them and does his own thing."

Having fended off the nuisance that was the self-proclaimed Chairman of the Educational Guidance Council, the *Naglfar*'s flight to Calaveras was uneventful and smooth, even as the air started to become visibly befouled. The evening came and went, and their approach into Calaveras started around the middle of the day.

"I don't recall it being this dirty last time we were there," Sebastian said, looking out the window. All but Matthias were gathered in the kitchen area, grabbing lunch.

"When was the last time we were here, though?" Basch asked. "Marianne tended to give this place a wide berth. And I'd be inclined to do the same, were we not asked to do something."

"What's in Calaveras?" Venser asked.

"Nothing. And that's the point."

"Calaveras is the other main mining city," Arycelle said. "It and Gran Moria are sort of the 'dirty' cities, to use a lazy bit of language, because their mineral deposits are valuable enough to justify exploiting, and exploiting those is not a pretty business. But Calaveras has built up even less than Gran Moria, focusing exclusively on extracting ores and processing them while the other has some diversity to what it does. Not much, but enough."

"It's not *all* bad news," Sebastian added. "We can usually get skystones and airship parts in Calaveras at a marked discount. Not enough to justify going there normally, mind."

"So, Venser's looking to meet with the leader of Calaveras, and we're doing whatever in the meantime," Basch said. "I hope we're not kept here too long."

"And here I thought you weren't excited about going to Balmung," Arycelle quipped.

"I most certainly am not. But it's marginally preferable to an extended stay in Calaveras. Not by much, though."

Calaveras started to come into view, and it was unlike anywhere else Venser had seen to that point. It looked like a single, monolithic shard of rock floating in the sky, with plumes of smoke spewing out from various openings. There seemed to be a perpetually dark pall over the entire rock, and Venser was thankful that the airship was resistant to the pollution outside, as he'd seen when they were in Gran Moria.

"Let's get ready for landing," Sebastian said, standing up. He and Arycelle headed out to get ready, leaving Basch and Venser in the kitchen area.

"How are you holding up?" Basch asked, putting a hand on Venser's shoulder.

"I'm...okay, I guess. As well as can be expected." Venser answered. "A lot's happened recently, I suppose. It's hard to find the time to process it."

"Take the time you need," Basch replied, kissing him on the head. "Do you want someone to go with you to see the lord of Calaveras?"

"That would be lovely."

"All right, then. Grab your scarf, as well. Calaveras isn't known for its particularly good air, unfortunately, and I don't want to hear you hacking up a lung while we're there."

The sky harbor of Calaveras was located right outside the mouth to the interior of the rocky shard, and they noticed a general dearth of airships. It was easily the harbor with the sparsest population that Venser could recall having visited, and barely anyone was present.

"They're not the most welcoming group," Matthias said, joining the rest of the crew as they emerged onto the deck. "But it's understandable enough. Calaveras hasn't always had the easiest go of it." As if to accentuate his point, a patrolman came out from the cave and scowled at them.

"All right, let's work on getting this delivery hammered out," Sebastian said. "Venser, you can go ahead and find who you're looking to talk to."

"We'll stay as long as you need," Matthias said, "but not much longer, if possible."

Venser nodded, and he and Basch got off of the *Naglfar* and headed into the mountain. Dimly lit and clammy, with a claustrophobic ambiance, he quickly understood why everyone was so low on the prospects of visiting Calaveras. It wasn't the same sense of lifelessness that he'd gotten from Aracoras, but there seemed to be very little joy and excitement. He drew his scarf up around his face as they walked.

"Looks like we might not need to go too far," Basch said, pointing. He was gesturing at a rather ornate-looking door flanked by guards. "I'd imagine that we'd have good results going there."

"I think we should start there," Venser nodded. They walked up, and the guards responded by broadening their presences, as to emphasize what they were there to do.

"State your business," one said. Their voice was terse, their tone blunt and to the point.

"I'm here to give a letter to the leader of Calaveras," Venser said. He pulled out the letter Elessa had given him, and the guard took it.

"The seal of Electrum. Please wait." The guard with the letter stepped into the door, while the other was left to leer at them.

Venser tried to survey his surroundings without seeming too suspicious. Tunnels snaked to parts unknown, most of them narrow and poorly lit. People scurried in and out of them in protective gear, some carrying carts of ores and stones to other parts. He tried to stay as far out of their way as possible.

The guard finally came back. "He says he desires to see you," they said, pointing to Venser. "I mentioned you had a companion, and he does not object to his presence."

"That suits me," Venser said. He tried to hide that he was slightly anxious over hearing this. "If you would lead the way, that would be appreciated."

They nodded, and Basch and Venser followed him through the door.

Another series of tunnels stretched out, though these had better lighting and were apparently taken care of better than the others. As the guard led the way, they passed by children and women, all of whom regarded their visitors with curiosity and surprise.

"We're here," the guard finally said, gesturing to them to go into a room. This was at the back of the tunnel complex, it had felt like. They acquiesced, and they came face-to-face with a rather solemn-looking man whose features were sharp. He did have an impressive head of hair, and his skin was nicely tanned.

"It has been a while since we've had visitors, much less a visitor like you, Venser of Aracoras," he said. He spoke deliberately, his enunciation very particular.

"I am he," Venser said, bowing respectfully. He wasn't sure what else made sense so far as an introduction.

"Your manners and appearance are certainly not what I'd expect, though the letter vouches for you. As does your necklace." Venser had taken his necklace out as they had made it to the back of the tunnel complex, suspecting it would be useful.

"I have heard that, sir."

"I do wonder why that may be the case, but that's an ancillary concern, one that's hardly pertinent. More interesting is that, recently, I got a notice of your wedding to Hessler's daughter, Leondra. Which suggests to me that there's a lot more going on than I've heard."

"You're correct, sir."

"How about you tell me what you know, then? Let's see what all I have missed out on."

Venser began to tell the man about the events that had transpired to that point. His betrothal to Leondra, the plan to open the Tomb of the Almighty, and the events that led to him escaping his fate…they all were brought up, and the man listened in silence. When he was done, the man took several moments to ponder, leaving Venser ill at ease.

"A fascinating string of events," he said, finally breaking the ice. "One that rings with plausibility, if nothing else. This isn't the first time I've heard of plans to open the Tomb of the Almighty, as a visitor told me similar things. Her tone was a lot more optimistic, as opposed to your skepticism."

"Her tone...was she named Hellvira?" Venser asked.

"That was her name, yes. She was dressed rather interestingly, I must say. I presume you all have crossed paths."

"A couple times, yes."

"She gets around. But the enthusiasm of her pitch, coupled with the lack of particulars, suggested that I should turn her down. Listening to you, I think that was the right decision. Especially in light of what I was able to find in our archives."

"That sounds interesting," Basch said. "I heard that Leondra was unable to learn anything from the resources in Lunaria, and Venser mentioned tight control and restricted access to books in Aracoras."

"What can you tell us, sir?" Venser asked.

Here, the man's expression turned dark. "This will be long, and you may not like what you hear," he said. "I will explain all that I have read, and it is on you as to if you believe it or put stock in it in particular."

"I think we should hear this," Venser said. Basch nodded in agreement. Despite how it sounded, knowing had to be better than ignorance, right?

"You've made your decision. Let's hope you don't come to regret it." The man took a deep breath, and then he started.

"The beginning of our story," he said, "has its roots in the time humans made their home on the lands below what is now covered by the sea of clouds. While many generations have known nothing but the endless sea dotted by floating islands, there were once civilizations on the surface, said to be radically advanced and in some ways ahead of the society we have made."

"Civilization beneath the sea of clouds?" Venser asked. "That sounds plausible enough."

"Unfortunately, those civilizations would attract the attention of those seeking to exploit them. It would come to pass that, after fending off many such threats, they were faced with one they found to be beyond their capabilities: a being of pure malice that apparently called itself 'Ack-Tar,

God of Darkness'.

"It became clear that Ack-Tar was a force too powerful to drive back, and in their desperation, the people called upon the power of the Almighty, the divine protector. The battle was long, arduous, and destructive, and Ack-Tar's onslaughts ruined the lands and seas. The two beings were evenly matched, though the Almighty ultimately was able to get the upper hand."

"So far, this sounds like the story we're familiar with, albeit with pretext for why we're no longer living on the surface," Venser said.

"That is fair. The part that follows may not be known, though. When the people rejoiced over their victory, Ack-Tar lashed out with one final blow, gravely wounding the Almighty. Without their power, the people could not defeat the self-proclaimed dark god, its malfeasance too powerful to be properly constrained.

"And so the decision was made: with both deities weakened, they would be entombed. The Almighty to recover their strength, Ack-Tar to hopefully ensure it could never be allowed to wreak havoc. The resting place of the Almighty is...*not* the Tomb of the Almighty."

"So, that would mean that the Tomb of the Almighty holds this 'god of darkness', right?" Venser asked. He thought he knew the answer, but he wanted to hear it for himself.

"Correct. I believe the calculation was that the land needed time to heal, and so they crafted a sarcophagus of clouds for the land and an elaborate tomb for the Almighty on the surface. I do not know where on the surface their resting place is. But the floating rock Aracoras keeps watch over, the Tomb of the Almighty, is indeed the resting place of Ack-Tar, the malign entity that forced this sorry state on all of us."

"So...they're walking into awakening a dark being, thinking that it's something else?" Basch asked, shaking his head. "What do we think happens when the Tomb opens?"

"I cannot say. Whether this Ack-Tar has regained its strength enough to make its return immediately disastrous instead of merely disastrous later is still to be discovered, something I was unable to further clarify."

"So, how can we stop them?" Venser asked. "I...well, my wedding was apparently to coincide with them opening the Tomb."

"It was, indeed. Would they still go through with a wedding, though?"

"I have a younger brother and a younger sister, and it's possible they may deem my brother suitable if they were set on a marriage happening."

"That sounds like what might just happen, then. The way for Aracoras to get the money they apparently seek is through payment of a dowry, and the tradition is that the bride's family pays the groom. How far away is the wedding, if you know?"

"I do not know…at least, not conclusively. My father returned to Aracoras shortly after our arrival, probably to secure some approval of some kind and begin preparations, and our…the airships used by Aracoras are slow and outdated. The journey to Lunaria took five days. I believe that he would have returned to Lunaria by now, and when the wedding actually is planned, they would need to fly everyone to Aracoras for the ceremony."

"Again, using the Aracoras airship for a good number of the wedding party, because of their insistence on it. From my interactions, they are *very* insistent on only using their airships, as they fervently distrust newer models. Presuming an immediate turnaround, which is unlikely, we probably have a couple of days. And we'd also get a wedding invitation when the time comes."

"They would probably want you there to see that," Basch said.

"Hessler most definitely does. He has always carried himself with excessive self-importance." The man grimaced as he recounted this.

"So, what do we do?" Venser asked.

"What were your plans?"

"Our intent was to visit the last of the great cities, Balmung, and appraise them of the perspective that we have." Venser thought he saw Basch flinch as he said this.

"I think that is a reasonable idea. Calaveras has little in the way of comfort and attraction, so I imagine you're not planning to stay long."

"We are not," Basch said. "Our captain plans to wait for as long as we need, but plans to leave shortly after."

"We shouldn't leave him waiting then," the man replied, a wry smile apparent. "Come back later this day. I will have something for you."

"So, if what he said is accurate, Basch started, "they're looking to awaken a self-styled dark god. Brilliant." The two had left the living quarters for now.

"I'm inclined to believe him," Venser said. "But I want to know where he got the information."

"My understanding is that there are lots of old caches of books scattered around. Lunaria is the exception, as they seemingly got rid of most of theirs long ago. Apparently, they only keep books on hand from recent history."

"That's interesting."

"And speaking of books, I think I know the cargo Matthias was keen on transporting." He pointed to a man walking by, clutching a shiny new copy of a book whose title looked to be *The Sluttacular Adventures of Breastarella and Her Haughty Harem*.

"Where *do* those books come from?" Venser asked, simultaneously amused and appalled.

"Never underestimate the market for literature of that inclination." They passed near a small stall that had been set up to peddle the aforementioned book and other works, and it seemed to be doing a good bit of business. A closer look revealed that the proprietor was none other than Matthias himself.

"Why does none of this surprise me," Basch sighed, the two walking up to the stand.

"Hey, literature opens minds or something," Matthias said, grinning broadly. "Arycelle and Sebastian are off checking the ore markets, I think. Did you two meet with who you meant to?"

"We did," Venser said. "And he told us some interesting things."

"We'll catch you all up on that later. But why are you selling smut to people in broad daylight?" Basch asked, picking up a book bearing the exciting title of *Breastworld 2: Chest In Show*.

"Broad daylight is relative, dear Basch, especially in a place such as this. And I had nothing better to do, so why not? The shipment was of fine literature, and while I could sell it to a distributor here in Calaveras, I wanted to see if I could sell some directly to the people as a fun activity,"

Matthias said. As he said this, someone paid for a small stack of books, walking away with a massive grin on their face.

"Those are some...interesting books," Venser said. The covers were all impressive, with rather eye-catching titles and plenty of scantily-attired women to lure in their intended customers.

"I can vouch for all of them personally!"

"I would ask, but I don't want to know," Basch said. "I don't think *any* of us really want to know."

Later that evening, Basch and Venser returned for a repeat meeting, to get what they were promised. It was just the man from their last meeting, this time with gifts.

"An interesting development happened while you were away," he said, not waiting for them to settle in. "A wedding invitation, specifically. It's to be held in Aracoras."

Basch and Venser looked at each other, sharing a look of surprise and curiosity. "What does it say?" Venser asked.

"I feel you would benefit from reading it." He passed the invite to Venser, and he and Basch started looking over it.

"So, the bride is Leondra, and the groom...they scratched out my name and wrote my brother's in, it looks like," Venser said. "'Velgrand, Esteemed Son of Victarion, High Priest of Aracoras'...so, he's esteemed now. I always thought he was a spoiled brat."

"I don't think it's good form to refer to one of the participants as a spoiled brat," Basch quipped.

"And what day does it say it's happening...that's about eight days away from the present day, correct? So the flight back to Aracoras, if it hasn't happened yet, will be departing soon. Eight days to get to Aracoras, then..."

"It's about a day and a half to get to Balmung," Basch said, "and the flight from there to Aracoras would be roughly that long. Ideally, we should have enough time to get to Balmung, deal with them there, and then get to Aracoras with time enough to figure out what we're doing with the nuptials."

"They did not mention anything here about the 'Tomb of the Almighty,'" the man said, "but there was an insert mentioning that this would be a 'ceremony none should miss, a great turning point in our history'. I don't think a mere wedding would rise to such lofty heights, particularly since Lady Leondra is unlikely to inherit her father's position and the groom is the tenth child in a large family."

"You wouldn't think so. Yet I've heard of some lavish productions that might almost rise to such promise."

"I doubt that this is intended to merely be a lavish spectacle," the man replied. "Still, it will be a show none of us forget soon, if we're correct. But I suspect we *are* correct."

"It's hard to draw the lines between all the points at times," Venser said, his brow furrowed. "But Hellvira's behavior is what seems to be the common thread, trying to get us to open the Tomb. Why would she want it, though?"

"She has answers, and she's not sharing. Anyway, take this with our blessing, and I hope we meet at a time that's less frenetic." The man handed Venser two things: a musty-looking book, and a letter stamped with the Calaveras seal.

"Is this the book you mentioned?"

"It is. Maybe you'll be able to glean more from it. It does me no good here. I trust you'll take good care of it."

"Of course. Before we take our leave, though…might I ask your name?"

The man smiled. "Here in Calaveras, we prefer to not share our names with those not of here," he said. "It is a custom of ours. I hope you're not too taken aback by this."

"That's fine, that's fine." Venser wondered the reasons for this, but he wasn't going to dig further. Such an investigation would be impolite, and he didn't want to come across as impolite.

"You four missed the booming business I had today," Matthias said, grinning broadly. The five of them were at supper in a small Calaveras tavern. The food was very hearty and unpretentious, far more about function than about form.

"We saw a slice of it," Basch responded, shooting a pointed look in his direction. "Surprised you didn't go for a more appropriate descriptor that fits in with your proclivity towards innuendo."

"There's always time for *blow-by-blow* commentary, dear Basch. But we can save it for later, right? I want to hear about what you talked about in your meetings."

"Yeah, bring us up to speed," Arycelle said, putting her fork down.

Venser sighed. "So, we learned two things of note today," he said. "The first is that there's going to be a wedding in Aracoras in about eight days, between my younger brother and Leondra."

"Well, they moved on quickly," Sebastian said.

"More like they *had* to," Arycelle replied. "They both have reasons for wanting the nuptials to happen."

"Speaking of that," Venser said, "we were made aware of a book that purports to know what's inside the Tomb of the Almighty. It's similar to one of the theories Leondra mentioned, and…it's apparently the self-styled 'dark god'."

"Oh, so that's what's in there after all?" Matthias asked, raising an eyebrow. "Probably not the most exciting response, in a sense. I was hoping they'd say it contained a cache of spectral strippers."

"How would those even *work?*" Arycelle asked. She managed to be surprised anew by the depths of Matthias's mind, as did everyone else.

"That's the fun part, they don't," he smirked. "We can talk about spectral strippers later, though. Our plan thus is to visit Balmung, bring them up to speed, and then hurry onto the wedding, right?"

"That's what we were looking at," Basch said. "Unless you have a different itinerary."

"I can save the Interplanetary Pagoda of Perpetual Pleasure for another time, so I suppose that works. It is a pity, though; it's been a while since I played the Stripper Slots."

"'Stripper Slots'? Where do you…you know what, no, I *don't* want to know."

"Suit yourself. You're missing out, though."

Venser smiled as he listened to this exchange. Despite Basch and Matthias sniping at each other, it did feel like they were amicable, at least. And while he was especially fond of Basch, all of the *Naglfar*'s crew were people he quite liked.

It was, he thought, almost like a family. It was weird to think that, given that his family was still off doing their thing in Aracoras, but even with this having been a short period of acquaintance, he'd felt more welcomed by the group he was sitting with.

Venser finally felt like he had found somewhere he belonged, like he had the family he'd never known he hadn't had.

13

Snowblind

At first light on the next day, the *Naglfar* bid Calaveras farewell, swinging its bow majestically towards Balmung. The air slowly cleared up as they flew, going from the dingy pall enveloping the city to a clear, clean sky.

"I believe we're on pace to get to Balmung around midday tomorrow," Arycelle said. She and Venser were in the kitchen, and she was doing some ordering and arranging of goods.

"Basch always seems to respond weirdly whenever Balmung gets mentioned," Venser said. "I heard he's from there, but he doesn't say any more."

"My guess is that he has a family he's not keen on seeing again," she answered. "He's spoken about having them, but never positively."

"Uh...do you have a family?"

"I do. My parents live in Lunaria. They weren't thrilled about me joining an airship crew, truth be told, but they got used to the idea. Mostly because they didn't really have a choice. Sebastian's parents also live in Lunaria, which is convenient enough. Matthias...no idea about his family, but he's mentioned that he's originally from Electrum, actually."

"So, you and Sebastian are from Lunaria, Basch is from Balmung, and Matthias is from Electrum. What about Marianne?"

"Honestly, no idea," she said. "If you thought Basch was tight-lipped, he has nothing on Marianne. I think she likes it that way, really. An enigmatic sky pilot with an aura of mystery, who swoops in on the wind and leaves with it."

"I suppose some people have pasts they want to leave behind."

"Like you?"

Venser sighed. "Maybe? I...I guess I haven't thought a lot about my future, but I really...I'm not going back to Aracoras," he said.

"That's a start, at least," she smiled.

"Getting outside has shown me just how deprived we are there. Not sure that's the perfect word, but I'd prefer the world outside to the cage I'd been trapped in."

"Well, as long as you need a place to figure things out from, I imagine all of us are happy to have you along for the ride, Venser."

"I appreciate that."

"So, while we're talking, I'm curious as to what life is like in Aracoras, if you want to share."

"I'm happy to talk about it, if you're curious. Where to begin..."

As Venser spoke of his time growing up in Aracoras, he reflected on how peculiar it all sounded. The isolation he described was all-encompassing; even with a family, they were hardly familial, treating him like an interchangeable piece in a machine. It was impossible to recognize from within, but he was happy to be out of it, and sharing the stories he had helped him realize how little he wanted to go back to any of it.

That evening, Venser was sitting at the desk in his room, reading the book he'd gotten from Calaveras. It was dense and dry, with plenty of florid opacity to go around. The language they used was very deliberately vague, he felt, and it seemed almost like they didn't directly want to address what was inside.

"How did anyone get anything out of this?" he asked, shaking his head. He closed it and set it down, needing to take a break from looking at it.

"Sounds like it's going well," he heard Basch say. He turned around to notice Basch standing in the doorway, watching.

"Very," Venser responded. "And by that, I mean it's not."

"Book's too hard to get through?" Basch walked over and sat down on the lower of the bunk beds.

"I don't exactly know. It's really convoluted and obtuse, a lot of particular turns of phrase and opaque language. Though it's been a while since I had to try and read something that dense and impenetrable, which might not be helping things."

"Try and tackle it again when you're well-rested, if you're not making any headway tonight. Sometimes a clear mind helps."

"You're probably right," he sighed.

"If it takes your mind off of it," Basch said, "I suppose I could…tell you a bit about myself. And explain why I'm not excited to go back to Balmung,"

"I'm interested," Venser said, perking up. Basch had always seemed reluctant to talk about it, so he was keen to listen.

"As I mentioned before, I'm from Balmung. My parents…well, my father is actually the paramount leader of Balmung. I'm his youngest child."

Venser suspected that something was there, but he wasn't expecting *that*. "Why did you leave, then?" he asked, raising an eyebrow.

"We…that is, my parents and I, we had a massive argument one day. It had been building to that point for a long while, but it finally boiled over, and all hell broke loose. It was explosive, things got broken, and words were shared that have stuck with me to now. The next day, I packed up and left without a word to them. I've been back to Balmung occasionally since then, but I've always given the palace a wide berth. I still try to keep updated on palace intrigue, though, since there's always a chance of it affecting me." He told all of this in a dispassionate tone, one Venser thought sounded practiced.

"What was the argument about?"

"It was the culmination of a lot of things, little and large. The crux of it was that, because I wasn't in line to succeed my father, my parents had plans to get me married off without my consent, both to strengthen diplomatic ties and to remove a potential obstacle to my brother's succession," he said, smiling. "Sort of like you were in Aracoras, only they were too sloppy to properly close the cage door. From what I've heard, though, my brother might be getting in the way of that himself."

"Really?"

"To be precise, I have two brothers, both older. The older one is Sigmund, and the younger is Richter. Sigmund has long been the designated successor to our father, but his antics apparently seem to be wearing thin, and what I understand is that Richter's seen this as a chance to try and maneuver into pole position. And by 'antics', I'm referring to feats of womanizing and debauchery even Matthias would not stoop to. Not that Richter is much better from what I've heard, but at least he hasn't been caught with his pants down *as* often."

"That's...frankly impressive." He wasn't sure what that all looked like, and he wasn't sure he wanted to know.

"I'm happy I'm not there in that maelstrom, but there's a chance we might be stepping back into the eye of the storm. Hopefully you won't need to deal much with them, but I'm sure they'll try to drag people onto their side."

"What are you going to do when we get there?"

"Well...I think it's time I made my peace with them and properly bid them farewell," he said. "It might be easier to keep hiding from them, but I think it's finally time to face what I've been running from."

"You're sure about this?" Venser asked.

"It'll be fine. Besides, you'll be there," Basch said, smiling.

Venser returned the smile. "I'll be there for you, Basch," he affirmed.

"Good." Basch drew Venser to him, and the two kissed. They retired to Basch's room, where the kissing intensified and the clothes came off anew. The book would be waiting for Venser, whenever he had the appetite for dry literature. He was more than happy to welcome a distraction, and sex with Basch had proven to be an excellent distraction.

The living quarters of the *Naglfar* were kept fairly comfortable, but Venser noticed the next day as the temperature started to dip lower and lower, to where he needed to put on another layer. They had thought ahead and gotten Venser a jacket in Electrum, so he bundled up in that as they continued their flight. The windows seemed to fog up appreciably, and Venser had to rub the windows to see out of them.

Finally, Balmung came into sight, and snow had started falling. Snow was not completely unknown in Aracoras, but it was definitely not a common sight, and not in the volume it was in here. A blanket of white covered what Venser could see, which appeared to be a lot of low-slung structures.

"Man, it's gotten cold here," Sebastian said, popping into the kitchen where Venser was sitting.

"Is it always this cold?" Venser asked.

"Not always, but Balmung is colder than anywhere else on average. Their warm days are akin to a cooler day on Lunaria, though Lunaria's gotten as cold as this on occasion."

"I see."

"Make sure you walk carefully when you get there. Ice is slick and unpleasant if you're not used to it. I should know, it always trips me up."

"Thanks for the warning."

He disappeared, and Venser was left to prepare for arrival. That happened smoothly and seamlessly, the *Naglfar* touching down gently in the harbor. The cold of Balmung greeted Venser as he stepped onto the deck, a whip of ice across his face that surprised him.

"So, you and Basch are off to the palace first?" Matthias asked. He was already standing on the deck, holding a box.

"I think so," Venser answered.

"Lucky you, I have a delivery to make to the palace, so I might be headed that way. The lordlings both recently requested…material. For anatomy study, you could say. One had a rather voluminous requisition sheet." He raised his eyebrows in a way that seemed to suggest the nature of the materials.

"Oh…like Isamu, right?" he asked.

"Exactly so. But a lot longer and more particular. Isamu kept his lists short and vague, which was appreciated. He was also…easier, shall we say."

"You have a client for your smut, Matthias?" Basch asked, emerging from below deck. He was wearing a long jacket that covered most of his torso.

"But of course, dear Basch. They're in the palace, so I figure I could walk with you there. Arycelle and Sebastian said they'd handle the other cargo."

"I see. If you're coming that way, I suppose it works out for us to go together." He looked over at Venser and raised an eyebrow, though this was less suggestive.

Just then, they heard a bit of swearing from below. They looked over the deck and saw Sebastian leaning against the hull, having lost his footing.

"He does that a lot," Matthias said. "Let's be off, then. Mind your step!"

Balmung was lashed repeatedly by freezing gusts, and the trio found that the path to the palace, while navigable, needed to be taken slowly. Buildings were set largely into the ground more than built up, and the overall effect was that the city was very weirdly flat, besides the hills that punctuated the landscape. Few people were on the street, but they largely kept their gazes down and their paces fast.

"There we are," Matthias said. He was carrying the box of "anatomy study material", and he pointed to the palace with his free hand. It kept with the low profile of the other buildings there, though with a couple of opulent-looking features that afforded it a bit of dignity.

"I don't think the guards are stationed outside," Basch said. "They control access just inside, because they'd rather not have people wait outside. Nor would they want to stay outside themselves."

"As they shouldn't. From experience, the cold's not good for my skin," Matthias quipped.

"Does it interfere with your skin-care routine?"

"You know it!"

Immediately inside the palace gate was appreciably warmer, but still cold. Guards were indeed stationed in front of the door, and they puffed themselves up upon seeing guests. Venser had noticed that Basch had pulled a scarf up around his face.

"State your business, visitors," one of them said, their tone curt and clipped.

"I am but a humble merchant, here to deliver to the venerated Sigmund, heir apparent to Balmung, the anatomy study materials he requisitioned from far-flung locations," Matthias said. His tone was comically overwrought.

"And I am here to, if possible, see the leader of Balmung," Venser said. "Much has happened that they should be made aware of, and I have letters that might explain everything."

He handed the letters to the guard, and they muttered among themselves in consultation. "Let us take the news inside," one of them said. "We need to see if such a meeting is amenable, as well as if the delivery was indeed requested." They slipped inside, leaving their companion to guard the doorway.

"Waiting, as usual," Matthias said, turning to his companions. "They do like their security. I wonder why they need it, though. Things have been peaceful for a good while, at least in the cities."

"It might be as much to keep people in," Basch said. "I've heard that the sons of Balmung's paramount leader have a tendency to…behave very badly."

The remaining guard huffed indignantly, as if to insert themselves into the conversation. "Who are you to speak ill of Sigmund and Richter?" they asked, adopting an appropriate tone.

"I know them. Like how those 'anatomy study guides' my friend is bringing Sigmund feature titles like *Fantastic Breasts and Where to Find Them*. His favorite, I do believe, is called *Mega Mazongas Monthly*."

"Aw, we're friends now," Matthias said, his tone teasing.

"Where do you come up with such titles?" the guard sputtered. "And how do you claim to make such claims?"

"I mean, you can look in the box and see for yourself," Matthias grinned. He opened it up and picked up the top article, featuring a lascivious-looking lady, with an ample chest, splayed out like a dining-table centerpiece and the title *Mega Mazongas Monthly* placed so as to preserve what modesty could be preserved.

"Did he *really* request such…filth?" The guard was looking closely at the cover, apparently trying to quantify just how filthy it was.

"Most certainly, he did. I even have his hand-written requisition sheet. There were five titles he specifically spelled out wanting, and the rest were left up to me. Within…certain bounds."

"I…I see. I may need to talk to Sigmund later and ask him just how… uh, how he uses these for anatomy study." The guard tried to recompose themselves, having been rendered nicely flustered.

"I suspect he might not want to share them, since he does like to *examine* them very closely. You might have better luck asking someone else to see them."

"I see."

As they stood there, awkwardly silent, Venser thought he saw Matthias with a glint in his eye. Something mischievous, no doubt.

"Pardon me, guard," Matthias said, "but I heard you mention two names with regard to the leader's sons, when my friend here mentioned them. Forgive me if I'm presumptuous, but weren't there *three* sons?"

Basch shook his head as Matthias said this. Venser wondered if Matthias actually knew Basch's identity, or if he was making the guard squirm. Maybe both.

"That is privileged information!" the guard snapped, still apparently uneasy from their past exchange. "How does a rat like…uh…I'm afraid I have no idea what you're talking about."

Basch signed. "I seem to recall this information as well, come to think of it," he said, glaring at Matthias. "Sigmund was the eldest, Richter the one in the middle, and…Basch the youngest. Yet you only mentioned the former two."

"How do you know about the third son? He left the palace ages ago!"

"Well…" Finally, Basch lowered his scarf, so that the guard could get a good look. "What if I were to tell you that the third son is standing in front of you?"

"I…I…I…" The guard was speechless, and they immediately scrambled into the palace, leaving the three in silence.

"Marianne owes me a pastry," Matthias said, finally breaking the silence.

"Did you know?" Basch asked, looking right at him.

"Know? No, I wouldn't say that I *knew*. I had my suspicions, and I had some lovely ladies do some investigative work to confirm those suspicions. Those brothers of yours have lips looser than those ladies' legs, it turns out. Your past doesn't matter to me, which is why I never cared to ask directly, but I like to know about my comrades."

"I'm not sure if I'm impressed or appalled."

"Both work well whenever I'm involved, Basch. You had your reasons for not talking about it, until now. What those reasons are, I'm sure we'll find out. But we are crewmates, and like it or not, I'll do what I can to protect all of you."

"Uncharacteristically serious, Matthias."

"Hey, sometimes you need to know when to be serious," he said, smiling. "As fun as fun is, sometimes the time for fun is not upon us. Anyway, I hear commotion on the other side of the door."

Venser was quiet in all of this, and he watched the two guards emerge from the door. They were both out of breath, panting heavily and seemingly having raced back.

"We apologize if we've kept you waiting," one of them said. "Two of you are here to see Lord Solvaring, yes?"

"I mean, if you have room for a third, I'll come with," Matthias said.

"That's fine, that's fine. Please, come this way."

The three followed them inside, and through a long hallway. The inside of the Balmung palace was cozy and warm, with many tapestries and wall decorations lining the corridors. Notably, a number of palace staff members seemed to be in the hallway, watching them as they made their way inside. They seemed to be murmuring and pointing, at Basch in particular. Venser noticed this and subtly squeezed his friend's hand as a show of assurance.

Finally, they arrived in the main audience chamber. Unlike their meetings with the other leaders, Balmung's leader chose to receive them in some manner of throne room. There were two thrones at the back, each occupied. The larger was filled by a broad, stern man, while the smaller held an equally-stern woman. Their sharp faces and gray eyes both resembled Basch's features, Venser thought.

"I bid you welcome, esteemed guests," the man said. "I am Solvaring, paramount leader of Balmung. I have read the letters you have brought to me, and I feel like we have much to discuss, Venser of Aracoras."

"I believe we might, sir," Venser responded, bowing.

"I believe that one of your companions and I may have much to discuss, as well," he continued, looking directly at Basch. "But that is something we can get to in time. I would ask that you tell me, from your perspective, all that has come to this point."

Venser began to, slowly, retell what had brought them there. His betrothal to Leondra, their investigation into the Tomb of the Almighty and their conclusion about its contents, and their relative misadventure aboard the *Naglfar* were all touched on, and Solvaring listened attentively, nodding and making noises to confirm what he was hearing. When he finished, it was Solvaring's turn to talk.

"What you're telling me is concerning, though not completely out of the blue," he said. Venser noticed that his voice filled the space of the room impressively. "Several things have happened in the past few days that line up with what you tell me. Hildegard and I received a wedding invitation to the wedding of Leondra and Velgrand, though it did look like another person's name had been hastily scratched out. Thinking on it, it looked an awful lot like your name."

"The leader of Calaveras also got such an invite as we visited him," Venser added.

"He did, then. And I imagine he also got this urgent letter, mentioning that Venser of Aracoras had been absconded with by malfeasant sky pirates in the dead of night, clearly seeking to hold him for ransom or to inflict emotional injury upon Aracoras."

"That's a colorful bit of phrasing, sir," Matthias said, raising an eyebrow. "I take issue with being called sky pirates and with being called malfeasant... and them saying we have absconded with him. He's a full-fledged member of my crew, not a hostage."

"A full-fledged crew member?" Solvaring repeated, "For someone with your...reputation, Matthias of Electrum, you appear to do things by the book."

"I have a reputation, now? I'm almost flattered."

"Back to the topic at hand, we were paid a visit by this...woman of questionable morals and even more questionable attire. She spoke about the opening of the Tomb of the Almighty, how this was a chance to be seated at the side of divinity. I had little idea what she was talking about, as the Tomb of the Almighty is not something we're familiar with on Balmung besides vagaries."

"Hellvira?" Venser asked.

"She said her name was such, yes. And my sons were quite smitten with her," he said, the distaste in his voice. "It sounds like you all have an idea of what you're doing, though. You mean to try and stop the opening of the Tomb of the Almighty?"

"If possible…yes, sir, we do," Venser said. Basch and Matthias nodded behind him.

"Balmung certainly will have no objections. That said, this is a subject I would like to talk with you more about tomorrow. We need time to discuss this at length. I presume you are not immediately leaving?"

"We were not planning to do so," Matthias said. "We are on a timer, though. We would like to reach Aracoras before the wedding, so we have only a couple days to spare."

"Time enough, then. There's plenty to be talked about. Including…with someone who has chosen now to show his face to me and his mother."

"Better now than never, I suppose," Basch said. Venser could tell he was nervous, and what he could make out of his body language was tense and uncomfortable.

Solvaring sighed. "Your disappearance came as quite a shock to us," he said. "I know what we said at the moment was…regrettable, to say the least. But when we woke up in the morning to continue the conversation, you had left."

"I didn't feel welcome here anymore," he responded. "I guess…it was the argument that really underscored it, on top of everything else over the years."

"Hildegard and I came to realize that. We had many sleepless nights wondering what ultimately caused you to disappear like that. We certainly could have been more supportive, I think. Our focus was always on your brothers, and…"

His voice trailed off as they heard a commotion coming from outside the audience room, an argument between two men.

"They sound rather animated," Matthias said.

"Rather," Basch repeated. He sounded exasperated.

The source of the argument was made manifest with two men coming into the throne room, yelling at each other. They both resembled Basch, Venser thought, but with enough differences to not be easily confused with each other. One was lanky, the other well rounded, and they both seemed to carry themselves in a "noble" manner.

"Father, Richter's being a little bitch again!" the well-rounded one whined. "He's been threatening my favorite poster!"

"Well, Sigmund is not supposed to have that poster of Carmelita the Cock Destroyer, *especially* where others can see it!" the other shot back. "Clearly you're more interested in ogling girls instead of being appropriately leader-like!"

"Who I ogle is none of your business, Richter! And, besides, I wasn't the one who got kicked out of the academy for being an obnoxious prat!"

"Those teachers didn't know what they're talking about!"

"*Enough!*" Solvaring thundered, bringing their argument to a momentary pause. "You're coming in here while I'm entertaining visitors, thinking your business is more important than anything else!"

"Aren't we, though?" the one named Sigmund asked. He looked over at the three visitors. "I have to say, they look *completely* unimportant."

"For once, Sigmund is right," Richter added. "They look like they got off of the street! How did *they* get an audience with you?"

"It's good to see some things never change," Basch said, speaking up so the two of them could hear. "And by that, I mean the two of you still are completely insufferable."

"How *dare* you talk to us like that!" Sigmund yelled. "Who do you think you are, presuming to know us at all?"

"Your brother."

"Nonsense! That blood traitor left us ages ago! We're the only remaining sons of Solvaring and Hildegard in good standing!" Richter retorted.

Matthias shook his head. "To briefly change the subject, Sigmund, I brought you your anatomy study materials from abroad, to practice your drawing," he said, holding up the box. "I made sure several copies of your favorite reference magazine, *Mega Mazongas Monthly*, were included."

Sigmund turned pale. "That's...uh, that's great," he said, clearly not wanting this to be said in front of his father. "But did...well, did you have to say that here, where everyone can hear it?"

"I maybe didn't *have* to say it here, like I didn't *have* to bring up that I also made sure *Slyemenestra Hymen's Breast in Show* and *Fantastic Breasts and Where to Find Them* both made their way in there, along with a copy of *Muffy the Vampire Layer*. But you also didn't *have* to be rude to my crew member and your brother, so here we are."

"Those are some *interesting* titles," Solvaring said, raising an eyebrow. "Would you be so kind as to bring that box to me?"

"With pleasure." Matthias handed the box of "reference materials" to Solvaring, and Venser noticed the sheer panic on Sigmund's face.

"I made sure there was also one in there for Richter," Matthias added, grinning in a way that suggested he knew exactly what he was doing. "It's harder finding the references that satisfy his particular...preferences in perspective, but I think the issue of *Buttstravaganza* I tracked down will do the job."

"Why do you have to mention that in public?" Richter whined, his face turning red.

"Excellent question. Maybe it's because you're a huge tosser?"

Solvaring cleared his throat as he picked up one of the magazines. "So *these* are what you have been using for your figure study," he said, his tone clearly dry and displeased as he looked over the issue of *Fantastic Breasts and Where to Find Them*. "This is the first I have heard of your artistic endeavors. Might I see some of your efforts? I'm *curious* as to how you both have developed an interest in the practice and how your studies are coming along."

"It's Sigmund's fault!" Richter yelped. "He set me up!"

"I did not set you up, you brown-nosing twit!" Sigmund snapped. "I clearly remember you asking for that magazine! *You're* the one trying to make me look bad!"

"Well, where are *your* drawings?"

"I'll go get mine if you'll go get yours!"

"You don't *have* drawings, do you," Basch said. "Neither of you could ever tell the pointy end of a pencil from the other."

"How dare you, you presumptuous cur!" Sigmund spat. "Who do you think you are?"

"*Will you two be quiet?*" Solvaring thundered, getting all of them to stop their quarrel. He turned to the pair of sons that were closer to him, both looking at their father with a mix of regret and remorse.

"Sigmund...Richter...you both *disappoint* me with your appalling behavior," he said, letting each word hang in the air. "You continue to quarrel like spoiled brats, in front of important guests from near and afar, and you treat them poorly besides."

"*Are* they important?" Richter asked.

"More important than you two are right now."

Sigmund couldn't help himself, and he puffed up haughtily. "More important than *me*?" he asked. "Your heir, soon to be paramount leader of Balmung?"

"If you continue to talk as if it's a given, it may not be the case," Solvaring said, his expression connoting a level of displeasure Venser could only recall having seen thrice before in his life. "If you two have any sense, you'll leave us alone for now." The tone suggested that this was *not* a suggestion.

"Uh...our study materials...can we..." Richter stammered.

"No."

The two brothers slunk off, and Solvaring turned back to the trio. "I regret that you had to behold that shameful and sordid display from my sons," he said, shaking his head.

"I don't recall them being this feisty in the past," Basch said. "Has something happened?"

"I'm not aware of such things having happened, but I suppose I have not been around as much as a father should. But enough about them for now. There is much to talk about, Basch."

14

Frozen Dominion

"Well, today's been interesting enough already, and it's not even lunch time yet," Matthias said. He and Venser stepped out of the audience room while Basch spoke with his parents alone. "I must say, though, the two lordlings seemed *especially* rowdy today."

"They weren't before?" Venser asked.

"Not that I can recall, but my interactions were mostly in passing. At most, it was just passing off their 'preferred anatomy study materials' and getting lists for more titles to procure. That said, we might want to continue this later." He held up a hand as the sound of fighting echoed through the hallways.

"Is that the two of them?"

"Sure is. They certainly wasted no time resuming their argument. Let's just wait here for when Basch gets done. I'd rather not get lost in this palace."

"They...sound hostile, if they do come this way."

"Don't worry, Venser. If they get rowdy, I'll rise to the occasion." He thought he saw Matthias smile.

Sigmund and Richter came into sight, still bickering about something. They paused when they saw their guests and decided to saunter over.

"Oh, Sigmund, it looks like those street ruffians from earlier," Richter sneered. "Did your friend already get kicked out?"

"Probably did," Sigmund snickered. "They probably got tired of his lies about being our brother. As if he'd come back looking like *that*."

Matthias sighed. "Are you two bitter that you got your tit magazines taken away by Daddy?" he asked. He made sure he was between them and Venser, which Venser silently appreciated.

"You bought those for *us*, you scam artist! We *paid* you for them!"

"Using Daddy's money, no doubt. And because you were rude to us, I decided to give them to the person who bankrolled their acquisition. You can ask him for them later."

"How were we rude?"

"You said we were street urchins, and you accused my crew member of lying."

"But why would Father want to meet with *you*?" Richter whined.

Matthias sighed. "We're here on business."

"What kind of business?"

"None of yours. Come on, Venser, let's go elsewhere."

"Hold up!" Sigmund hissed. "You do *not* get to do that to us! We want answers, and you will give them to us!"

"Well, what answers do you want?"

"For starters, who's your friend there, and why are they important?"

"Why don't you go ask someone else for that information? We're not your subjects, and I'm certainly not inclined to answer after you two have been so thoroughly unpleasant." Matthias had a bit of a harder edge to his voice than Venser usually heard.

"You *will* tell us!" Richter and Sigmund spread out as if to obstruct the hallway.

"Looks like we're at an impasse, then," Venser said.

"Oh, *now* he talks! I thought he was mute," Richter said.

"Come on, rat, out with it! Who are you, and why are you here?" Sigmund asked.

"Why should I tell you?" Venser asked back. He was annoyed, and he fought against his urge to give in to their queries.

"Why *shouldn't* you?"

"Way to deflect without answering the question," Matthias quipped. "You two are going to be *wonderful* leaders some day...and by that, I mean you're not. It was sarcasm, since I figure you two are too dense to pick up on it without being told."

"We know what sarcasm is, you jumped-up scamp, and we're not going to let you keep mocking us like this!"

"It sounds to me like you are." They all turned around to see Basch walking up to the group of them.

"Ah, Basch, perfect timing!" Matthias called out, waving. "Your brothers are being *so* incredibly rude to me and to Venser."

"How unsurprising," Basch responded. He was glaring at his brothers.

"Wait...you're *actually* our brother?" Sigmund stammered.

"I didn't realize I was so forgettable that you two would have completely lost track of what I looked like. I haven't changed that much. I'm not back for good, so you two don't need to break out your mourning clothes just yet."

"Where have you been all this time?" Richter asked.

"Elsewhere. I've gotten around."

"That doesn't answer our question!"

"I told Mother and Father about what I've been up to. You want to know so bad, you can ask them. And didn't Father say he wanted to see your figure study drawings?"

Both of them flushed red with embarrassment. "Uh...yeah, he did, I guess," Sigmund muttered.

"We can talk later after you show your drawings to him. It wouldn't do to keep him waiting, after all, and I imagine they're interested to see what's come from their sons' acute interest in anatomical studies." Basch motioned Venser and Matthias to follow, and they did without the two brothers following.

"I don't remember them ever being this insufferable," Basch said. The three men were in a small conference room not far from the main entrance. "I did ask that Sebastian and Arycelle were sent for, so they should be here before too long."

"Your brothers do seem lively," Matthias said, smirking. "I knew they were the scions of the leader in my past dealings with them, but I didn't conclusively know you all were brothers. Who's the oldest?"

"That would be Sigmund. I've heard he's…behaved rather badly of late, and apparently Richter doesn't want to pass up the opportunity to outdo him."

"Define 'badly'."

"The climax was that he was caught in the middle of an orgy at a brothel here, concurrent with what looked to be a 'triple-X bondage party' hosted by a particular, trouble-inclined coven. The details were horrifying."

"I can see how that would cause *quite* the scandal."

"Why would he go to an orgy?" Venser asked, confused. He had never heard good things about orgies, or about whatever that other thing was.

"Why would *anyone* go to such occasions, dear Venser?" Matthias asked. "The promise of pleasure beyond mortal measure, of course. They're not my thing, but they're appealing to people with such inclinations. But I'm surprised that your brother would think he can get away with it here in Balmung, as small as it is."

"They sometimes have done things under the belief that their stature will let them get away without consequences," Basch said. "I should know, I've done that trick myself once or twice."

"Ooh, Basch was a bad boy. Nowhere near as bad as those two, though, from what I can tell."

"I've only scratched the surface with their misdeeds, but Mother and Father are…not pleased by them. Very much not pleased. That's the sense I've gotten, anyways."

"You're going to be promoted to the favored son status, is what I'm hearing."

"As if."

"So, when were you going to tell us who your parents were?" Arycelle asked. She and Sebastian came in just then, and the query was aimed at Basch.

"When it was relevant," Basch said. "Which is now, I suppose."

"Let me guess, you didn't want to be known as the scion of a prominent family," Sebastian said, smiling lightly.

"People treat you differently when they think they can be advantaged by you or your position. I wanted to be known for who *I* am, not who my family is."

"Not to mention you and your parents haven't been on the best terms of late," Matthias added.

"That, too, I suppose. And don't get me started on my numbskull brothers."

"Those are all fair points," Arycelle said. "I imagine Marianne might have responded differently if she knew who you were, trying to get a bit extra out of your position."

"Anyway, back to things at hand," Basch said. "My parents have said that we're to be permitted to stay here at the palace."

"Aw, yeah!" Matthias grinned. "A nice, soft bed with all the trappings of luxury."

"It's not that luxurious. They only have one room to spare, so between that and my old room, we have two rooms for five people."

"Look, as long as I get a bed, I don't mind."

"There are two beds in that room from what I recall, so if Arycelle and Sebastian want to share a bed, that would mean you get your own."

"If the result is 'Matthias gets his own bed', I don't care too much about the particulars. Unless it involves rooming with your brothers."

"It shouldn't come to that. I wouldn't want to subject you to that, especially with Sigmund being a loud snorer."

"So, the three of us in one room? You have room enough for Venser in your room, Basch?" Sebastian asked.

"I should, unless they decided to extensively renovate the place."

"That suits me well," Venser said, nodding.

"Sounds good, then. We're looking to be here…three nights, I think?"

Matthias pursed his lips, thinking. "We want to have a bit of lead-in to be there the day before the wedding," he said. "It was eight days from when we arrived in Calaveras, correct?"

"It was," Venser said. He closed his eyes to try and recall, and that did sound right.

"A day in transit before this, and now today. If we want to be there in advance, we can stay up to four days, but I think three is better."

"I'd definitely like more time to get there, in case people are difficult," Arycelle said. "But I don't think we should get there *too* early."

"Will Balmung be sending a delegation to the wedding?" Sebastian asked. "We might figure out when they're leaving, as a guide."

"Good idea, that."

"On the topic of delegations," Basch said, "we have been invited to dinner with my parents. All five of us."

"Free food is always a good plan," Matthias said, grinning. "Count us in."

Venser nodded. Supper would be a nice time to sit in and interact with the leaders of Balmung on a more casual level, hopefully without interruption.

"So nice you all could join us," Solvaring said. The seven of them, Basch's parents and the crew of the *Naglfar*, were all gathered in a small dining hall. "I apologize if our fare is lacking somehow."

"Simple food has its own pleasures," Arycelle responded. It was hardly a lavish spread, but a suitable one, filled with hearty fare.

"We appreciate it all the same, sir," Sebastian said.

"Such politeness from you," Hildegard said. She and her husband were seated at opposing ends of the table; Basch and Venser were on one side, while the other three were on the other. "I see Basch's companions are all rather reliable."

"I should think so," Basch said, nodding. "We don't always get along completely, but we've been there for one another."

"Admittedly, Basch has been warming up a bit more ever since Venser joined us," Matthias quipped. "Though whether that's because we deposed our previous captain around that time or not, who knows."

"Deposed your previous captain, you say," Solvaring said, ignoring the slightly murderous glare Basch had aimed at Matthias. "That sounds… interesting. I did hear word that there was an aviator who was looking to take revenge on some people who had wronged them."

"That sounds like something Marianne might do," Sebastian said. "She was intending on turning Venser over to the people in Aracoras, even though it was an awful idea."

"That does strike me as…foolish. Aracoras is notoriously hostile to outsiders. I recall hearing years ago about an expedition that set out to explore the Tomb of the Almighty. They were ultimately unsuccessful, and I don't know if any of them made it back."

"I thought I heard one of them escaped," Hildegard said. "He was pretty shaken up by the entire experience, and it was nearly impossible to get him to talk about it. He passed away some time after that."

"Your memory's better than mine in that regard," he chuckled.

"I don't recall hearing about that," Venser said. "Any time people trespassed, it was usually a massive spectacle, usually culminating in a public execution of some kind."

"It would have happened a long time ago. I forget how far back it was, exactly. It might have been from before when you were born." Hildegard's face showed displeasure at hearing about the public execution.

"Quite a while ago, then. It probably was before I was aware of such things, then."

"On a related topic, we do probably have to consider who we'd send to represent us at the wedding. You all are already accounted for, right?"

"Lady Elessa said we could attend as part of Electrum's delegation," Sebastian said.

"So that's good. Basch wouldn't be an ideal representative, because he has duties to attend to with you as part of your crew. So I feel like it should be Sigmund or Richter to represent us at the wedding."

"It sounds like it might be wise to not be there yourself, sir," Arycelle said. "If they do open the Tomb of the Almighty, it might be dangerous to be there, if whatever is in there winds up hostile."

"That is part of it, as well as that travel and I don't get along as well as we used to," Solvaring said. "I'll inquire as to which of them will want to go, though I suspect neither of them will show much enthusiasm for the task. And in the case your affiliation with Electrum falls through, we'd be happy to offer affiliation to you as to protect you."

"That's appreciated," Matthias chirped. "Any time we're dealing with those nuts in Aracoras, surety is welcome."

Venser nodded between bites of food. He knew he didn't want to risk his friends' lives any more than necessary, and an extra bit of protection that way was good.

"I'm sure we'll have other things worth mentioning," Solvaring continued, "but you all might benefit from some time to relax and rest until it's time to head to Aracoras. As long as you behave better than my other sons, I imagine we'll have no issues that way."

"I think we'll be able to clear that *incredibly* low bar," Matthias said.

"No thanks to you," Basch shot back.

"Hey, I *can* behave myself! Emphasis is on 'can'. I just choose not to most times."

"That might be an understatement," Sebastian chuckled.

"Not you too!"

As supper wrapped up, Solvaring and Hildegard made a request: they both would like a chance to speak with Venser alone. At least, the two of them together with him. They all agreed (some more reluctantly than others), and they filed out of the dining hall.

"First of all, Venser," Solvaring started, "we want to thank you. It wasn't your intention, as I understand, but you helped to open the door for us to reconcile with our son. That's a relationship that will need time to be repaired, but you've given it a chance to happen, and for that we're grateful beyond what we can express."

"I…I think I understand," Venser said. "I'm happy that it's gone well."

"I'm happy Basch seems to be willing to give us another chance. With justifiable trepidation, but that's on us to nurture what we ruined."

"We asked him to catch us up on his travels beyond what you told us in our first meeting," Hildegard said. "He seemed to light up a bit when he talked about you. More so than the other companions he's had, at least."

"We are good friends, that is true," Venser said. He didn't think it prudent to mention his proclivity towards naked cuddling with their son.

"Good friends, indeed," Solvaring repeated, a slight smile on his face. Venser had the feeling they had figured out their relationship was more than merely friendly, but didn't want to pry. He did wonder if the impetus for the initial souring of their relationship was Basch striking it up with someone else and them disagreeing, but that was a query for another time.

"Besides thanking you," Hildegard said, "we did have something we wanted to talk to you about. In private, because we're unsure enough of particulars to want to keep this rather tight-lipped. As I'm sure you heard, you don't look like people from Aracoras normally do, a place known for homogeneity."

"That's something I've always heard, both there and since I started out," Venser said. "My mother insisted on dying my hair blond so that I wouldn't stick out as much, but it was never a good job, and it always looked really bad."

"Trying to help you fit in, I see."

"Part of why we mentioned this," Solvaring continued, "is that we think you look like someone we knew. In particular, you look like one of the adventurers who set out for Aracoras so long ago to explore the Tomb of the Almighty."

"Really?"

"I asked Hildegard to find the photo of them that they had given us before they left. We didn't condone their operation, but we wanted proof that they existed in case things went awry."

"I did find it," she said, pulling out a weathered-looking picture. It was in black and white, but it depicted a band of five men, each with some manner of smile. One caught Venser's eye in particular: a rather dashing man whose features resembled his.

"We can't be sure of what we're thinking," Solvaring said, "and the only person who would be able to tell us anything concretely would be your mother. The man who looks like you never came back, and the one who did return descended rather quickly into madness, unable to communicate and having passed away some time ago."

"I feel like Mother might not want to discuss such things," Venser said, frowning as he thought about the woman. "She was always very dodgy when I asked her about why I had to have my hair dyed, though. It was like she was hiding something she didn't want to tell me. Or tell anyone, I suppose."

"So, you see what we're insinuating," Hildegard said. "I do apologize, this is a lot to be confronted by."

Venser sighed. "I think I understand," he said. "I look different from the others because my father might not be Victarion. It would be…whoever is in that picture. I guess this answers and raises questions in equal measure, if this is correct."

"We don't raise the theory baselessly or aimlessly. I feel like that might provide some explanation as to your seeming expendability, that they're willing to marry off the one who stands out. I suppose this also is to show that you have roots outside of Aracoras, roots that you can choose to turn to if you want."

"After the wedding, I have no intention of staying in Aracoras at all. I…I have plenty of reasons to leave. And no reason to stay, I think."

"Do you want to talk to your mother about this?"

Venser whistled. "I don't think much would be gained from a conversation, but I think it *could* help to answer the lingering questions I have. I'm not going to try to speak with her, though, and I'm definitely not going to endanger any of my crewmates. If they figure out who I am, that would be very perilous for all of us."

"You seem to have taken quickly to being part of that group," Hildegard said, smiling. "That's good."

"I'm surprised, myself. And it has been a bit of an adjustment. But they've been good for me. I've…grown a bit since I started traveling with them."

"Experience is a great way to learn who you are and what you want to do," Solvaring said. "I think that's been a great boon to Basch. And while I think my wife and I would prefer him to stay with us, it's better for him to follow what he wants to do and pursue what he wants…and, in turn, I think it's ultimately better for us and our relationship at the end."

"I think we've kept your ear for long enough, Venser," Hildegard said. "We'll be free if you want to talk at any point in your stay."

"I appreciate that," Venser nodded. He had a *lot* to think about.

"As far as revelations go," Basch said, "that is a doozy." The two were settled into Basch's old room; night had fallen, and snow continued to drift down lazily outside. Venser told Basch about what his parents had told him.

"I'm not shocked," Venser said, "but I…guess I don't know where my head is right now. It should be shocking, but it all sort of makes sense…my parents' relative indifference towards me, all the bad hair dye, and just a weird feeling of isolation I've had. Like I was an outsider in my own home."

"Isolation, huh? I can relate. Not the same way as you, probably, but I know I had those feelings. Laying in bed, staring up at the ceiling, wondering why I was different, wondering why my parents favored my brothers…"

"They favored them, then? Seeing how they're behaving, that seems like it didn't go well."

Basch tried to suppress a laugh. "I suppose so," he said. "It was mostly Sigmund who got the favorable treatment, since he's the oldest and the presumed heir, but there's often one kid who gets lost in the mix."

"You were that kid?"

"Not for lack of trying. When it came to studies, I outdid my brothers handily, and I kept pace with Richter in physical competitions. Sigmund… let's just say that was never his strong suit. But it felt like I had to do twice the work for half the attention. The final straw was when my parents decided to arrange a marriage without my consent. We had an argument that night, and the tone of the argument was that they didn't understand me and didn't respect me as an individual. I left that night, and this is the first time I've seen them since then. In my absence, several of my distant relatives passed away, others got married, and my brothers got steadily more obnoxious."

"They did seem to imply that they want to repair your relationship."

"I'll always be a bit skeptical, but they seem sincere enough, and I'll give them a chance until they prove my trust is misplaced. I don't *want* to, necessarily, but with as awful as my brothers have been and their seeming sincerity, I owe it to them to try."

"They felt sincere in my conversations and dealings with them. It didn't seem like an act they were putting on, but I could be completely wrong."

Basch shook his head. "They're not great liars. They were bad at hiding when they had surprises for us. So they might not be lying here, unless they've picked up that skill in the years since."

"What about your brothers?"

"Eh, they can rot for all I care. They've been insufferable before, and it likely won't change. They *have* gotten worse in recent years, though."

"How so?"

"They're more brazen with what they try to do and get away with. They might try to be a bother to me during the rest of our stay here."

"Whatever happens with your family," Venser said, "I'll be here for you if you want me to be, Basch." He moved closer and put an arm around him.

"I know, Venser. And I appreciate that." Basch leaned his head against Venser's, and they continued to watch the snow fall.

Venser wasn't entirely sure why he and Basch got along so well, and with such chemistry, but they did. The prickly, brusque man he'd initially met had a sweet, soft exterior that he seemed loath to let others in on, but it felt like that was changing for the better. There was that spark of interest from their first meeting, but it had slowly developed into a full-blown affection.

Moments like this, he thought, were more than worth the journey. He turned and kissed Basch, a kiss that was returned in short order, and the two men started to make out passionately. Their clothes made their way onto the floor, and their naked bodies pressed warm into one another.

The falling snow outside made for a serene backdrop as they had sex, with Basch sliding into Venser for the first time. To Venser, it felt *right*. His mind flickered back to his past experimentation, surreptitious and fleeting encounters with boys that were forgotten about immediately afterwards, and he found all of those memories were getting washed away with his present pleasure. He tried to not be too loud as Basch's cock thrust inside him, his own rock-solid member leaking profusely.

The way they were positioned, he had the chance to look up into Basch's eyes. They seemed to have a very distinct light to them, a twinkle that was captivating. Even feeling Basch thrusting into him, there was a sense he had of peace. That this was the place for him and the man for him, a feeling that was accentuated when he leaned over to kiss Venser squarely on the lips.

Not long after that, both men erupted, Venser's cock shooting a load up his torso and Basch's inside where it was ensconced, as they both found themselves unable to contain their euphoria. They were breathing heavily from the high they had just hit. After another kiss, Basch flopped down next to Venser, and the two men fell asleep cuddling.

The next morning, Venser woke up to see Basch standing by his window, looking out it. Snow was falling outside, making for a cozy, peaceful ambiance. Basch was completely naked, and Venser took a moment to silently admire his form.

Venser got up, stretched, and walked over to Basch. He was also naked presently, which he found he didn't mind all that much, at least not with the present company. He walked up behind and wrapped his arms around Basch.

"Good morning to you," Basch said, putting his hands up to where Venser's hands were. "Slept well?"

"Quite," Venser answered.

"Good. Yesterday was a lot for both of us to take in."

"I agree."

They kept standing there, bodies pressed against each other and just enjoying the moment. Venser knew he'd have to confront the past he'd gotten away from, so that the present he was enjoying could persist, but that all seemed so far away.

"Basch?"

"Yes, Venser?"

"Uh…how do I put this? Are we…are we boyfriends?" It was a weird thing to say. The idea of having a "boyfriend" or "girlfriend" was positively scandalous in Aracoras, as romance was never a factor in the arrangement of couples and marriages, and he'd only heard about them in illicit books he wasn't supposed to have or read. He also had not really known that men could have boyfriends (or women could have girlfriends), but the word felt

right for what they had.
"I think we are."
"I like that. I think we are, too."
"Then why'd you ask?" His tone was jovial.
"I wanted to make sure."
"I'm pretty sure we are. It's what it feels like to me, at least."
"That's good, then."
They fell back into silence, watching the snow fall.

15

Winds of Winter

Venser and Basch emerged from their room and immediately happened upon quite the spectacle: Richter and Sigmund were rolling around like quarreling children, screaming at one another and trying to land blows on each other. The two beheld the tussling men in the hallway, watching them writhe around in some approximation of an arcane mating ritual as a gathered crowd spectated.

"What's going on?" Venser asked, confused. Basch just shook his head.

As the two continued to fight, it became clear what the subject of their quarrel was: who would have the "privilege" of representing Balmung in Aracoras for the wedding. Sigmund obviously felt Richter would be the worthy choice, Richter thought it was on Sigmund to represent them, and their father's instructions were to "figure it out for yourselves".

"Looks like you two got here to watch the show," Sebastian said, walking up to them. "They've been going at it for a while now. Nobody wants to stop them."

"Of course they don't," Basch sighed. "But knowing them, they're not going to stop on their own."

Venser watched as Basch stepped forward and inserted himself between the two brothers, both still howling and flailing.

"Would you two just *shut up for one minute?*" he roared. They both quit their largely incomprehensible screaming and looked at him.

"That worked," Venser whispered to Sebastian, impressed.

"He started it!" Richter whined. "He's claiming I have to go to Aracoras!"

"Why can't you go instead, Basch?" Sigmund whined.

"I have a job I can't step away from, and I thought you two didn't think I was on the same level you were on," Basch answered.

"You're not! I mean…uh…" Sigmund realized he had said something he probably should have not spoken.

"I suppose I should tell Father, then, that you *both* have decided to go." Basch let them go and stepped back, greeted by a look of horror from both of them.

"He won't believe you!" Richter said, his tone nicely unctuous. "Not if *I* go to him first and tell him Sigmund volunteered!"

"You won't get the chance! I'm going there right now and telling Father *you're* going to Aracoras!"

Basch sighed and motioned for Sebastian and Venser to follow him, leaving the two to their quarrel.

"Have they always been this…animated?" Sebastian asked. "One of them tried hitting on Arycelle earlier this morning."

"Please tell me she slapped them," Basch said. "They would deserve it."

"She was tempted to, and I certainly wouldn't have faulted her, but no. I think she and Matthias have gone off to offload the cargo we've picked up from Electrum and Calaveras, as well as anything else worth liquidating."

"We should probably go down to the market, then, and see if they're there. I doubt Arycelle would want to stay here with the threat of my ogling brothers."

"I wouldn't want to, either," Venser said. "They don't seem like people I'd want to spend time around."

"I'm *sure* they have redeeming qualities. I just forget what they are, and I'm not sure who'd know at this point."

Stepping outside, Venser was greeted by a wall of cold, and he drew his jacket around him as tightly as he could muster. They stepped carefully on the pathways and through the snow, winding around snow-dusted trees and inundated structures. There was a weird sense of idyll here, between the general dearth of people on the street and the snow-covered environs. The crunching of snow under their shoes was the only sound Venser could presently discern, a rhythmic cadence as they walked.

"This should be the marketplace," Basch said. They had reached a long, low-slung building, and they stepped inside to be greeted by both a wave of warmth and a proverbial wall of sound and smell from people inside.

"Hey, you got here," Arycelle called, walking up as they stepped inside. "Sorry Matthias and I left so quickly. Those brothers of yours, Basch..."

"I know, I know," he said, shaking his head.

"Good to see you," Sebastian said, giving her a kiss. "I take it Matthias is off doing his thing?"

"Yep. He's selling all the goods we picked up on the way or have had for a while. Skystones, his...literary acquisitions, and anything else left over from the reign of our last captain he felt was worth liquidating."

"You mean that he's selling his smut," Basch said.

"He'd come up with some extravagant sobriquet for those books, but yes, his smut," she nodded. "Among other things. We do have two days before we need to be off, so it made sense to offload what we could before we head over to Aracoras. Partly because we think it'd be a terrible idea to carry the *Ogler's Digest* into that place."

"I'd agree with that," Sebastian said. "And, besides, I think we all wouldn't mind a bit of a breather."

"Anyway, I think Sebastian and I will go look at vendors," Arycelle said. "We'll find you later." They disappeared into the crowd, leaving the two men behind.

"The market's like how I remember it, more or less," Basch said. "It's good to see some things don't change all that much."

"I see," Venser replied. It was an interesting mix of smells and sights. "When things are changing, it's nice to have constants. The opposite is true, though...when nothing changes, you like to have something to liven things up."

"I suppose you would be more familiar with the latter. Let's check the market out."

The actual stalls of the market were a dizzying array of vendors, offering all sorts of products and goods, along with vendors selling exciting and tantalizing foodstuffs. The wares ranged from the mundane to the exotic, often with florid descriptors to match. It was a stark contrast in activity to the outside world of Balmung, cozy and warm and energetic. It reminded Venser of Electrum and Lunaria, albeit with its own particular flavor.

"Do you think we should get some kind of wedding gift?" Basch asked. "You know, something that would lend credence to us being part of the entourage."

"I think that would work," Venser said. "That said, I…don't like my brother, and I really don't want him to get something nice out of this from me."

"I see," he chuckled. "I don't think I'd get my brothers a nice wedding gift. If, of course, they found someone who could put up with them."

"So, something that's a joke would work?" Venser was smiling lightly.

"I think we can figure that out. I'm guessing your brother would get all the gifts?"

"In Aracoras, all property belongs to the husband. So, yes."

"Talk about sexism. You know…Matthias might have an idea. Something really inappropriate would be right up his alley. Speaking of which…" He pointed to a stall they were nearing, run by Matthias. It had plenty of livery suggesting a "limited time sale". Like in Calaveras, he was selling books and other literary products, each of which was more horrifying than the last.

"Good to see you," Matthias said, waving to the two of them. "We got off to an early start, thanks to Arycelle needing to get away from those disgusting brothers of yours and their rather foul hands."

"They are something, all right," Basch sighed. "I didn't realize they had gotten this bad."

"Nor had I. I may enjoy literature of a particular bent, but I draw a firm line at non-consensual touching." As he said this, he accepted money in exchange for a recent issue of *Ogler's Digest*.

"We were thinking," Venser said, "we should figure out a wedding gift. I don't want it to be anything nice, because my brother is…very unpleasant."

"I'm going to guess you can't just give something to Leondra?" Matthias asked.

"Nope. All property goes to the husband."

"Well, that's a bit archaic, isn't it? A gift for a sexist, immature, and unpleasant twit...I have a couple of ideas, each one more terrifying than the one before. When I've closed up shop, I'll take a look around and see what I can find."

"I'm sure we all will inevitably regret letting you pick it out," Basch quipped.

"Eh, it's more fun that way! Speaking of fun, I think I saw the Coven of Unholy Nocturnal Terror has set up shop here. I saw one of their posters advertising an upcoming 'triple-X bondage party' and a concurrent 'bacchanal of ceaseless pleasure', if nothing else. They also had their own books, purportedly penned by their leader, but I don't think their particular brand of bodice ripper has broad appeal."

"They're out here, too?" Venser asked. He didn't want to know about the party. Basch just sighed and shook his head.

"Hey, they have services and spectacle to offer and plenty of places to plunder and pilfer, and I'm sure Basch's brothers have checked them out aplenty."

"Don't remind me, Matthias. They seriously think they can get away with anything these days, which isn't too different from when I lived here. I wouldn't be surprised if Sigmund made his way down to the party to see what was going on."

"I'm curious as to why your parents haven't tried to rein them in. Or maybe they have, and they're just too good at bucking those reins. It also could be in the middle, or we can just blame the schools. Regardless, I'm just a humble peddler of fine literature, so I should probably not offer parenting advice."

"Humble and fine are *relative* terms here, Matthias, terms you're stretching to their breaking point," Basch said, pointing to a book cover depicting a woman being accosted by tentacles.

"Even the humble and pure of heart have their vices at times," he grinned.

"Of all the terms I would use to describe you, those two would be towards the bottom of the list."

"At least they make the list."

That evening, the crew of the *Naglfar* had converged back on the Balmung palace, and Matthias had mentioned that he had found a gift suitable for their purposes. It had already been gift-wrapped, a fairly tall and narrow box with some heft to it, and everyone was examining it.

"What *is* in here?" Venser asked, weighing the box as he held it.

"Secret," Matthias grinned.

"Of course it's a secret," Basch said, shaking his head. "It's more fun that way when we all get into trouble over it."

"It's something they will absolutely *love*, I assure you!"

Venser set the box down carefully. "That's either a good thing or a bad thing, and I'm not sure which one it is anymore," he said. "Which probably means I've been hanging around Matthias too much."

"Finally, he gets it," Sebastian joked.

"I'm not *that* bad an influence! I don't think so, at least," Matthias said. "I can tell you what it's not: a copy of *The Fisherman's Wife 3: The Doors of Moan*."

"Please tell me that's not an actual title," Basch sighed.

"Well, it's not out yet, but they keep saying it's coming! They've been saying it for a long while, but who even knows if is still being worked on. Maybe the author found more interesting avenues to pursue, who knows?"

"Speaking of gifts, and to change the subject away from unreleased literature only Matthias is interested in, have we figured out which of those two is going to Aracoras to represent Balmung?" Arycelle asked.

"Haven't heard yet," Basch replied. "They might still be arguing over who's not going to do it."

"I did see one of Basch's brothers earlier while I was at the market," Matthias added. "I think it was Sigmund, and he had a female companion with him. That companion was really annoying, though."

"How so?" Sebastian asked.

"She spoke in this high, cutesy voice. Almost like a baby. And she had this awful enunciation, adding in weird sounds to all of her words. It sounded a bit like 'owo', if I had to characterize it?"

"Funny you should mention that," Arycelle whispered, dropping her voice. "I think I hear someone. Might be them." Two voices could be heard, and it was indeed Sigmund and his female companion of the day, walking into the room they were gathered in. His lady friend was short and had big eyes and blonde pigtails, and she wore a bright, frilly dress with gratuitous ribbons and bows.

"Oh, look, it's my brother and his ruffians," Sigmund scowled.

"Hello, Sigmund," Basch said, his voice stiff. "I see you have a companion today."

"That I do! Her name is Zsa Zsa, and she's been someone I've been *seeing* of late."

"Awe these those vewy wude peopwe you towd me about, owo?" she asked. Her voice *was* an obnoxious infantile squeal, one that seemed to turn every "r" and "l" sound into a "w".

"I'd hardly characterize us as rude. More rude is your presumptuousness, little girl," Matthias shot back. Venser noticed a strange, dull headache starting to take root behind his temples, but he didn't want to alarm anyone.

"Oh-em-gee, you awe *so* wude, uwu! Zsa Zsa is nyot a wittwe giww, owo." Venser noticed another of her *charming* speech quirks, and he could tell she and he were not going to get along.

"Don't mind these scoundrels and their jealous whining, my little Snuggle Muffin," Sigmund said, his voice thoroughly patronizing. "Anyway, *dear brother*, you might be amused to hear that Father dearest has dispatched both of us to the wedding."

"I thought it was just to be one of you," Basch replied. "Did he change his mind to get rid of you both in one fell swoop?"

"As charming as ever, *brother*. Richter insisted that he come along if I was to go there. It was something about not wanting me to get all of the experiences for myself, which is probably just his jealousy talking. I wouldn't be alone, of course, as I asked Zsa Zsa if she wanted to go with me."

"Zsa Zsa woves weddings, owo! Thewe's gonnya be so much cake and so much dancing, uwu!" She bounced up and down as she said this.

"She seems excited," Sebastian said.

"I'm not sure there's going to be a lot of cake or dancing there," Venser said, trying to keep his voice low. He tried to recall all of the other weddings he'd sat through over the years, and they were all bereft of cake and merriment.

"Don't tell her that," Arycelle muttered. Zsa Zsa showed no signs of having heard this, and she continued to squeal and bounce around giddily.

"Are you two planning to stay for that 'big event' they have planned at the end?" Basch asked.

"Zsa Zsa *woves* big suwpwises, owo! Awawawawawawa!" She spun around as she uttered the last bit.

"But of course we are, as such merriment seems well-suited for us. At any rate, Zsa Zsa and I should leave you to keep planning whatever vile shenanigans you have planned," Sigmund said, puffing up. "I do hope our paths cross as little as possible, little brother."

"The feeling is mutual, asshole."

"Oh-em-gee, so wude, uwu."

Sigmund put an arm around Zsa Zsa and led her away, and Venser noticed that his headache started to fade as she walked away.

"I don't think I have ever met a woman I have been less attracted to," Matthias said. "I am impressed."

"You, turned off by a woman?" Arycelle quipped. "Mark it on the calendar."

"Something felt *off* with her," Venser said. "It felt like an act, and there's something unnerving to me about how she was behaving."

"One my brother's bought hook, line, and sinker," Basch growled. "You're right, though. There was something about her I couldn't quite put my finger on, but it's something I don't like."

"Hopefully we won't have to deal with her again, given that literally none of us can stand her, but if Sigmund's calling her his girlfriend, that might not be something we can avoid," Sebastian said. "Anyway, let's get this gift put away and clean up for supper."

As they dispersed, Venser thought back to the strange headache that surfaced while he was around Zsa Zsa. The last time he'd felt something like it was when he was face-to-face with Hellvira in Electrum. Was it related somehow? He couldn't rule it out, but it was something he didn't know enough about to want to bring it up just yet.

"You've been quiet all evening, Venser," Basch said. They had gotten through with dinner, a larger affair with Basch's brothers in attendance and doing their usual bickering and brown-nosing. Zsa Zsa was also there to fawn over Sigmund and provide obnoxious commentary, causing Venser's headache to creep back in and drive in jagged points any time she opened her mouth. Richter had mentioned that his current girlfriend was unable to attend, which got snide remarks about him *having* a girlfriend that livened up the proceedings rather nicely.

"Have I?" Venser asked. They were both back in Basch's room, and Venser was relieved to notice that his headache had gone away.

"You have. Is something troubling you?"

"It...yeah, I've been a bit concerned. It's about your brother's girlfriend."

"She does concern me as well, but I'm guessing your issues with her are a bit deeper."

"When I was around her...I noticed a headache setting in. Sort of a dull ache near my temples. It's not the first time it's happened, either. I noticed it when I met with Hellvira, both in Sorocco and in Electrum."

Basch frowned. "That's very concerning," he said. "I don't know what it means, but if they gave you a similar sensation, there might be something going on there that they're both involved in."

"I didn't want to trouble anyone, or raise any suspicions around her, so I just...kept quiet."

"I get that, and I definitely understand not wanting to make trouble. Zsa Zsa...she is certainly concerning to me, with all of her particular quirks and the things that give me pause. Her demeanor seems comically fake, and listening to my brother fawn over her was a bit nauseating."

"Do you think there's something there?"

"Yes, almost certainly. Between what you've told me and what I've seen, I suspect she's certainly not benign. I'll try to keep an eye on her, of course, but I don't know if we'll learn anything more about what's up with her before we leave."

Venser sighed. "I guess there's so much we don't know and have no real way of knowing about," he said. "Not yet, anyways."

"Hopefully there are answers to be found soon," Basch said, drawing him in for an embrace. "I just hope it's not after they succeed in opening the Tomb of the Almighty."

"Can we stop them?"

"I don't know. I'm not sure how we would do it. I guess interrupting the wedding might be a start, since they're not going to open the Tomb until after the nuptials finish."

"It might delay them, maybe," Venser said. "There's usually a part in the ceremony where objections can be voiced, but nobody ever speaks up during them."

"Well, that sounds like the opening we need. I don't know if it will actually stop them, but it's as good an idea as we have."

"If we can delay, that might be a start."

Basch kissed him, drawing him in tight. "We can figure it out when we get there," he said. "I'll be here to help you."

"I know you are, Basch."

He returned Basch's kiss, and the two started making out, the first part of what had become their regular evening ritual.

There was one final day for the crew of the *Naglfar* to rest and prepare before they headed to Aracoras, and so they took advantage of it as best they could. Basch took the day to show Venser around the palace properly, to give him a tour of all the nooks and crannies he'd grown up in and around. His brothers apparently had set off for Aracoras earlier, and Venser appreciated that he wouldn't need to see Zsa Zsa again.

"It's weird to revisit all the places I thought I'd left behind forever," Basch said. "I don't know how often I'll be back here, but that's something we'll discover later."

"A reason to go home is nice at times," Venser said. "I don't think I'll have one of those after we're done at the wedding."

"I suppose that's not a bad thing intrinsically. I didn't have a reason to go back to Balmung until recently, and even that reason is still a fairly narrow one. But Mother and Father will want to see me more, I guess, and I can occasionally agree to that."

"I understand that." They passed by what was a training hall, with guards practicing combat maneuvers and drills. Venser did wonder if it was for anything particular or just general preparedness.

"Look at that, it's little master Basch," they heard. A stern, grizzled man walked up to greet them. "I had heard you had returned, and it's good that I got a chance to see you before you left anew."

"Sorry I haven't run into you before this," Basch nodded, shaking his hand. "Venser, this is Captain Regulus. He's in charge of the Balmung guard."

"So, you're Venser," he said, shaking hands. His grip was firm, and while he was imposing in form, his eyes twinkled with a bit of kindness he didn't like to show off readily. "The palace has been atwitter about a visitor from Aracoras. You must be him."

"That I am," Venser nodded. "It's a pleasure to meet you."

"I must say, you're a lot nicer than the other Aracoras louts. The last time I dealt with one, they had this air that I was wasting their time, that I was inconveniencing them somehow."

"To them, you probably were. They…have a high opinion of themselves."

"So I could tell," Regulus chuckled.

"Regulus was responsible for training the three of us," Basch said. "Father felt it would be useful to have some combat training in case we needed to defend ourselves or others."

"Basch was the only one of them who was any good at it," Regulus said. "I probably wouldn't hire him on as a soldier, mind, but Sigmund was useless and Richter complained all the time, so he stood out in a good way."

"That sounds like my brothers, all right."

"Take good care of him, will you, Venser? He's always been a bit soft and sweet under his exterior."

"I'll do what I can, sir," Venser said, pretending to ignore the mortified

213

look on Basch's face.

"Good. We just got him back, and we'd like to keep him around, so to speak. Even if he won't actually be here much of the time."

As they walked away, Venser noticed that Basch's face was flushed red. "You seem embarrassed," he said.

"To say the least. Wasn't expecting the old man to say all of those things."

"It seems to me that they like you and they legitimately feel bad for driving you away, Basch."

"I *know*," he sighed. "They're trying, and I'm trying as well. It's hard to forget the scars brought by the past when they happened to you."

"Take the time you need for it, Basch. I'm here, like you are for me."

"I know that, and I appreciate it." They exchanged a quick kiss.

As night fell, Solvaring asked for one final meeting with Venser, following dinner. Basch was explicitly invited, and Matthias invited himself, Sebastian, and Arycelle. Solvaring was more amused than annoyed by this.

"So, you leave for Aracoras tomorrow," he started. They were in the throne room, with Hildegard there as a mostly silent observer. "My other sons have departed in advance, as you know. Whether or not you interact with them there is up to you, but I do have this." He handed Venser a letter bearing the official seal of Balmung.

"That's a letter to affiliate us with you, right?" Matthias asked.

"Indeed, it is. You might not need it, but it's better to have and not need than to need and not have."

"I appreciate it," Venser said.

"I don't know what, exactly, Hessler and his cadre are planning," Solvaring continued. "Be on your guard, though. He's up to something, something we're not entirely sure of, and I don't think he's left any details up to chance."

"Given that he wants the Tomb of the Almighty opened," Basch said, "I wouldn't be surprised if he had all the minutiae planned out already."

"I do want to impress on all of you that you are welcome back here any time. You have been lovely guests…aside from someone bringing my delinquent sons a wide array of 'anatomy study materials', but I suppose it helped to show just how poor their behavior has been."

"Glad it worked out," Matthias said, grinning.

"I don't think he's happy you brought *The Fisherman's Wife 2: The Re-Tentacling* into his palace, Matthias," Arycelle glared.

"The particulars are...unnecessary," Solvaring said, raising an eyebrow. "One thing I did want to tell you, Basch, is that, while you are still free to travel as part of the crew of the *Naglfar* and wherever else you might go, you are always our son, and I hope that we can get to a better place than we have been before this."

"I...thank you, Father," Basch said. "I promise it won't be so long before I come back."

After a final set of farewells, including some hugs between Basch and his parents, everyone started retiring for the night. The last to leave were Basch, Venser, and Solvaring, and the last stopped Venser one final time.

"I do not know if the lead I gave you is accurate and your father is not Victarion," he said, "so feel free to validate and make use of that information as you will. But whether your blood is of Balmung or not, you are always welcome here, Venser."

"Thank you, sir," Venser nodded.

"I presume you have no intentions to return to Aracoras?"

"After the wedding, absolutely not."

"That is reasonable. Find the place you belong, and the people you belong with. I do hope it's with us." Solvaring winked at Venser, and he got the sense that they had figured out his relationship status, particularly how it pertained to their son.

That night, Basch and Venser made love and retired in each other's arms. As he drifted to sleep, Venser had the sense that he might have figured out somewhere he belonged. He just hoped Aracoras wouldn't do anything to shake that.

The Tomb of the Almighty awaited. For the first time since early in his journey, it loomed large in his dreams. A monolith of stone, inscrutable and daunting. This time, though, he felt a strange chill as he watched it from his dreamscape.

A wave of darkness radiated out from the towering tomb, and faint laughter echoed. Where was it coming from? He had never before heard the voice that was laughing. One voice was joined by others in a cacophonous chorus, and the nightmare ultimately faded away into the abyss of his mind.

16

Contest of Clouds

As the sun rose, so did the *Naglfar*. The airship ascended out of Balmung's harbor as its bow swung at a sharp angle, setting a course for Aracoras at first light.

Venser remembered hearing that Aracoras and the Tomb of the Almighty sat at the center of the other major cities, and the other five formed a ring around it. They were thus headed towards the center of the ring, about a day and a half of flying time if everything went according to plan. The first day was, indeed, uneventful, and Venser took the day to write heavily in the journal Leondra had given him. He hadn't had much time to write in it previously, besides a couple of quick notes, but it was reasonable to put what had happened down while still fresh in his memory.

The idyll was not to persist, and the next day was definitely not uneventful. Shortly after he'd gotten breakfast, Venser ran into Arycelle and Basch, who were a bit frantic.

"Venser, we have trouble!" Basch yelped.

"What kind?" he asked.

"It looks to be an airship conspicuously approaching us in confrontational fashion," Arycelle said. "Possibly more than that, but Matthias just saw the one when he sent us to send word."

"I'll go tell Sebastian and take my station," Basch said. "Can you take Venser to the bridge, Arycelle?"

"Can do. Thanks, Basch."

The two men had time to exchange a quick kiss, and Basch scrambled below deck while Arycelle led Venser to the bridge. The rush of the breeze was cold and exhilarating, but Venser still wasn't keen on having his eyes open while crossing the deck.

"Good, you're both here," Matthias said, addressing his company. "I think I figured out who's approaching us." He pointed to the screen that showed *three* approaching vessels, one large one and two smaller ones.

"Who's chasing us?" Arycelle asked.

"Guess."

Venser frowned as he thought about who it could be, and finally he got his answer as the communication channel crackled to life.

"Long time no see, Matthias. I would say it's nice to see you again, but we all know that's a lie, you treasonous weasel." It was Marianne. At long last, the time had come to settle that score.

"Come now, Marianne, that's not particularly polite, even if you think it's true. It's...*lovely* to see that you got your wings back," he replied. Venser noticed that Matthias was a bit paler, even if his voice tried to convey the usual bravado.

"Sure it is. Would rather it have been with my ship, and not the replacement. I heard you even renamed it after you made off with it. And all this fuss and this bother over a boy...I thought he wasn't your type, Matthias."

"He's definitely not my type, fair Marianne, lovely company though he might be. My type is more...buxom. Far, far more buxom. Bounteous bosoms, breastacular, breast-in-show, and all that. But I feel like I, and we, all made the right decision in the end."

"Was it, now? I was intending to deliver him back to his home and get nicely rewarded for it, and then we could go about our merry way. I quite dislike being caught up in politics like that, as good rarely ever comes from being ensnared in the disputes of those who see themselves far above us, and I definitely think Leondra misled us when she tasked us with ferrying her fiancé away from the wedding venue."

"You were just delivering us to our doom, Marianne! They wouldn't deal with us. They'd execute us, and that would be that!"

"You're just justifying your treason to yourself, and it's not working on me, you treacherous weasel."

"Venser told us as much, and he's from Aracoras, so I'd trust *his* word about what they would do over your naive sense of optimism!"

"Naive, am I? We'll see just who's naive when I punch some holes into that commandeered vessel. Hate to damage her, but bullet holes buff out nicely with the right treatment."

Venser took a look out the back of the bridge and had a view of the approaching vessel. It looked comparable the *Naglfar* in terms of size, a broad and sleek ship with menacing curves and threatening armaments, and it certainly looked like a formidable opponent from what little he knew about airships.

"Seems like you got yourself quite the ship," Matthias replied. "Might be more formidable than the *Naglfar* if you believe in yourself, even. What did you call it this time? The *Sexecutioner*? Maybe the *Vulvatron*?"

"Your names are as appalling as your taste in literature and women, Matthias. It's called the *Angel of Retribution*, if you need to know what's going to finally pop your treasonous ass for good."

"Not as florid a name as I was expecting."

"Who cares about florid when it's…" She was cut off by another voice entering the communication channel with a long, drawn out scream of "Wooooooooooooooomaaaaaaaaaaaaaaaaan!"

"Oh no," everyone groaned in seeming unison, from Matthias to Marianne to even Venser.

"Most radiant Marianne, buxom beauty and boundless treasure of the skies, I finally have caught up to you in order to aid your chastisement of the transgressing vermin that have absconded with the *Alamithea*!" came the familiar, unctuous whine of Archduke Emperor Pope Guillaume XIII. "At long last, larcenous scamps, your crimes shall be brought to light and smote under a bathing rain of heavenly bloodshed and *glo*rious violence!"

"I noticed," Marianne said, her voice clearly displaying annoyance.

"Who were you, again?" Matthias asked. He had a grin that would betray to everyone that he was doing this for comic effect.

"How *dare* you forget my name, the identity of the one who is going to finally bring to justice your sin-clouded existence! Like a flower that blooms in the soil of our carnal and corrupt society, I shall administer retribution to the straying vermin that graze upon the land! For I am the Chairman of the Educational Guidance Council...*Archduke Emperor Pope Guillaume XIII!*" As always, this was a monologue delivered with maximal sanctimony.

"Nope, still doesn't ring a bell."

"Why did you come here?" Marianne asked. "I have business with them, and the business does *not* involve you, Guillaume."

"You needn't tax yourself, my chaste and delicate Marianne! I shall be the one who shall properly punish this pernicious posse, and my reward shall finally be administered in the form of my ensconcing my exalted head in your ample and voluminous bosom!"

"Will it, now." Marianne's tone suggested that this was not going to happen regardless of outcome, and Matthias was trying to suppress laughter.

"Verily it will, most voluptuous and vivacious Marianne! The *Divine Divinisher of Divine Divinity* will be the instrument that cleaves their desecrating existence from this mortal coil, staking a grand and glorious victory for the Educational Guidance Council and morality as a whole!"

"We've finally found you, Archduke Emperor Pope Guillaume XIII!" This came from a *fourth* party, a lisping female voice that sounded vaguely familiar to Venser. "You have fallen afoul of my Coven of Unholy Nocturnal Terror, and it has come to collect on your debt to us!"

"I have no business with you, trollops, and I take great issue with the insinuation that I might be even tangentially associated with you!" Archduke Emperor Pope Guillaume XIII had dropped the lecherous, brown-nosing whine and had reverted to his equally whiny regular speaking voice.

"We beg to differ! My Coven of Unholy Nocturnal Terror keeps *precise* receipts, and we have your entire unpaid tab right here! You have yet to pay for thirteen Cleavage Divinations, nine Black Magick Lap Dances, seven Entrails Auguries, four Death Tarot readings, three Purification

Séances meant to expunge the persistent taint of the aspect of the mating fire eel from your aura, and, most egregiously, one instance of our most premium offering, the Dance of the Blood Rivers! Blood Countess Erzsébet Báthory has come to *personally* collect, be it with monetary compensation or sanguine compensation!" She punctuated this proclamation with a laugh, a shuddering giggle that sounded like she was climaxing then and there.

"Well, this all just escalated," Arycelle whispered. Matthias just shook his head, trying not to laugh. Venser wasn't sure if he should laugh or just be appalled. All of their services had extravagant names that seemed deliberately overwrought, and he couldn't help shake that he had heard the voice elsewhere.

"Your fabulism cannot conceal the vacancy within your soul, you amoral trollop! I shan't be blackmailed by a hare-brained hag and her harem of hussies and harlots!"

"If you refuse to acknowledge your indebtedness, it falls upon Blood Countess Erzsébet Báthory to punish *you* for your transgressions! Fortuitously, my Coven of Unholy Nocturnal Terror is well-equipped for such aboard our majestic craft, the Vessel Attaining Grand Impressive Noble Achievements!" She punctuated this with another quavering, orgiastic laugh.

"That name is a mouthful," Matthias muttered. "Why would you call it 'Vessel Attaining...'" He trailed off, and broke into badly-suppressed laughter.

"Grandiose titles can neither mask nor quell your innermost squalor, hussy! But if you too desire the light of heavenly retribution, Archduke Emperor Pope Guillaume XIII will be happy to administer it to both you and the larcenous weasels I have apprehended!"

"Would you two just *shut up* and piss off somewhere far away from me?" Marianne yelled. "I'm trying to deal with these nimrods, and you're both annoying me profusely!"

"Buxom and radiant Marianne, bounteous treasure of the skies, you needn't exert yourself unnecessarily in the devastation of these craven curs!" crowed Archduke Emperor Pope Guillaume XIII, adopting his brown-nosing tone once again. "Observe closely my divinely-guided actions as I rain divine retribution upon both the absconders of the *Alamithea* and the hemophagic trollop's pernicious posse!"

The familiar "rat-ta-tat-tat" cadence rang out as the *Divine Divinisher of Divine Divinity* attempted to barrage both vessels with bullets. As always, though, no damage seemed to be done by the measly munitions.

"Is that all you have?" squealed Blood Countess Erzsébet Báthory. "You're as cheap with your vessel as you are in other regards! Looks like it's time for us to collect our payment! Full speed ahead, cultists! Aim right for that gibbering, sanctimonious gasbag! *Bring me his blood!*" She laughed again, a sound that would never not perturb Venser.

"Looks like it's time to book it, as amusing as this conversation has been," Matthias whispered. He tapped several buttons and pushed forward on a lever, and the *Naglfar*'s engines roared to life at full force, lurching forward and accelerating markedly.

"Get back here, Matthias!" Marianne yelled. "We're not done here!"

"Stop in the name of divinity, scou-" Archduke Emperor Pope Guillaume XIII was cut off by a loud *crunch*, letting out a squeal as the sound of something being impaled filled the air.

"Direct hit! Excellent work, my cultists! You honor Astaroth through your divinely-guided actions! Now, make after that fleeing vessel! And bring me that insipid twerp who dares impugn the good name of the Coven of Unholy Nocturnal Terror, so that I may personally exsanguinate him and sup upon the crimson rivulets that course through his fetid person!" Another shuddering, orgasmic laugh punctuated this, and Venser realized he *really* didn't want to know.

The *Naglfar* continued to pull ahead in their weird race through the skies, though they were unable to shake the *Angel of Retribution*, which leered menacingly from a distance too close for any sort of comfort. Meanwhile, the *Vessel Attaining Grand Impressive Noble Achievements*, apparently with the *Divine Divinisher of Divine Divinity* stuck to it, continued to give chase, albeit poorly.

"It appears that we are losing pace with them, cultists!" proclaimed Blood

Countess Erzsébet Báthory. "Full speed ahead, so that we may apprehend them! If they get away, so goes the bounty for returning that wayward son of Aracoras! Imagine all of the bacchanalia in honor of the majesty of Astaroth, the celebratory orgies and bondage parties, we can put on with that windfall!"

"Oh, so they heard," Venser muttered.

"And where might you have heard such salacious rumors?" Matthias asked. "Whose business were you up in, bothering them for information?"

"Blood Countess Erzsébet Báthory doesn't not need to obtain information through the fetid pools of information you dredge, you disgusting lizard! The information we seek was ascertained divinely, a revelation imparted through the quivering of my clitoris in consonance with his virginal aura!" She followed this with another shuddering laugh.

"Her *what*!?" All three of them shared a look of profound disgust over this newest proclamation.

"The quivering of my clitoris has never led me astray, and the Blood Countess Erzsébet Báthory and her Coven of Unholy Nocturnal Terror shan't be kept from the bounty awaiting us!" Another laugh punctuated this.

"Look, I don't know what you think you're getting out of all of this," Matthias shot back, shaking his head in disgust and trying to stifle his horror and annoyance, "but you and…your quivering clitoris and your vagina can all putter on home with your recent conquest."

"You sanctimonious, sexist old codger! How *dare* you!?"

"Hey, *I'm* not the one who brought their clitoris into this, nor am I the one who named their vessel in a way that has the acronym spell out 'vagina'! Quite an eerie coincidence, that! Much like how I'm *sure* it's a coincidence that your group's name can be contracted down to…"

"Your blasphemous screamy-screams end today, demeaning and chauvinistic blood banquet! You deserve precise punishment by my Coven of Unholy Nocturnal Terror! Alas, due to what is clearly your malfeasant alliance with forces in opposition to our grand and glorious benefactor, we evidently are unable to keep pace, as we are not directly aided and abetted through the blessings of the waxing blood-stained penumbra of the virginal crescent moon! Accordingly, it's time we deployed our secret weapon to thumb the scales of justice forever in our favor! A gift from the great and terrible Astaroth, ruler of all and font of boundless malevolence!"

"Waxing blood-stained *what*?" Arycelle repeated, still shell-shocked over the previous disclosures. "I swear, they just came up with something that sounded florid and grandiose."

"And that weapon is *what*, exactly? Flashing your tits?" Matthias was having fun with this, now able to add "demeaning blood banquet" to the list of rude things he had been called. As this was happening, Arycelle explained what Matthias was insinuating to a confused Venser, and he tried to avoid laughing over the absurdity of their nomenclature.

"*Shut up*! I tire of your demeaning, condescending tone! A foul-tongued snake like you deserves punition of unerring and utmost precision! It is time we deployed the Astaroth Engine, the most sacred treasure of my Coven of Unholy Nocturnal Terror! He must be punished for his incredible rudeness, and he must be punished *immediately*! I shall personally unleash the crimson rivulets that course through his fetid personage and subsequently gorge upon his blood until I am sated!" Another climactic laugh punctuated this.

Slight mechanical sounds could be heard. Venser looked out the bridge to see what he could find: the *Angel of Retribution* continued to loom large, while the smaller vessel that was struggling to carry the wreckage of another on its bow struggled to keep pace. It did look like *something* was happening, but Venser couldn't make anything specific out.

"The time has come! Deploy it *now*!" she thundered, accentuating this with another of her shuddering, climaxing moans.

A loud whine cut through the air, and they saw a ship zip past them, missing the *Naglfar* by a substantial margin. It was a pitch-black vessel that was apparently decorated with sufficiently sexual metaphors, and the lurid orange-and-blue vessel impaled on the bow refused to move.

"We've overshot them!" they heard Blood Countess Erzsébet Báthory scream. "Cut power to the Astaroth Engine! We need to…*what do you mean, it can't be turned off!?*"

"Well, that's one way to get rid of them," Matthias said, their screams of panic fading away as the overclocked airship flew towards Aracoras.

"I think you're forgetting about someone," they heard Marianne say, her tone melodic and mocking.

"I could *never* forget about you, Marianne. No matter how much I might want to."

"Let's prove that, then. Here's something you and your treasonous scamps won't ever forget." The cadence of gunfire filled the air anew, and Venser felt stronger shocks, but Matthias didn't seem panicked at all.

"Is that all, dearest Marianne? Don't worry, happens to a lot of girls."

"You reinforced the ship's armor. I'm impressed. Turns out you might not just be a proverbial pretty face."

"Oh, I'm pretty now?"

"I said 'proverbial'."

"Indeed, I took care to add some thickness to the ship. I figured you'd calibrate to counter the last-known specifications of what *was* once known as the *Alamithea*, since you're on a relative budget and are more interested in revenge than in making the shiniest ship known to the skies."

"I've noticed you haven't been firing on me in return. Performance issues?"

"I'm fairly confident your hull thickness is enough, dear Marianne, to repel any attack. I focused more on upgrading our armor than our armaments. Unless you *want* me to see if Basch loaded the *special* shells today."

Venser looked quizzically over at Arycelle, who shook her head as if to indicate that there were no special shells.

"And how, exactly, are these shells *special*, Matthias? Are they shaped like little dildos?"

"They might *penetrate* your armor all the better, but bullets hardly keep their shape when fired, so I wouldn't spend the time turning them into bespoke little dildo-bullets. But if you're unwilling to bring us down, we have a wedding to get to."

Marianne sighed. "I suppose I miscalculated my ability to get you this time, Matthias," she said. "We'll have to settle this later, though. A skirmish near the airspace of a city proper is not my jam, nor is an unplanned stay in Aracoras without reason."

"And here I thought you wanted to go there at one point. We can try to settle this amicably later. Or try to, at least. I doubt it'll be all hookers and sunshine again."

"I'll take you up on that. Don't die before I can kill you, Matthias."

With that, the *Angel of Retribution* dipped and backed off from its pursuit, falling back towards another city. Matthias breathed a sigh of relief, just happy that this had ended without incident.

"That didn't go as badly as I was dreading," Arycelle said.

"You're telling me," Matthias said. "We're lucky that those two other losers showed up to provide distraction. We're close enough to Aracoras that I don't think Marianne would want to risk their ire, and I'm not sure I want to see everything she has on offer on that new ship of hers."

"I'm surprised she backed off without being fired at."

"What happened to those other two ships?" Venser asked.

"They went zipping towards Aracoras, so I presume they landed there."

Matthias smirked. "If what Venser's told us is true, I suspect they're in for a rude awakening on arrival," he said. "We should make ready for our landing, though."

The gleaming white parapets of Aracoras loomed large as the *Naglfar* descended into the harbor, lined with vessels bearing all sorts of interesting livery. Venser watched the ground approach with a strange sense of dread. He'd finally come back to Aracoras, though not like he could have imagined.

He took a moment to look at himself in the mirror. He looked little like he had when he set out: the eyes were the same, but he had developed sideburns for the first time (after being forced to shave them off), and his hair settled into a messy brown tousle on top of his head. The only constant had been his eyes, still the emerald green he had always known. Venser didn't look like he was from Aracoras, and that was a good thing.

The engines wound down, and he got up, grabbing his bag. Time to go. He stepped onto the deck to see his fellow crew members, and the Great Cathedral of Aracoras loomed front and center in their line of sight. A massive building with ornate carvings into a brilliant white façade, it attempted to command respect and attention from the get-go.

"Well, we're here," Arycelle said, looking around. "This place creeps me out." Everyone had, under Venser's advice, gotten out their best clothes, so as to leave a good impression; Basch had even put on a shirt.

"Don't let them hear that," Sebastian said. "I agree, though."

"Looks like we have company," Matthias said. "Look alive. I'll handle this." A posse of white-clad men came up to the airship, seemingly ready to apprehend them.

"State your business in Aracoras, the cradle of divinity and pinnacle of light," one of them said. His voice dripped with condescension and disdain, his blond hair shining bright in the sun.

"We are guests for the upcoming wedding of Lady Leondra and Lord Velgrand," Matthias said. "We were invited at the behest of the leadership of Electrum, and we have these articles to prove our affiliation."

"I do recall being told that there were other guests from Electrum," another of the posse said as the leader took their credentials, the medallion and the accompanying letter. "They are shabbier than I was expecting, but I suppose this is them."

"So it would seem." He handed back the articles. "It appears that you are indeed guests at the wedding. Follow us."

They walked off, and everyone dutifully followed. Venser kept his gaze ahead, while everyone else took in the sights and sounds. The city had a sterile feeling, with a general dearth of noise and activity, and immaculately-trimmed and kept bushes and livery lined the narrow thoroughfares of the city.

While it was obscured by the cathedral, the Tomb of the Almighty loomed large on the other side of the island, and Venser caught a glimpse of it. It looked like it had when he was last here, a monolith of stone that floated somewhat separate from the rest of Aracoras, with a small bridge and a path that led to a shrine at its peak. It was a place of great power and significance, and people were not freely allowed there outside of very particular occasions.

"You are among the final guests to arrive ahead of the wedding," said the leader of the entourage. "And just in time for our pre-wedding address, at that. The wedding ceremony is scheduled to be held in two days time, and it will be a grand and glorious event that honors the Almighty utterly."

"The address is to be held in the Grand Cathedral," another added. "Take your seats at the back of the room, and we shall commence with the introductions."

The quintet were ushered into the Grand Cathedral and into the main audience room, and everyone but Venser took a moment to soak in the grandeur. It was a deep, cavernous room with austere decoration and a raised dais at the back that was already being decorated for the wedding. The back wall of the Grand Cathedral contained a giant window with ornate, stained-glass depictions of some manner of divinely inspired tableau, and Venser could see the Tomb of the Almighty through it.

On the dais was a small group of six old men, and Venser recognized all of them. One was Hessler, and the other five were members of the Council of Elders. Victarion, his father, stood at the front of them, watching the last people file in. Venser hoped that he didn't look too familiar to the people there, though he was far enough back in the hall that they might not notice. They took their seats and waited for them to begin.

"It appears everyone is here," Victarion said, his voice carrying through the hall and bouncing off the walls. "I do hate repeating myself, so it is good to deliver this once and be done with it." He cleared his throat, glared condescendingly, and started into his spiel.

"Esteemed guests," Victarion started, "we welcome you to Aracoras on the most sacred of occasions: the uniting of Lunaria and Aracoras, our two great cities, in marriage. In two days, we will welcome Lady Leondra of Aracoras into our family as she accepts her role as the wife of my youngest son, Velgrand. While this happens in the wake of the unfortunate disappearance of her intended fiancé, Venser, this shall still be cause for celebration all the same, bringing our cities closer together and ushering in a new era of prosperity and collaboration."

Dutiful applause followed this, and Venser looked across at his companions to see how they reacted to this. Nobody looked particularly pleased, and Arycelle's look of distaste was most pronounced of all.

"Following this sacred ritual, the union of man and woman in the most sanctified, glorious, and consecrated bond of holy matrimony under the eternally watchful purview of the Almighty themselves, we will have another sacred ritual to attend to. It has come time to open the Tomb of the Almighty, returning to the world our most benevolent and beneficent Almighty, to shower their blessings upon us!"

Murmurs of interest rippled through the cathedral, breaking into dutiful applause. Venser thought he saw Hessler's face light up a bit more from this, but it could have just been a trick of the lighting.

"As for the festivities. Tonight, we shall have a banquet in honor of the bride and groom, and there will be optional entertainment opportunities for you on the morrow you may choose from. To avoid perturbing the sanctity of our noble and sacred activities, we would like to offer to you guided tours of our exalted paradise so that you may get to know Aracoras better, and you will only be allowed to explore our sanctified paradise within one of these organized and curated excursions."

There were murmurs from the crowd, but nothing beyond that. Venser wasn't surprised by this.

"Hessler, do you have anything to add?" He received a head shake in negation. "That can be good for now, then. Remember that your conduct reflects on more than just yourselves, and it should always be in honor of the Almighty, both here and elsewhere. We should clear out while the administrators and arbiters of justice set up, as well as to allow space for the trial of those intruders."

"Intruders?" Matthias whispered.

"Should you want to watch that, you may. For now, we are adjourned. Speak to a guard if you desire to be shown to your quarters for the nonce."

Most people remained seated, out of curiosity for the trial that had been promised, and the men on the dais left the room. Before anyone had time to really get up and interact, another man came into the room, dressed in a way that suggested he was a magistrate or judge of some kind.

"All rise for the convening of the Court of the Divine Order," he thundered. "You are guests to a sitting of the most exalted court of them all. Take notes, if you will, as you may learn much from our proceedings."

They had all risen, and Venser thought he recognized the man in the robes. It looked like one of his brothers, which didn't surprise him.

"Bring forth the sinners, the unwashed swine who have wrought grievous offenses upon the sacred idyll we have swathed ourselves in!"

Commotion could be heard from the side of the room as guards ushered in a group of people. It appeared to be fourteen in all: thirteen were clad in black robes that looked familiar, and the odd one out was an extravagantly-dressed and markedly diminutive man whose attire screamed out in a desperate play for authority and plea for attention. They were escorted to right in front of the dais, and the man on it glared down at them. His expression was one of utter contempt.

"You stand before the paramount magistrate of Aracoras, Vectoringame," he said. It *was* his brother, Venser thought. Second-oldest out of the ten of them. "State your names for the Court of the Divine Order, so that we may know the identities of the sinners in our presence."

"You speak with such condescension towards the great and terrible Blood Countess Erzsébet Báthory, High Priestess of the Coven of Unholy Nocturnal Terror and prophetess of Astaroth, the one true god!" squealed the leader of the black-clad gang, her red-framed glasses perched precariously upon her proboscis.

The other members of the Coven of Unholy Nocturnal Terror gave their names in turn, along with threats of divine retributions upon the proceedings by Astaroth. Venser thought he heard them offer names like "Thrussy" and "Bussy", each of them ending with the same last sound. He glanced over at Matthias, who was trying to not laugh.

"Archduke Emperor Pope Guillaume XIII refuses to acknowledge the feigned authority of a weasel borrowing the robes and trappings of justice and morality!" thundered the man. "He stands above this shambolic attempt at morality, this play at justice without the backing of true divinity!"

"*That's* what he looks like?" Venser whispered. He wasn't sure what he was expecting the man to look like, but this was not it.

"I know, right?" Basch replied. "He's certainly a piece of work."

"You stand before me having committed a grievous sin against Aracoras, blasphemy and desecration through incursion upon our sacred grounds without leave," Vectoringame said. He leered menacingly from the dais as he said this. "Your crimes are clear, your blaspheming presences sufficient proof of your transgressions. Do you acknowledge the unmistakable weight and gravity of your guilt?"

"We are innocent of all things you accuse us of!" Blood Countess Erzsébet Báthory whined. "We are a pious and well-behaved organization in service of the infallible and omnipotent Astaroth, induced to sin by this morally and fiscally bankrupt crook!" This was met with murmurs of concurrence from the fellow members of the Coven of Unholy Nocturnal Terror.

"Archduke Emperor Pope Guillaume XIII will not debase himself and the dignity of the Educational Guidance Council! Accordingly, he will not partake in this charade, this masquerade, this hollow play! He is a great distance above the self-styled court you pretend to administer your flimsy attempts at justice from!"

"It is clear that you do not accept your guilt, and so thus your sentence must reflect as such. In seventy-two hours, you shall be returned to the loving embrace of the Almighty, their mercy and their benevolence washing away your sins and granting you absolution in the process. You shall be detained until your sentence is to be carried out. So it has been proclaimed, and so it *will* be done." Vectoringame brought down a gavel to signal the finalization of their sentences.

"We are innocent! Innocent, we say! Astaroth shall not take your farcical play at justice lightly! May his return come quickly, and may he devour you all for being unworthy!"

"Archduke Emperor Pope Guillaume XIII shan't accept the so-called judgment of a sham court, one not guided by divinity!"

They were hauled away, and Venser noted that they were scheduled for execution after the wedding. The florid language hid that this was, indeed, them getting their heads lopped off, either literally or figuratively. Mustn't let a little bloodshed spoil a wedding, though.

17

Luminescent Spires

"As far as trials go," Matthias said, "that was the shortest one I've ever witnessed. Called them guilty, sentenced them, and hauled them off." People had begun to filter out of the cathedral, and they wanted to not be among the initial crush.

"The verdict is always guilty, and the sentence is always death," Venser said. "To face a trial before the magistrates of Aracoras is to have your fate already decided."

"Presumption of irrevocable guilt *would* certainly expedite the legal process. How do they meet their ends, anyways?"

"I don't know for sure, actually. Executions were always a closed affair. I know that the bodies were dropped into the cloud sea in the dead of night."

"I'd say this is all the more reason to not draw their ire," Sebastian said. "On an unrelated note, did you bring our gift?"

"They already took it away," Matthias said. "They wanted to get it ready for the 'presentation of tribute', as they apparently called it. *Unfortunately*, they insisted that any markings as to who gave the gift be removed, so as to not allow attention to be drawn away from the couple."

"And I'm sure whatever you got them is going to go over *so* well," Basch said.

"I think *one* of them will like it." The grin Matthias had on his face was as mischievous as they got.

"So, next on the agenda is supper, right?" Arycelle asked.

"It should be," Venser said. "It's late enough that they'd want to get to it once everything is ready."

"Let's go see if it is, then," Matthias said. "I'm certainly up for a good meal."

The banquet hall was already packed by the time they arrived, and the group was led over to join the Electrum delegation at their table. As they walked over, a thin young man rose to meet them, his bearing like Elessa's.

"You're the guests my sister told me about," he said, shaking their hands vigorously. "I'm Erdrick, her brother. Elessa's brother. She asked me to attend the festivities in her stead."

"A pleasure to meet you, Erdrick," Venser said.

"You must be...ah, are you using that name here?"

"Oh...just call me Victor for now."

"I see, I see. Anyway, have a seat, have a seat. The bride-to-be and groom-to-be have yet to make an appearance, but they should show up soon."

They joined the Electrum entourage, and each of them tucked into the food on hand. It reminded Venser of that first banquet he had in Lunaria at the start of his journey, though worse. It was all very bland, the meat texture felt a bit rubbery and unpleasant, the sauce was flavorless and congealed, and the garnishes were limp. It looked the part, but failed to deliver.

"Don't tell them," Arycelle said, "but this food isn't that good."

"It's like they went through the motions, but didn't know what they were doing," Sebastian added.

Basch set down his fork. "I don't think I've had food this bad in years," he said. "It's bad in an interesting way, so I guess that's remarkable?"

"It feels a bit like Lunaria told them what to make, and they didn't know how to make it," Venser said. "These dishes feel a lot like the ones I had in the palace in Lunaria, back when I got there. The food they'd make on their own here is a lot simpler and heartier, with much less meat than this."

"I see, I see," Erdrick said. Venser took a closer look at him, noting the angular features and black hair framing his face. He looked reedy, for lack of a better word, but his demeanor was friendly and warm.

The din of the dining room dropped off markedly, and everyone instinctively turned to the front of the room. Into the room came the bride and groom, Leondra and Velgrand. Leondra had been made up to have an appallingly pale complexion, and her hair had been pulled into the beehive hairdo that Aracoras women often kept. All in all, she looked thoroughly miserable. Velgrand was short and plump, with stringy blond hair and an unpleasantly ruddy complexion. Following them were Victarion, Hessler, and Venser's mother, who joined them at the front of the room.

"We present our soon-to-be bride and groom, Leondra and Velgrand," boomed Victarion. Dutiful applause followed this proclamation, and they had a seat.

The meal continued, and Venser occasionally glanced at the front table where the guests of honor were located. Velgrand was chatting animatedly with their mother, Hessler and Victarion were talking, and Leondra looked like she wished she was anywhere but here. He felt bad, but what could he do?

As the evening wore on, Victarion got their attention once again. "I believe," he said, "we should allow the betrothed pair to open one of the pieces of tribute afforded to them on the occasion of their nuptials." He motioned, and a wagon containing all of the wrapped boxes was wheeled into the dining room.

"Ooh, prethenth!" Velgrand exclaimed. He had a marked lisp that made it sometimes hard to make out what he was saying, and Venser recalled that their mother was vehemently against any sort of training to remove it, because it would "tire out her baby".

"Yes, presents. Pick one, and you and Leondra can open it. The rest will be opened later."

"There are tho many giftth, I have no idea know which one to open firtht!" He got up and perused the wagon intensely and intently. "Ooh, I wanna open thith one!"

The box he procured was the long, skinny one Matthias had shown them in Balmung. As soon as he grabbed it, Matthias tried to stifle a snort of laughter. Venser had no idea what was in there, and his laugh suggested that whatever it was would be a *spectacle*.

"All right, sit down and open it," Victarion said.

The audience raptly watched as Velgrand flailed around with the wrapping paper, finally tearing it off and getting to the box. He opened it up, reached in, and pulled out...

"What ith *thith?*"

Velgrand was holding a large stone, phallic in appearance. Made of a delicate pink skystone, its shape was unmistakable, a thick shaft that made women *shudder*.

"Did you buy him a *dildo?*" Basch whispered to Matthias, his voice a mix of shock and amusement. The audience began to murmur with laughter, and Matthias was trying to not talk, lest the laughter consume him.

"Thith lookth like a paperweight," Velgrand said, turning it over. He was oblivious to the wide-eyed horror on his parents' faces. "It doeth not look like any paperweight I have ever theen before. It even vibrateth a bit."

Venser looked at Leondra, who was trying to stifle laughter of her own. Her eyes lit up a bit, and the misery wrought on her face had abated somewhat.

"Why are you laughing?" Velgrand demanded, turning to Leondra. "What ith tho funny?"

"Someone got you a dildo," she answered. "It's not a paperweight. It's... meant to pleasure someone, and it's shaped like a..."

The realization slowly dawned on his face as the laughter became more audible, the audience unable to contain their amusement over the son of the High Priest of Aracoras getting a sex toy as a wedding gift. Velgrand turned red, and he burst into sobs over the thought of people laughing at him. Instinctively, Venser's mother took him and ushered him out of the room, consoling him. Victarion followed, along with Hessler and Leondra. It had happened quickly, but they got the feeling that the banquet was, by and large, over as Velgrand's sobs faded.

"That was...something," Erdrick said, trying to rein in his laughter.

"I'll say," Venser said. "He was not happy, and my mother certainly was not thrilled."

"Fancy that," Basch said. "No wonder *someone* didn't want us to see the gift before he opened it."

They all looked at Matthias, who was trying to quit laughing. The gift of a giant dildo had seemingly had its desired effect, on both the gifter and the giftee.

The guest quarters were located not too far from the dining room. Much to their chagrin, they were strictly segregated by sex, and so Arycelle had to split up from the group. Matthias and Sebastian were to room together, and Venser and Basch had the other room.

"What an introduction," Basch said. They were in their room, having locked the door. "I hope Matthias doesn't get us in trouble for his little stunt."

"They'll have trouble tracking the gift back to us," Venser said. "Unless he takes ownership, all they know is that it was a black-wrapped box with no other identifiers. Gifts are stripped of their identification for these ceremonies, as the deliverer is insignificant…in theory, of course."

"That's a relief, at least. You saw Leondra, though, right? She did not look happy."

"Not at all. I feel bad for her, having to deal with my brother. Looks like Mother's still protective and coddling towards him."

"Very much so, from what I saw. Has she always been like that with him?"

"So far as I can recall, yes." Venser frowned as his memory churned, remembering all the times his mother had protected Velgrand from any sort of adversity. It had gotten to where the threat of a single tear put his mother into full protection mode.

They fell into silence, and Venser thought about his room. It might not be impossible to get into it, but he'd have to plan carefully to sneak around. He could do that tomorrow night. For now, though, he wanted to sleep.

He yawned and laid down in his bed. There were two single beds in their room, clearly meant to dissuade people from any sorts of shenanigans, as they were. They were certainly not comfortable, with an extremely firm mattress and thin pillows, and Venser found himself wishing he had his bed on the *Naglfar* again.

"You don't seem comfortable," Basch said. Venser rolled over and saw Basch laying there, clearly wishing the same.

"I forgot how awful these beds are."

"I wasn't expecting it myself."

Venser tried to drift to sleep again, but it proved elusive. His mind kept wandering, a strange sense of unease haunting his dreams and permeating his thoughts. Finally, he got out of bed and stretched, trying to shake the thoughts away.

"You too?" Basch was still awake, and Venser nodded.

Despite the bed being small, Basch drew Venser to him, and the two found sleep in each other's arms. It was weird, Venser thought, how well and how quickly they had grown close, but there was something there he really liked. Basch liked it as well, else he wouldn't have stuck around.

The day before the wedding was a day filled with several exciting activities, or activities billed as such. First on the agenda was a guided tour of Aracoras, to see all of the sights that they wanted their visitors to see. They were taken in groups of six, and their sixth was none other than Isamu, sent by his father on the occasion of the wedding.

"Fancy seeing all of you here," he said, enthusiastically greeting all of them. "It's been a while, hasn't it?"

"That it has," Matthias said. "You've been keeping out of trouble, I hope?"

"Relatively." He had a smirk that suggested that he hadn't been doing that…more that he had gotten better at not being caught.

"Your father sent you to represent Sorocco at the wedding, then?" Venser asked.

"Yes, though…I kinda insisted that I go as our representative. I'm not thrilled about the wedding, and I want to stop it if I can." Isamu's voice almost contained hints of longing.

"So you can marry Leondra yourself?" Matthias teased.

"No! Uh, I mean…if she asked me, I wouldn't say no." He was blushing. "We've been friends for so long, and she gets me, and I don't know if she has anyone else in her life..."

"Ooh, you *fancy* her. We can talk about it later, though. Let's focus on the tour."

"Oh, yeah! Right. The tour. How...exciting."

The first stop was the Garden of the Heavenly Ideal, done up in full livery. This was definitely a "good" year for the gardens, Venser noticed. Many lavish plant arrangements were on hand, all immaculately trimmed and with flawless white blossoms. Their guide explained how only the purest, whitest blooms were allowed to adorn plants in the Garden of the Heavenly Ideal, a reflection of the intangible virtue that exuded from every soul and every heart in Aracoras. Venser added, quiet enough so the guide couldn't hear, that any blooms that didn't meet their exacting standards were excised.

"Truly, this garden is a reflection of our inner piety and unimpeachable virtue," the guide crowed.

"They're pretty," Arycelle said, "but it's all so boring."

"Silence, woman!" he hissed. "Speak not on matters about which you lack knowledge."

"I agree with her," Sebastian said, glaring pointedly. "And don't insult my girlfriend like that. Not very virtuous to try and punch down at her, is it?"

The guide's response was to sputter and disengage, clearly not keen on further conversation with people he viewed as beneath him. While he sulked, Venser quietly told them about how the garden's extravagance waxed and waned as a reflection of the city's fortunes, and that this appeared to be a rather bountiful period.

The next stop on their tour was passing by the Pillar of Purification, which was a glorified name for their jail. They didn't go inside, though they noticed guards stationed outside it. This was where Archduke Emperor Pope Guillaume XIII and the Coven of Unholy Nocturnal Terror were being held, awaiting the enactment of their *final* judgment. Venser thought he heard commotion from inside the Pillar of Purification, and he wondered how lively the prisoners were.

Past that, they stopped at a fountain, and their guide gave its name as the "Vestibule of Divinity". Ornate and elaborate, it was meant to convey a sense of opulence and power. This was where they encountered another of the touring groups, composed of Basch's brothers and their female companions.

"Looks like our brother made it after all," Sigmund scoffed.

"And here I had hoped he would have found some tail to chase far away from us," Richter sneered.

"I suppose that's what passes for a greeting from you these days," Basch sighed. "I even see you have your trollops with you. We met Zsa Zsa, though I don't think we had the chance to meet Richter's victim."

"Oh-em-gee, you awe *so* wude, uwu," Zsa Zsa replied. Her pigtails had extra ribbons in them today, and nobody wanted to tell Sigmund that she looked especially like a little girl.

"Like, oh-em-gee, such a presumptuous boor," the other woman with them scoffed. She was also vaguely evocative of a young girl, albeit with a short bob instead of pigtails in her hair, though her vocal patterns were more akin to those of a teenager. "Do you *know* these people, Snuggle Bear?"

"Uh...yes, I unfortunately know them, Magdalyna," Richter answered, blushing.

"Such a tragedy that you know us, Snuggle Bear," Basch said, smiling. "You wouldn't want them to listen to your brother tell them about your fondness for...literature of a certain persuasion, I imagine."

"*Don't call me that!*"

"Zsa Zsa doesn't think you was supposed to caww him that in pubwic, owo."

"Keep your cutesy nicknames to the bedroom," Sigmund glared. "You're going to embarrass us."

"Like, don't talk back to Magdalyna! Why are you being *so* mean to me?"

"How am I being mean to you?"

"Did you not or did you not come for me just now?"

"I'm not entirely sure what's going on," Matthias said, raising an eyebrow. "But it sounds like Magdalyna might not have gotten up on the right side of the bed."

"Like, why would you say something like that to me?" Magdalyna whined, starting to sound more flustered. "Why are you attacking me like this?"

"Calm down, Magdalyna!" Richter pleaded. "Don't mind my brother and his ruffians! They're not attacking you!"

"*I feel very attacked!*"

"...owo, what's this?" Zsa Zsa squealed, grabbing at Sigmund's crotch.

"Not now, Snuggle Muffin! Not in public!" Sigmund whispered. He blushed and tried to get her to not grab him like that in public, hoping that their guide wouldn't notice.

"Anyway, we should probably continue our tour," Richter said, trying to console Magdalyna and calm her down. "Hopefully Magdalyna will calm down when she doesn't have to see your face. Hope we see you never, little brother."

"The feeling is mutual," Basch growled.

As the other group walked away, Venser noticed his headache, brought about by Zsa Zsa's presence, had abated. It was more intense this time, though, and he wondered if Magdalyna had the same thing about her as Zsa Zsa did. Whatever it was, it did not bode well.

"Have your brothers always liked girls that looked like they were still teenagers?" Matthias asked.

Basch groaned. "Yes," he said. "Sigmund has, at least. Just…please don't remind me."

Following an explanation of the innermost virtue of the fountain, the last stop on their tour was a glimpse of the Tomb of the Almighty. It was separated off from the main body of Aracoras, a tall monolithic shard with connecting bridges drawn to it. It was massive, and guards flanked it to ensure nobody could sneak up to the shrine at the top.

"And this is the heart and soul of Aracoras. You look upon the Tomb of the Almighty, resting place of the one true divinity," the guide said. "The shrine at the pinnacle is the closest one can get to the Almighty, and only occasional forays are permitted for the occasion of veneration. May their return come quickly and shower us in the blessings that we are due."

"That's certainly an impressive hunk of rock," Matthias said, looking up at it.

As Venser stared at it, a strange feeling washed over him. It was almost like he could hear a throb, the sound of something *inside* the Tomb of the Almighty. His mind tried to plumb his memories to remember this happening before, but he was drawing a blank.

"Are you okay?" Basch asked, noticing Venser's intense stare.

"I...I think so. We can talk about it later. It's just...there's a strange feeling I get when I'm looking at the Tomb of the Almighty." Venser finally took his eyes off, realizing that he wouldn't get much from continuing to stare at it.

"Me too," Matthias said. "In particular, I feel hungry."

"You ate three massive plates of food for breakfast!" Arycelle retorted.

"Still hungry. Those pastries were very dry."

"You're going to have to suffer until lunch, then," Isamu said. "As will I, it turns out. Who knows, maybe our suffering will make us better people. That's what they espouse here, right?"

"How *dare* you presume such things!" the guide sputtered. "Aracoras is an enlightened city bereft of suffering and squalor, unlike the filthy demesne that is your abode!"

They turned to Venser, who quietly nodded to affirm Isamu's statement.

"What would *he* know about the innermost workings of our sanctified paradise?"

"More than you, it seems," Venser responded.

"And what does *that* mean?"

Nobody responded, leaving the guide to sputter further and bring them to the ending point of their tour.

Following the lunch that Isamu and Matthias desired, which did little to abate their hunger, the next event was the production of a play. Venser explained, as they finished food, that they often put on "divinely-inspired plays" as means of entertainment, supposed to provide their audience with insights into the nature of true virtue and piety. His mother was a prolific writer of such plays, and the title to be put on today was one of hers, the delightfully-named *Heaven's March 18: Chastisement of the Sinful Swine and Ascension of the Heavenly Ideal*.

"Who comes up with the titles?" Basch asked in a whisper as they took their seats.

"She does," Venser replied. "The longer the title, the more feted she thinks they ultimately will be."

The play began, the story of which ostensibly followed the travails of a chaste maiden (whose name was never given, as to allow the audience to directly relate to the protagonist more) as she attempted to fend off suitors who tried to drag her into a life of sin and squalor. Or, rather, she was tempted towards such by each of them, but the personifications of virtue and chastity pulled her back from the brink each time, reaching out like a *deus ex machina* to open her eyes and throw off the yoke the temptations attempted to thrust upon her.

To call it "flimsy" would be accurate, as the plot was plodding, the pacing was ponderous, and the characterization was thin and one-dimensional. The dialogue was artless, the stage direction was wooden, and there weren't musical numbers or points of comic relief, features that Venser's mother thought were clearly beneath her talents. The sum was something that *resembled* theater, but had nothing theatrical. As a child, Venser remembered being compelled to sit through showings of his mother's other plays and sometimes take part in them, and the ones he remembered were all similar to *Heaven's March 18* in style, structure, and intended moral teachings; they also all were beset by the same issues of stilted dialogue, poor stage direction, and heavy-handed moralizing at the expense of everything else.

He looked across at the group he was with. Isamu, still seated with them, was bored out of his mind. Sebastian and Arycelle had gone for a nap. Matthias seemed to be fiddling with a sketch pad and a pencil. Basch also looked impressively bored, and he and Venser had taken to surreptitiously holding hands and playing with each other in lieu of actually being entertained by the performance.

After what felt like an eternity, the play concluded, and polite applause emanated from the crowd, applause that caused everyone who had lost interest to snap to attention. Venser's mother then stepped onto the stage that had just been vacated. She bore a triumphant smile, clearly pleased with how her production had gone.

"Thank you for your warm reception," she said. Her voice had always been oddly cold, lacking maternal warmth to Venser's ears. "I am Lady Venaria, wife to High Priest Victarion, and mother to the groom-to-be in tomorrow's festivities, Velgrand. I am also the author of *Heaven's March*, both this play and the seventeen that preceded it. Writing has always been my passion, my drive beyond serving my role as the faithful partner to the High Priest, and I hope to bring to the masses a sense of morality that is sadly nowhere near as prevalent as it should be in today's society." This was met with further polite applause, and she waited before continuing.

"The ideas of *Heaven's March 18* came to me in the throes of…grief, I suppose you could say. It was not supposed to be my little Velgrand who was to be married on the morrow. His brother, Venser, was betrothed to Lady Leondra, but he has been…abducted. No news has come back as to his whereabouts, the identity of the scoundrels who could have made off with him, or if he is even still alive. But the marriage…it must happen, and it has come time for my baby to be wed to fulfill a greater role in the sanctity of our sanctuary."

Basch squeezed Venser's hand protectively, and Venser squeezed back. Hearing his name in such a context was still odd. His mother was tearing up, but he knew it was over the prospects of her little baby, Velgrand, getting married off.

"This installment of *Heaven's March* is one that might be…a direct response to this adversity. My emotions poured forth into this piece, and I hope that all of you were able to grasp the depths of my despair, the valleys of my sorrow, and the pits of my woe."

"I don't think I grasped much besides boredom," Arycelle muttered.

"You and I both," Isamu added.

Polite applause carried through the theater as she bid them farewell, and everyone got up to leave. As they did so, Venser looked up at his mother on the stage, wondering if she recognized him. The gaze he was met with was unfamiliar and cold, suggesting that she did not. Had he changed *that* much, so as to be unrecognizable to his own family? He didn't mind that, but it was still a weird thought.

The evening came and went with a banquet, and everyone had finished up for the evening. Velgrand had gotten to open another of his presents, and it looked like it was hastily re-wrapped, much to the amusement of Venser and everyone else; it was a gaudy tapestry woven with some manner of vague landscape depiction in mind, the kind of gift one gets so as to not think too hard about the act of giving a gift. Eventually, the wedding party retired to continue preparations, signaling everyone else to leave. As they prepared to do so, an attendant came up to the group, seemingly from Leondra's retinue.

"You are part of the delegation from Electrum, correct?" he asked.

"That is correct," Matthias said.

"I was asked by Lady Leondra if she could have a chance to talk to one of you, in particular. She told me that they are a dear friend, and a chance to talk to them would put her mind at ease before tomorrow." He pointed his finger at Venser, having picked out who she wanted by physical description.

"Me?" Venser asked. "If she wants to talk to me, I'm happy to have a word with her. Uh...can I bring a friend?"

"You may, but all of this needs to be done quietly. She is not supposed to see anyone, much less men before her wedding day. But she was insistent, and I suppose I can keep a secret." He had a wry smile on his face.

"All right. Basch, if you would?"

"Certainly." Basch stepped forward and followed Venser, while the rest left for their quarters. They were taken to a small drawing room not far from the banquet hall, one with a guard stationed outside. With a nod, the two men were ushered inside, the attendant waiting outside.

Leondra was sitting in a chair, waiting for them. Her hair was in the ludicrous beehive style women were forced to wear, portrayed as a sign of piety and devotion in Aracoras, and her dress had been swapped out to a formless, billowing white garment. When the door closed, she rose to meet them.

"Venser!" she exclaimed. It was certainly not amorous, more the sound of someone reunited with a friend they'd been separated from. All the same, she couldn't help herself, and she rushed over to hug him.

"It's good to see you, Leondra," Venser replied.

"I'm so sorry about all of this," she said. "I...we have a bit to discuss, and not much time to discuss it."

"It's okay. You don't need to apologize."

"I know, I know. It's just..." She sighed heavily, trying to fend off emotion.

"I know. A lot has happened. I have much to tell you, as well."

"I imagine." She turned to Basch. "And I see you've been taking care of him. Basch, was it? We didn't talk much during my travels."

"You remember correctly, lady," Basch said, smiling. "And that's on me."

Venser sat down with Leondra, and they began to talk. It turned out that, right as Leondra prepared to return home, the deepest parts of the archives held information that matched what Venser had learned on Calaveras. That is, the Tomb of the Almighty actually held not the convalescing Almighty, but the remains of the dark god, Ack-Tar, and the whereabouts of the Almighty were unknown. What Venser wasn't prepared for was the other tidbit: the Tomb of the Almighty's seal was not meant to last forever, and it had begun to weaken at an accelerating pace from what people could glean. It would naturally open if given enough time, but the tomb could be opened with a bit of a proverbial nudge, which was the intention of the "big event" after the wedding.

"My father is obsessed with opening the Tomb of the Almighty, and the ceremony tomorrow could be a ritual sacrifice for all he cares," she said. "The intensity of his focus and his mania...I've begun to wonder if there's something else pulling the strings."

Venser frowned. "Someone pulling the strings..." he repeated. "Do you think...that Hellvira's involved?"

"I'd bet money on it, Venser. My father's been keeping counsel with her consistently, so long as I can remember. She loves to talk about how the opening of the Tomb of the Almighty is the elixir to cure the ills of the world, quashing all of the discord and ushering in a new era of peace."

"If this Ack-Tar is entombed inside," Basch said, "then it's clear she's lying to all of us."

"I'm curious as to *how* she's doing the manipulating, though," Leondra said.

"You mean besides the trick where she makes every man nearby go googly-eyed over her?"

"That *is* an interesting trick, but I don't think it properly explains how she's gotten into my father's ear like she has. If we knew how she did it, I suppose it could prove useful." She smiled as she thought about it.

"Unfortunately, I think we're out of time," Venser said, shaking his head. "We can try to make a scene at the wedding, but will that help?"

"I don't know, but it might. We're low on time and light on options. If we can keep them from opening the Tomb of the Almighty, it's a chance worth taking."

Basch whistled. "I suppose it would also have the upshot of potentially keeping you from marrying that insipid moron," he said. "No guarantees, though."

"*Are* there guarantees?"

"Oh, yeah," Venser added. "Isamu's here as well. He's hoping the wedding goes poorly."

"I bet he is," she smiled. "He always was bad at hiding his emotions. I…don't know if I feel about him like he does about me, but we can figure that out. Let's get through tomorrow first."

"Right, tomorrow."

"I'm guessing you haven't gotten to speak to your parents yet?"

"I…I have not, and I don't know that I want to," Venser said, wincing. "They seem to have moved on from me, and…"

"Is something wrong?"

He sighed. "When I was in Balmung, the leader told me that I looked like an adventurer who had gone to Aracoras in search of the Tomb of the Almighty. The timing of the excursion…it happened before I was born, by a bit less than a year."

Leondra frowned, as if to process the information, before gasping. "You think…" she started.

"I'm wondering if my father is *actually* my father, yes. There's a lot of circumstantial evidence that lines up. I look different, my parents have always treated me coldly, and...I guess I've always felt like I don't *belong*. Like a stranger in my own land."

"I see. I guess, then, it was almost good that we were betrothed at one point. If not for me, then for you. That you were able to find something approximating home."

"I'm not there yet. I think I'm getting there, though. But were it not for you, I'd never have gotten that chance. For that...thank you, Leondra."

The two hugged again. Venser knew it was time to part, as there was only so long one could evade the gaze of the guardsmen of Aracoras.

That night, Venser had managed to collect the small amount of belongings from his old room, the spoils of a surreptitious nighttime excursion. He encountered no resistance and no trouble, using the secret corridors and passageways he had learned of as a youth, and he had come away with a couple small trinkets and his childhood journals. The rooms were empty at that time, his family members attending a late-evening service or something of that nature in advance of the wedding tomorrow.

All the same, he didn't want to linger. The memories he had from his life in Aracoras weren't particularly happy ones, and he didn't want to risk running into his family and forcing an awkward confrontation. Outside of possibly his younger sister, with whom his relationship was at least not entirely negative, he didn't want to deal with any of them and would not particularly miss them after he'd made his final farewells to Aracoras after the wedding.

The journals, though, he wanted to keep. Those were memories he could revisit with time. That time was not now, though, and he fell asleep in Basch's arms after a brief bout of passion with his boyfriend. There was something almost exciting about doing it in Aracoras, a place that actively tried to suppress any sort of emotion and romance, and his climax felt like a last shot of defiance against a place he had chosen to leave behind.

The moon looked similar to the day he'd arrived in Lunaria. He realized that he hadn't needed to look at the moon much; the people on the ground were more interesting anymore, and his life satisfying enough that he didn't need such distractions.

18

The Pinnacle of Light

"I've always hated weddings," Basch growled. "They're always a show of style over substance, and the style is always very dubious."

The crew of the *Naglfar* were at breakfast, enjoying a meal before the festivities. They had been warned both that they would be leaving shortly after the ceremonies and that there would be no occasions for food during the wedding, so they saw fit to load up on food while it was available. Even with as dry as they were, a pastry was still a pastry.

"I would say 'look at the upside: free food'," Matthias said, "but it feels like we're not getting even that afterwards. They're kicking us out after the ceremony and the 'special festivities to follow'. I wonder what *those* could be."

Venser frowned. "Weddings in Aracoras are normally turgid, dry affairs," he said. "Don't look forward to excitement."

"Even with who's getting married?" Sebastian asked.

"That wouldn't change much about the program. While there's always clear favoritism, and I feel like Mother would go all-out to make her little treasure's 'special day' as special as possible, they have a general script they follow. Lots of dry and dull hymns, preaching about the various roles of husband and wife, and all that."

"I'm looking forward to their reasonable and progressive take on what women should do," Arycelle said, her tone suggesting that she was very much not looking forward to this.

"I bet you are," Matthias grinned. "I recommend ignoring all of their advice."

"One step ahead of you."

Venser smiled. "Coming back here's been enlightening for seeing the face they present to the public," he said, "as well as how I've changed."

"You *have* changed," Matthias said. "You're nowhere near as scared to talk to people, and you seem a bit more sure of yourself overall. Still scared to be on the airship deck, though."

"We…can work on that." They all had a laugh over this.

"Let's see how this wedding goes," Arycelle said, frowning. "I'm hoping everything goes like we're hoping, but with a ceremony like this, who knows?"

As they sat and ate, people started filtering out and to the Grand Cathedral. When they were the last people there, they knew it was time to go. The wedding they had hoped to stop was beginning, and while he was not optimistic, Venser still held out hope that there might be a way to stop what might be coming, for both Leondra and the unsuspecting people who thought it would be simple nuptials.

Among the final people to arrive at the Grand Cathedral, the crew of the *Naglfar* were seated in the back of the cathedral. The pews were uncomfortably familiar to Venser, stiff and claustrophobic. He wound up sitting between Basch and Matthias, and he took a moment to survey the room and see who was where. He thought he saw Isamu near the middle-front of their side of the pews, and he thought he could see Sigmund, Richter, and their "companions" on the other side of the room.

At the front of the room in pews were his eight siblings uninvolved in the wedding, as well as the spouses to those who had been married off (everyone but his younger sister). His father and mother sat on one side of the dais, with Hessler on the other and a disgruntled-looking priest in the middle to officiate everything. The rest of the Council of Elders was seated at the front, though separate from his siblings.

Venser looked at Hessler's face...or tried to, a hard task from where he was sitting. The man seemed impassive, oddly disinterested in the impending nuptials and a contrast to his mother's rapt sorrow and excitement. He looked *bored*, a weird reaction for someone whose daughter was getting married. Was he only interested in the opening of the Tomb of the Almighty?

Once everyone had gotten seated, the officiant cleared his throat. "Esteemed guests, gathered from near and afar," he started, his unctuous tone an interesting choice for a wedding, "I welcome you to our sanctified sanctum, to bear witness to the ceremony of holy matrimony we have gathered for today. By the end of the day, the houses of Lunaria and Aracoras will forever be united in the sacred bond known to us, that of marriage, as Lord Velgrand takes Lady Leondra to be his wife."

The tone and tenor of the invective that followed was familiar to Venser. It was a detailing of the virtue of the sacred marital bond between man and woman, how the man was akin to a pillar rising tall and supporting the fabric of morality, while the woman was the foundation, protected by the man's form from the squalid excess of reality. It was the usual patriarchal content, and Venser noticed Arycelle had a look of disgust that was shared by everyone else in his group.

He would have been expected to absorb all of this sermon without question at one point. One didn't have the liberty to question their view of how men and women were meant to associate with one another. Yet all of his travel and experience had rendered the sermon meaningless noise to him, a web of propaganda and half-truths easily confuted, and he wondered if anyone who wasn't from Aracoras actually took anything meaningful away from this.

The man stepped back, and a small choir took the stage to sing a hymn. It was one Venser knew by heart, and he tried to not sing along, settling for inaudibly mouthing the words. The words were in an ancient, otherwise-forgotten language that only resurfaced for ecclesiastical purposes in Aracoras. What they *meant* had also been lost to memory, and they just cared to repeat the sounds that they had been taught. Words that once had intent and purpose, now reduced to sounds that meant whatever the listener thought they meant or wanted them to mean, and Venser wondered if they even meant anything at all.

"How long is this supposed to go?" Matthias whispered.

"As long as they want it to," Venser replied. "It's usually a couple songs between parts of the sermon."

"*Parts* of the sermon?" Basch asked, appalled.

"They like to hear themselves talk. And with the High Priest's son being involved, the ceremony needs to be long enough to match his importance."

As promised, the choir gave way to a resumption in the sermon, this part talking about the virtue of the union and how this would inevitably bring all parties together in harmony. It wasn't anything new to Venser, the same platitudes about harmony and peace, but it all rang weirdly hollow. It was like the officiant hadn't been told that the point of this was to give Aracoras a fat sum of money and to give Hessler access to the Tomb of the Almighty. That a wedding was happening besides was almost incidental, he felt.

Following yet *another* musical number in the divine tongue, the officiant returned to the stage. "It is time," he said, "to commence the sacred duty with which we have been charged today! I bid you, please rise to your feet to honor Lord Velgrand, the man who will be united in the most holy of bonds today, that of matrimony!"

All rose out of their pews as the groom entered the cathedral. Velgrand walked into the hall between the pews, dressed in pure-white robes with minimal ornamentation. He had what looked like a tiara on his head, a brilliant piece that reflected light in a very distinct way; Venser recognized it as the Sun Crown, one of the relics occasionally worn by the High Priest of Aracoras in their ministerial duties. He was amused that his little brother got to wear the Sun Crown, when none of his siblings had gotten that privilege for their weddings. Truly his mother's favorite, he thought.

Velgrand slowly, ponderously made his way down the aisle. It seemed like they had put him in platform shoes, since Leondra was a fair bit taller and it would be poor form to have her kneel for the entire ceremony…even if Venser's mother wouldn't mind. His gait suggested as such, and it felt like the better part of an eternity for Velgrand to totter his way to the dais. Once he was there, he positioned himself in front to await his bride.

"Now, please remain standing for the honoring of Lady Leondra, the one who shall be completed by Velgrand as they enter in the most holy union we celebrate on this day!"

Leondra walked the same path Velgrand did into the cathedral. Her dress was relatively plain and modest, with a wedding veil draped over her face and a plain silver circlet atop her head. Her face was stony and betrayed no emotion, though Venser had an idea of the displeasure and distress she was battling. Her walk up the aisle was far more deliberate and measured, taking much less time to reach the dais. She took her spot, facing Velgrand, and it was time. The attendees all sat down at the bidding of the officiant, leaving just the prospective partners standing at the altar.

The next stage of the officiant's sermon was describing the merits of the rulers of both Lunaria and Aracoras. Praise was slathered over the Council of Elders and its luminaries, with particular focus on Victarion's benevolent leadership and great wisdom bringing the two families and great cities together. Velgrand listened to this all with a look of excitement, while Leondra's face was inscrutable. Venser's parents both looked raptly and with great pleasure, and Hessler looked disinterested. After a winding and droning recitation about the perceived merits and virtue on display, focusing on those of Aracoras most of all, the next part was yet another hymn sung in the incomprehensible language, though Venser thought he could pick out the names of Leondra and Velgrand. This was said to be a directed benediction, to plead to the Almighty to sanctify and consecrate this most exalted of unions.

Finally, as the choir took their seats again, the officiant returned to the dais and got to the question Venser knew was part of the program and had been, in equal parts, looking forward to and dreading.

"The light of the Almighty has illuminated the way forward, and they deem it to be the shared road to divinity drawn out for Velgrand and Leondra," he said, letting each word hang in the air. "I ask you all in the audience: do any of you see a reason that this exalted ceremony should not be brought to its natural conclusion, that these two should not be united as husband and wife? Speak now, or forever hold your peace." He settled back, allowing for silence. Objections weren't expected, of course, but it was thought impolite and an affront to the Almighty to not allow for a perfunctory period.

Venser knew there were at least two people with reason to object. Isamu would, as would he. He looked over at Basch, as if to ask for guidance.

"Do what you need to, Venser," he said, squeezing his hand.

Venser took a breath and, ignoring all the reasons he might have to stay silent, rose out of his pew.

"I object."

"Who thaid that?" Velgrand yelled, looking around. He had clearly been told that this was a perfunctory formality. "Who would object to thith wedding?" A murmur from the crowd met this, breaking the solemn silence that had held up to now.

"I do. I object to the marriage, to the union proposed to us," Venser said, projecting his voice as best as possible. Everyone snapped to attention to look at who said it, and nobody seemed to betray any sort of recognition as to who said it.

"I also wish to register my objections to this!" Isamu exclaimed, jumping out of his seat. "I, Isamu of Sorocco, cannot idly stand back and watch as my dearest friend gets married off to a doddering, lisping twit!"

"How *dare* you!" Venser's mother shrieked, her response instinctual and visceral. She rose out of her seat, though restrained by her husband. Venser saw Leondra's eyes light up as the two men rose out of their pews, hoping to bail her out of the fate foisted upon her.

"You will not defame my son like that, you cretinous, craven whelp!" Victarion thundered, standing to address the offending party. "We will not countenance the objections of a lovesick puppy, and you *will* know your place in these sacred halls!"

"What of *my* objections, though?" Venser asked.

"And what could they *possibly* be?"

"How about that I was originally the one betrothed to Leondra, a betrothal apparently overwritten when it was deemed convenient?" The ring Venser had been gifted by Leondra as they parted was not a ring of engagement, but they needn't know that, and he held his hand up to show the ring.

Victarion laughed. "You are a foolish child, an attention-seeking scamp who claims to have knowledge when he is truly ignorant!" he scoffed. "Velgrand was always to be Leondra's wife!"

"That's a lie, and you know it!" Venser shot back. Gasps rose from the pews, especially near the front, and Victarion turned a lovely shade of crimson.

"You will *not* accuse me of lying, contemptuous little shit!" he screamed, the choice in words getting even more gasps. "I am the High Priest of Aracoras, infallible arbiter and representative of divinity, and you will *not*..."

"I know who you are, *Father*, and I'm almost disappointed you wouldn't recognize your own son, Venser! Not when he's been here this whole time, hiding in plain sight!" Now Venser was mad. He had hoped to keep his emotions in check, but being accused of lying by his father right after the man had openly and outwardly lied to everyone in attendance was the last straw.

Even more gasps rang out, accompanied by the apparent fainting of someone in the front rows, and murmuring broke out. The officiant started to look distressed; this had not gone to plan at all, and they were supposed to be back to more hymnals by now.

"You sit there and spew falsehoods and spin mistruths fluently, like it is ingrained in your very nature! You are clearly a lowborn scoundrel in a masquerade of his own making! No son of mine would *ever* resort to cavorting with such sinful, lesser beings as those you are sitting with!"

"Maybe it's because he's *not* your son and your wife couldn't keep her legs shut!" Basch yelled, jumping out of his seat in anger. More murmurs erupted from the crowd, a mix of entertainment and confusion, and another fainting spectator livened up the front of the cathedral.

"*What*!? You *dare* accuse the exemplar of virtue, Venaria, of anything like that? How *dare* you! Apprehend those heathens, those scoundrels who lob baseless accusations and interrupt this sanctified ceremony!" Victarion's face was as red as Venser could ever recall it being, and his fingers pointed threateningly in their direction. For her part, Venaria looked like she wanted to murder Basch. yearning to see him disemboweled from toe to tonsil.

Leondra scoffed. "Still blind to it all, old man," she said flippantly, making sure she was audible enough for the people to hear.

Victarion wheeled around. "What did you say to me?" he hissed. He was not used to a woman talking to him in a way that was anything but wholly deferential.

"Oh, so you didn't know? It turns out that your wife apparently had a fling with an adventurer from Balmung a bit before Venser was born. It'd explain a lot, like why he looks so different and why he isn't an insufferable little *bitch* like the man you're trying to marry me off to! And for my part, I might have…also helped a bit with getting him out of Lunaria, which goes to explain why he's over there."

Venaria had listened to this silently, but she had heard enough from Leondra and her foul, forked tongue, a tongue that dared to slander her, her husband, and her precious little angel. She shook free of her husband and strode over to her soon-to-be daughter-in-law.

"You gussied-up, immoral, slavering little *whore!*" she screamed. She reared back and prepared to slap Leondra, but Leondra responded by ducking out of the way, such that Venaria slapped the officiant. More gasps rang out from the audience.

"What is going on?" Hessler demanded, standing up. "Can we get this ceremony back on track?"

"*Excuse you!?*" Venaria shrieked. "Are your ears not working? Are you blind? Have you been paying attention to *any* of this? Your vile, wretched *skank* of a daughter is a disgrace to you and your city! She's responsible for *all* of this, for her trying to take my little angel away!" More gasps met this, and Venser thought he saw one of his sisters faint in one of the front pews. This was at least the third fainting person he had noticed, and there well could have been more.

"What does any of this matter? This wedding, it is but window dressing to what truly matters here! We have the Tomb of the Almighty to attend to! Every moment we delay finishing this…ceremony, they yearn further for the release they seek! They can't be allowed to suffer any longer in their imprisonment!" The way Hessler said this sounded really weird to Venser's ears.

Here, Leondra rose up. "That's all you cared about, isn't it, Father?" she asked. "I was just a pawn to you so that you could open the Tomb of the Almighty."

"Do *not* speak to your father like that!" Victarion bellowed. "Why I even agreed to allow my youngest son to marry such a vile shrew, I will never know!"

"Clearly you didn't have a problem with the money that was being offered! Should I be sorry for not being on my knees like your daughters are?"

"You filthy *bitch*!" Venaria screamed. She again moved to slap Leondra, another miss. The officiant had given up and had retreated, not wanting to get slapped.

"And I can affirm that the man who says he's Venser is, indeed, Venser," Leondra continued. "Rather pitiful that neither of you would recognize your own child, is it?"

Here, Victarion turned to Venser, who was still standing besides Basch. "Impossible!" he spat. "No son of mine would *ever* debase himself like…"

"Cut it out, Father," Venser glared. "I understand your need to feign moral superiority, but you're not fooling me or anyone else here. Besides, you've always treated me badly, so I suppose your treatment of me now is in character."

While the argument on the dais had happened (and Velgrand had sat down to cry, displeased by his not being the center of attention and having his big day ruined), Venser had pulled out his symbol of devotion, and it hung over his shirt. Victarion finally saw it and gasped, joined by Venaria's stunned reaction.

"You see?" Isamu said, having chosen to not sit down after having his objections dismissed. "He's who he claims to be. The symbol of devotion is unique to the people of Aracoras, and it's impossible to counterfeit."

Victarion shook his head, then pointed to Venser. "Apprehend him and his accomplices!" he roared. "He has violated our tenets by straying from the path of divinity and enlightenment! He has been shepherded along the wide and pleasant and chosen to cavort with sin! He is *unclean*, contaminated and led from his ordained path, and he *must* be punished!"

Matthias rose up in response to this. "You will not do such a thing! Venser's part of my crew, and if you want him, you're going to have to go through me," he said, his voice deadly serious. "I might not look like much, but you're not going to get to him without a fight."

"A part of your *crew*? Whatever do you mean?"

"Explaining it to you would be far above your level of comprehension, you self-absorbed asshole!"

"How *dare* you! Erdrick, how did you let a nasty, foul-tongued parasite into Aracoras?"

Erdrick stood up angrily. "Maybe you should look at your own faults before you lob accusations at us!" he snapped.

"How dare you! You will know your place, and you will not talk back to me!"

Venser had gotten the feeling that this wedding had completely gone off script, and in between the shouts at one another, bedlam had started creeping into the Grand Cathedral. Parties screamed at each other in the pews and on the dais, and the whole business of marrying Velgrand and Leondra had completely been forgotten about.

The din of the Grand Cathedral abated abruptly as clapping rang out sharply from the back. Venser turned to see where it was coming from, noticing that he had developed an intense headache rather suddenly. It was no ordinary headache, and seeing who had stepped into the fray made it all make sense.

"I must say," Hellvira purred, her voice carrying, "I was not expecting the wedding to be this...chaotic. Are all weddings in Aracoras this much of an unhinged comedy of errors?"

Basch quickly ushered Venser to sit down. Matthias had gone comatose, as had much of the audience. Much of the dais had not, though, with only Velgrand transfixed by the busty babe before him. She was dressed as always, an absurdly inappropriate dress with immodest cuts that would appall everyone in Aracoras utterly.

"Begone, trollop!" yelled Victarion. "Why do you desecrate these halls with your impure mien? How did you even get in here? And why were you not accosted?" Venser was curious as to why his father was unaffected, and he had noticed that the Council of Elders had seemingly not fallen under her spell, tittering worriedly.

"Why would I be? I have an invitation. Mind you, I invited *myself*, because I will not allow such trivial things as 'invitations' to stand between me and where I mean to be. But I imagine Hessler's happy to see me, right?"

"I was waiting for you, Hellvira!" Hessler exclaimed. His joy unnerved Venser, the first time the man had shown anything besides indifference. "It's so good to see you. Are the preparations ready?"

"But of *course*, Hessler! Have I engendered so little faith from our time working together?"

"Of course not!"

"Excellent."

Hellvira strutted up to the dais, rapt gazes following her. She motioned as she walked by, and Venser noticed that Zsa Zsa and Magdalyna rose out of their seats, abandoning their dazed dates to join her walk. She reached the dais, ignoring the horrified looks of everyone standing up there.

"The time has come," she exclaimed, "to open the Tomb of the Almighty! At long last, the Almighty shall return to us and shower blessings upon their faithful! And Hessler, as the one who has worked most tirelessly to make this happen, you shall be the one who sets foot in it first!"

"How *dare* you…" Victarion started.

Hellvira turned to face him, a steely look on her face. "You will learn your place, old man, and your place is on your *knees*," she hissed. She snapped her fingers, and Victarion was thrown to the ground into what looked like a groveling position. Another pulse of pain rippled through Venser's temples when she did this, and he tried to shake it off.

"Zsa Zsa? Magdalyna?" she continued.

"Wight hewe, owo," Zsa Zsa squealed.

"Like, reporting for duty!" Magdalyna said, saluting.

"It is time. I have brought with me the *key* to the Tomb of the Almighty, and all it needs is a little…help. Please lead Hessler outside to the Tomb, so that he may enter *immediately* upon its opening."

Her two flunkies obeyed, and Hessler was led outside, ignoring everything else and the protests of Victarion. Hellvira turned to face the Tomb of the Almighty, pulling out from her cleavage a sinister-looking sword of crystal. It was, from what Venser could see, an unsettling black, weirdly absorbing and reflecting light in a way that was mesmeric and unnatural.

"The day has come for the Almighty's return!" Hellvira proclaimed. "I bid you rise off your feet and to your knees as the Tomb of the Almighty opens!" She reared back and threw her sword towards the monolith. It shattered the window as it flew through it and, true as an arrow, embedded itself into the Tomb of the Almighty.

Cracks and fissures started to emanate from the point of impact, and a small door-like structure popped open at the base, right where the bridge connected to the Tomb of the Almighty. They watched as Zsa Zsa and Magdalyna led Hessler out to the Tomb, with the guards no longer there, and bade him to go inside. Hessler moved as quickly as Venser had ever seen anyone move for anything, disappearing into the hole in the rock.

"I *do* so wonder what Hessler will discover in there," Hellvira purred. "Don't all of you?"

"What do you mean by that, harpy?" Victarion yelped. "How did you do this?"

"Oh, why would I tell such a *disgusting, sexist* pig what's in there? Not when you can find out when Hessler comes back out."

"You…" Victarion tried to get up, but whatever Hellvira had done kept him rooted to the ground.

"I told you, your place is on your knees, and you will *obey*. You were going to be here as the Almighty awakened from their long slumber, so why not stay there?" she chuckled.

The sense of dread Venser had was palpable, and it intensified with each passing moment. Cracks began to propagate from the openings of the Tomb of the Almighty, becoming more pronounced as they spread. Finally, chunks of the Tomb began to slough off, falling into the cloud sea.

As the tomb fell away, a loud, strangled scream cut through the air. Beams of dark light began to pour out of the fissures in the Tomb of the Almighty, and Venser tried to hide the searing pain that throbbed intermittently. The disintegration of the monolith accelerated, a spectacle of lights and thunderous noise.

"The Almighty is upon us!" Hellvira yelled. She laughed, a dissonant cacophony that chilled Venser to the bone.

"That's not the Almighty!" Leondra shot back.

"...what did you say, little girl?" Hellvira stopped laughing and glared at her.

"I know what you've unleashed! The Tomb of the Almighty never held the Almighty...it held a dark god, and you tricked my father into opening it!"

Hellvira laughed. "Tricked? *Me?* Your father wanted to open the Tomb all on his own! Well...maybe not all on his own, but what does that matter when divinity is upon us anew?"

Before anyone could ask more questions, the disintegration of the Tomb of the Almighty hit its climax, shedding all that surrounded it and leaving nothing of the stone monolith behind. What remained was Hessler, only something was off about him. He was being suspended in the air by a strange, swirling presence, a dark miasma that fluctuated viciously and malevolently.

"Where is the Almighty?" Victarion yelled. "Where are they?"

"You behold them," Hellvira cooed. "Well, it might be more accurate to call it an aspect of them. I believe they have chosen to use Hessler's body to fuel their return, to drain what remains in the man to reignite the fire that had been quashed. A continuation of, and conclusion to, what was started years ago, but..."

"What do you mean by that, you two-timing hag?" Leondra yelled.

"I shall choose to ignore your disrespect this time, *little girl*. Your father... he has been lost for many, *many* years, corrupted by the glimpse of majesty he beheld when I first offered him a peek. His heart yearned to be filled, and I offered him that which he sought." She chuckled malevolently, content with how her plans had all panned out to this point.

"You are a wicked charlatan, hussy!" Victarion screamed, still on his knees.

"And I thought you were supposed to know what you were guarding all these years! I suppose legends have a way of rewriting themselves with time and a bit of encouragement from others. It's not good for business if the Council of Elders is guarding the tomb housing a god of darkness, so why not tell the tale in an ambiguous way? A half-truth gives way to a lie, that lie blossoms into a tree that looks like the truth, and the fruits of it are being born as we speak!"

The miasma finally jettisoned itself from Hessler's body, and the corpse fell into the sea of clouds, disappearing into the abyss. It swirled and flowed, pouring into the Grand Cathedral through the hole in the window, while Zsa Zsa and Magdalyna excitedly followed it back inside.

"This is so exciting, uwu!" Zsa Zsa squealed. "The God of Dawknyess is awmost back, owo! Awawawawawawa!" She spun around like someone had given her too much sugar.

"Oh-em-gee, you, like, weren't supposed to say that, Zsa Zsa!" Magdalyna said.

"But Zsa Zsa's so excited, owo! Awoo!"

The mist swirled as it coalesced and congealed, finally settling into a corporeal form. Emerging from the shadowed miasma was a creature unlike anything Venser could have ever imagined, and he desperately tried to ignore his throbbing headache. Its form resembled that of an anthropomorphic great white shark, albeit with a majestic pair of horns. Its hollow eyes brimmed with evil, an obsidian crown sat on its head, and a thick fur robe draped across its towering frame. One hand bore a massive, sinister-looking crosier with chains trailing off of it. It would almost be absurd, were it not so horrifying. As its limbs coalesced, the fiend took a moment to stretch each one, shaking off years of incorporeality.

"It has been so long," it said, "since I enjoyed my physical form. Too long, to be honest." Its voice was a grating, shrieking cacophony, the anguish of a small dying forest creature mixed with nails being dragged across a chalkboard.

"That it has, my liege," Hellvira said, performing a curtsy. "I am happy to have contributed to your release from that prison."

"Your contributions were invaluable, Hellvira."

"The God of Dawknyess is finyawwy back, owo! Awawawawawa!" Zsa Zsa squealed.

"Like, you have *no* idea how excited we are!" Magdalyna said, jumping up and down.

"Ah, my faithful servants, Zsa Zsa and Magdalyna. You, with Hellvira, shall also be rewarded. I do not forget those who have done well by me…nor do I forgive or suffer the slights and the misdeeds of the past."

"What misdeeds?" Victarion yelled, trying to reclaim control of the situation. "And where is the Almighty, you fiend?"

The fiend laughed in response, a chilling sound that rang odiously. "You're really slow to arrive at the party, deluded gasbag!" it snarled, throwing out the calm that had punctuated its initial statements. "Let me spell it out for you in terminology you might be able to understand: *there is no Almighty!* There never was some being of light, neither entombed here nor anywhere else! There is but one god, the god of darkness! Never mind who you thought I was…I'm Ack-Tar, *bitch*! And it has come time for me to get my revenge and assume my mantle as the lord and master of this world!"

It punctuated this with another laugh, and Venser felt his blood run cold as needles shot into his head. He grasped onto Basch's hand in fear, his gut telling him that things were about to get much worse.

19

The Door of Destiny

Standing on the dais, Ack-Tar surveyed the room with utmost contempt. Its eyes brimmed with the malice gained from centuries of imprisonment, and its expression betrayed a deep loathing it fully intended to act on. Venser tried to make himself as small as possible; he knew escape was preferable, but they couldn't just leave and abandon Sebastian and Matthias to whatever was going to happen. Basch and Arycelle were both trying to compress themselves into the pews as well, not wanting to let Ack-Tar know they were fully conscious.

"I believe," Ack-Tar said finally, "it has come time to put some more plans into motion, plans that have long yearned to be executed. Hellvira, you know what is to be done, and I shall leave you to do it."

"Of course, Your Malevolence," Hellvira purred, bowing. "I shall take my leave. Should I take Zsa Zsa and Magdalyna with me?"

"I believe their presence might be an *asset*. I would rather they stayed, for now."

"Indeed. With that, my liege, I shall be off. " Hellvira took this opportunity to make as flashy an exit as she could, opting to jump through the cracked window and get sputters of horror from all relevant parties. Her departure caused her enthralling hold over the audience of the wedding to finally lift, and they slowly came to.

"Hey, who invited the freak?" Matthias whispered, shaking off the stupor rather quickly. Basch, Arycelle, and Venser all shushed him, while Sebastian was slower to come to and just as appalled.

"Foul beast, desecrate this hall no longer!" Victarion roared, finally able to rise to his feet with Hellvira gone. "In the name of the Almighty, I…"

"The 'Almighty' you cling to is merely a fairy tale, a construct of your ancestors trying to hide the error they made in calling me to this world!" Ack-Tar snarled. "There will be no salvation coming from whichever manner of fictional creature you place your faith in! Once, I erred in allowing myself to be vanquished and subsequently sealed in that accursed rock, the product of earned hubris having been turned against me, but this time *will* be different!"

"The end is nyigh, owo!" Zsa Zsa squealed. "Beg fow mewcy, uwu!"

Sigmund cleared his throat, rising from his pew nervously. "Uh, Zsa Zsa? My little Snuggle Muffin?" he asked. "What's going on? Why are you up there?"

"Zsa Zsa is nyot youw snyuggwe muffin, owo! Zsa Zsa sewves the god of dawknyess, uwu! Awawawawawawawawa!" She spun around excitedly.

"Looks like that relationship just ended," Basch muttered.

"Oh, you came here as his date, Zsa Zsa! I must ask, did he treat you well?" Ack-Tar asked, the tone clearly suggesting something in the works.

"Absowowutewy nyot, owo! He was totawwy condescending to Zsa Zsa and he tweated Zsa Zsa wike a wittwe giww and wike Zsa Zsa was his puppet, uwu! Zsa Zsa was *so* offended, awoo!"

"Well, that's…disappointing." Ack-Tar rose up, making its presence even more threatening. "Had you treated her well, I *might* have been willing to offer you a chance to serve me. But I don't think you've earned that, the privilege of serving the god of darkness…all you've earned in your mistreatment of my subordinate is a quick *death*."

"What do you…" Sigmund started, only to be cut off. He put his hands around his throat; he appeared to be choking, induced by what looked like dark waves of energy emanating out from Ack-Tar. Venser's headache flared up, and he tried to rub his temples to reduce the discomfort.

"What are you doing to my brother?" Richter demanded, jumping up.

"Oh, you're his brother? That's almost quaint! You know what they say…the family that thrives together *dies* together!"

Richter turned as white as a sheet, sputtering aimlessly as his brother continued to be strangled by the dark god's power, flailing and thrashing as he tried to get air he was being cut off from.

"Not even trying to help your brother, I see. Such a pity…such a pity," Ack-Tar laughed.

"How *dare* you!"

A sanctimonious shout came from the back of the cathedral, and Ack-Tar released Sigmund from its strangulation spell to see what merited attention. Venser looked back as well, and he was appalled to see a particularly short, unpleasant figure in the doorway, one he'd seen in passing and thought he'd never see again. With the attention of all in the building, a rapt audience quiet enough to allow a falling pin to be heard, he saw fit to introduce himself.

"Like a flower that blooms in the soil of our carnal and corrupt society, I shall administer retribution to the straying vermin that graze upon the land! For I am the Chairman of the Educational Guidance Council…*Archduke Emperor Pope Guillaume XIII*!" His usual spiel was this time delivered with some manner of interpretive dance, assuming a series of poses that culminated in what he thought was a sufficiently-imposing battle stance.

"What an absurd bit of theater!" Ack-Tar sneered. "Is this what passes for theatrics among you maggots these days?"

"Malevolent and maleficent malefactor, a malfeasant monstrosity manifesting a mien most malign, it has come time for you to be met with a rain of heavenly bloodshed and *glo*rious violence at the hands of Archduke Emperor Pope Guillaume XIII, vanguard of morality and guardian of all that is divine and divinely buxom! Verily, this shall be the final day of your existence!" This proclamation was met with more posing, culminating in a strange pirouette.

Ack-Tar met this with a defiant laugh. "You claim yourself a vanguard of morality, yet all I see is a skirt-chasing little rat with a feigned sense of superiority! I'm certainly not inclined to regard the deranged gibbering of a parasite, but if you wish to meet your demise before the god of darkness, I'll happily provide it to you!"

"*Silence*! Your bravado and your pathetic ploys to project puissance shan't be observed by the one clearly aligned with the full backing of divinity and the light of righteousness! In the names of the Educational Guidance Council and Marianne, bounteous bosom and treasure of the skies, I, Archduke Emperor Pope Guillaume XIII, will knock you down!" With a final, valiant scream, Archduke Emperor Pope Guillaume XIII charged down the aisle, armed with a especially pointy stick that he had found on his way to the venue.

He had made it barely to the dais when Ack-Tar, weary of this charade, responded. It pointed its crosier at Archduke Emperor Pope Guillaume XIII, and his forward momentum was immediately arrested as dark energy crackled from the tip. Venser winced in pain, each crackle sending a sharp sensation through his head.

"Unfetter me, fiend! Allow your demise to come at the hands of divinity, without relying on cheap parlor tricks to save you!" He flailed against the formless fetter, refusing to consider retreat as an option.

"I have a better proposal. How about I just kill you? You're not really worth it, if we're being honest, but you're *so* annoying!"

Ack-Tar laughed as it conjured a mass of dark energy in its free hand, drowning out the insipid whimpering of its self-proclaimed nemesis. Venser noticed his persistent headache intensified as the darkness coalesced, and he tried to rub his temples to relieve the pressure. Once the dark mass had reached a suitable size, the dark god threw it into the ground at the feet of Archduke Emperor Pope Guillaume XIII, and a massive obsidian spike erupted from the ground and impaled him. After a short pause to allow for suitably horrified gasps, the spike exploded, eviscerating the freshly-slain corpse and raining down blood and innards upon those nearby. Venser's head felt like it was going to explode in the meantime, and Basch grabbed his hand to try and provide comfort when he saw his discomfort.

"Not the most subtle trick, but it gets the point across!" Ack-Tar sneered.

"That was amazing, owo! Zsa Zsa is in awe of youw mawevowence, uwu!"

Zsa Zsa twirled around excitedly.

"Like, how he blew up was *so* fetch!" Magdalyna was bouncing up and down giddily.

It was here that Velgrand decided it was time to try and take back control of his wedding. "Excuthe you," he said, rising up and trying to get their attention, "what maketh you think you can come in like thith and ruin my wedding?" He ignored his mother's attempts to get him to try and lay low in the interest of self-preservation.

Ack-Tar turned around and laughed. "Oh, you little numbskull, it was never about you or about your parents marrying you off!" it said. "My return was the main point on the agenda, and whatever they decided to do on top of that was a sideshow!"

"But I wath thuppothed to be married!"

"And who'd want to marry a coddled little shit like *you*, still clutching to his harlot mother's bosom whenever he had a chance?"

"You will *not* impugn my wife's good name, fiend!" Victarion roared, and Venser saw all his brothers jump up to defend their mother's honor.

"I suppose 'harlot' might have been a bit erroneous, considering the word implies a more transactional nature, but it might still be sufficient verbiage to underscore her lapses in judgment! *Particularly* with regards to the black sheep of your family! I wonder, when she came to the Tomb of the Almighty praying that the child she bore had the parentage she had hoped for, if she got the answer she wanted…oh, wait, I know the answer to that! She came back later and prayed all of you would never find out!"

Ack-Tar laughed, and Venser saw his mother had lost all color in her face. So it *was* true.

"What do you mean by that, fiend?" Victarion asked.

"I've already said all I plan to on the matter, and litigating the harlotry of your wife is quite boring in my eyes, so why don't we move on to more exciting topics? Like how your son could marry one of my associates instead! Zsa Zsa and Magdalyna would both make for excellent brides! I hear they're *otherworldly* in bed." It looked directly at Sigmund and Richter as it said this, and they both looked uncomfortable.

"My son will *not* be corrupted by those hussies!"

"You huwt Zsa Zsa's feewings, owo."

"The decision is not yours to make, old man!" Ack-Tar snarled, turning back to Velgrand. "I think it should fall to the little groom to make a decision for the first time in his life, made without Mommy or Daddy to hold his hand!"

Velgrand looked absolutely petrified. "What…what thould I do?" he asked.

"Look deep in your little heart! What do you *want* to do?" Venser saw Velgrand looking at Zsa Zsa and Magdalyna, who were both trying their best to look as seductive as possible in spite of their seeming prepubescence.

"They are tho pretty," Velgrand said, swooning over them. Victarion was still trying to get his son's attention, to get him to reject his suitors outright.

"But before you decide, I should ask Zsa Zsa and Magdalyna, because it's only polite to ask *them*! Zsa Zsa, Magdalyna…do either of you like him and want to marry him?"

"Absowowutewy not, awoo!"

"Like, absolutely *not*! He's *so* not fetch!"

Velgrand's face fell, and he started crying again.

"What even was the point of that, you fiend?" Victarion yelled. "You made him cry for no reason!"

"Reveling in the anguish and suffering of others *is* the point, you stuffy twit! I have been trapped in that miserable stone prison for far too long, stuck listening to your insipid paeans and entreaties to a god that never even existed, an existence almost dire enough to make one yearn for death! Now that I'm free, it's time to catch up on what I've missed all these years! And inflicting anguish is *far* more fun and satisfying than just settling for mere gratuitous bloodshed!" Ack-Tar laughed again.

Commotion could be heard at the back of the cathedral, and the nature of it was made clear as the Coven of Unholy Nocturnal Terror tromped into the hall, led by the inimitable Blood Countess Erzsébet Báthory.

"Most…gasp…malevolent deity and incarnation of…gasp…evil, I, the…wheeze…the Blood Countess Erzsébet Báthory, head of…wheeze…my Coven of Unholy Nocturnal Terror, have come to…gasp…offer our services

THE DOOR OF DESTINY

to you in the...wheeze...in the name of malfeasance!" Blood Countess Erzsébet Báthory and her thralls had run there, and she was completely winded from the light exertion. "We...gasp...we have escaped the prison those...wheeze...those foul creatures threw us in, and we...gasp...pledge to aid and abet the evil you choose to wreak!"

"Parties willing to join the winning cause, I see!" Ack-Tar said. "I do like volunteers! It's so much easier to subjugate those willing to bend their knees!"

"How did those hussies escape?" Victarion roared, still desperately trying to seize control of the situation. Ack-Tar chose to ignore him.

"We...we beg you, take us into your bosom!" Blood Countess Erzsébet Báthory squealed. "Fill us with malfeasance most majestic and evil unending!" She punctuated this proclamation with a shuddering, orgasmic laugh.

"If that's what you want, who am I to deny you? Willful subjugation, forced subjugation...all of it serves the same end!" Ack-Tar held out its hand, and waves of darkness started projecting outward, washing over the Coven of Unholy Nocturnal Terror. Venser felt more intensifying head pain as the Coven squealed in libidinous euphoria, disappearing into the intensifying miasma.

"What is going on? What are you doing to those...those trollops?" Victarion demanded.

Ack-Tar ignored him and continued to laugh as the darkness pulsed and throbbed. When it finally cleared up, the Coven of Unholy Nocturnal Terror had all been turned into smaller versions of Ack-Tar, squat anthropomorphic sharks with horns and a forked tail. They all gargled out vague noises symbolizing gratitude and prostrated themselves before their god.

"Oh-em-gee, that's so amazing, uwu! Zsa Zsa is totawwy impwessed, owo!" She and Magdalyna were both bouncing up and down giddily.

"Behold, the newest additions to the forces of darkness at my beck and call! It's good to see I still have it," Ack-Tar chuckled. "Enough of that, though...I think we get on with some *real* entertainment now!" Its voice took on a very sharp edge that suggested things were going to get even worse.

"Have you not already done *enough?*" Victarion yelled.

"Enough? I've only just begun, you insipid moron! I think I know what would make for an *excellent* bit of entertainment: destroying this pathetic little city! What purpose does this miserable hunk of rock serve now that I have awakened? It might be more useful to take on a new purpose, to warn all humans of the fate ultimately awaiting you at the end of your despair, once your suffering has reached its zenith!" Again, Ack-Tar laughed.

"You will *not* destroy this city! I, Victarion, High Priest of Aracoras and paramount of the Council of Elders, will not allow it!" He rose up to his full height, trying to present an impression of bravado.

"I think you don't understand: I care not for what you'll allow, because I'm going to do it anyways! And I'm tired of you talking back to me and telling me all the things that I, a *literal god*, cannot and will not do!"

It held out its crosier, much like had happened with Archduke Emperor Pope Guillaume XIII, and tendrils of agony reached up and wrapped around Victarion. He tried to talk, but his mouth was quickly bound by a shadowy limb, and all he could do was scream into it as Ack-Tar charged up another ball of energy in its free hand.

"Victarion, High Priest of Aracoras, paramount of the Council of Elders… it is time you bid this plane of existence farewell! I, the god of darkness, sentence you to *death*! I hope you and your family have made peace with this, because you're now on the one-way ride to damnation!" Venser's brothers (besides Velgrand) had all gotten up by now and were trying to get to their father, impeded by a barrier of dark energy Ack-Tar had thrown up.

Finally, Ack-Tar threw the orb into the ground, and a spike of malice erupted forth to take Victarion's life in an instant. The primal screams that followed the spike's explosion and showering of the audience in more viscera shook Venser to the core, almost as much as the debilitating pulses of pain that accompanied it.

"I think it's time we left," Matthias whispered, motioning that they needed to creep out as carefully as possible. "I've seen enough of this bloody spectacle."

Venser didn't respond audibly, nodding as he tried to drive his headache away. It had gotten far, far worse, a stabbing pain that intensified right as his father exploded into bits of human.

Ack-Tar laughed once again. "If you want out before this place comes crashing down, I recommend you flee now!" it sneered, turning to face the crowd. "Of course, what fun would that be to just *let* you go? Get them, my minions! Water the soil of this forsaken rock with their blood, and fertilize it with their entrails!" It laughed again.

The transmogrified Coven of Unholy Nocturnal Terror immediately leapt into the pews, and everyone screamed in a mad dash to get out of the cathedral. Venser saw Leondra making a break for it at the back of the room, while his brothers continued to try to get revenge for their father's gruesome execution. With Basch's hand on his shoulder and the rest of the crew by his side, they made a break for it, occasional slices and screams filling the air as Ack-Tar sought to show Venser's brothers the error of their ways.

As the party stepped outside the Grand Cathedral's main hall, they felt a disconcerting rumble underfoot, a persistent tremor that pulsed through Aracoras.

"I don't like any of this," Sebastian said. "We need to get to the harbor, and we need to get there now!"

"The front door's been destroyed!" Arycelle yelled, pointing out a door that would no longer budge for anyone. "Venser, can you get us out?"

"I can," Venser answered, trying to focus. This was no time for uncertainty. They were counting on him, and it was time to deliver.

The Grand Cathedral was a series of snaking pathways and halls, and they scrambled through as the rumbling continued. Screams of panic made it hard to hear much of anything else, but Venser remained unbowed, desperately trying to push his headache out of his consciousness. He pushed back all the thoughts he'd need time to process later and focused on getting them out, on finding a path that would take them out of there.

The solution was through the office of one of the members of the Council of Elders, via a window. It wasn't his father's office; Venser thought it had belonged to Quintavius, a weak and subservient man who had always allowed Victarion to have his way. All of them had been that way, to be honest. Basch grabbed the chair in the room and shattered the window in one swing, and they cautiously made it outside. The rumbling had gotten worse, and Venser took a moment to get his bearings.

"That way!" he said, pointing. He was correct, and they came upon the harbor. It was a place of utter bedlam, everyone scrambling onto airships desperately and departures happening at a steady clip.

"Going somewhere?" they heard. Magdalyna had emerged in their path, with a look of satisfaction on her face.

"We are, and you're getting out of our way!" Basch roared. They didn't slow down, and Basch delivered a running kick to Madgalyna, who was knocked backwards with a yelp.

"You filthy *bitch*! How could you do this to me?" she screamed as they continued past her. "*I feel very attacked!*"

They got to the harbor, and the *Naglfar* was in shape to take off with little effort. As they got there, two familiar figures ran up.

"Have space on board for some extras?" Leondra asked. It was her and Isamu, the latter having caught up to her in the chaos by following her path out.

"Gladly," Matthias said. We have room, but we don't have time, so I recommend you get on posthaste!"

As they started boarding, Venser turned to Leondra. "Did you see anything else that happened in there?" he asked.

"See anything, Isamu?" she asked. "I got out of there as fast as I could."

"Right as I left the room, I heard that Ack-Tar had just bashed your brother's head in. Velgrand, the one who was supposed to marry Leondra. Your other brothers had been cut down before that. They threw themselves at Ack-Tar to avenge your father, and…" Isamu looked disgusted as he retold this.

Venser gasped. "What about my mother and sisters?" he asked. It was instinctual, asking the fates of his family even if they'd not have cared about him.

"No idea. I heard screams, but I have no idea what came of your sisters or mother."

"Hear anything about my good for nothing brothers?" Basch asked.

Isamu made a sound, like sucking air through his teeth. "Richter got away, I think. Zsa Zsa caught Sigmund and wanted to 'punish him personally'. I think that's what I heard, anyway. I could barely understand her."

As they got on board, Matthias and Arycelle broke for the bridge while everyone else scrambled below deck. Venser noticed that his head was still throbbing with marked intensity, and he hoped that clearing out of the condemned city would abate it somewhat. The engines soon roared to life, and the *Naglfar* took to the air again.

The vessel rising gave Venser a good idea of what was happening on the ground, and he saw parts of the Grand Cathedral crumbling away while other buildings cracked. Screams on the ground continued as airships joined them in taking off, everyone desperate to avoid death at the hands of a self-styled dark god.

As they rose, though, Venser noticed that the screams below had gone silent. A purple fog started to coat the ground of Aracoras as the last shrieks dissipated. The gas then began to rise skyward and expand, racing outward. One of the airships Venser saw behind their pace met the cloud, and he saw it stall before falling ignominiously from the sky. The next couple ships met with the same fate, and soon it approached them with horrifying velocity, faster than even the overclocked engines could muster.

"Is that a *death cloud*?" Isamu screamed.

"Son of a bitch!" Leondra swore. She, Venser, and Isamu were in the guest room, watching. "Talk about toying with its prey before it closes the trap."

Venser didn't reply; his headache had gotten worse, and he tried to massage it away. It was like a thousand needles were being driven into him at once.

"Venser?" Leondra asked "Your eyes...they're glowing. What's happening?"

"I...I don't..."

Venser's eyes had ignited with green fire, and he felt the pressure mounting. Finally, he screamed. It was a primal scream, one he'd never let loose before, and a green flash raced outwards from the *Naglfar*. It met with the death cloud, and the cloud broke. The purple cloud in pursuit no longer followed them, the last airship left escaping Aracoras.

As it broke, so did he, and Venser fell. He collapsed, hearing Isamu and Leondra frantically calling for him. What hold he had on consciousness slipped away, and he felt all go into darkness…

"So, Venser's alive, at least," Leondra said. They were all gathered on the bridge, night having fallen on their escape from Aracoras. "But he's been out cold ever since this afternoon, when he did what he did and the death cloud dissipated."

"I suppose he did save all of our lives," Matthias chuckled. "There was something special about him, after all. Pity it took us nearly being brought down by a death cloud to find out."

"So, what now?" Isamu asked.

"I think," Basch said, "we should return to Balmung. My parents will help us with getting things sorted out, and hopefully Venser can wake up soon when we get there." His tone was noticeably despondent.

"Your parents?" Isamu asked.

"He's the youngest son of Balmung's leader," Arycelle said.

"Oh, *you're* him! I should have recognized you!"

"It's fine. Let's…let's just go there," Basch said.

Matthias sighed. "This all certainly didn't go to plan, whatever was entailed in the plan" he said. "The best part of it all is that there are now even more questions than when we started. We got *some* answers, but I've got a bad feeling about what is to come."

"Don't we all," Sebastian said.

Leondra shook her head. "I know I'm not guilty," she said, "but I can't help feeling like I am. They would have opened the Tomb of the Almighty anyways, wouldn't they?"

"Don't look back on what could have been, Leondra," Arycelle answered. "Look at what *is*. We're still alive, and tomorrow's a day we have ahead of us, another chance to figure everything out."

She smiled. "You're right. We should all get some rest, shouldn't we? This has been a long, unpleasant day."

They all filed out of the bridge, except for Basch, who continued to stand there sullenly.

"Need to talk?" Matthias asked.

Basch grunted. "You know why I'm so down," he said. "He…I don't know if he'll wake up. I don't know what happened to him. And I hate feeling like this. So powerless."

"You've really fallen for him, haven't you?"

"…yes."

"He'll wake up, Basch. He's not dead. There's a lot of questions we have about what happened, but I think that much is something we're all confident about. He's just exhausted, I imagine. Venser needs to sleep off his saving all of our lives. Hopefully he won't be out of it too long."

"You're right. I'm just…I suppose I'm being dramatic."

Matthias smiled. "You know, if you ever need to cry, I promise not to tell anyone."

Basch allowed himself a small smirk. "I'll consider it, though I won't trust you to not tell people if you won't get a good story out of it," he said.

"Probably wouldn't be all that interesting a story, mind. 'Grown man cries over his boyfriend getting knocked out after saving us from a death cloud'…not a real page turner in my eyes, but what do I know?"

Basch bristled a bit. "Boyfriend, huh?"

"That's what you and Venser are, isn't it?"

"…it is, but I didn't think that was public knowledge."

"It's not public, but it's plain as day from how both of you talk about each other. There's a bit of lightness and joy in how you speak of the other, and I know you *definitely* don't talk about me like that."

"No, I don't. Still, I suppose I shouldn't be surprised, given that you seem to have a knack for figuring things out."

Matthias smiled in response. "Information is the key to a lot. And while I don't have answers as to what would wake Venser up, I suspect he'll find his way back to us, and to you, soon enough," he said.

Basch just nodded and left. Matthias looked out at the horizon as the ship continued on its course, flying above a dark sea of clouds illuminated by the cloud-covered moon.

"There's so much I don't think any of us knew," he murmured, looking out over the horizon. "And I reckon that we're about to learn a lot more, none of it things that we want to learn."

Epilogue

The moon rose over the ruins of Aracoras. All life on the city had been quashed by Ack-Tar, god of darkness, and the forces of darkness at its beck and call, and it surveyed its conquest with contempt and satisfaction. It had sent Zsa Zsa and Magdalyna off to wreak havoc elsewhere, joining Hellvira in the grand plan to bring the skies under its rule, and it would have time alone to reflect on the totality of its victory in Aracoras.

All things considered, the day had been a successful one. It finally was free of that accursed tomb, the prison where it had been forced to, for generations, listen to the hymnals and the prayers of the people it had just brought ruin to.

In spite of all of this, Ack-Tar couldn't help but feel a bit dissatisfied. The death cloud it had set after those fleeing had been broken somehow. This setback led it to remember the circumstances that saw it be defeated so long ago…at the height of its triumph, a flash of green, a sealing chant, and an eternity in stone.

It sighed, stretching its limbs. Ack-Tar's long imprisonment had not been shaken off completely, and devastating Aracoras had taken almost all of the energy it had. The fleeing rats need not know that, of course, but it knew that time was what it needed to fully regain strength and continue to enact revenge for the humiliation from ages past.

As it surveyed the landscape, it thought ahead. Hellvira was busy working her magic to fill a power vacuum that had opened up in Lunaria. While she did that, Ack-Tar could take the time to recharge, recuperate, and begin its reign over the dark empire that was its due. They would *rue* the day they invited Ack-Tar to this forsaken planet.

Then, it laughed. A cold, pitiless laugh that echoed into the darkness.

Their end was coming, a long night of panic and terror. They would tear each other apart in the carnage to come, which Ack-Tar enjoyed the idea of. And when all was said and done, it would finally be the ruler of its dominion, a throne long denied to it and one that it would not have wrested away again.

About the Author

James is a peddler of bespoke cardstock and small independent game developer who lives in North Carolina with his three cats and a geriatric parakeet. He aims to provide the top-shelf kibble to his cats through book sales.

You can connect with me on:
- https://bsky.app/profile/acktar.bsky.social

Also by James E. Honaker

Worlds of fantasy, realms uncharted.

Beyond Good & Evil: The Future Past
The conclusion to Venser's story, as he and his companions race to fight the darkness before it consumes them all.

Made in the USA
Columbia, SC
07 April 2025